Praise for *Daughters of the New Year*

"Wildly imaginative, rich with humor, and unafraid to dive into the histories that are woven through the threads of our family life, E.M. Tran's *Daughters of the New Year* is the kind of story I love: A novel unabashedly American as it is Vietnamese. Through Tran's utterly unique and richly drawn characters, she is able to fully embrace the thick complication of family, diasporic community and the pain and resilience that it takes to rebuild in the wake of devastation."

—**Xochitl Gonzalez, author of *Olga Dies Dreaming***

"*Daughters of the New Year* is engrossing and exhilarating, traversing between countries, generations, and the myriad lives in between. Tran's prose rings throughout, weaving together laughs and chills and tears, unifying and contorting a family tied by love, debts, humor, and ghosts. With hundreds of threads in between, *Daughters of the New Year* is both thrilling and sobering, enthralling and awe-inspiring, and Tran has turned the question of what a family can *be* into a complex, heartfelt mural of possibility."

—**Bryan Washington, author of *Lot* and *Memorial***

"E.M. Tran writes with such a unique sense of imagination and insightful observations that have the power to bring generations together and to illuminate the complex Vietnamese history and culture. Fresh, innovative, poetic and captivating, *Daughters of the New Year* is a book that deserves its place on everyone's bookshelf."

—**Nguyễn Phan Quế Mai, author of *The Mountains Sing***

"This is the kind of book about existing between cultures that makes me wish I could reach back through time and hand it to my younger self. E.M. Tran has crafted a story as ferocious, brave, and big-hearted as the women within it."

—**Violet Kupersmith, author of *Build Your House Around My Body***

"E.M. Tran confidently leads readers into the hearts of her characters, but the world she writes of is much larger than that. The legacy of colonialism, the history of women warriors, the mythology of a culture—it's all here. Intimate yet epic, *Daughters of the New Year* is a remarkable debut."

—**Eric Nguyen, author of *Things We Lost to the Water***

"Polyphonic, epic, and tender, this searching portrait of three sisters moves fearlessly back in time, unearthing legacies of colonial violence and war. A haunted story of resilience and survival."

—**Meng Jin, author of *Little Gods***

"The Vietnamese American family that opens this novel—three daughters and their mother—are richly brought to life, but the only thing better than meeting and loving those four women was meeting their fierce women ancestors. From contemporary New Orleans to colonial Vietnam, this compelling epic shows us both the big moments that are recorded in textbooks and the quiet moments that are recorded in the human heart. E.M. Tran has crafted an original and unforgettable debut."

—**Beth Ann Fennelly, poet laureate of Mississippi and author of *Heating & Cooling***

DAUGHTERS
OF THE
NEW YEAR

A NOVEL

E.M. TRAN

HANOVER
SQUARE
PRESS

**HANOVER
SQUARE
PRESS™**

ISBN-13: 978-1-335-42923-0

Daughters of the New Year

Hanover Square Press
22 Adelaide St. West, 41st Floor
Toronto, Ontario M5H 4E3, Canada
HanoverSqPress.com
BookClubbish.com

Printed in U.S.A.

for my parents

DAUGHTERS

OF THE

NEW YEAR

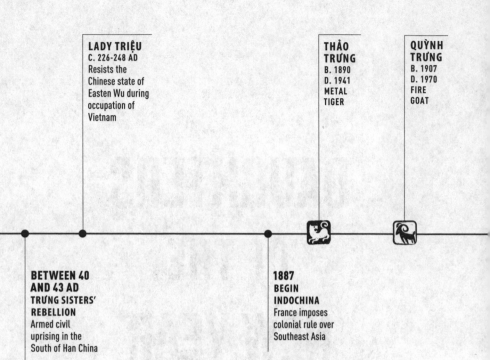

LADY TRIỆU
C. 226-248 AD
Resists the
Chinese state of
Easten Wu during
occupation of
Vietnam

**THẢO
TRƯNG**
B. 1890
D. 1941
METAL
TIGER

**QUỲNH
TRƯNG**
B. 1907
D. 1970
FIRE
GOAT

**BETWEEN 40
AND 43 AD**
*TRƯNG SISTERS'
REBELLION*
Armed civil
uprising in the
South of Han China

**1887
BEGIN
INDOCHINA**
France imposes
colonial rule over
Southeast Asia

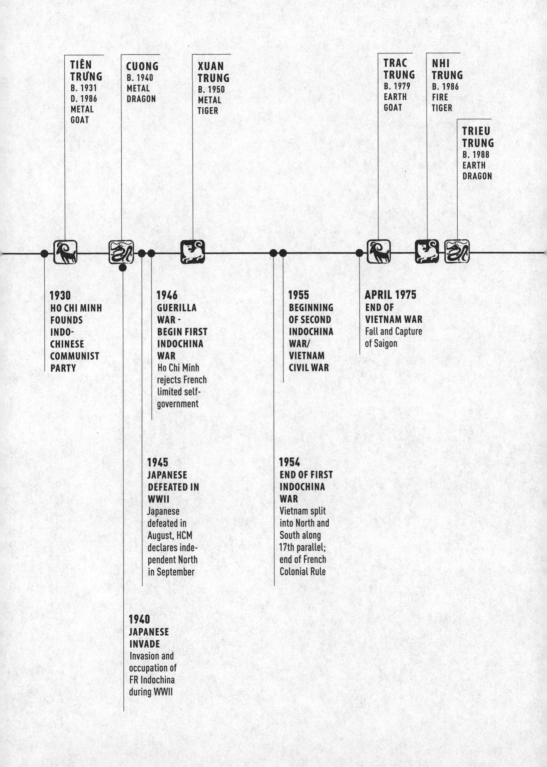

TIÊN
TRƯNG
B. 1931
D. 1986
METAL
GOAT

CUONG
B. 1940
METAL
DRAGON

XUAN
TRUNG
B. 1950
METAL
TIGER

TRAC
TRUNG
B. 1979
EARTH
GOAT

NHI
TRUNG
B. 1986
FIRE
TIGER

TRIEU
TRUNG
B. 1988
EARTH
DRAGON

1930
HO CHI MINH
FOUNDS
INDO-
CHINESE
COMMUNIST
PARTY

1946
GUERILLA
WAR -
BEGIN FIRST
INDOCHINA
WAR
Ho Chi Minh
rejects French
limited self-
government

1955
BEGINNING
OF SECOND
INDOCHINA
WAR/
VIETNAM
CIVIL WAR

APRIL 1975
END OF
VIETNAM WAR
Fall and Capture
of Saigon

1945
JAPANESE
DEFEATED IN
WWII
Japanese
defeated in
August, HCM
declares inde-
pendent North
in September

1954
END OF FIRST
INDOCHINA
WAR
Vietnam split
into North and
South along
17th parallel;
end of French
Colonial Rule

1940
JAPANESE
INVADE
Invasion and
occupation of
FR Indochina
during WWII

"I only want to ride the wind and walk the waves, slay the big whales of the Eastern sea, clean up frontiers, and save the people from drowning. Why should I imitate others, bow my head, stoop over and be a slave?"

—Lady Triệu

PROLOGUE

XUAN

The night before the first day of Lunar New Year, Xuan called her children to give them their horoscopes. She did this every year: for at least a week, she pored over the gigantic book with each sign's annual predictions and star positions, and the daily zodiac calendar with its moon phases, both of which she bought at the Vietnamese bookstore across town at the strip mall in New Orleans East.

Xuan always called her children in the same sequence: first Trac, the oldest, then Nhi, the middle child, and finally Trieu, her youngest. Every year, she had a private laugh about calling them in their birth order because it reminded her of the zodiac origin story. Her own mother used to recite it every Tết when they lived in Vietnam. Myth had it that the Jade Emperor beckoned all the animals to participate in a race. It was an invitation to be inducted into the zodiac for all of time, but there would only be twelve victors. The order in which they each crossed the finish line was the order in which they would be immortalized into the zodiac. But, of course, the race was treacherous, requiring the animals to cross every kind of terrain in every kind of weather predicament. The final and most difficult hurdle was traversing the Mighty River, to enter heaven, where the Jade Emperor awaited their arrival.

In the private joke she had with herself, Xuan was the Jade Emperor, and her own children the scrappy animals fighting and clawing their way to heaven to be first, second, and third in the zodiac. Of course, Trac, Nhi, and Trieu cared little about this myth and never noticed that Xuan got a kick out of it. No doubt, they would be annoyed, as they inexplicably were, about anything and everything Xuan did.

Xuan had been at Trac's house just a few days ago, only because Trac had insisted she come for dinner. Xuan didn't want her children to cook for her. They didn't know how to cook, not any of them, despite Xuan's insistence all their lives that they learn.

"I'll teach you to make wonton soup," she'd say to one or another of them. Sometimes it was wonton, sometimes it was glass noodles, sometimes it was beef stir-fry. It didn't matter, because they all responded with traded eye rolls and vague avoidances. "Your mom know how to make the best soup in town. She the best cook in the world," she'd say, and still, none of them would seem keen to take her up on the offer.

Yet, she had been pressured to come to Trac's house, which was in a part of town where Xuan hated driving, and was expected to behave politely about her eldest daughter's cooking. Where she'd learned this cooking, Xuan had no idea. The internet, she was sure, some website for Americans. This was why Trac wasn't married—what man would marry her when she couldn't cook a decent meal? And *then*, and this was the worst part, when Xuan offered help, Trac replied, "I know how to do it," followed by *"God,"* disguised under a sigh, as if she was deaf. There was that annoyance again—it cropped up in unexpected moments. She could never manage to prepare herself. It was a kick in the gut. Her children never seemed to notice, always wrapped up in their own defensiveness.

"Are you sure you want to add the pork so early?" she asked Trac.

"Yes, I want to add the pork this early," she said. And when dinner was ready, Xuan thought the pork was tough, dry, and too salty.

She wanted to tell her children the directions they should each go for good luck on the first day of Lunar New Year. She wanted to tell them to avoid risky ventures and the color white. She wanted to tell them the recipe for stuffed bitter melon soup. She wanted them to listen, but she knew they wouldn't. She told them anyway. She told Trac while choking down tough, dry, too-salty pork; she told her youngest, Trieu, while she sat, unresponsive, at the computer; and she even told Nhi, who was in Vietnam filming that horrible reality show about American women fighting over a mediocre American man. She had been mostly out of reach for three months shooting *Eligible Bachelor*, and must now be nearing the end of the process.

"I don't think you're allowed to call her in Vietnam, Mom," said Trieu, who was currently living in her old bedroom in Xuan's house.

"Why not? I call her, I'm her mother."

"You haven't spoken to her in months."

"I don't need reason. I call my child whenever I feel."

"She's filming the TV show. I don't think she has her cell phone."

"How you talk to her, then?" Xuan asked, and felt a twinge of satisfaction at Trieu's guilty expression. She'd heard her daughter talking on the phone in her bedroom, speaking so loudly, she was surprised Trieu thought the simple fact of the door being shut was enough to muffle the conversation.

"She only calls me when she has a chance. It's always from a different phone number."

"You tell me how to call her," said Xuan.

Trieu gave Xuan the phone number for Nhi's agent in Los Angeles. "It's just some woman in LA. I don't think you should call her. What are you even calling her for?"

Xuan went into her room with the cordless phone. When the woman picked up, she didn't say hello. Her voice had a fried, dry quality to it, which reminded Xuan of Trac's pork.

"Angela Weiser," she said.

"Hello, this Xuan Trung. I am Nhi Trung's mother."

"Oh—hello, what can I do for you?" Brisk and already aggravated, Angela Weiser was apparently not accustomed to unannounced callers.

"I want to speak to my daughter, but I have no way to contact. Do you have the number I can call?"

"Is there something wrong? A family emergency?" The sharp edges of her words had dissolved. Her greeting had begun so efficiently, but now Xuan could hear the core of her. She was happy that Angela Weiser was her daughter's agent, whatever that was.

"No, there is no emergency, I just need to speak with her about something."

"I'm so sorry, Mrs. Trung, but we're not allowed to contact the contestants. She has designated phone call time, and she only checks in with me every once in a while. I can tell her to call you when we next talk?"

"I can leave message with you, and you can tell my daughter, okay?"

"Sure," said Angela Weiser.

"Do you have a pencil? Do you write it down?"

"Yes, I have paper and a pen."

"Tell my daughter that it will be Year of the Monkey, a very bad pairing for a Fire Tiger like her."

"I'm sorry?"

"It will be Year of the Monkey," Xuan repeated. "Tiger and Monkey never get along. They always bicker and fight, so this may be a bad year for my daughter. They have very clashing personality and cannot agree on anything. She may see a lot of conflict this year." Xuan could hear the pen scratching the paper.

"Is that all?"

"No, she also has to be careful, because the Monkey can be a tricky animal. She should watch out for small tricks or deceit."

"Small tricks...or...deceit," she mumbled. "Okay, got it."

"Also, if you wish for luck in money go to the south direction. If you wish for luck, fame, prestige, go to the southwest. Maybe she should do this because she actress, no?"

"Mm-hmm, I think you might be right about that," said Angela. "Should she go southwest on a walk, or does it not matter?"

"Yes. First thing in the morning. If you wish all kind of luck, go to the east or west. Overall, east, west, south, southeast, southwest—lucky star move to these direction."

"So, don't go north, northeast, or northwest?" said Angela.

"Yes, that right. You should also do this for luck. Only for the first day of Lunar New Year, though."

"There's more than one day?"

"Yes. Tuesday the second day of New Year. If you wish luck in money, go to the east. If you wish for all the good news go to the southwest."

"Wow, okay, so—"

"Wednesday the third day of the New Year. If you wish for all the good news, go to the south. If you wish for a mentor, go to the east."

"Is that the last day of Lunar New Year?"

"Yes, only three day. You tell my daughter that, okay? If she can, she should celebrate in Vietnam with the correct food. She should not work on New Year, it bad luck. Please tell my daughter that for me, okay?"

"I'll tell your daughter," said Xuan's daughter's agent in Los Angeles.

When she hung up the phone, Xuan went to find Trieu and tell her what Year of the Fire Monkey had in store for an Earth Dragon.

The story went like this:

Ngọc Hoàng, the Jade Emperor, or in some versions, Buddha, invited all the animals of the kingdom to participate in a race to heaven. The race took them across mountains and desert, jungle and tundra, through air and underwater, rain and snow and hail. Bitter cold and scorching hot, animals of all kinds dragged their way toward the finish line, which lay across the Mighty River, the most difficult obstacle of all. They competed for one of the coveted and honorable positions in the zodiac. Only twelve animals could be initiated.

Cat told his best friend, Rat, about the race, and they agreed to be a mutually beneficial team. They were wily and creative, and faster than all of the other animals. But both of them were terrible swimmers. So, when they arrived at the Mighty River, they hid until Ox (sometimes referred to as Water Buffalo) arrived, jumping on his sturdy back as he waded easily through the treacherous current. Rat, sneaky in nature, pushed Cat into the water, thinking he would drown. (This explains Cat's eternal dislike of Rat, and why he still chases Rat to this day with intent to kill.) When Ox reached Heaven's shore, Rat jumped ahead of Ox to be first. The winner, the first initiate of the zodiac, became so through cunning, secrecy, and betrayal.

After Ox, Tiger was third in the zodiac. In the Chinese version of the tale, Cat does not make it in time to be included. But in Vietnamese versions, he surprises Rat by knowing how to swim after all, and crawls ashore as the fourth animal in the zodiac. In every version of the myth, Tiger's story is left off the page. Tiger is third, without much explanation or fanfare, the attention diverted to Cat's comeback story.

Then there is Dragon, the most revered sign of the zodiac. Dragon could've been the winner, as he could fly, but he stopped for some philanthropic reason or other, sacrificing first place to protect and serve. Sometimes the story is that Dragon noticed the people below him were dying of thirst, so he stopped to create rain for them. Other times, the story is that Dragon stopped to extinguish a fire terrorizing a village. Regardless, Dragon is portrayed as self-sacrificing, protective, and as creative genius embodied, his mind brimming with ideas waiting to come to fruition. He is the only mythical animal out of the twelve zodiac signs.

Horse came soon after, but Snake had been hiding behind his hoof. Snake slithered out, spooking Horse and cutting the line, coming in at number six, and Horse at number seven. In some varieties of the tale, Snake and Dragon are good friends and arrive in Heaven at the same time as travel companions. Unfortunately, because of Dragon's size, the Jade Emperor sees Dragon before he sees Snake.

Goat, Monkey, and Rooster collected reeds and built a raft together on the riverbank. They worked as a team to cross the Mighty River: Monkey using his hands to propel them forward, Rooster crowing so loudly, the air expelled from his chest pushed them onward, and Goat using her horns to fling off any passing debris that might capsize them. Dog, despite being the best swimmer of all the animals, was eleventh in the race. He had been covered in dirt and grime from the grueling terrain, and when he dived into the Mighty River, the water invigorated him. He was such a good swimmer that the river's current made no impression on Dog, so that he only noticed how cool and refreshing the water was, how it washed away the filth caked in his fur. He frolicked and lollygagged his way to eleventh in the zodiac.

And just before the closing of Heaven's gates to the great race, Pig squealed and kicked his way through the river, bursting out just in time before the end of the competition. He was the twelfth and final zodiac animal, having been so behind due to his tendency for snacks and naps.

And so, the gates closed, and the Jade Emperor welcomed these animals to their rightful places. That Mighty River the only thing separating them and us, Heaven and Earth, eternity and now.

Xuan herself was a Tiger, born in the element of Metal. Those under the sign of Tiger are competitive and confident. They are charming and popular, bold and natural leaders. They can be bad-tempered, overindulgent, stubborn. Tigers are judgmental. Metal traits include inflexibility, rigidity, firmness—what one might associate with literal metal. People of this element possess a strength of will, determination. They are ambitious, set in their ways, and loath to accept help. They like to do things on their own.

Xuan always took offense to the lack of Tiger narrative in the myth. On the first day of Tết, when the cleaning had been done and all there was left to do was eat and relax, Xuan would ask her mother to tell the story. At first it had been a childish desire, an obsession with searching for herself in it. Where was Tiger? How was she just like Tiger? When Tiger's part came and went without much flourish, Xuan would demand her mother say more, to make up the parts she wanted to know. Did Tiger help Cat? Did the Jade Emperor ever confuse *them* as he had confused Dragon and Snake? What was it about Tiger that allowed him to be third overall in a very difficult and competitive race? Of course, Xuan's mother had no answers. The myth was the myth. She couldn't change how the story was told, could she? She simply delivered the tale as she had received it from her own elders.

But Xuan would rewrite the myth herself when her mother refused to indulge her, filling in the gaps. Tigers were important, sacred animals in Vietnamese culture, after all. They deserved to take up more space in the story. And as Xuan got older, she insisted on continuing the tradition of her mother sitting down to tell the tale every year, partly out of nostalgia, but also because she never quite outgrew the need to search for herself in it. There was an ego, she was ashamed to admit, involved in her consumption of the story.

Now she obsessed over the yearly horoscopes, thinking that if she ever decided not to consult them one year, that would be the year they'd all regret it. They'd miss out on opportunities, they'd be killed or bankrupted by disasters easily avoided. She thought of all the grief she could've escaped if she'd just read horoscopes in 1975 as diligently as she did now.

But then, Xuan could admit, she was stubborn. She was a Metal Tiger, after all. They'd all known Saigon had an expiration date. But Xuan didn't want to believe it. When anyone had brought it up in those days, she changed the subject, even getting into several disagreements with her sister over her own refusal to discuss the matter. It seemed, increasingly, the only solution was to escape, to leave behind their home for something unknown, for the rest of their lives. It was impossible for Xuan to understand. Back then, she could not imagine her life as anything other than what it was. Before the fall of South Vietnam, Xuan had been in a beauty pageant. She'd won, too. How could it be that her home, her friends, all her things would disappear in a few years when something as normal as a beauty pageant had happened not that long before? She had left the pageant trophy behind, and thought about it all the time. Even after forty-one years here, she wore American citizenship with discomfort, like a pair of shoes half a size too small. The shoes could fit, yes, but every step reminded her she should not be wearing them, that she should be wearing something else.

When she and Cuong had bought their first, and only, house in America, those first days in their new home while sitting at the fold-up plastic table in the still-empty living room, all she could think about was that trophy. Gleaming silver, metal, displayed in the room where the light was best. She went to a trophy store, but all the trophies were plastic, multicolored, ugly. They were meant for karate achievements or school art show awards. She bought one anyway, one with a large cat figure on the top. She bought a spray can of metallic silver and covered the trophy in a fine mist of paint. On the base, she'd written in black permanent marker *Miss Saigon 1973* and placed it on the fireplace mantel, where the afternoon light made its silver polish glow.

She turned on the television at seven every Monday night and watched her middle daughter shine like a star on television, competitive and ruthless and charming against these other women. She was a Tiger, just like her mother.

PART I:
2016—1975

1

NHI

It was ten in the morning in Saigon, and already the summer heat was steaming up from the damp cement. In front of Notre Dame Basilica, the women pushed and shoved each other. This was always how it was when they were told to stand together for a group photo. Nhi jumped up front, trying to get to the middle where Ben was, saying loudly that she was short and couldn't stand in back. The photographer stood behind his camera and cleaned his glasses with the hem of his shirt, indifferent to the internal drama of the show's contestants. They did these photo ops at least twice a day, and even more if they'd just arrived at a new destination, which happened weekly.

"*Girls*," the producer shouted. They called them girls even though they were all women. "Hold those smiles!"

After the photo shoot, Ben, the show's Eligible Bachelor, left with producers for his hotel room. Nhi wandered from the girls, staring up at the alien city. The other contestants stood together like corralled cows, waiting to be sequestered in their own hotel, which they were not allowed to leave unless they were filming on-site somewhere. They didn't like Nhi, which likely would cast her as *Eligible Bachelor*'s villain for the season. Even though they were, all of them, filmed every moment of the day, she noticed the cameras lingered on her especially. Whether it was because the showrunners could tell she would attract trouble and filmed her all the time in anticipation of this, or because the other women noticed the cameras and therefore brought the trouble to her, she didn't know. It was a chicken-or-the-egg situation. The fighting was exhausting and sometimes even degrading, but there was also, Nhi was abashed to admit, a wretched feeling of satisfaction being the center of attention. Even if what they saw was not quite accurate, didn't it still mean being seen? She was the show's only nonwhite contestant. Maybe the producers would make her story line more memorable for viewers. When she'd called her older sister, Trac told her to take advantage of this unexpected gift.

"It might mean you'll stay on the show longer," she'd said.

"I'm sure Mẹ and Ba will love that," Nhi said.

"You might as well commit, if they've already disowned you."

Nhi agreed, although hearing Trac say it so bluntly still stung. Her parents had refused to speak with her since their fight about Nhi's acceptance onto the television program. While she hadn't spoken to them in the two months or so since she'd been on the show, she was sure Trac and Trieu had told them both by now that Nhi was in Saigon, a fact guaranteed to drive the wedge between her and her parents even further. Her mother had, for the past five years, suggested they all take a trip to Vietnam as a family. Nhi hadn't been opposed to this, but the family vacation never happened because Trac, a corporate lawyer, was "too busy" trying to make partner at her firm. While this was true, the real underpinnings of Trac's refusal lay in her dread at the thought of going on an extended trip with their parents.

Holiday after holiday, Trac would volunteer to work often and late on purpose, shooting down every possible date for the trip. Nhi knew this because Trac had told her she'd rather get fired and then run over by her boss's G-Wagon than go on an international family trip.

"If we go to Vietnam, we go the whole month," their mother had said. "Too far to fly and stay shorter than that." She reiterated this point often, as if she suspected her children were always on the verge of suggesting less time together.

"Oh, I bet Trac won't be able to come," said their youngest sister, Trieu. She avoided Trac's glare as she poked grains of rice around with her chopsticks in one hand and her bowl cupped in the other.

"How you know she won't be able, huh? We don't even have a plan. She can come."

That had been a few years ago. They'd been discussing the trip over a Christmas dinner of fish and rice. Their cousin Vinh had given their mother a large red snapper and three pounds of gulf shrimp because he always caught enough for her when he went fishing. She had panfried the fish and caramelized the shrimp instead of making a turkey or ham. When they were kids, she used to try traditional American holiday dishes, except everything had been soaked in a Vietnamese soy sauce marinade. They used to set the table just like white people did, with lots of forks and plates of varying sizes and fancy cloth napkins. The table would be laden with mashed potatoes and oyster dressing and green bean casserole alongside animal organs and bánh cuốn and banana-leaf-wrapped sticky rice. But that had been when they were young, when their mother was still interested in the charade of American life, as if they could be included in it if she made a turkey on Christmas Eve. Now that they were older, she didn't bother. Perhaps it was because her children's absence left nothing behind for her to dress and feed and speak to in American. When they came home for the holidays, she made whatever catch Vinh had given her, and that had to be good enough.

Nhi thought of this as she sniffed the fetid air of Saigon. She felt seduced by the city, both a stranger and an intimate. Something about its modernity surprised her and yet felt inevitable, the modern edges of new buildings not quite able to stamp out the old, crumbling ones cast in their shadows. As the girls followed a shouting producer who was directing them toward the bus, Nhi looked around, realizing she had become enveloped in a bustling crowd of people, people who looked like herself, dark haired and brown skinned. The producers did not realize she was missing, could not tell her apart from this crowd. It was equal parts funny and offensive. She stole one last look at the bus-boarding gaggle of girls, turned and plunged deeper into the streaming mass of people without a second thought.

She paid the entry fees to the Saigon Zoo and Botanical Garden, ambling in a daze past the colorful, loud carousel, right through the throngs of screaming children without really realizing where she was. The babble of Vietnamese pushed her into a familiar dreamlike state, one which she had been accustomed to entering as a child, a survival technique around adults at family gatherings. She could hear them, at least, a vague buzzing she could break through when she tried, which was at least something in comparison to Trieu, who, as the youngest, knew the least amount of Vietnamese. When they were kids, Trieu would block out the noises her mind couldn't translate, which is to say everything, and sometimes their father would hit her if she didn't respond to the questions she didn't realize he had asked, mistaking her silence for insolence. Trac, on the other hand, could not ignore a single word, which Nhi thought explained a lot about Trac's quick irritation and, underneath it, her sensitive nature toward their parents. She heard everything that was said about them.

"The worst part," Trac had once said as a teenager, "is that they're completely unconcerned about whether we hear or not. Because, who cares, right? Who cares what we think?"

Nhi exited the botanical garden and eventually ended up at the famous and crowded Bà Chiểu marketplace. She strolled through the open-air market, fresh fish gleaming in the sunlight, unintelligible shouts in a mother tongue she had never properly learned. People were cooking and eating everywhere, at stalls and outdoor restaurants. She even passed a group of middle-aged women squatting on the ground, shoveling rice and fish into their mouths with chopsticks. *Rice is a dietary staple of the Vietnamese people*, she thought, the phrase rising to the surface of her mind from a middle school history project about Vietnam she'd had to do. Walking now through the city, through this marketplace, she marveled at how the near-forgotten textbook information from her childhood had managed to flatten out all the intensity of the place, the sense of wonder and opportunity, the feeling of electricity frizzling between bodies.

The smells of the market were salty and raw, less rotten than the reek of the Asian grocery store their mother frequented in New Orleans, although the sweet scent of decay did still linger on the edges of lemongrass and beef broth and browned seafood. While the foul smell of dead fish was the same, she wondered if it didn't quite trigger the same sense memory as Phuong's Oriental Grocery because she was strolling under the bright morning sun in Saigon rather than under the flickering fluorescents in that dingy little strip mall grocery on New Orleans's West Bank.

Nhi gaped at the bustling market around her, noises and smells jolting her out of her walking reverie. She was so eager to get away from the other girls, she had rushed off without any company, without any thought of the possible consequences she might face for breaking the rules. She'd never considered it before— in Brussels and Bogotá, she'd been afraid to get lost, the sudden fear of being misplaced overwhelming her, the reality of being a foreigner prickling at the back of her neck. In Saigon, however, she walked easily, the same way she walked through her neighborhood in New Orleans or through aisles at the grocery store.

The comfort was an illusion, she knew; Saigon was no more home to her than Bogotá or Brussels, the streets and the people and the language no more familiar. But Nhi felt her family ancestry here—that genealogy of Vietnamese crawling back like tangled vines on a sturdy camphor tree, even if its original root system was lost in the jumble—it somehow fixed her to the people currently shouting from market stalls, to the children peddling for money, to the young lovers zooming past on mopeds on the nearby thoroughfares, and she felt that they knew this about her, too, that indelible tie.

It was foolish and imaginative. She was not one of them. Yet she could not shake the confidence from her shoulders as she pushed through crowds. A woman wearing a purple shawl sat alone behind a small wooden stand. She was serving hot banana dessert from a large steaming tin pot. The coconut milk was mauve from purple yams, filled with floating clear tapioca pearls and slices of bananas.

"One bowl, please," Nhi said in her best Vietnamese.

The woman stood up to stir the pot (which was nearly the length of her entire torso) and ladled a healthy portion into a Styrofoam cup.

The woman opened the palm of her hand and told Nhi the price, which was more than twice the amount handwritten on a small yellow piece of dirty paper affixed to the wooden counter. Nhi looked at the sign but didn't argue as she pulled her purse to her front to get the money. She had never been one for confrontation, preferring to let conflict ferment into bitterness. This was part of her problem on the show, in fact—the other women perceived her actions as manipulative and mean-spirited because Nhi refused to engage in their conversations. She didn't instigate, and didn't need to. Several other cast members had cornered her with the cameras present to ask about her intentions, which she had only deflected. Nhi could only imagine how that might appear on the film when editors went through it. But she did not mind being cast as a villain by the show or by the other women, hoping that it would give her more screen time.

She plunged her hand into the abyss of her purse, but found only debris. Gum wrappers and pens jostled against her fingers, none of the loose bills where she had put them earlier when she'd exchanged money at the airport. She looked up at the woman, who already realized Nhi had no money for the dessert. She had sat down and started eating from the Styrofoam cup herself, no longer interested in Nhi.

"Chị," a girl said from behind her. She wore a large T-shirt and dirty white tennis shoes. Her voice sounded oddly distant, like an echo. Nhi wouldn't have even heard her if she hadn't tapped her hand, insistent and aggressive. "Chị," she said again. She looked up at Nhi, wide innocent eyes, and waved the bills of money, so stiff and new that they crinkled as they bent back and forth in the air.

"Hey!" Nhi said. "Is that mine?" She had reverted to English out of anger.

The little girl turned and dashed through the crowd, yelling "Chị, chị, chị, chị!" as she went. Nhi ran after her, but the task of pushing through the bodies proved much more difficult for her than it was for the girl, who wove between legs and in opportune spaces that opened and disappeared with the movement of the crowd. Soon, Nhi reached the edge of the market, the girl more easily visible on the city streets where the crowd was less dense. She ran, thankful she'd worn tennis shoes, chasing after the little girl, who continued to dart through pedestrians and over sleeping hobos, occasionally glancing back at her. She was making sure she was followed, Nhi realized. This thought should have made her stop. But it didn't. She continued running, a breeze cooling the sweat beading along her hairline. Nhi followed the little girl's disappearing form around corners, past shops and restaurants, through frenetic crowds and across busy streets. Drivers swerved, almost clipping her. How was the girl going so fast?

Soon she was met with the scent of water and mud, the Saigon River's current a low murmur. Down an alley, the shadow from two tall, modern buildings cast a cloak on the street. And when Nhi emerged at the end of it, the wide river ran before her, its supple bosom keeping boats afloat, the slosh of water and wind enveloping her in a warm, womb-like embrace.

When she got back to the hotel suite later, the other girls had already drunk eight of the twelve bottles of wine provided by the producers. "They'll get us more if we ask," said the Professional Dog Walker. "No point in rationing." The cameramen hovered behind the couch and near the curtained window. They never ceased filming in the sleeping quarters because that was where all the disagreements occurred—where the girls felt most cooped up, irritable, and lonely. The place where they had time to overthink, about Ben, about their families, about the jobs they'd left to be here. It was an intense two- or three-month filming spree, and they didn't get paid. But the exposure was worth it, and if they got eliminated, they had the chance to be invited to one of the show's spin-offs. At least two assistant producers were always there sitting in the corner of the suite with their headsets on, bored and ambivalent, directing the cameramen and pulling girls aside for individual interview footage.

"Where have you been?" said the Visual Artist. Nhi had learned the Visual Artist was actually a hair stylist, but the way she'd described it, it was more of a side gig. "My *main job* is being an artist," she'd said. "I specialize in abstract art and acrylic paints." This was hilarious to Nhi at first, and it definitely still retained its comedic appeal. But the Visual Artist had smuggled in a traveling watercolor set, and she sketched and painted sometimes at the dining table. She was actually a good artist. They had the peculiar relationship, as all the women had with each other, of being amiable friends who sometimes chatted about their favorite hobbies one moment, and the next, they turned into hostile competitors who had no problem launching the most personal attacks.

"Sightseeing," said Nhi. Eye rolls rippled around the room. They all thought she was trying to create her own story line on the show, trying to stand out from the crowd. She didn't bother explaining that it really had been an accident, a spontaneous decision born of her desire to get away.

"I'm glad to see you made it back all right," said the Taxidermist. There were snickers. "You were gone for a long time. You know we're not allowed to leave, right?"

"I was trying to get away from everyone here," said Nhi. She had to stand up for herself, even if she didn't like to, even if the others misinterpreted her actions as snobbishness. Lashing out made everything worse, but she felt unsettled that day, more reactionary. The little girl was nowhere to be seen at the spot by the river, and when she had put her hand in her purse, crisp bills brushed against her skin once again.

"Whoa," said the Taxidermist, "aren't we feeling cranky."

"We're all here for Ben," said the Entrepreneur from Dallas. Nhi felt the tension frizzle again. "What would Ben think if he knew you were leaving? If you can't handle it, then I don't know what to tell you. This is serious, and Ben is here to find his wife." There was a purr of agreement. Nhi hated the Entrepreneur from Dallas, a genuinely dull woman who had started a line of hair ties that supposedly didn't stretch out after multiple uses. The Former Ballerina had pointed out they were simply scrunchies, which had been the source of a huge house conflict resulting in the Former Ballerina's elimination from the show.

"I'm here for Ben, too," said Nhi. This wasn't at all true, nor was it true for most of the other women, who were all really models, actors, musicians, or various other occupations in the entertainment industry. But there was an unspoken agreement that this charade was indispensable, that they had to keep up the ruse for their own benefit, or else all this had been a waste of time. A larger audience for their social media accounts, more opportunities for sponsorships, a greater chance at being cast for other shows. At least, that was how it had started. They weren't allowed to use their cell phones or bring books. They weren't allowed to watch television or use the internet, either. The producers plied them with alcohol and forced them into small quarters together. But Nhi began to suspect that the charade was no longer a charade for most of them, that somehow, the show had become reality. It was why Nhi could barely stand to be in the room with everyone these past two weeks. Even so, she, too, felt the disconcerting nerves, the butterflies in her stomach when she saw or spoke to Ben, a man to whom she normally would never be attracted. It was like Stockholm syndrome, a captive to the well-oiled machine of *Eligible Bachelor*, and she could feel it happening but was powerless to stop it. She was afraid that it might become real for her, too, out of pure circumstance and inevitability. She knew her mother would have something infuriating to say about it all, probably attributing her difficulties with the other women to unlucky star positions for Tigers, or an inhospitable year for anyone born in the element of Fire. She imagined her mother flipping through her astrology book, searching for Ben's birth chart, and clucking unhappily, conveniently interpreting their signs as incompatible.

Nhi was an aspiring actress and had lived in Los Angeles for the past ten years, but for every contestant living in LA, the information bar on the screen instead said their hometown to make the cast appear like a collection of America's sweethearts rather than another Los Angeles casting call. For every model (of which there were at least sixteen in the original batch of twenty-five girls), an alternate occupation was used. The show producers wanted the cast to appear more diverse: they'd asked Nhi if she cared if they used "Vietnamese Food Critic" as her occupation, because in the contestant questionnaire, she'd said pho (along with pumpkin ravioli, seafood paella, and fried chicken) was one of her favorite meals, and because she'd written a few posts for a now-failed food blog. Nhi wasn't sure why, but she told them it was fine, even though it wasn't.

There was a knock on the door. The Professional Dog Walker went to answer and came back clutching a white envelope. She flipped her bleach-blond hair over her shoulder and fumbled with the seal. She opened the card, scanned its message, and then looked around slowly at the circle of women, their breaths held in anticipation.

"Nhi," she said. She pronounced it *Knee*, unable to make the nuanced grinding of the letters *n* and *h* against each other. There was a disappointed exhalation from everyone when they heard it wasn't their own name. "'We're going to have a *pho*nomenal time tonight in Vietnam! Love, Ben.'"

Nhi took the invitation from the Professional Dog Walker's hands and read it over. The handwriting was rounded and girlish, clearly written by an assistant or a show producer. Inside the envelope was a sheet of paper with details about what she would need to wear, and a reminder to pack her suitcase in case she was sent home, eliminated from the show because of her performance on the date.

"You are so lucky you get to go on a solo date with Ben," said the Marathon Runner. "All of us would kill for that."

"It's really not fair. Just because we're in Vietnam," said the Real Estate Agent. Nhi actually agreed with this. What could be more conspicuous than the Vietnamese girl going on the date in Vietnam? She wished she could have been invited to the zip line date in Bogotá, or the shopping spree when they'd still been filming in Los Angeles.

She left the room to get ready for her date, the cameramen and a producer following close behind to document her makeup routine, her outfit selection.

"Take a bit longer to put your blush on," said Assistant Producer #3. "Arnie, can you turn the lights up and then do the shot again?" Nhi pursed lips and sucked in a bit to accentuate the hollows above her jaw, lightly tapping her makeup brush against the apples of her cheeks. She put on a new set of false lashes, trailing the glue along the strip and waving it in the air to get the glue tacky. She pressed them to her eyelids with tweezers, fluttering her weighted lashes. It would have to do. She hated her eyes because, more than anything else about her, they immediately gave away to everyone that she was Asian. While she could cover her straight, thin lashes with artificially thick, curled ones, she could never make her eyes any larger than they were, not even with surgery. She would never be a doe-eyed Marilyn Monroe, even if she bleached her hair with dye and bleached her skin with whitening cream. When she stepped back from the mirror, however, she still couldn't recognize herself, the contours of her face sculpted by skin-colored liquids and powders, an illusion that gave her cheeks and nose and jaw the kind of angular structure she had always envied in high fashion models.

"Look in the mirror again like that," said Assistant Producer #3. "You're thinking about Ben!"

Nhi flinched, remembering the cameras. She felt embarrassed to have gazed at herself in such a moment of genuine vanity. She supposed, in a way, she hadn't gazed at herself at all, but at another woman who lived a different and wonderful life, who had a different past and a different future and a different family because of how she looked. "Sure," Nhi said, "I can look in the mirror, again."

Ben and Nhi were ushered into a black SUV and driven toward District 1. A producer with curly hair sat in the front passenger seat, rattling off talking points for the segment.

"Make sure you face the camera, Ben. You keep turning away and we get all this footage of your back," she said.

"Yeah, sorry about that," he said. "I was a little too into the dodgeball game on the last group date, I guess."

"How many times do I have to tell you it doesn't matter if *you* are good at the activities? Just be more aware of the cameras, man."

Ben said sorry, but turned to Nhi, winked with a small, conspiratorial smirk. In spite of herself, Nhi's stomach did a small flip. When the car pulled over, they exited, greeted by Assistant Producers #1 and #4, who were guarding a red moped. The filming began when Ben and Nhi straddled the seat, Nhi in the back with her arms wrapped around his waist as they maneuvered around the hundreds of other mopeds weaving among the stream of never-ending traffic. Nhi could hear, even over the roar of drivers on every side, the helicopter hovering far above them for bird's-eye footage. The producers had Ben drive around the same traffic circle three times before they were directed to the date location, which was a small pho restaurant nestled among the tourist shops of District 1. Mopeds and bikes were parked out front, and Ben led her by the hand around the back of the noodle shop, where they entered the hot kitchen.

An old Vietnamese woman waited for them there, an array of ingredients splayed out next to her on the table. She wore a large Hawaiian shirt and wide leg pants, hot pink flip-flops exposing a bejeweled pedicure, and her long, gray hair was twisted tightly into a bun. She looked to be at least seventy years old, and when she spoke, it was in Vietnamese accented by a hint of Northern roots. Although Nhi hadn't noticed it before now, she realized this woman was the oldest person she'd seen since they'd arrived in Saigon. Most of the city was young, frenzied and coursing with the busybody energy of youth.

The Old Woman continued speaking, motioning toward the table.

"Nhi?" said Ben. "I think she's talking to us." It took Nhi a moment to notice that there was no translator in the room.

"Ben, I'm not fluent," she said.

Assistant Producer #4 stepped in. "You mean you can't understand her?"

"Unless 'not fluent' means something else to you." A beat of silence in which both Assistant Producer #4 and Assistant Producer #1 shared an impatient look. "I can only understand some phrases, or words here and there. I'm not conversational."

"We don't have a translator for this date because we assumed you wouldn't need one," said Assistant Producer #1. She seemed to be talking more to herself than to either of them.

"Listen, why don't we just keep filming and see what happens?" said Assistant Producer #4. "It could end up being a cute conflict in the episode's narrative." They continued to talk among themselves about the chances of finding a translator at this late hour versus the option of filming without one.

"It'll be fine. It's fine," Assistant Producer #1 said to them. "It's really fine, you guys can do it. Carry on."

Nhi wanted to tell them it would not be fine. That she didn't understand much Vietnamese beyond numbers and simple phrases, that the Vietnamese she heard most often growing up was her mother criticizing her figure or her father dangerously warning her to be silent while he watched *The Price Is Right*. How to explain that she could discern the general flavor of her mother's gossip, the intensity of her father's commands, but could not now, under pressure, translate with any precision this old woman's instructions? It was amazing to her that for all the show's meticulous planning, scheming, and manipulations, this breakdown in language based on an assumption about how Nhi looked and how Nhi must speak was *fine*. But they did not appear concerned, and they did not ask.

The cameras began rolling again.

"I think she wants to show us the ingredients," Ben said. She smiled up at him, a terror seizing her insides, the kind of simple, familiar dread she felt at family events where aunts and uncles ridiculed her bad accent. *Americanized*. The word seemed to float up from the floor.

"Yeah," said Nhi. Ben rubbed her back, a comfort. She was reminded, then, of the strange fact that she had only these people—Ben, and the Visual Artist, and the Taxidermist, and everyone else on the show—to really understand the weird and taxing experience of this fake reality. She looked at the ingredients arranged on the large metal table: a bag of onions, cinnamon sticks, licorice, star anise, a pile of fresh bean sprouts, bundles of mint and Thai basil, hulking beef bones, and a large slab of beef. *We're going to have a pho-nomenal time.*

"She's making pho," Ben told her.

Obviously, Nhi thought but did not say.

"I think she's going to teach us how," said Ben. "I love trying new things. Have you ever had pho?" *Foe*, he pronounced it.

"Yes," said Nhi, "my mother makes delicious pho. It reminds me of being home."

"Wow!" said Ben. "I love that you're different. You're just different from the other girls."

Any affinity she had felt to him dissipated as quickly as it had appeared. He beamed, blue eyes shining. She looked at his boyish, handsome, all-American face. So placid, the hum of thought completely absent. It made her feel more confident even now, in this most unstable of settings.

A man nearby gave them aprons that, inexplicably, said *Pho* on one and *Eligible Bachelor* on the other. The Old Woman motioned for them to pick up a pair of tongs and begin cooking with her, searing cut vegetables on a hot grill. They tossed blackened onions and spices into a giant pot already simmering with beef bones. The Old Woman spoke rapidly and often, and Nhi fell into the rhythm of her voice, both hearing it and not hearing it, going through the motions of cooking she'd learned from her own mother. Sometimes the Old Woman would correct her by pointing at a different ingredient or moving her hand to the intended spot. Ben splashed chunks of ginger ungracefully and giggled at the awkwardness of this foreign task, but Nhi did not participate as she normally would have for the cameras. She didn't even notice him as she pressed her onion half onto the smoking grill, as she flipped the delicate, blackening cinnamon, as she studied the pot of bones. Periodically, she looked up through the steam, near the propped-open kitchen door, at the dirty little window above the sink, her eyes scanning the small, cluttered room, and thought she saw that little girl creeping on the edges of her vision, peering inside.

When they sat down for the dinner portion of their date, it was within an empty restaurant. The floors were dirty and the one-room establishment itself was ramshackle. Nhi suspected the restaurant had been bought for the night in order to film. Furniture had been pushed to the edges, outside of the camera's frame, with the exception of a single table covered in a white linen, its surface adorned with greenery and tapered candles. Two large, steaming bowls sat ready for them when they walked in. She was sure these meals had previously been prepared, because they had only just left the pot of simmering bones they'd been cooking. It wouldn't be surprising if the shop owner gave their haphazardly made batch of soup to some homeless kids, unwilling to serve it in the restaurant.

"I'm really glad you're here, Nhi. I think we have a strong connection. You're so unique. You're really your own person."

"How so?"

"I don't know," he said. "I've never met a girl who, like, can do this with me." He motioned to the bowl and the surrounding restaurant.

"You've never cooked?"

"No, I've cooked. I mean, I've never cooked this way before." He laughed.

Nhi knew what he meant. He'd never done anything as adventurous as preparing unfamiliar food with a girl who looked unfamiliar to him. She wished she could eat her pho, which was enticing and aromatic and only inches from her, but she knew that none of the girls actually ate on these dates. In fact, she rarely saw anyone eat at all, unless it was a shake or a granola bar or a boiled egg in the early morning. She almost laughed thinking about how unsightly one looked slurping down noodles and broth. She thought of her father, splattering broth all over his shirt and belching afterward.

Nhi looked up from her bowl to see the little girl gazing at her through the glass front door. Nhi noticed now that she got a good look at her, that the child looked familiar. The soft and feminine curve of her jaw, rosebud lips, almond eyes, an expression of appraisal. She gazed back at the girl.

"Are you okay?" Ben said.

"What?" said Nhi. She turned back to look at him, but the presence of the girl at the door was like an anchor on her eyes.

"I asked about your other relationships. Why didn't they work out?"

The truth was mundane, so she offered him a streamlined cliché. "I guess I just haven't met the right person." Ben agreed with this explanation and began to talk about his own romantic struggles. The source of her failed relationships could easily be traced to the fact that she had lived in Los Angeles for most of her adult life—that she had dated men like Ben, men who said they were creative directors and acting-workshop managers, but who were really social media influencers or club promoters. Ben was a former professional baseball player, but less famous than his older brother, who was a current major league baseball star. Now that his baseball career was over, Ben did guest spots on ESPN talk shows and made money off the pictures he posted on his personal social media accounts. On *Eligible Bachelor*, he talked about his failed baseball career as if it weren't over, and the other girls all did, too. Nhi could not deny that she had participated in this. She did, after all, want to stay on the show for as long as possible.

"But my mother has always been my rock. I know if I can find a girl like my mother, I'll have found my soul mate," Ben said.

Nhi hadn't been listening. She had been looking out the front door again, but the girl was no longer standing there. "You want to marry your mother?"

Ben did not understand that this was funny. "No, I said I want to find someone like her. I love my mother."

"That's sweet," said Nhi.

"What's your mom like? Your parents?"

Nhi knew the appropriate answer to this question. There were two options. She could take this moment to gush about what a supportive and traditional family she had, or she could gravely reveal the trauma of divorced or distant parents that undergirded her fear of never finding love. The question seemed so innocuous and direct, and yet Nhi could not find an honest way to tell Ben about her parents, about her mother, about the way she hoarded food in the refrigerator, how she used to record household phone conversations in secret out of paranoia, how she bought gold bars and stored them in a safe-deposit box, how she did this because she didn't want any of her children to go hungry if everything went to shit. Or about her father, who worked forty-hour work weeks and came home, sullen and unhappy and still needing to edit the Vietnamese newspaper he published, and who asked for dinner and silence and *Wheel of Fortune*, who had been incredibly demanding of his children but who always assured them they were better than they had allowed themselves to be. These things made her parents sound difficult, which they were, but these were tender things, too, things they'd done because they had nothing and wanted everything for Nhi and her sisters.

Behind Ben, sitting at one of the tables pushed against the wall, the little girl had slipped inside. She smiled at Nhi, a mysterious, closed-mouth arc. Ben waited, a quizzical expression on his face. "What are you looking at?" he said, twisting around in his chair. His voice, for a moment, sounded like it must in real life, off-screen. The sugarcoating that accompanied their forced small talk had washed away. The girl hopped onto her feet and waved, running past them through the kitchen entryway, her sandaled feet pattering.

Nhi stood up, her chair crashing back onto the floor. She vaguely recognized her own legs moving, her mouth saying *Sorry* as if she was a ventriloquist dummy, and pushed past a cameraman to follow the girl through the kitchen. The men holding cameras and large hanging mics tried to follow her, jogging through the narrow door and maneuvering around obstacles. The little girl was standing on the kitchen stove, arms akimbo, when she burst into the room. There was dirt under her fingernails and a smear of what looked like dried blood on her shirt. Jade bracelets hung on her slender wrists. Dark eyes sparkled behind the wisps of wild hair covering her face. She jumped down and exited out the back.

Nhi followed her into an alleyway and into the pulsing crowds of people along the main thoroughfare filled with street hagglers and makeshift food stand vendors milling around. Nhi pushed through them all in pursuit of the girl. She glanced back briefly at one point to see the cameras bobbing above the sea of black hair getting farther and farther away.

The girl took her down the main road, zigging into alleyways and zagging out onto other high-traffic streets. They passed parks and old French colonial buildings, statues of communist heroes, women crouched at their portable grills trying to pull themselves up by their bootstraps, beggar children, and smoking men playing cards. They had both slowed to a brisk walk, and Nhi wondered why the girl would not simply let her catch up. She wanted to know how she knew her.

When they arrived back at the river, Nhi was not at all surprised. Somehow, she'd known this was where they'd end up all along. She walked toward the little girl, who stood at the river-bank's edge and watched over her shoulder as Nhi approached.

"Chào em," Nhi said. *Hello, little sister.*

The girl turned and jumped, and then she was gone, the ghost of her closed-mouth smile an impression on the air. Nhi ran to the bank and watched the dark river flow. She thought she saw the girl's wild hair tangled in the stream of water. Where would the river take her? For a moment, she wanted to follow.

2

TRIEU

The dragon dance, which was the only reason Trieu had wanted to come here, was not going to happen. The MC had shuffled onto the stage and announced that one of the dancers sprained his ankle playing basketball on the church's court fifteen minutes ago. Her mother sighed, in that annoying way that said without saying, *I told you so.* Trieu repressed the snappish retort aching to escape. She had wanted to go to one of the several Tết celebration fairs across New Orleans's Vietnamese neighborhoods, hoping to write an article about the dragon dances. She'd never written an article before, had never pitched to a magazine or newspaper or to anyone, anything. For the past two years, she'd been fully content to live in her mother's house and work as a towel girl at an overpriced gym up until a few months ago, when her sister Nhi joined the cast of *Eligible Bachelor.* Trieu wondered if it was jealousy, this feeling, but she knew that wasn't quite right. It was a weight against her chest, trapped beneath her collarbone, making it hard to sit still, making it hard to wake up on time for work, making it almost impossible to ignore her mother as she normally did.

She got the idea in her head that she'd write this article, even though she'd only ever written insignificant little short stories as a creative writing major in school. She had taken the classes because, in a conversation about choosing a major, her college counselor asked her what she was good at, a question that Trieu found stupid and useless. She was good at a lot of things. In fact, almost everything Trieu had been interested in trying, she was "good" at. She'd won first place in an art contest in third grade because she thought the theme (pastels and superheroes) was fun, beating out other kids who had to test into their school's visual arts program, and which Trieu's parents had considered but could not afford to pay the testing fee. For her birthday one year, Trac bought her a cake-baking workshop as her gift, and by the end of the session her cake looked professional sitting next to the other participants' drooping layers and untidy icing jobs. She could rarely think of a time she had really failed at anything new, and this, perhaps, was the reason Trieu had little interest in any one thing more than the other.

"Dragons are very good at many creative endeavor," her mother bragged to another parent when she'd won the pastels art contest. Trieu sometimes considered this a curse, that expectation of success from her mother. Was she inherently good because she was a Dragon, or was her mother's expectation of her goodness a self-fulfilling prophecy? Trieu thought it was more likely the latter. Her mother bought markers and crayons when Trieu had asked for them, thinking she would be the next Van Gogh, when really, Trieu's art was good because she had new markers and new crayons. And anyway, was it good? Or was it just better than what her sisters used to create, because they drew with old broken crayons, free from Shoney's, and dried-up markers filched from school? She thought now that she had always been destined to disappoint her mother. She wished she had the dogged determination of her eldest sister, Trac, or the single, focused talent of Nhi.

She would never live up to the fantasy her mother had invented, fed by horoscope books and star charts. She twisted her daughters into the shapes she wanted, to make these stories about the zodiac feasible, even if it was clear to everyone they weren't. Xuan wanted Trieu to reach the promised heights of a Dragon, and when she didn't, she made excuses—her Earth element, *that* must be it. It's true that Trieu was indecisive and fickle. Whether or not that had anything to do with her Dragon sign, she doubted it. There were many things she was *good* at, but was that a reason to devote your life to it? She had told her college counselor this, who responded, "Okay, what do you *want* to be good at, then?"

"Writing. English," she said, for no other reason, she realized later, than that maybe it was the only thing she had tried and truly struggled with. Maybe it was her own generally twisted relationship with language, her discomfort with words, that made her say it. Maybe it was that, in her own home, Vietnamese felt like a stranger, and out in the world, English felt unsure. Maybe it was that, no matter how good something might appear when she first wrote it, there was always a place to be improved, some revision that proved Trieu's earlier hopes wrong about the possibility of ever arriving at a place of success.

"Don't you think that could be true for many of the other things you're good at?" the counselor suggested. But, even if that were true—Trieu had never felt insecure enough about those things to try. In writing, on the other hand, she never felt fully stable. The challenge was the only thing she could cling to for purpose or reason, the only thing that scared her. Now, she devoted herself to it only reluctantly while working at a gym, greeting patrons who ignored her, their ears stuffed with music, while her own life remained paralyzed. Despite knowing her mother's beliefs were akin to fairy tales, in her daily paralysis, Trieu thought often about her own zodiac sign as if it were something real. She couldn't help it. Maybe it helped her feel some semblance of control when she had none. She could see why her mother clung to it. In the middle of wiping down yoga mats or medicine balls, mopping the always-grimy floor, organizing the front counter, surrounded by grunting gym goers, Trieu saw herself as a Dragon, undulating body soaring through the sky. Decisive and powerful, she always knew where she was going—a village to create rain, a fair to bring music, a feast to provide bounty. She reimagined herself differently each time, maybe red, maybe green, sometimes glowing like the sun.

Trieu had become especially enamored with the topic of the dragon dances when Nhi called from Bogotá to inform her their next destination was Vietnam. And afterward when she walked into her mother's room to find her asleep at her computer, a digital slot machine still whirling and clinking, Trieu thought she'd take her along to the fair, get her out of the house and walking, socializing with other fairgoers while she herself took notes on the dragon dance.

The outing was a total failure, though. The dragon dance could not go on with one of its four dancers missing. Who would be the butt in the second dragon? Surely they could not have the second dragon's butt dragging on the dirty asphalt of the Holy Name of Mary Woodmere Catholic Church parking lot. And her mother did not walk about and socialize. In fact, she'd dragged a chair close to Trieu and sat, hovering in her blind spot, arms folded and an empty smile for any of the neighborhood women who approached to say hello.

"I told you, these people are trash," said her mother. "They never do what they say they will do. I knew the dance would not happen."

"One of the dancers sprained his ankle, Mom," Trieu said.

"Exactly. He play basketball with Black boys."

"Jesus, Mom. Don't you want to try any of the food? I heard someone say the bún riêu is good."

"It's no good. I already know. The woman who cook is no good. I know her. She's a bad woman."

"How do you know her?"

"I know her. She had a very success restaurant, you remember Pho Ha Long? It use to make a lot of money, but she gamble it all and lose it."

"She could still be a good cook," said Trieu.

"Now she cook at the New Year fair for people like this," said her mother, motioning to a group of teenagers milling around. Trieu could discern what pop song was playing from the headphones they shared. "How she can be good cook if this the best job she can get?"

"I think it's all volunteers here, Mom."

"Even worse! She make no money."

Her mother had not acknowledged or greeted any of the community women as they wended their way through the crowd, browsing the fair stalls. She made Trieu sit with her in a high-traffic spot near the frozen coffee vendor so that she'd be in clear view of anyone entering the row of food stalls, yet her mother refused to circulate the event, and she didn't need to. Every woman came to her, exclaiming that they hadn't seen her in ages, asking how she was, mistaking Trieu for Trac or Nhi. Her mother was always polite, a gracious pageant smile at their approach. Even if they thought she was arrogant, even if they later gossiped that she was unfriendly and uptight, hands shielding their mouths, her mother knew they couldn't resist coming. They were drawn in like insects to a bright, dangerous light. Trieu sighed. Her mother loved manipulating people to bend to her unspoken and arbitrary wishes. These women who came up to them had fallen into a trap that they didn't know existed, only to prove the whole exchange had been successfully engineered by her skillful hands.

Trieu wouldn't care about this, except that in every instance, the women tried to speak to her in Vietnamese, and when she couldn't respond in the correct language, their clucks of shock made Trieu feel a crushing disgrace. Her mother would say in Vietnamese, "I don't know what's wrong with her." And they'd laugh together about their children, how stupid and simple they all were, but also how their child was smarter and more successful than everyone else's children, of course.

While it stung to hear Vietnamese elders talk so openly about her deficiencies while she stood less than a foot from them, the sting itself was a familiar feeling, as if she was handling an unfriendly pet hamster and had come to expect its bite, not fooled by its innocence and yet still fool enough to desire its affections. What hurt more were the judgments of her peers, their casual cruelty. She'd come to the Tết fair thinking she would observe, disregarded by the fair's attendees. It was evidence to how little she interacted in Woodmere's clique of Vietnamese that she erroneously thought she could pass by unnoticed, an unfamiliar, almost faceless person who only happened to look like them. Her adolescence, if she stopped to remember it properly, had been a series of experiences where Vietnamese people simply stared at her entrance into their spaces.

When they first arrived at the fair and walked to the entrance at the church gates, where the ticket table was, a boy she'd gone to middle school with, Van, gave her an up-and-down glance. He greeted Trieu's mother with respect, addressing her formally in Vietnamese. Everyone in Woodmere knew her parents, the snobby couple who was divorced but still went to events together and ran the local Vietnamese newspaper, *Ôi Chúa Oi*.

"How your mom?" Xuan asked.

"She's good, Bác Xuan. She's in the fair if you want to speak with her," he said.

"Okay, con," she said, calling him *con*, affectionately, as if Van were her nephew. Her mother plunged into the fair and left

Trieu behind. Van cocked his chin up and said, "Sup, mỹ trắng. Didn't think we'd see you at a Vietnamese fair." *Mỹ trắng*, white American, slapped her in the face before she could prepare herself. *Viddameez*, Van had pronounced it, an affected urban lilt to his accented English. She envied the traces of bilingualism in his speech, the inflections that made him belong. Her own Vietnamese, when she had tried to learn it, had been clumsy, its nuance encumbered by the lumbering American English to which her tongue was accustomed. She couldn't get her mouth to comply, and was ridiculed for it when she tried. "That accent!" her aunt had once said. She couldn't even bring herself to practice, knowing that it meant she would be derided in the process.

She smiled at Van. *Chúc Mừng Năm Mới* danced on her lips. Would she say it right? Would her voice go down enough for *Mừng* or up enough for *Mới*? A nauseating venom swirled in her gut. "Happy New Year," she said, instead, not even daring to say *Tết*. Van smirked. Trieu hurried away from the ticket table, shame welling up inside her. She was happy her mother hadn't been near to witness.

She knew exactly what she'd say: "You use to know Vietnamese. You forgot because of American school." Trieu had been fluent in Vietnamese as a young child, supposedly, and heard the same story told so many times, she could recite it mentally while her mother retold it. According to her mother's recollection, Trieu's grandmother, frail and sick, had been walking through the doorway over an uneven threshold at Kim Pham's Restaurant one night for dinner. Terrified she would trip, Trieu shouted from across the restaurant, "Coi chừng, bà nội!" who, in response, looked up and laughed at her grandchild's endearing concern for her. All the patrons at Kim Pham's laughed too, reminded for a moment of their home country, where children spoke in tongues they understood. "Bà nội loved you the best. And bà nội was mean, bà nội didn't like anyone. But she loved you best," her mother would say at the end of these recollections.

Trieu could not remember her bà nội, her father's mother, because she'd died when Trieu was only five. Trieu also could not remember this moment in time, this person who had shouted across a restaurant in a language she could no longer recall, concerned for a person she didn't know any longer, if at all. When her mother told this story, it was as if she were hearing an anecdote about someone else, a younger acquaintance that her mother wished Trieu would model herself after. Trieu suspected this memory had never happened at all, or her mother was mixing her up with Trac or Nhi. Or perhaps it had happened, but it covered up a larger truth: that Trieu had never spoken Vietnamese fluently. The memory served to make her mother appear better, that she had dutifully taught her daughter how to speak in the correct language, but to no avail—it was Trieu's fault, and Trieu's alone, that she spoke only English.

The children at the Woodmere Tết Fair lit Chinese firecrackers and ate Andy Capp's hot fries with melted Velveeta straight from the bag. Trieu left Xuan sitting, unable to bear her mother's crowding.

"Where are you going?" her mother said.

"I'm just walking around."

"Be careful. *Trieu!*" she said, suddenly. She snatched Trieu's purse, which she'd left on the ground near her mother's chair, and shoved it into Trieu's hands. "*Never* leave your purse like that. Hold it tight. Someone will steal from you here." She eyed the children playing nearby as if they might suddenly charge at them.

Trieu took her purse without a word, suppressing an eye roll. Her mother's paranoia got worse every day, in deceptively ordinary ways. When Trieu tried to explain this to her friends in college, they would always, well-intentioned, say something like, "Oh, moms are like that. It's really annoying," or "She's just worried about you." But Xuan was not a normal mom. Trieu laughed thinking of her white friends and their white mothers, how they chatted on the phone about boyfriends and discussed the particulars of Weight Watchers or dating apps, how they sometimes got irritated when visiting at the holidays and their mothers asked them what time they were coming home.

Xuan also asked what time Trieu was coming home. And she also asked for the exact address of where she was going, and the phone numbers of who she was with. She told her not to drink. She warned her not to eat too much at dinner, or she might get fat. She asked if Trieu really was sure about that lipstick shade. Trieu had long ago learned to lie. She always said she was coming home at one, even if she had no idea. She started putting lipstick on in the car so her mother wouldn't see. She always gave the address of a restaurant near where they were going out, even if she knew they would bar hop all over the city. She always gave her the phone number of the same friend, regardless if that friend was coming. Xuan had never once called, even when Trieu didn't come back until sunrise, but she insisted on having the number, as if that might make everything less dangerous. The irrationality of this worsened Trieu's impatience. Trieu had tried to explain once that she didn't *know* where they'd end up going or at what time they would be done, but this only served to confuse Xuan more—how could they not know? What could Trieu be hiding from her?

"Mom thinks you're dealing drugs," said Trac at dinner one day. She wore a Brooks Brothers suit and burgundy lipstick. They were eating at a pizza place in Mid City because Trieu had called her oldest sister, desperate for food that was not Vietnamese. They both knew their parents would not come to the meal if they ate American food.

"Why?" Trieu said, incredulous.

"She said you're going out late at night with strange people, and not telling her where you're going." They exchanged looks of exasperation—Trieu's sisters were the only ones who could understand their parents, the precarious balancing act of making them happy, a task at which they all failed often.

And now, as Trieu strolled the Vietnamese Lunar New Year's fair, farther and farther from her mother's seated figure, she let out a long, low, and tense breath, her purse still clutched to her torso like a newborn baby. Heads flicked her way like falling dominos as she walked. Trieu regretted the decision to come, her article now an ill-formed blob in her mind.

Nhi's success at being cast on the television show had destroyed the equilibrium among the Trung sisters, at least the one that had existed privately for Trieu. Nhi and Trieu, who were only two years apart, had both always been floundering together, their careers nonexistent. Trac was a lawyer at a big New Orleans law firm, one of the few women and the only Vietnamese person there. Trac had always felt the most pressure as the first child in the entire family who was born in the US. But now Nhi, who so badly wanted to be an actress, had actually done something big, and Trieu was forced to abandon her illusions.

The worst part, Trieu thought, was realizing that she had viewed Nhi's career aspirations just as her parents had: a joke, a passing whimsy, an impossible indulgence. And now that it was clear Nhi was doing real work for the career she wanted, Trieu felt a roiling humiliation, acutely aware of how pathetic her own attempts seemed. *Writing*, she'd said to herself, *this was what would make her equal*. But now, at the Woodmere Fair, that declaration seemed silly.

Underneath the shade of a tent near the church's side entrance, the dragon costume pieces lay crumpled on a tarp. Trieu circled around them and crouched to touch it. Both costumes were red, with feathery embellishments scalloped all across the body. The eyes bulged out of the head like a chameleon, its face bearded with the same plumed material. The whole dragon looked like he was wearing feather boas.

"These costumes are new," said Van. Trieu hadn't seen him

sitting at the collapsible table in the corner of the tent. He was wearing a white undershirt and the matching dragon pants that paired with the costume. "The church had to raise money to order a new one from a specialty store in China."

"I didn't realize you were one of the dragon dancers," said Trieu.

"You know, the múa lân's not really a dragon dance. A lot of people mistake it for the dragon dance, mỹ trắng."

"Don't call me that," she said. Van may have bullied her in middle school, but she was an adult now, and she didn't have to tolerate it. "What do you mean it's not really a dragon dance?"

"It's a lion dance," he said.

"They look nothing like lions. How did you become a part of this?"

"I volunteered when they asked at church. A long time ago, when I was still fifteen and in Sunday school, I taught two younger guys how to do it. I might quit soon. Getting too old. The other guy my age sprained his ankle."

"You act as if twenty-seven is like being a hundred years old."

"It is, when you're doing the múa lân. That shit is labor-intensive."

Trieu bent down again to run the costume's fabric between her hands. It was less delicate than she had expected, sturdier than it looked. She lifted up the lion head with both hands, bringing it to eye level. The lion stared back, eyes strange and malevolent. They had always frightened her as a child, so looming, the dancing and drums so aggressive. She looked at Van, who shrugged as though giving her silent permission. Trieu lifted the head over her own and held it up on either side. It wasn't heavy, but cumbersome enough, her arms and shoulders straining under the weight. She understood how this would be laborious to dance in, especially with a partner.

Inside the lion, the sun shone through, casting everything in red tint. It was hot, with no airflow circulating, and the costume smelled of sweat and vinyl and fish sauce, perhaps the remnants of the last person's breath lingering in the crevices. It was suffocating to be in there. Trieu was disappointed by this, had been expecting something more. She thought, naively, that she would feel mighty, for once like her supposed Dragon being. That something inside her might grow to match this exterior costume, like someone on a makeover show. Anything but this anticlimactic indifference. She had romantic notions about everything, and they always let her down. Instead, she felt only trapped and hot. For a moment it seemed there were dozens of people around her, jeering as she struggled to lift the lion head off of her shoulders. Where had they all come from, these people? There was a buzzing in her ears, a low hum. Behind her, she felt the breath of someone on her neck, and when she turned her head to look, a woman was lifting the butt of the costume, as if the two of them might trot off to perform a New Year's dance together.

Trieu shoved the costume off, only just hanging on to its edges to prevent it from crashing to the ground. When she blinked, all that was around her was dragging fabric. Van had gone. There wasn't anyone there. Fairgoers walked leisurely in the sun, or sat on the sidelines eating. Trieu laid the lion costume gently on its side before returning to her mother and asking to leave.

At home, the New Year's fair left Trieu feeling irascible and tired. She wasn't sure who was at fault—she liked to think it was Van or her mother, who both made her feel the starkness of her difference from people that were supposedly her own. In some ways, it was her fault for thinking belonging was a birthright. She had gone out of her way to avoid Woodmere and its people for so long that she'd forgotten that unique feeling of exclusion.

In the kitchen, cuts of pork belly, salted and marinated in fish sauce and garlic, sizzled in a large pot. Xuan was peeling a bowl full of hard-boiled eggs as the pork belly seared. The house smelled of caramelized meat and the sweet-savory scents of Trieu's favorite meal. Xuan poured a can of coconut soda onto the hot pan of rendered fat and pork belly, a satisfying hiss steaming into the air. Xuan was comfortable in the kitchen, moving quickly from cutting board to stove, a large butcher's knife in her stiff left hand the whole time. Her body moved impressively in the space, like a familiar speech memorized to thoughtless mechanics.

Her knife hand was the only part of her body that resisted the natural flow of the ritual. Xuan had fallen a few months ago, landing on her left hand. Trieu had been at work and Xuan didn't tell her about it. Trieu had only recently noticed that her mother could not fully bend her middle finger or rotate her wrist.

Xuan didn't tell Trieu, Trac, and Nhi lots of things. This was something that drove all her daughters crazy, but they did very little to change it. Finding out that Xuan was not talking to her sister, or that she couldn't find the key to her safe-deposit box with the gold bars, or that she had dozed off at the wheel for a few seconds while driving down their empty, residential street, only happened on accident, an occasional slip of Xuan's tricky tongue, and to find out any earlier would require them to spend more time with Xuan. Such a chore it was to sit through their mother's nagging, her unsolicited fortune-telling about the economy, medicine, and weather, in her uncomfortable and crowded home.

The kitchen around her was packed full of things, counter space covered in bowls and platters of snacks or dried goods, tins of tea, bottles of cooking oil, fruit and vegetables, many about to go bad. It was as if the room had been turned on its side, and all the things had tumbled out of their hidden places, except that those hidden places were still full, no extra space to be found. There was an assortment of Asian goods, dried herbs and dried shrimp and dried squid, the kitchen smelling vaguely like a stale fish market. The refrigerator was no better. It, too, was packed from top to bottom, front to back, with old produce, old holiday treats, and things Xuan refused to throw away but would never eat: American cheese slices, Activia yogurt, and Jordan almonds that were bonbonnieres from a cousin's wedding.

Trieu watched as Xuan opened the refrigerator, unfazed by its controlled disarray. She shifted the pickled quail eggs and garlic, peering past a carton of soy milk, to find an old jar repurposed as a fish sauce mixture. She'd made it herself, adding sugar and vinegar, ginger and garlic, shredded carrots and chili peppers. The rice cooker emitted a short song. The pot of pork belly and boiled eggs simmered in honey-colored liquid, the sweet licorice odor of star anise lingering underneath salted meat. It was Trieu's favorite meal, and her mother knew this.

They sat at the table, the two of them, holding bowls of rice and chopsticks. Trieu's rice and boiled egg yolk soaked up brown drippings. Her mother dipped pieces of pork belly into a dish of fish sauce.

"You go back to the fair next week. A different fair, the one in New Orleans East," Xuan said to her daughter.

"I don't think I will," said Trieu. "You were right about the fair. It was a waste of time."

"No," said Xuan. "You go to the Tết fair. We will go."

Trieu ate the food Xuan had cooked for her, the dish her mother had known would fill her with warmth. Trieu's tongue knew the dish, its taste, its feeling. Her body greeted it fluently as an old friend.

"Mom, is it a lion or a dragon? The dance they do at Tết. Was it always a lion?"

"If you think it a dragon, then it a dragon. If they say it a lion, it a lion. It both. Who care what it is? It look the same no matter what."

She sat up a little straighter. Her mother's words seemed to harden with the food in her belly as she pictured the costume.

The ritual loomed large in her memory. When she was young, she was proud an entire dance revolved around her sign—there was no tiger dance, no goat dance—but as she got older, this prerogative became a burden, perhaps imagined and invented in her own mind. The fact that she was a Dragon, that they gathered to watch and celebrate this dance, seemed so important to her mother, and by association, an entire culture. Now she wondered if that, too, hadn't been built up in her own mind. Trieu called it the dragon dance as a child, pleading with her parents to take her to the show, even though it frightened her. She had always thought it was a dragon, her whole life. Yet the costume didn't look like a lion or a dragon. It looked like a friendly beast, some nondescript, monstrous wonder of the East that jumped and wiggled, its feathered face and body blustering in the breeze. If she thought it was a dragon, then it was a dragon. If they said it was a lion, it was a lion. Who cared? It looked the same no matter what.

3

TRIEU

The athletic club, aptly called the Athletic Club, was one of the oldest in America. It was housed in its original historic building, an imposing downtown structure with tall arched windows and elaborate crystal chandeliers, under which patrons would pound into oblong punching bags or stretch into downward dog. There was an indoor pool that the city elite had frequented for decades, and was still the venue for the mayor's annual Spring Azalea Ball, in which local politicians and New Orleans socialites would wear pink and sip craft cocktails.

Two months before the Tết festival, Trieu was scheduled for the opening gym shift, which meant she was supposed to be there with a key-holding manager to open the door so that they could enter the gym together. Something about legal liability and witnesses. Trieu hated the morning shift, which was before dawn, and she was always late. On this particular morning, Farrah, the assistant manager, was in a bad mood.

"I wonder if you'll ever show up to a single shift on time?" she said, without any greeting. Trieu thought this was unfair, especially considering the fact that Trieu requested that she not be scheduled in the mornings. Farrah regularly expected employees to stay late assisting customers and cleaning, but had the gall to be upset when they shaved a few minutes off from the start of their shift.

Farrah was also mercurial. She might start the day surly, but an hour later, tell Trieu all about her online dating adventures unprompted, as if they were the best of friends. She talked incessantly. Trieu once conducted an experiment during a shift where she refrained from saying a single thing during Farrah's rambles, and it became clear that Farrah did not need or even notice Trieu's silence. By the time she was done Windexing the mirrors (if not sooner), Farrah would always come out to her trapped audience of one.

That morning, she had a small red gym bag on her shoulder, which Trieu suddenly noticed was shuddering. "Farrah, your bag," she said.

Glancing down at the trembling pouch, Farrah's haughtiness melted away. She gave her a conspiratorial smile and shushed Trieu, putting a finger to magenta lips. Trieu imagined that Farrah was the only gym manager who wore lipstick to work every day. "Come with me," she said, lateness seemingly forgiven.

In the staff room, Farrah scooped a mewing gray kitten from the depths of layered blankets in her gym bag. It squirmed in her hands, black eyes shining above a tiny pink nose.

"Oh my god, how old is it?" Trieu said.

"Less than two weeks, maybe? I don't know, I looked her up online and guessed her age. She's so small and can barely walk, but her eyes are open. And, sometimes when I put her on the ground she stumbles around and explores."

"Don't you need to like, feed it special food?"

Farrah took preportioned bottles of milk from the side pocket of the duffel. "Already on it! That's why I had to bring her to work."

Trieu was almost entirely sure their manager, Doug, would not be okay with this arrangement. Doug was very invested in maintaining the Athletic Club's atmosphere, which evoked the peculiar combination of a modern, sanitized spa that was also kept inside a crumbling historic Victorian building. This likely was not the ideal setting for a newborn kitten being fed hourly from a duffel bag. The kitten was suckling from the nipple as Farrah held the upturned bottle and cooed at the tiny creature nestled against her abdomen.

"I'm going to vacuum the weight area," said Trieu. "Do you mind if I turn the TVs on and play last night's episode of *Eligible Bachelor*?"

"You shouldn't watch trash television," Farrah said absently.

"It's the first episode, and my sister is in it."

"Wow, really? Who's your sister? Maybe I voted for her last night. I just downloaded the app."

Trieu pulled up the app on her own phone while rolling the Oreck vacuum to the second floor. She wanted to try to vote for Nhi, but she couldn't connect to the gym Wi-Fi, and gave up. Because the episodes were filmed live each week, the audience had to submit votes by midnight before each one aired, making her attempt useless.

The weight area was upstairs, the entire floor like a wide upper balcony around the perimeter of the gym so that one could overlook the railing and see into the glistening pool below. Now, the water was glass-like and blue, the chlorine undisturbed by the musky sweat of gym patrons. The pool was bordered on all sides by delicate, multicolored tiles that were original to the building. Trieu imagined a Turkish bathhouse might look like this. She had never traveled outside of the United States, though, despite having nursed a long-held desire to leave on the cheapest flight she could find without telling anyone. She harbored a lot of fantasies like this that she had yet to realize.

She withdrew the weight area TV remote from her pocket and pressed the power button. Every TV on the floor flickered on. Trieu selected episode one of *Eligible Bachelor*, which she had scheduled to record during her last closing shift, and began vacuuming as a dozen televisions played the same episode, mouths moving in unison to a chorus of echoes.

Barry Michaels, the *Eligible Bachelor* executive producer and host, stood in front of a glowing Mediterranean-style villa. It was nighttime, but the orange tile roof, the white stucco facade, and Southern California desert landscaping were still clearly visible under the production lighting. Barry Michaels's straw-colored hair was combed over, and he held his hands demurely in front of him, legs at ease like a soldier.

"Tonight, Ben meets his women, and possibly his future wife," he said. "This is night one of *Eligible Bachelor*'s most dramatic season yet. Who will Ben make a connection with? Will it be Sarah H., the kindergarten teacher looking for love? Or, will he fall head over heels for Becca M., our career-focused wedding planner? You'll have to tune in to find out. Meet Ben's women and vote for your favorite!"

Trieu pushed and pulled the vacuum across heather-gray carpeting. This was a futile exercise and did little to improve the carpet's odor. They needed to steam clean it in order to absorb the sweat of the hundreds of gym patrons, but this had not happened at all since the carpet's installation. So, she still vacuumed every morning shift without complaint, knowing any suggestion she made would be ignored.

Ben now stood in front of the Los Angeles mansion. He was a handsome, brown-haired man whose story line included an absent business magnate father, an uneventful pro-baseball career, and a well-publicized failed engagement to a YouTube star. A limousine pulled up to the mansion packed with the other women, each of whom stepped out one by one to greet Ben. Some tried to be memorable, delivering jokes or one-liners to entice him. Others diverged from the limo arrival by galloping in on a horse or pulling up in a sports car. One woman was delivered in a box that said "Emotionally Fragile," and that Ben had to open to meet her.

Trieu liked to catalog what kind of women were on the show. She imagined what went into casting decisions: Ben's stated physical preferences, possible standouts and crowd favorites, ready-made villains. Most of the women were at least a foot shorter than Ben and expensive-looking shades of blond. Did they make him fill out a questionnaire about his type? Did they interview him? Did they not consult him at all, and instead trawl through his personal history and social media, making decisions based on their own inferences of his type? She was willing to bet Ben had no part in casting. Otherwise, how did her black-haired, brown-eyed older sister get on the show?

"Hi, I'm Monica." A woman wearing a gold-sequined gown. Her thigh flashed through a high slit as she walked down the winding path to Ben. Her smile was large and toothy. She held a small statuette of a squirrel.

"Nice to meet you, Monica. You look gorgeous!" Ben said. She handed him the squirrel statuette.

"One thing you'll learn about me is that I'm a taxidermist. I made you this little guy so you can remember me," Monica said. The squirrel was wearing a small wreath of wildflowers around its neck. At the bottom of the screen was a ribbon with her name and age, "Monica 24," and her occupation, "Taxidermist."

As she sashayed to the house, Ben said in a low voice, "Okay, a taxidermist. What is that, exactly?"

He had met at least fifteen women so far, some of the introductions quickly glossed over. A few women had much more screen time, side interviews and reels of them packing at their homes before leaving to be on the show. As Trieu vacuumed near the balcony railing, she peered into the gleaming pool below. A tile mural with the Athletic Club monogram, paved into the concrete bottom, rippled under the water's surface.

Trieu's mind wandered to the annual Spring Azalea Ball. She'd never been, but had seen many photos of the event in the newspaper, the posed and grinning locals clutching craft cocktails in front of the pool. She hadn't worked at the Athletic Club long enough to be invited as part of the core staff. There was really no reason for any of the staff to be there since the city hired their own event planners, caterers, and party vendors. Really, the only person who needed to be there to monitor setup and takedown was Doug, but Farrah and the other assistant manager also attended. Trieu hoped her tolerance of Farrah might secure her an invitation this year.

A woman on-screen screeched to a halt in a faded red antique Ford truck. Ben let out a whoop. "Yeehaw!" she said, swinging open the truck door. Ben lent her his hand to help her down. She had on a white cowboy hat and red cowboy boots with her floor-length metallic blue dress. She looked like a sparkling American flag.

"I need to know your name," Ben said, almost greedily.

"I'm Mary Catherine, and I'm from Clarksdale, home of the blues!" She had wavy blond hair down to the small of her back, and wide, sparkling eyes with long, spidery lashes that seemed to take up half of her face. "Y'ever heard of Robert Johnson?" she said. Trieu wondered if Robert Johnson could ever have imagined his name floating out of the mouth of this pale, Mississippi pageant queen, or if Mary Catherine had ever actually listened to any of Robert Johnson's music.

"Who's Robert Johnson?" Ben said.

"I guess you'll have to find me later so we can talk about it!"

Trieu attached the small brush to the extending hose for precision vacuuming. She began cleaning between the railing spindles and stared again at the pool waters below. Light from the small skylight windows near the ceiling was beginning to stream in as the morning wore on. The surface of the pool gleamed bright so that she could no longer see the tiles at the bottom.

The kitten stumbled into her view, sniffing curiously in the wet corners of the pool room downstairs. Its fur was striped gray and the texture of an angora sweater. Trieu had always wanted a cat. When she was ten, she once begged her mother to buy *Everything You Need to Know about Cats* from a bargain book bin. The hardcover was thin and had the glossy feel of a textbook. Xuan conceded the purchase, which Trieu took up to her room, determined to read. The back of the book had a glossary of breeds, and Trieu lingered here the longest because there were lots of color photos. Her favorite was the Siamese, because its name looked Asian, because seeing those words, however Thai they were, gave her a thrill, as if it were she, herself, featured in the book.

"I promise to take care of it," Trieu had said to her mother, pointing to the images in the book glossary.

"A wild animal should not run around the house with us."

"It's small. You wouldn't even know it was there."

"An uncontained pet will poo and pee inside. They are animal, not people."

This, to Xuan, was her central fear: a pet that lived inside with them would leave them unlucky turds in places they wouldn't find in time. But, to Trieu, the primary appeal of a pet was the idea that an animal could roam the house just as they did, be their friend and equal, be a comfort and a companion despite that they didn't speak the same language, weren't human—this made Trieu ache, she wanted a pet so badly.

"We can teach the cat to use the bathroom in a box."

"Okay, we get a cat," Xuan told her daughter.

"When can we go?" Trieu was shaking with excitement.

"In three months, we go," said Xuan, thinking she would forget. Trieu was horrible at keeping track of time. She was slow and distracted and dreamy. But, she stole the small desk calendar Trac had received for Christmas and counted out exactly three months into the future. She wrote the date down in her journal and tallied each day that went by. On the day she had been promised a cat, she approached her mother, dressed and ready to go.

"Can we go to get a cat today?" said Trieu.

Xuan was frying tofu. Her apron was covered in grease splatter. She frowned at her daughter. "What you talk about?"

"You said three months ago we could get a cat. Today it is three months."

"No cat," her mother said. Her voice was flat and left no room for debate. Trieu, though now twenty-eight, never let go of this disappointment, this empty promise. For all the ways her mother let animals dictate the fabric of their years—cats and dogs, goats and tigers, snakes and dragons—the irony was that animals had no part in their actual lives. Only the fiction created by her mother had mattered. God forbid Trieu have an actual cat to care for when she could simply worry about the catastrophe sure to befall them during Year of the Cat. As she watched Farrah's newborn kitten totter here and there, she wanted to run down and snatch it away, to hide it in her childhood bedroom, where she still slept as an adult woman.

"Wowza!" said a dozen synchronized Bens on all the gym televisions. It was Nhi stepping out now. She had opted for a traditional limo entrance. There must be a dozen other women waiting in the same limo Nhi had just exited. She imagined her sister was probably making lots of friends, that she had been sipping champagne easily with the other girls as they waited their turn to meet the Eligible Bachelor, as confident and charming as her Tiger sign.

"Hi, there, Ben," said Nhi sweetly. Her voice had taken on a melodic overtone several pitches higher than her normal voice. She wore a flowing, emerald green dress that bared her collarbone and shoulders. She looked incredible, was oozing such star power that Trieu sincerely wondered how they could be related. Ben took both of Nhi's hands and held her arms out to examine her more closely. Nhi's laughter was girlish and seductive at the same time.

"I'm Nhi," she said. At the bottom of the screen, in white sans serif font, "Nhi, 30," and "Vietnamese Food Critic." Trieu blinked, briefly closed her eyes, and reopened them to check if she had read correctly. The information bar had disappeared, though.

"What is it again?" Ben said.

"Nhi," she said, more slowly, drawing out the word.

"Nee," he said. "How do you spell that?"

"N-h-i."

"Wow, that's not how I thought it would be spelled! You're so beautiful that I'm weak in the *knees*," he said, and Nhi laughed. "Where is your name from?"

Trieu watched as the kitten stumbled along the tiled floor. Patches of fur were sodden from brushing up against standing puddles or wet walls. Farrah had said they weren't able to clean themselves this young, and it occurred to Trieu that the kitten had probably been soiling itself in the red duffel.

"I'm Vietnamese," she said. "But, anyway, I'm so excited to finally meet you, Ben." She kissed him on the cheek, leaving behind a bright red imprint of her lips.

The kitten poked the water's surface with its pink nose, withdrawing quickly as if shocked by cold. It swiped its paw in the water, like trying to catch some errant, buzzing bug.

Ben watched Nhi as she turned and walked toward the *Eligible Bachelor* mansion. Trieu watched as the kitten teetered on the pool ledge, reaching for some invisible string. It stretched, then crashed ungracefully into the water, a small splash that sent ripples across the glass surface.

"She's hot," said Ben. "*Nee*. Nee-Nee! That's cute. Really cute."

The kitten was mewing, paws thrashing. Its wet, flattened fur made it look like a rodent.

Trieu ran down the stairs two at a time and almost fell as her sneakers slid on the wet tile floor. She could not remember if she had even turned off the vacuum. She thought she could hear its white noise humming, the vacuum hose snaking on the floor.

The cat's small face was no longer above the water's surface. Trieu plunged into the pool, swimming breaststroke underwater like a frog. The chlorine stung her eyes as she swam for the gray kitten, suspended and drifting slowly toward the pool's filtration system, its fur fluttering like seaweed. The water, though seemingly still when viewed from above, now rushed around Trieu's ears in great whooshes, as if other bodies were thrashing and darting all around the floating cat, creating a storm of motion leading her to it. Trieu could hear the television audio filtered through pool water.

"It's crazy to think I might have met my future wife tonight," said Ben.

"Ben's really handsome," said Nhi in what Trieu guessed was a cutaway interview. "I'm not exaggerating, but I feel a really crazy connection. Maybe it's love."

Her drenched clothing dragged, but she was buffeted up, the force of a thousand hands lifting her through the water. She cradled the limp kitten in the crook of her elbow, using her free arm and legs to propel herself to the surface.

4

TRAC

Trac tugged on the top drawer of her filing cabinet. The metal was dented where her boss had punched it in the day before, and now it had trouble opening. He was enraged that Trac had not gotten bankruptcy paperwork in on time. It wasn't her fault—the papers were given to her at three forty-five, and the courthouse closed at four on business days without fail. They were literally across town. Trac broke the speed limit and took every short-cut she knew to get from uptown to the middle of the French Quarter. She left her car unattended, illegally parked on the curb in front of the courthouse. In the time it took for her to run up the courthouse steps, yank on the locked front doors, and run back to her car, the violations officer had finished inputting her license plate into his electronic device. The small slip of paper printed out as she jogged up, waving her arms.

Francis did not care about these inconveniences, though. He only cared that Trac had not done something fast enough, a common complaint of his, despite the fact that Trac often got impossible tasks completed on time. She smothered her resentment, letting it sit there like a stone in her chest. It wasn't even her job as an associate to deliver the paperwork—the intern should've done that. While Francis yelled and raged about Trac's performance, the truth was that he trusted no one else to do the things he wanted done.

It was an incredible and impressive place to work right out of law school, though, and Trac didn't want to get derailed from her career trajectory. She'd had a clerkship with Francis, who took her on in the beginning of her 3L year only because she had an excellent recommendation from her law professor, who knew Francis from their tennis meetups at the Athletic Club and New Orleans social circles. Francis, while extraordinarily successful in his field, was known for being unreasonable, a former federal judge who stepped down from his position to go back to his firm.

"Is that normal for a federal judge to step down?" said Nhi. "I mean, he obviously didn't retire." They were out to dinner when Trac told her about her first month on the job.

"Federal judges have their judgeships for life. He was *asked* to step down," said Trac, "because of his anger issues. He had some kind of rage meltdown in the courtroom one day."

Trac was able to deal with Francis's "rage meltdowns" quite well, considering that these meltdowns sometimes included him punching her filing cabinet or slamming her door or yelling at her so loudly that flecks of spit landed on her face. At first, she would sit through it without a word, and call Nhi during her lunch break to complain. She never once cried. But then, more recently, she started retorting in ways that made him stutter, forcing him out of her office in bafflement. Once, he stood behind her and said, "Go faster. I swear to fucking god, Trac, a goddamn loggerhead turtle moves faster than you. Are you a lawyer or a loggerhead turtle? Can't you go any faster?" She admired the specificity of his references, even in an insult.

"I'm a loggerhead turtle if you keep doing this," she said flatly.

Internally, she laughed, thinking for an absurd moment about the taxidermized sea turtle her mother had purchased illegally and hung on the wall in her childhood home. Francis stalked out of the room fuming, but her point had been taken—did he want productivity or did he want to yell in her face? He wanted both, of course, but could not stand to be exposed as a hypocrite.

She worked a lot of hours, often on Saturdays and Sundays, and last year her bonus check alone was more than thirty percent of her annual salary. She was twenty-eight and she wanted to buy a house before she turned thirty. The housing market in New Orleans was ripe for picking. Katrina had flooded eighty percent of New Orleans only two years ago and people had fled in waves, afraid to return to their drowned city. She could buy a house in whatever neighborhood she wanted. She currently rented one-half of a duplex. It was a classic double shotgun in the Irish Channel that was, truthfully, a very beautiful building that was also a very shitty apartment. But, she loved it more than she could explain to anyone, especially to her father, who never understood why she had chosen to live there, and who also did not understand her present wishes to buy a historic home.

"You should live with your mother," he said. "You have to live with her until you get married." He had suggested this once before, when she first graduated law school and was about to move back to New Orleans. He had sent her an email, which she received while packing up her one-bedroom New York apartment, containing a color-coded list of requirements for post-grad life (and which she eventually had openly rejected):

1. You must move in with your mother.
2. You must pay 50% of your mother's utilities.
3. You must put the rest of your earnings
   in a savings account.
4. **You must quit smoking cigarettes.**

This last point was written in bolded, red font and highlighted in bright yellow. It was, evidently, the most important.

"You smoke cigarettes. Why can't I?" said Trac, confronting him at a Sunday dinner.

"I'm an old man. If I quit, it kill me. You can quit because you a young lady. Young lady don't smoke."

Trac allowed this point to go unaddressed. "I'm not moving in with Mom. I'm starting my job and need my own space."

"No. You move in with your mom," he said. "She getting old. Her children should live with her, take care of her. Vietnamese responsibility is to care for parents. You care for her until you get marry. Why don't you get marry?"

In a moment of wild delusion, she envisioned sitting down to dinner with her family, and with Belinda. Just as quickly, the freedom of that small act dissolved in her mind, as she looked at her father, gray haired and stubborn. She wondered about the hopeful expectation in his eyes, what image he had conjured of her future, what proud fantasy about his daughter's life he kept close to his heart.

Trac was afraid to get married for many reasons. She imagined everything she had built disintegrating around her like a sandcastle in water, replaced with children and a faceless man. She had seen her own mother's failed attempts to transcend the home, create a career for herself despite the demands of three children and a tired, overworked husband. Xuan's odd collection of jobs aside, she spoke often about how she wished she'd started a Vietnamese grocery store when she had the chance. Another woman they knew had taken her idea and now owned a successful chain of Oriental markets. She lived in Houston and managed her groceries from afar. Trac knew she wasn't condemned to her mother's fate, knew that they no longer lived unstable, immigrant lives in the margins. But she could never relieve that weight of expectation, both her own expectations and her parents' expectations for the kind of life she owed them. A dutiful

Vietnamese daughter and wife. A son-in-law who was a pharmacist, a doctor, a professor, an engineer. She wondered if her mother might finally be proud of her for doing that one thing, because her career achievements never seemed to be enough.

Xuan wasn't cruel, but she said small things about her sign that Trac absorbed growing up—Goats are unlucky, she'd said once, to explain why a toy Trac had brought to school in second grade was stolen. Perhaps it was worse what her mother *didn't* say. When Trac's teacher suggested she test into the Talented in Arts Program after being impressed by her illustration of women swimming at sunset, Xuan did not say anything, didn't even notice the drawing when Trac came home with it, nor did she ever take the teacher's advice. When Trieu, years later, won an art contest, Xuan told everyone her Dragon daughter was an artist, so creative and imaginative. If Trac married whoever they imagined she should marry, she wondered if they would even notice, or if she would simply be fulfilling another thing they expected of her, not knowing nor caring about the exceptional effort or sacrifice made.

It didn't seem quite fair—that Nhi and Trieu, just because they were younger and still in college, didn't have to deal with this. Their parents acknowledged her accomplishments the least and expected the most from her. Trac did everything before them. She had to because she was first in the line of fire. She dived right into the overgrown jungle and forged a path for the rest to follow, hacking away at cloying vines and smothering greenery. Sometimes she didn't make it, caving into the wishes of her antagonists. But even that made it easier for Nhi and Trieu, for once their parents got what they wanted from Trac, they became more amenable to all other requests. Her sisters had no idea, really. Trac was seven years older than Nhi and nine years older than Trieu. Sure, they'd witnessed these instances of inequality (they weren't blind after all), but seeing was different from being. And being Trac was exhausting.

"I'm not moving in," said Trac. "I won't."

Her father gave her an inscrutable look. He got up from the table and went outside to smoke. Her mother scowled.

"Don't listen to him. He just want to control. I not control my children. It not good," her mother said. "I don't know why he want you to move in here. You should find husband and move in there."

"Is he mad?" said Trac.

"Who care? He don't even ask what I want! I don't want anyone move in. I need my space, too," her mother said. She took out her yearly almanac, which lay on top of a tottering pile of mail and loose paperwork on the kitchen table, and pointed to an indecipherable chart in a chapter about the fortunes of Goats during the Year of the Ox. "This year, it bad for you to live in the southeast direction. I don't think it good for you to live in my house because we in southeast part of the city."

Trac wished her mother had said all of this during her father's lecture. It would've made everything so much easier. But Xuan had waited for Cuong to go outside for his Marlboro Red, sat in skulking silence until she'd heard the front door shut. Her mother always did this and had the irritating habit of complaining to her children about her ex-husband only when he wasn't around to hear it. Cuong had a horrible temper, and Xuan had often been on the receiving end of it. Well, this used to be true, anyway. When Trac was young, her father could barely contain his rage—rage at the missing remote control, rage at rush hour traffic, rage at the broken toaster, rage at a too-early or too-late dinner, and most of all, rage at his family. The only thing at which he did not seem to rage was his wife's bumbling, vague astrological predictions. Trac wondered if he, like her mother, found comfort in this one thing, however unreliable it was.

But now that he had retired, had begun to age toward a point one might deem elderly, his temper receded into the murky waters of buried memory. At first, there was a gradual shift in how often he would get angry, until one day, Trac noticed that her father did not shout at Nhi for putting her chopsticks directly into the communal plate and taking all the best pieces of shrimp before anyone else had the chance. If this had been a decade ago, Cuong would've barked at his daughter in a flash of heat, perhaps even snatched the chopsticks from her hand and thrown them on the floor.

But Cuong had aged into a tired and resigned older man. He no longer felt outraged by the daily injustices that no one told him would greet him in America. What remained was the disappointment: Trac recognized it when her father returned smelling of tobacco and old coffee and sweat. It was perhaps worse than the rage of her youth, which she had grown familiar with and had come to anticipate. She was an adult, now, and this disappointment was jarring. She didn't expect she would ever grow accustomed to it.

Cuong did not bring up his demands again that night. He came in from his cigarette break, flip-flops dragging on the tiled floor, and turned on the local news station. He slouched on the couch and drank his mug of hot tea without looking at Trac. There was not much he could do about his American daughter—it was his fault, anyway, for giving them American opportunities, raising them to expect American prizes, American money, American success. How could he expect them to care about being Vietnamese when he and his wife had worked so hard to create this American life?

So, when Trac began looking for houses, she thought the conversation had ended that night she'd rejected her father's emailed list of conditions. She was searching for a house in parts of the city she had always dreamed of living in. Not the barren outskirts where her family and other Vietnamese families lived, but in the center, in the middle of the city she had always called home but had never really lived in. She wanted a historic home, the kind that people thought of when you told them you lived in New Orleans. She wanted a front gallery she could adorn with greenery and rocking chairs, the underside of the porch overhang painted baby blue. She wanted Greek Revival, Italianate windows, wooden ones with original glass. She wanted hardwood flooring, Doric columns, high ceilings, gas lamps. She wanted ironwork and brick walkways.

Her realtor, Vanessa, had shown her several homes in the Garden District and Uptown. The homes were smaller than she liked, even with how affordable the market was, but Trac didn't care. She wanted to live where those beautiful homes were, wanted to walk outside every day and see she was surrounded by, included in, the version of New Orleans she had always romanticized.

"The homes in Lakeview are really affordable right now, and that neighborhood is coming back strong. I'm telling you, you could get double the space for the same amount of money," said Vanessa, after Trac had looked at a two-bedroom home that needed some renovations near Audubon Park. Vanessa was an attractive woman whom Trac found untrustworthy.

"No," said Trac. "I don't want to live there. I want a historic home. All those houses in Lakeview are basically new."

"How about Algiers Point?" said Vanessa. "I see that neighborhood getting very popular in the next few years. It's the city's second oldest neighborhood."

"No," said Trac, again. Algiers Point was across the Mississippi River, on the West Bank where her parents lived, where she'd grown up. While the Point was an old neighborhood, the rest of the West Bank was suburb and corporate development, the homes built in the '70s and the Best Buys and Targets built in the late '90s. Trac and her family lived in a subdivision called Quartier Mignon, a neighborhood whose street names were all in French, and whose houses were clapboard cutouts of each other, constructed in the early '80s. The use of French street names was a glimmer of what the neighborhood architects had hoped it might become; yet streets like Rue Monique and La Cour Yvonne were poor impersonations of the actual French New Orleans streets. As a child, it was to Trac a charming task, having to memorize her street name. Her rounded lips smoothly sounded out Rue du Canard. When she got older, became a teenager, it mocked her, reminded her that the New Orleans she lived in was not the sophisticated, European New Orleans everyone knew, but a cheap and poorly rendered imitation.

It was not a fancy neighborhood by any means—they lived not far from Woodmere, the Vietnamese community which was situated underneath a bridge. Xuan had insisted when they bought a house that they not live in Woodmere.

"I don't want to live in that neighborhood," she said. "Those people are low." And so, Cuong bought them a house outside Woodmere but still nearby, in the faux-French subdivision just five minutes away down the main thoroughfare. The children of Woodmere were not kind to Trac for this fact. On that first day in second grade, while Trac wrote her address on large-lined paper for children learning primary handwriting, the student sitting next to her peered at her work.

"What's that say?" said Vu. He had wide-set eyes and little gaps between his baby teeth. Trac could still picture those teeth because they'd reminded her of an illustration she'd seen in a book of a goblin. Vu had tiny little goblin teeth.

"It says my street name," said Trac. "Rue du Canard." *Roo doo ca-nar*, was how her mother, who used to speak French in Vietnam, had taught her to say it.

"Where's that?"

"In our neighborhood, Quartier Mignon," said Trac. *Kah-tee-ay Meen-yon*. "It's French."

Vu moved his chair back to examine her. He was only seven years old but had already learned the habits of his parents, of adults. "You Americanized, huh?"

"What's that mean?" said Trac.

"It means you're not like us," said Vu.

If it was not clear to Trac immediately, it would become so in the days and years to come. The kids of Woodmere heard about Trac's "fancy" French neighborhood, and her family's refusal to live in Woodmere (this was mere speculation, never confirmed, but Trac knew it was nonetheless accurate in the case of her mother). They heckled her on the bus, gabbing away in loud Vietnamese about her as if she couldn't hear them, saying mean things, the kind of mean that only children can manage. As they got older, the words became less cutting, but the taunts became more energetic, bolstered by hormones and routine.

"Rue du Canard!" they chanted when the bus came to her stop. Eventually, they would simply quack like *un canard* when she exited, head hung in shame.

She wasn't quite sure why it was so degrading to her. There were no vulgar words, no stinging attacks on her looks or intelligence. And yet, the mere name of her street was enough for a lifetime of bitterness.

When Trac told her parents about her house search, her father glowered and waved his finger. "No, no, no," he said. "You should not buy house over there. It is dangerous." His *g* in *dangerous* was a hard sound, like in *girl* or *gun*.

They were at a pho restaurant across town in New Orleans East, where the rival Vietnamese neighborhood was, called Disneyland. It felt like a remote country, the kind of place where people had started paving roads but had given it up as a futile project. The whole drive to Disneyland felt like this, that barren, eerie feeling of desertion. Its nickname was partially credited to the theme park right outside of the neighborhood, Blues Playground, which was built in the early '90s, but to a tepid citywide response. It shut down a few years later as a result, and the skeleton of the theme park was still there along the flat expanse of below sea-level highway. It still stood, even after being submerged completely in Katrina's floodwaters. The theme park seemed to be a permanent fixture, a landmark alerting visitors that they had arrived in the neighborhood, a derelict welcome sign to a neglected place.

Trac used to go to Disneyland a lot as a teenager because she delivered her father's newspaper out of the family minivan for fifty dollars every Saturday morning. She and her father would drive to the airport, where the shipment of newspapers had arrived from the printing press in Southern California, and they loaded up the minivan front to back, top to bottom, with stacked issues of *Ôi Chúa Ôi*. Then Trac would drive by herself to Disneyland, parking the car in the strip mall lot and running to and from the van with papers for Trang Mai's Video Store, Viet Nam Herbs and Medicine, Van Vu Dental, Saigon Grocery, Red Dragon Restaurant, Chiropractor Tran, Linh Vy Hair Studio—Trac would take the car every few feet down the strip mall parking lot, delivering the papers methodically. Disneyland was a strange combination of energies, being simultaneously abandoned and bustling. Every property in the strip mall was occupied by a different Vietnamese-owned business, and yet, Trac only ever saw a few people milling around, one of whom was almost always a homeless man wearing a Tasmanian Devil T-shirt. Many times, a business would be closed when they delivered the papers, and Trac might never have seen it open. But they continued to order newspapers.

Now that she was here again, at lunch with her father at a new pho restaurant she'd never had to visit with newspapers, Disneyland struck her as perhaps even more depressing than she remembered it. She hardly ever drove out there anymore. Her father had now hired the son of the owners of Saigon Grocery as a delivery boy.

Driving on I-10 East that far, the land felt lower, if that were possible, lower than other neighborhoods in the city. There was something about the air that felt wet, like they were crouched over a dark swamp. As she exited the highway, the silhouette of Blues Playground sat shrouded in humid mist. Dilapidated old apartment complexes, gas stations, and fast food drive-throughs dotted the landscape as she drove on the wide, empty, four-lane street spread with potholes and cracks, uneven drops where the road had fissured. Some of the homes appeared to have inhabitants, but were next to others that were gutted and hollow. The oak trees that used to grow out of the grassy neutral ground were gone, drowned and fallen from the storm. There were plenty of empty lots where houses had been bulldozed all together. Angry ghosts flitted along her periphery, following her car, trying to see who dared enter their forgotten graves.

"Do you like the new restaurant?" Cuong asked his daughter now. There were few people willing to open new businesses in the area, the memory of Katrina still too fresh. Cuong didn't seem to notice this. "They advertise in the newspaper. Very good pho. Many new businesses open here, it good for the newspaper."

"I like it," said Trac. The restaurant had the gleam of an immigrant's business, the strange, echoing emptiness of cold tile and sparse decor. There were silk paintings of women in áo dài and cone-shaped rice field hats and scenes of rural life. Various jade statues of dragons were displayed throughout. A four-foot-wide aquarium sat near the register and contained a gray fish resembling a miniature eel.

"New Orleans East come back real good," he said. "A lot of people come back. I know because they read my newspaper. All the papers are gone, I know they come back to town and read them."

"But how do you know?" said Trac. "Are there official numbers from the city?"

"I know because I know Vietnamese do not like to leave their home. If they can stay, they will stay. Who likes to move away from their home? They have already been forced out of their first home. Vietnamese do not like being told what they allowed to do or where they allowed to be."

Trac did not push this. She knew her father was thinking only of himself, of his experience and his preference. He had a point, though—Vietnamese people did seem to be returning. Indeed, it appeared they'd never left, stubbornly waiting through the violent downpour, wading through the wreckage, rebuilding their homes, intent on staying put. She wondered if they did this because they refused to be cowed, or because they did not have the means or the heart to leave. It was possible the answer was a marriage of both.

"I looked at two houses last weekend," said Trac. "In the Garden District and Uptown."

"Those are not good parts of town. It dangerous to live in the middle of the city like that."

"They're in a very nice area."

"Listen, you do not need to look at any more houses."

"I'm going to. I want to see more in those neighborhoods."

"You already have a house."

"I'm not living with Mom."

"No, I got you a house. You have a house now. Do not need to live with your mom."

Trac stared at her father in confusion. "What do you mean?"

"I bought a house here in New Orleans East. You said you want to live on East Bank, away from your mom and West Bank, so I buy you a house on the East Bank."

"I don't want to live in Disneyland, Dad," she said.

"I buy you a house. That's why I take you to lunch here today. We can go see it after. I buy it for a real good deal. The owner before couldn't pay his mortgage, so I buy the house for real cheap from the city."

"Dad, I don't want to live here," she said.

"Just look. No harm in look."

Their food came out. Her father took meticulous care preparing his dish. They never spoke—no one in the family did—when the food came out. Everyone ate in silence, any talking deferred for after the meal.

He had ordered bún bò Huế. The broth was a deep orange, the sheen of oil collecting along the top. It was full of fatty meat and thick, slippery noodles. Cuong took the pig knuckle out and placed it on a separate plate. He lifted each piece from his bowl and inspected it, carefully cutting off the thin sinews of fat from the thinly sliced beef shank. Gelatinous brown cubes of pig's blood floated among the meat debris. He added finely shredded purple cabbage and squeezed the juice of two lime wedges. Trac watched her father do this as she ate her vermicelli bowl. She was halfway done, already, and her father had not yet begun. He did this every time. She wasn't sure why he insisted on ordering the meal with the fattiest cuts of meat, only to spend so much time shearing away its most delectable feature. He slurped the noodles and broth. Sprays of orange dotted the napkin tucked into his collar. He picked up the knuckle and chewed away the soft bits, gnawing on cartilage and sucking the bone, extracting the flavor of home. He still finished eating before Trac did, taking large chugs of lukewarm jasmine tea before getting up and shuffling to the door to smoke a cigarette out front.

Trac finished her food to the sound of boiling pots and muffled chatter from the kitchen. The restaurant had no ambient music, and only a single man sat at a table across the restaurant from her, reading the latest copy of Ôi Chúa Ơi.

She was frustrated, caught off guard, but ultimately not surprised. It was exactly the type of thing her father would do. He had bought the house as a gift, yes, but also as a form of control. He wanted a say when his daughter had refused him one. Here was authority disguised as a well-meaning bestowment. And how was Trac to refuse it? He had already bought the house. To refuse a house would mean an outright dismissal of her father's wishes, the harshest rejection. She wondered if they could ever recover from such a thing.

Suddenly, music filled the restaurant. Someone, a waitress or maybe the owner, must have remembered they were supposed to play it, and the volume dial had been cranked to its highest setting. A Vietnamese ballad reverberated in the tiled restaurant. The man across the restaurant did not react, and Trac wondered if he even heard it. The woman singing had a longing in her throat, the steady, nasal pitch of her wail like a brick dragging across Trac's chest. She wished she could know what the woman in the song was saying, but the words meant nothing to her. She could've been speaking German or Spanish and still, she would've understood the same.

Trac let her father pay, knowing he would not allow her to do it. She'd had an old boyfriend a long time ago, once, who paid for the bill while out to dinner with her family. Her father's anger had been shocking. She knew he would be upset, but his ire was intense, far beyond the reaction she thought he would have. "I am the oldest member of the family, so I must pay," he said. Trac thought a lot about what this meant, being the oldest herself among her siblings. The most responsibility, surely, which her father seemed to suggest would eventually be her duty to take on once he was gone. The most responsibility had to be reiterated through payment. But, Trac had come to realize that any claims about age, respect, or responsibility were only a cover. Her father's motivations in anything boiled down to control, even in something as innocuous as paying for a meal.

"I will drive with you," he said. His old, gray minivan was parked illegally in the handicapped spot. It was the same minivan her father had when Trac was a teenager delivering his newspapers. The sliding back door had become difficult in recent years, sticking in place whenever someone tried to pull it shut. Cuong shut it by driving very fast and slamming on his brakes, an abrupt halt that made the door speed forward and smash shut.

Trac couldn't help but feel ashamed about her shiny black Mercedes. Despite her previous self-congratulatory sentiments on buying a "low profile" luxury vehicle, it seemed ostentatious in the empty, trash-strewed parking lot next to her father's old car.

Cuong shuffled to the passenger side of the coupe and pulled the door handle, a futile effort as it was still locked. "It very expensive car," he said. "Why the door not working?"

Trac unlocked the door and they both got in. She'd gotten the cognac leather interior because she thought it was a sumptuous color. The kind of brown you looked for in a nice handbag or a work pump. That she could have the leather of those handbags and shoes in her car was, however, an impractical fancy.

"I like leather interior," her father said. "You should have a cover on it."

"I don't want a cover. I like that people can see it." She looked over her shoulder to reverse from her parking spot.

"If you don't put on a cover, it will make your car look old."

"Then I'll just buy a new one," she said.

They drove down the main highway, passing entrance ramps built above low-lying bog. Trac turned into a subdivision entrance which had an empty security booth. The gate was open and looked to be permanently withdrawn. Trac paused her car near the booth to look in. The brick, painted white, was peeling, and a few roof tiles had fallen off, littering the grass around the booth. Trac pulled forward and allowed her father to direct her to the home. They passed medium-sized houses for small and growing families. Here and there, the fresh exterior of a newly built home stuck out amid the gloomy and drab landscape. A family that had returned and rebuilt, had the money to come home.

Cuong pointed to a beige brick house, telling Trac to pull into the driveway. "You should park all the way in," he said. "Don't block the sidewalk. More. A little more. More," he said, as Trac stopped and started, inching forward in the driveway at inconsequential distances. Her bumper was almost touching the hedge at the end.

They got out of her car and walked up, her father leading the way with the keys jingling in his hand. The roof was made of green metal, hurricane-proof. It was a ranch-style home with a bay window on the right side. She hated how the house looked.

"The owner rebuild but could not afford to pay. The insurance trick him, and he don't have cash." He laughed heartily. "Only trust cash, never trust insurance. In Vietnam, we don't have insurance. You buy something, that's the risk you take."

He opened the door, taking off his shoes at the entrance. The floors were tile that looked like wood flooring. The windows were new, their plastic white frames standing out against the painted green walls. The front door led directly into the living room, and the kitchen was visible right away in the open floor plan.

"I paint it green because your mom say it good luck. Green bring money."

"How long have you had the house?" she said.

"I buy last year. I fix it up more for you. I buy it last year, when you finish your first year at your job. Your mom say face east is good. This house face east."

They walked through, and Trac saw more and more the traces of her father's yearlong work and dedication to the place. The double locks on both the front and back door, the surface-mounted light fixtures (he detested how ceiling fans and hanging fixtures gathered dust), the popcorn ceiling, the laminate kitchen counters in a granite pattern.

The house looked exactly how she knew he would have wanted it to if he lived there. His own one-bedroom apartment did not look like this, and instead had the bare-boned, sterile feeling of an uninhabited bachelor pad—the house their mother lived in, on the other hand, was like a mirror to this place. He had paid for its renovation before their divorce, and insisted on deciding its each and every feature. They would often get into arguments at Home Depot, until finally her mother would give up, sulking behind him as he rolled the cart aisle to aisle.

"You will live here," he said, knocking on the wall with his fist. "I spend a lot of time and money to make it nice for you."

There wasn't a trace of her personality in the walls, the floor, the yard, the roof. She hated its location. It was one thing to purposefully erase her from the decision, to dismiss her. But Trac wondered if it had even occurred to him to ask her what she wanted. That she would have an opinion, a preference, at all, perhaps did not exist in her father's thought process.

"You will live here?" he said. He phrased it as a question this time, an uncertainty and small fear in his voice. He had never *asked* her if she wanted anything. There was a tenderness there. She suddenly felt ill, the way she had sometimes when she was homesick at summer camp as a kid. Her parents never sent her any letters or care packages like the other kids' parents. She doubted whether they even knew that was an option. They thought the summer camp itself was a gift—why did you need to send presents to your kid when they had already received the biggest reward of an experience? Trac had hated camp, how hot it was and how bossy the counselors were. She hated how displaced she felt, not really knowing, as a child, how much longer it would be unfamiliar, how much longer it would feel uncomfortable, before she could be home. That nauseous feeling, like her guts were sinking through her organs and into her legs. She had wanted to go home then, and she wanted to go back to her childhood home now. The problem was, her home no longer looked the way her father thought it should. She wished he had never bought this house for her so that she didn't have to disappoint him.

"No, I don't want to live here. I don't think I can, Dad."

He exhaled a long, slow breath, expelling something deep from his chest. On the way back to the restaurant, where Cuong would get dropped off at his minivan, they did not speak. He fiddled with the air-conditioning vents and adjusted the temperature dials. He ran his hand along the black dashboard, inspecting it. Trac pulled up next to his car.

"Dad, I'm sorry," she said. "I just don't want to live there. You didn't even ask me my opinion before buying it."

"Why do I have to ask your opinion for a gift?" he said. He had difficulty getting out of the car. He was growing older, after all. She couldn't help but notice how suddenly tired he looked. He shut the door without another word, and leaned against his gray van. He lit his cigarette, one hand to shield it, and the other to flick his lighter, and watched as his daughter drove away from him.

5

XUAN

Cuong had finally moved out of the house. They'd gotten divorced more than a year before, in secret, and had planned to break it to the kids—especially to Trieu, who still lived at home—when the time was right. But then the storm happened, and they were forced to tell the truth, there in that stiflingly hot house in Baton Rouge. Lan, her sister, had let them stay there during the flooding, but it was not without its sacrifices. They'd had to watch, for instance, Lan's fourth husband work out on his Bowflex in the living room, even though it was ninety degrees inside. His grunts wriggled into the crevices of the home, no matter which room Xuan went to find peace. She'd brought her annual astrologer's almanac and had spent several hours flipping through the Bible-thin pages, searching for answers about what might come, but could not focus with Lan's husband's noise. Her almanac had pointed to some disaster that year, which Xuan had taken at the time to be the hurricane. But she had not seen that the real disaster, spelled out clearly in her chart, was her marriage.

And then, when they were finally allowed back into the city through checkpoints and underneath the hovering of helicopters, around the large, fallen oak trees—they pulled into the driveway to a house untouched. The trash cans were knocked over near the back gate, and a decorative shutter had blown off. But otherwise, it lay on the lawn intact, not a splinter out of place. While neighbors and friends around them rebuilt their lives brick by brick, shutter by shutter, the Trung family simply walked into their home and resumed their personal dramas. It all seemed so stupid in comparison to what the Vietnamese in Disneyland had had to endure. Everything in New Orleans East had been submerged. On the West Bank, there was no flooding, but some people lost their roofs, rainwater leaking inside and soaking family photo albums, heirloom quilts, prized pianos, or couches that had been dutifully and proudly paid off.

Before leaving, Xuan had painted the front door with blessed oil. She had printed out protective symbols and laminated them, hiding them under mattresses, in closets, and above doors. She sat at the altar, lighting prayer candles, and asked the universe to shield them from harm. All these things, she knew, were the reason their house still stood, their things preserved, their bodies unharmed. And yet, Xuan could not shake the feeling that horrible things were in store for them, that somehow, because they were not being punished now, they would be later. Her chest was always cramped, as if her heart had grown too big for her body, swelling up from worry. The sounds of the helicopters over their home reminded her so much of Saigon.

When she had watched the rain at Lan's, it was oddly comforting. The downpour made her think of wet season in Vietnam, when the earth never felt solid, always soaked with water. This was Xuan's biggest complaint about their house here: there was no large, green backyard, and so, there was no earth. The orange tree had been planted in the small patch of dirt against the house. A stretch of concrete dominated the space, and Xuan had tried her best to fill it with flower pots and hanging plants. But when it rained, the concrete garden simply filled with water, rather than soaking it up. The ground was always hard. Cuong refused to put anything in, saying grass was too much maintenance, too much effort. Xuan sometimes thought that the yard was the reason they got divorced, though she knew it was much more than that. Nonetheless, she loved the little acts of care required in cultivating nature. In Vietnam, her mother put her in charge of the entire garden, and Xuan spent hours planting and pruning. The yard was lush and green, and it smelled like wet earth.

So, the day that Cuong moved out, he told her she could do what she wanted with the yard. "Add grass," he said, infuriatingly. He'd found an apartment underneath the expressway. It was a one bedroom above the flower shop advertised in his paper. He told her she could have everything—the house, the furniture, the money, and he said to tell the kids he'd finally moved out and left it all to her, so that they knew he wasn't a bad guy like she said he was. He was always so concerned with how everyone viewed him, making sure they all understood the divorce wasn't his fault, that nothing was ever his fault.

It was probably the private investigator she hired that had really done it. Cuong lived in their house for a year after the divorce, but he went places without telling her, sneaky and suspicious. She wanted to know. And when she asked, he yelled at her, saying it was none of her business. But it was her business; after all, being married for twenty-seven years certainly meant it was her business. The private investigator was a man she found in *Ôi Chúa Oi*. He had placed an ad for his PI services, and after a week of detective work, he came back with two online profiles. One, from his America Online member account, and two, a Match.com profile. Why did he have these pages? Who did he want finding them? She shoved the printouts in his face and asked him. It was her business, after all.

Trieu had walked in on it, and Xuan showed her, too. Wouldn't anyone see what she saw? This man who sulked in secrecy, never telling her the truth.

"Mom, I made this AOL profile for Dad," Trieu said. "And that Match.com profile is a different man. It's a different name and there's no picture."

Xuan's neck was hot. Her children always did this—they treated her like she was an idiot. Whenever she tried to respond in English, her tongue betrayed her, bumping clumsily in her mouth, her mind falling blank to the words she could so easily conjure in Vietnamese.

"I hire a detective to find this," she said. A professional. How could her daughter not believe her? "Look, look again," Xuan said, waving the papers closer to her daughter's face.

"Mom, stop it, I don't want to talk about this," she said. She shoved Xuan's wrist down, away from her.

"Why not? I am just showing you the truth," said Xuan. Trieu ran up the stairs. Cuong's mouth twisted into an ugly shape.

"You're ridiculous," he said. "You act like a child."

That next week, he told her he found a place. He took her to come see it after he moved, which didn't take long because he left everything for Xuan and bought new furniture. There was no yard, only a small parking lot he shared with the store where she'd once bought her pageant trophy. They had to climb a set of metal stairs to get to his door, and when they walked in, Xuan saw he'd set up his desk in the front room. It looked to be a workspace, as well as a waiting and sitting area for newspaper clients. A small kitchenette was behind his desk. There was no stove or oven, only a microwave and a hot plate he'd purchased.

"The rent is five hundred dollars a month," he said. He led her through the apartment, showing her a second office, and then his bedroom and bathroom. "That's it. I did not want to spend a lot, because I plan to buy a house for Trac."

"What house?" said Xuan.

"I drove through New Orleans East. I looked at the properties the owners can't afford, and I thought about buying from the state at auction. It's much cheaper. The houses are dirt cheap because it's in a barren area. No one thinks it will recover from the flooding, but I know it will. Give it a few years."

"Why are you buying her a house?" Xuan said. Of course he had separate funds to do this, outside of her purview. Her children told her she was crazy, but she knew better. She knew him better than anyone. She wasn't the least bit surprised to discover he had done things without consulting a single person whom it might affect.

"I'm buying her a house because she's the oldest. I will buy houses for the others when the time comes. Our children won't fight after our deaths over property."

"How do you know the area is safe? Will it ever be safe again? Disneyland was destroyed during the storm. Completely obliterated. It still looks that way."

"I can tell from the newspaper. People who owned businesses there are coming back. They're putting ads in the paper again. Where there is business, there will be development."

"What if she doesn't want the house?" said Xuan. She knew her daughter. Trac was willful. She was an Earth Goat, although Xuan could tell her daughter was doing things with her life not suited to the Goat sign. Yes, Trac valued practicality above all else, as Goats do, which was also why Trac was working as a lawyer in an extremely stressful environment: not because she loved it, but because she had a vision of her life, a life filled with convenience and comfort and luxury. But the Goat could be stubborn, even against the force and power of a Metal Dragon. Xuan knew Trac and Cuong would not agree on this issue. She saw firsthand how Trac's immovable ideas about career stood in the way of a family, even if her sign, which was characteristically nurturing, dependable, and calm, would be best suited to motherhood.

Xuan wished she would've taken her own mother seriously when she'd told her about her sign.

"You are Year of the Metal Tiger," her mother had often said. "You must pick a mate who complements your strength." But Xuan didn't believe in it then. She wished she had. Maybe she could have avoided the disastrous decision of marrying a Dragon in the same element.

"A Metal Tiger and a Metal Dragon is asking for a clash," her mother said, when Xuan first began dating Cuong. And she was right. They clashed, metal against metal. For a while, he over-powered her, reining in her ambitions to work, to go to school, asking her to remain at home with the children. After all, the Dragon was the most powerful sign. What a Dragon couldn't achieve with charming persuasion, he could with brute will.

But, again and again, Xuan pushed against the walls of her tiny pen, doing things against his judgment. Even though he told her no, she applied for and got the job as a secretary for the Anthropology Department at the community college, where she worked until she had Nhi, and it was cheaper to be a stay-at-home mom. Even though he said she shouldn't, she bought a foreclosed house by putting aside half of her secretary paycheck every month until she could buy it, and then she turned it into a rental. She wanted to make her own money, and to possess a little bit of something outside of Cuong, and to have some-thing to hand down to her own daughters. (And now look at him—buying foreclosed homes for their children when it was her idea in the first place!)

But he was constantly moving the measuring tape, telling her what she could and couldn't do based on an arbitrary and ever-changing set of rules. He always told her she was controlling, but she knew his criticism of her was just a reflection of himself. It made so much sense why their children could not stand to be near them, could not stand to listen to them. Cuong made it too difficult, and their children saw them as one person.

"You know Trac won't like whatever house you buy," she said. "Trac only likes what she herself has chosen. This is why you always disagree."

This was also why, Xuan thought, Nhi moved a thousand miles away for school. This was why Trieu was not living up to her many potential talents—spiteful defiance. This was why Trac didn't like coming home for dinner. And perhaps if she came home for dinner more, Xuan could tell her about all the men who would jump at the chance to marry her.

At their last dinner, she had tried to introduce the topic, and Trac seemed responsive. While mostly silent, she at the very least did not immediately repudiate the idea.

"I know a man who work for the lawyer. He translate for Vietnamese immigrant who want to come here," Xuan said. "Maybe you want to meet him?"

"Maybe," Trac said. "I'm really busy at work, lately."

Xuan knew they would get along. He was an Earth Horse—responsible, extroverted, and decisive. Horses and Goats complemented each other, and both of their Earth elements would meld. She knew others, too, who would be compatible. If only Trac came around for dinner more. She was the child most determined to impress her parents, and still always avoided being in the room with either of them. Her absence was what made Cuong so confident. If she was not there, he could fill in the empty space with his own assumptions, take action without consent.

"You shouldn't have bought her the house," Xuan said, again, as they walked through his new apartment.

"She will like it. Of course she will. I bought her a house. If she respects me, she'll accept the house," Cuong said.

Xuan walked through both his offices and to the front door. The apartment was bare and stark white all around. The walls had a fresh coat of paint that still smelled. The floor was a speckled white laminate tile, what you might find in a gas station or a hole-in-the-wall restaurant. She didn't feel like she thought she would. Cuong moving out on her terms was a rare victory. She thought she'd feel triumphant and righteous, like she'd proved something. All she felt was sad.

For weeks after Cuong's departure, she feared the house might cave in on her, smother her to death. Its overabundance was all the more pronounced having come from the sparsity of Cuong's apartment. Every wall, every corner, every cabinet and cranny here was stuffed full, overflowing with the things she knew she didn't need but also knew she couldn't throw away. The problem was utility—she could *use* anything. And who knew what she would need, and when? She might eventually use the life jackets or cans of Spam she'd bought in preparation for Y2K. She didn't want to get rid of Trac's dollhouse because what if Trac one day had a daughter and wanted her to have the dollhouse, too? All the girls had left some of their belongings behind when they departed for college. The closets were full of knock-off Delia's catalog clothing and adolescent detritus that they did not want but could not find the effort to clear away. And what was Xuan to do? She could not be expected to donate or trash clothing that any one of them could wear again.

It was the height of arrogance, Xuan thought, to toss away the possible instruments of survival. It was the kind of arrogance only her children could have, never knowing what it was to be without. A shirt was not just a shirt, but a makeshift sack to hold your belongings; an old bedsheet was not dirty, silverfish-eaten fabric, but a covering when you needed to hide and the mere existence of your breathing body betrayed you; a package of expired American cheese (did it ever *really* expire?) was the difference between dire hunger or simple longing, plain death or meager life.

Xuan knew what her children thought—that she was crazy, that she had a problem. When her daughters visited, they would wait until Xuan left the house to run errands. They would ask her when she was going to Wal-Mart or if she had to check on one of her properties. They pressured her to leave, asking her about Bac Linh and when was the last time she'd seen her? And then Xuan would leave, already knowing what they would do. It was an act, all of it, a play that Xuan had been cast in, where she was assigned the role of the unknowing and trusting mother. Xuan played her part well, and when she came home from wherever she had been pushed out to, she would open her refrigerator and count the things that were missing. The most common absence was produce, vaguely wilted lettuce or tomatoes whose only crime was being too ripe. Trieu was often the culprit, so self-absorbed she would never consider that her mother might want what Trieu would not, plucking from the depths of the refrigerator and pantry things she thought Xuan would never notice: macarons or chocolates she'd gotten as wedding favors; pickled quail eggs that, to her daughters, looked simply unfamiliar and therefore rotten; sealed packages of cured meat whose printed date said it was bad, but whose appearance told the real truth. She'd look through and tally the damage, and then she'd go to the trash can in the backyard and try to salvage the unsullied items.

Xuan and her children never talked about this dance. They did it over and over again, playing their parts faithfully and acting as though the other had not transgressed.

Trieu, the youngest, was an Earth Dragon. She was most like her father. It made sense that Trieu and Xuan would come to clashes in a passive-aggressive way. The Dragon and Tiger got along, but only if they both allowed the other their personal freedoms. Xuan had been seduced by Cuong's excitement and power, their verbal sparring and banter, but eventually, it was clear, this Metal Tiger and this Metal Dragon did not understand how to concede space and willpower. But Trieu's Earth and Xuan's Metal did not clang and clatter like Metal on Metal did.

Their disagreements occurred in silent battles, unacknowledged but consistent combat. If Xuan had been wise, she would've chosen the birth years of her children more carefully, as her mother had warned.

She bolted the door and peeked out the front window curtains. It was only past 1:00 p.m., but she felt exhausted by the day. The neighborhood was getting worse and she worried about the Black boys who sometimes rode their bikes in front of her house. She worried herself into exhaustion. She couldn't help or control it. When the boys were out there, when someone pulled into her driveway to turn around, when the streetlight flickered on and off—her mind burrowed into the darkness of her fear, swelling and pulsing so that it was difficult to breathe.

When she and Cuong first bought the place in Quartier Mignon, the neighborhood was brand-new. It was well less than a decade old by the time they began house hunting, in search of a home for their growing family. It was January, an auspicious month to buy a house that year. Nhi kicked and tumbled in her belly, a Fire Tiger on the way. Xuan remembered how active she was, hot and uncomfortable there in her claustrophobic womb. She should have known then that Nhi would feel trapped wherever she was, always seeking the better place. But at the time, the neighborhood seemed perfect for Trac and Nhi to grow up in. The neighbors were white and middle-class. The school around the corner was small but highly regarded. The houses were newly built, and what could be better than something new? In Vietnam, if you had something new, it meant you were rich. If you had something old, it meant you were poor. If you had nothing at all, it meant you were nothing. Simple as that.

But then Katrina happened and many of their neighbors fled. Their housing value dived and remained low. People from bad neighborhoods who'd been flooded out came to Quartier Mignon because they could afford it. If Xuan had known how the neighborhood would change, she would never have bought the house. Dangerous people were making her home dangerous. She never took walks anymore because she was afraid. And now that Cuong had left, she was truly alone. If she was attacked or robbed or murdered, who would know? Surely not her daughters, who checked on her only if it was a matter of convenience or guilt.

She slid the chain on her door, deciding she wouldn't leave the house again that day. The air inside felt hot and still. She had turned the AC off. The moisture from outdoors seeped in through the cracks, sitting in the air and making her overstuffed home feel more oppressive than ever. Her childhood home in Vietnam had never held the air like this. That house was grand, in the French colonial style of their homeland's white-faced visitors. The windows had been large and always flung open, allowing the heat to blow in from the oncoming storms that sometimes only threatened to appear. Her mother kept the house cluttered, not intentionally but in the messy way of utility, of having people constantly in and out.

She never threw anything away, like Xuan, but in her mother's case, those things were truly reused and continuously replaced, renewed and repurposed. If not recycled for one of her children, then one of the neighborhood families might have need of the spare cloth to make a quilt, or of the old chess set, even with pieces missing. People came to her mother for help, for money, for advice. They shared their water well with others, they accepted household work from kids down the street. They sold books and herbal medicines from the side of the house. Their family name had meant something in Saigon.

But that house was gone now. Her sister, Lan, went back a few years ago and visited the site of their home. They heard after arriving in the States a lot of different things: that it was burned to the ground, that it had been seized and occupied by a high-ranking Việt Cộng officers, that it was left to rot. But Chi Lan confirmed it was no longer there. The method of its disappearance was unknown to them, but Xuan didn't know if that mattered to her. Who cared how it vanished if the end result was the same? The site of all her memories, the place where she became a woman, the location of her first kiss, first heartbreak, first friendship, first loss, first delight—it had evaporated, just like all the other material belongings of her youth.

In Vietnam, the family altar had had an entire room to itself. In America, the small altar honoring her parents and Cuong's parents was wedged between the dining room and the kitchen. Black-and-white photos of austere faces stared back at her as she lit a stick of incense for them and swiped some ashes from the bowl full of oranges. She knelt down and prayed for their souls. The picture of her mother was one as an older woman. She sat at the stand-up piano, which Xuan had purchased at a yard sale in the neighborhood when they first moved to Quartier Mignon. Xuan remembered that day well—the neighbor, Bernice Langois, lived three houses down in the yellow-with-blue-shutters colonial-style house. Collapsible tables were laden with clothes and housewares. Two perfectly fine armchairs upholstered in green corduroy fabric also sat on the lawn. Xuan couldn't believe this woman was getting rid of these belongings, all in fine condition.

A stand-up piano sat on the porch, as if the Langoises had started moving it outside without realizing how heavy a piano really was, and only getting as far as the front steps. The music rack was a faux-weave texture, and the bench was walnut with an orange velvet seat.

"It's. A. Kimball," said Bernice. She spoke very slowly, enunciating each word. Xuan was embarrassed for both this woman and for herself. She knew what Bernice was saying. Sure, when she had first arrived in the United States, she was so scared of failure that she learned just enough to get by. In Vietnam, she'd taken English in school, but to hear it spoken by native speakers was not at all like it had been in her classes, which she came to realize had not prepared her in any way. It wasn't until she had

Trac and attended a parent-teacher conference, barely able to ask about the math homework, that she understood how much she would never be able to do for her children if she didn't try. The math teacher, a woman wearing an embroidered sweater decorated in cartoonish numbers and crayons, had looked at her with such annoyance and disdain, Xuan could think of few other instances in which she felt as incompetent.

She watched American television during the day to try to become more proficient. She heard if you knew how to sing in a language, then you really knew the language, so she listened to American pop songs over and over again, but didn't think it was working. It was getting better, though—Trac learned English in school, and they practiced at home when Cuong was not there to hear. She had trouble responding quickly, but not with discerning tone and speed. Bernice was simply doing what so many others did, including what her own children would do when they became older. She was accustomed to this response, at the bank, at the grocery, at Trac's school. But what did *Kimball* mean? Trac was seven at the time, her hand clasping Xuan's like a lifesaver trailing at her side. Xuan's belly was full of Nhi, only two months away from childbirth.

"Do. You. Like. It? *Kimball*," said Bernice. "You. Must. Be. New. Neighbor. Hello. I. Am. Bernice."

"Hi, Mrs. Bernice. I'm Trac, and this is my mom, Xuan."

"Oh, my, aren't you cute!" said Bernice.

"My mother wants to know how much the piano is," said Trac. She spoke in a level voice, used to conversing with adults for her parents. She'd had to call the doctor's office the week before to schedule her own appointment for a vaccine.

"It's two hundred dollars. A steal, for a piano. Solid walnut, and I just got it tuned. The only thing is, you have to find a way to transport it. My husband didn't realize professional piano movers have to be hired." Bernice's laugh was tinkling and disingenuous. Xuan didn't need to understand English to interpret this woman's character.

"Hai tram đồng, mẹ," Trac said.

Xuan took two hundred dollars in cash from her wallet and handed it to Bernice. "It nice to meet you," she said. "Very beautiful home." Bernice gave Xuan a business card for a professional piano moving service, but Xuan just gave fifty dollars to some of Cuong's friends, men they'd met at the Vietnamese Catholic Church, and they moved the piano from Bernice's porch three houses down to the red brick Trung house. The men, Minh, Binh, Viet, and Bao, showed up wearing wifebeaters and car-oil-stained work pants. Bernice, not realizing who they were, called the neighborhood police on them, creating a stir and forcing Xuan to run out of her house with Trac so they could explain the situation. Minh, Binh, Viet, and Bao were very dark-skinned, the kind of men who labored in the sun, the kind of men she would never speak to if they were in Vietnam, but who, out of necessity, she had to befriend here. The nuances of Xuan's life flattened or disappeared in America, a fact that her children would never be able to recognize. They would not ever know, for instance, the sound of a piano as it vibrated in the cavernous ceilings of their home in Vietnam, the particular warm echo that was made.

Her mother loved the piano. Toward the end of her life, she became increasingly bitter and mean. She said cruel things to Xuan about the life she had built, how Cuong was not good enough, how the children were too American. But when she sat at the Kimball, she became softer and kinder. She stopped remarking on Xuan's mistakes. The music she played soothed her irritated and unsatisfied spirit, and it filled their claustrophobic rooms with nostalgic yearning. Even though the sound in their new American house was muffled and flat, penned in by low ceilings and closed windows, it still reminded Xuan so much of home. The thought of it being burned to the ground or occupied by Việt Cộng or rotting with wet, these thoughts never came to her when her mother played piano. She only remembered how happy and safe they had been.

In the altar photo, her mother has her gray hair tied in a tight knot at the base of her neck. She faces the camera, her right hand resting on piano keys. Her eyes look out somewhere behind the photographer. Her face is mournful, a deep wistfulness. Xuan gazed at her mother's face in the photo and longed for her presence, a gripping ache that made her throat seize. She realized she couldn't conjure an image of her mother outside of this photo, could not imagine her face on her own without the help of a picture. She could hear "Für Elise" being played on the Kimball, but could not hear her mother's voice, could not remember its sound, that familiar cadence, that familiar language. Xuan prayed again and again that she might remember—a selfish prayer, but one she hoped God would hear.

Xuan went upstairs and sat in Nhi's old room. She sometimes lay on the bed in there because it was bathed in the most natural light from its large, south-facing window. The silence of the house emphasized more than ever its emptiness. She lay down on the mattress, Nhi's patchwork quilt fuzzed over with a thin layer of dust from disuse. She stared up at the popcorn ceiling, shadows cast by the little bumps. A brown, crusty lump, a trail of dried dirt, nestled itself where the ceiling met the wall. It was right above a poster of Yosemite National Park. Nhi had plastered the whole white wall in magazine cutouts and posters, trying her best to cover the room with personality. Xuan stood beneath it, her head thrown back as she examined the stain. She dragged the desk chair over and stepped up.

Even on the desk chair, Xuan did not come to eye level with the brown mass. She reached up, tracing her finger gently along its trail. It was both hard and crumbling beneath her touch. She followed the brown mounds with her finger from the corner onto the ceiling.

The attic was above Nhi's room. Xuan had not gone into the attic for over a year. The last time she tried, it was to retrieve the Christmas decor from its plastic storage boxes. The door pulled down from the ceiling, and a stepladder unfolded. Xuan found that she was not strong enough to bring the plastic boxes down the attic stairs alone. She'd gotten as far as the first step, but could feel her arms failing as she attempted to balance both her body and the box. Cuong did not care about decorating the house, and her children did not come home for Christmas that year. Trac was still in law school and was busy, Nhi did not want to purchase a plane ticket home, and Trieu went on a winter ski trip with her friends. When Christmas happened the next year, a few months ago, she didn't even bother going up for the boxes, even though the whole family had Christmas at the house.

She felt the need to investigate, an inexplicable fear. She tugged on the string dangling from the attic door and pulled it down. She unfolded the stiff, wooden stepladder, placed each foot steadfastly on the grooved step before advancing to the next. She held on to the railing on the right side. The possibility of falling frightened her.

The attic was dark, except for the beam of sunlight falling through the small, circular window set in the house's front gable. The Christmas decorations sat exactly where she'd left them. Afternoon light illuminated the small space and seemed to catch and cling onto the edges of things, so that out of the corner of her eye, she thought she saw shadows fluttering in and out of the room. When she turned to look, there was nobody, but the sound of whispers filled her ears with static.

A fine wood powder sprinkled the top of the boxes, a dry pulp that coated the attic floor as well. Her eyes followed the dust, and she looked at the support beam next to the Christmas storage to find thin, finger-shaped, earth-colored hills trailing all along the beam, up onto the attic rafters, a network of packed mud, dust, and wood. These paths wound and sprawled all along the roof, along every beam and strut, every exposed wood surface, like Medusa's hair enveloping the house. Xuan knocked her fist against the wood and heard the hollow thump of her knuckle. In the cobwebs draped from beam to beam, dozens of clear wings the size of rice grains fluttered, twirling and dancing in the wind caused by Xuan's breath.

When the pest control inspector arrived the next day in his khaki shirt and stone wash jeans, he looked about the house wordlessly. Xuan had told Chi Lan a man was coming into her home, in case he attacked or kidnapped her. He did not do those things, but he was not friendly. He broke the second-to-last step of the attic stairs and did not apologize. He spoke to Xuan in a slow, elevated voice, as Xuan was used to hearing these past three decades.

"Ma'am, when was the last time you got your house inspected?" he said.

"I don't remember, but I think maybe I got inspect around ten years ago," she said, although this was a lie. She had never had the house inspected.

"New Orleans is home to Formosa termites. They're most active in the hot weather. Their swarming season is March to July, and they look for wood structures to burrow into and build their nests. You have to get your house inspected every year." Xuan nodded her head, but knew she would never do such a thing. She hated paying for annual inspections. And anyway, she felt lucky to have discovered this before it was too late, led there by destiny. She didn't need the inspection. They were a scam—she much preferred to call when the issue became apparent. The pest inspector seemed to know she was lying.

"Ma'am, you really do need a yearly preventative inspection, especially in this region. It looks like if you had waited another month, or even week, your attic would have collapsed. The infestation is advanced. Almost the entire roof is hollow. The nest covers every inch of your attic."

"What does this mean?" said Xuan.

"It means you need to have your roof replaced and the house fumigated."

"But how they get in?" She felt violated. The cave she had filled with things, walls of things to protect her from the outside world, had been invaded. She felt ill thinking about how easy it had been for them to burrow into the ramparts and eat away from the inside the structure that was supposed to shield her from harm.

"They get in through gaps in the foundation. A pretty good guess is that they came through your chimney, which may not be properly sealed."

Xuan saw him out. He gave her a list of recommended companies who specialized in termite damage. He scheduled another visit to deal with eradication of the infestation. After he left, she sat down at the walnut piano and ran her hands along the ledge where sheet music sat. She played a C major scale, but the piano was out of tune. No one ever played the piano now that her mother had died and the kids had stopped lessons. Xuan wished her mother was there. Perhaps she was lurking in the crumbling attic, had been this whole time, waiting for Xuan to go up there to find her trapped in the infested room. Maybe the infestation was her mother, an expression of her anger at being forgotten. She struck her fist against the piano, an opaque knock ringing out in the empty house.

6

NHI

The television volume was turned all the way up. Nhi could not stand to be in the living room. The newscaster's voice rang louder and more unbearable within the house's cramped living room. It was both cool and warm, the porcelain floor tile emanating a chill, but the late-August New Orleans heat finding a way in through old window gaps all the same. The effect was a bodily discomfort that would not allow Nhi to sit still, even as the warmth caused a desire to lie down. Her mother paced between the kitchen and the living room, her cork slides flapping against the floor. Her jade bangles clanked against each other. She banged the kitchen cabinets as if to make sure the entire house knew she was there, could not ignore her. Nhi loathed the racket. She was home for a visit on summer vacation and had been for weeks now. She was convinced her normal threshold for her parents could not exceed four days. After that, she became too irritable and impatient. She would fly back to California in three days.

Her parents did not know that she had dropped out of school

this past semester. She had been failing, on notice with UCLA. The only course she enjoyed was the acting class she had taken as an elective. Her father insisted she choose a practical major, but she wanted to act. He told her no, flat out.

"You can be prelaw. Going to law school is okay. I will pay for it," he said. "Or you can be premed. You can also work with computers—my friend say you make a lot of money work with computers."

"Maybe you can major in business," said Xuan. "Tigers can do business very good. I have my house rental, and look how success I am. Imagine if I go to business school for it!"

That had been when she was a second-semester freshman the year before, when the university required her to state a major. Her semester grades had been sent to New Orleans, the permanent address listed in her student information, and on the transcript was the major she had confirmed with her academic adviser: theater, with a minor in film and television. She had to declare right away because admission into the School of Theater, Film, and Television required an audition, and they had a limited number they could admit into the college. When Cuong saw what she'd done, he called her and told her it was not realistic. Nhi did not respond to his suggestions of law, medicine, or computer programming, nor did she voice any affirmative understanding of his demands. She remained silent, which her father interpreted as submission. He assumed he had beaten these thoughts of acting out of her.

In truth, Nhi had learned something crucial. She realized that she didn't care anymore about the burdens he had invented and put upon her shoulders. The resentment she felt boiled over after that phone call. She'd spent her whole life pacifying him, molding her own will into his so that it didn't fully defy his wishes, toeing the line between obedience and insubordination.

His wrath was no longer a sufficient form of control. She changed the declaration of her major to prelaw and sent him the document to prove it. She enrolled in the required courses, but failed them all, except her acting class elective. She updated the mailing address in her student account, so her father did not receive any of her transcripts. And then, that past semester, she withdrew from school. She saved up the money her father sent for expenses, and spent it on an acting and improv class in the city. She got a job waiting tables at a sushi restaurant in West Hollywood, an attempt to be in the thick of all the action.

Nhi had forgotten how suffocating home could be, there with her parents, who hovered over her, searching for reasons to suspect her deviance. She couldn't wait to leave; she'd already printed out her boarding pass and started packing up her suitcase for when she flew out of MSY airport in two days. If possible, the atmosphere in the house was made more intolerable with the news of a hurricane that had been brewing, slow and menacing, over the hot waters of the Gulf of Mexico. Nhi really felt bad for Trieu, who had to stay behind with their parents.

"It's going to be fine," said Nhi. They stood outside in the small, concrete backyard, looking out through the gate into the street. "Remember Hurricane Ivan? They said it was going to kill us, and all we got was some gusts of wind and a day off from school."

"Some of my friends are having a hurricane party tonight because school was canceled," said Trieu. "Their parents don't care. Meanwhile, *our* mom has been listening to doom and gloom. It's driving me crazy. She keeps telling me I need to pray."

The term "doom and gloom" was an umbrella expression for anything related to their mother's exhaustive worrying. Their mother could both *be* doom and gloom, and also consume the doom and gloom fed to her from the local news station or gossip from her friends. They had coined this term years ago, when their mother stockpiled the house with a year's worth of canned Spam and bottled water in anticipation of Y2K. Trieu and Nhi, being closer in age and having lived together at home more recently, shared these kinds of inside jokes with each other more than they did with Trac, who moved out for college when Trieu and Nhi were only nine and eleven years old.

"Mom wants to evacuate," said Nhi.

"That's not happening. I already heard Dad yelling about how he doesn't have time to pack up and go. He's worried about getting the newspaper done in time."

"She already packed her bag. Did you see her loading up all the china? She's covered them in pillows in her closet. If a hurricane rips our house apart, I'm pretty sure cardboard boxes and pillows won't protect her china."

"She also filled all the bathtubs," said Trieu. "Even though the garage is still stockpiled with gallons of spring water."

"I know," Nhi said, commiserating. "And you know what I saw her doing after Dad told her he wasn't leaving?"

"What?"

"She took out her big-ass horoscope book and started yelling about how we were positioned for really bad fortune this year, saying there was an unlucky star in the Water element and that our house is facing a direction that's 'combative' or something. She lost it." Nhi could not help laughing. She wondered what it must be like to believe something so much, in the way her mother did, something that was so clearly made up, that she would organize her entire life and her family's around it.

"I bet Dad loved that," said Trieu. "Dragons love being yelled at."

The air was warm but outside didn't smell fetid as it normally did from the humidity. There was a steady breeze, and a calm, an uncharacteristic silence free from the typical buzzing of insects, croaks of frogs, cacophony of birds.

Inside, their mother had piled all her luggage near the front door. She had two large suitcases, one full of clothes and the other full of food and bottles of water. Her hot curlers and professional grade makeup kit were in their travel cases. Her silver-spray-painted plastic trophy also sat on the ground next to them.

"Your dad agree to evacuate. We will leave in half hour," she said.

"Mom, I have a flight in three days," said Nhi.

"That is in three days. The storm happen tomorrow and we be back before you have to fly. School cancel for Trieu, so she don't miss school, either."

Nhi did not want to bring her entire suitcase. She borrowed a tote from Trieu and packed two pairs of underwear, one change of clothes, and her toiletries. Trieu did the same, packing a small backpack with the bare minimum necessities and privileging entertainment, books and comics and her Game Boy, which would fill up time at Aunt Lan's house.

"Think we'll need shampoo?" Trieu said, holding a full-size bottle of Pantene with reluctance. She really did not want to carry it in her bag.

"Aunt Lan will have stuff. We might not even have to wash our hair since we're coming back in less than three days."

Trieu tossed the shampoo on her bed. Later, when they put their things in the trunk of the old minivan, all the floor space was already occupied by their mother's luggage. Their father brought only his teal toiletries case and a pair of underwear, both shoved in a plastic grocery bag.

"Why do I need to pack when your mom bring anything I need to survive? I don't need to bring clothes, what wrong with the clothes I'm wearing?" he said in the car. Their mother clicked her tongue and told him in Vietnamese it never hurt to be prepared.

"I'm prepare. If something happen, it happen. I have no control. I will react if I need to react, but prepare is pointless. It mean nothing in the end. How can you prepare for a disaster?"

Xuan did not respond, but Nhi could see her expression in the car's passenger side sun visor. Her jaw clenched, physically holding the response she wished to make. They drove over the Mississippi River bridge. Below them was the water, the tail end of a river whose choppy and dark surface hid secrets and sediment from all the places it ran through. Nhi saw women swimming in it, tiny figures gracefully dividing the water with each stroke of their arms. But, they were gone in a flash of light as a cloud drifted, the sun reflecting briefly on the river.

Her father cursed and slammed on the brakes. Someone had cut in front of him. Cars on the bridge inched forward. It was surprising to see people out so close to the arrival of the storm. Nhi thought many would have already left if they were going to at all. As they drove to the outskirts of the city, lines of stationary cars in each lane gleamed under the bright, overcast sky. The car was filled with the blast of the AC, which their father had put on its highest setting in order to circulate air. She could smell her father's aroma of old cigarettes which he had tried to mask with Old Spice. The silence among the car's occupants made Nhi wish she were already on the plane to California. Her mother turned on the radio and clicked the preset for NPR, moving the volume dial up so the radio hosts could be heard over the roar of the air vents.

"Doom and gloom," Trieu said, under her breath.

"Dad stinks," Nhi said, under her breath. Trieu pretended to gag.

They both silently laughed, their backs hunched and shaking. The combination of smell and sound, the jerking of the car, was altogether nauseating, but Nhi laughed anyway, she and her sister clutching each other's hands.

When their father got the chance, he exited the interstate and drove onto an unfamiliar road. It took them into a rural area with a lot more traffic from people who'd seemed to have the same idea as Cuong. They drove and drove and drove, and Xuan asked if he knew where he was going. "We drive in the direction of conflict," she said, cryptically.

"We drive west. It toward Baton Rouge," he said.

They stopped at a small gas station which had a sign that said Out of Gas, but whose parking lot was still full of cars, their owners milling outside, speaking to the gas attendant. When Cuong got back in the car, he did not talk or inform them of their whereabouts. He simply started the car and drove again. No one asked. It took them eight hours to arrive in Baton Rouge, which was only eighty miles away. They lost four hours to traffic and the rest to the detour.

Aunt Lan's house was big but tacky. It was full of the things Nhi found in many other immigrant friends' homes: tiled floors throughout, uncomfortable leather furniture, the salty odor of boiled bones and fish sauce, taxidermized sea creatures hanging on the walls, painted silk images of Vietnam and its people. Aunt Lan fussed over them, speaking so rapidly in Vietnamese that Nhi had more trouble than usual discerning what she said. She went to the kitchen and began preparing large bowls of soup for everyone, which she stewed all day in preparation for their arrival.

Aunt Lan's fourth husband, Dr. Danh, stood to the side, nodding and smiling. He wore gym shorts that hit well above the knee, exposing a liberal expanse of thigh. Dr. Danh had the peculiar look of someone aged and waning, but also fit, like a military man gone to seed. His tanned, square face was wrinkled, his neck and hands veiny, betraying how old he might be, but his arms were muscular, legs stout. His ten-year-old son, Phuoc, sat behind him on the olive leather couch playing on a laptop, not looking up nor saying hello.

They sat down to eat together. It was the most Nhi had heard her mother speak all day, talking freely with her sister. They laughed and joked, sometimes lowering their voices to gossip right there at the table. When her mother spoke in Vietnamese, it was natural and without self-awareness. Nhi sometimes forgot she only heard her speak in a language that made her seem clumsy and dim. She suddenly felt bad for the petulant way she'd spoken to her mother all day, her voice slow and loud. Her mother had a whole life outside of her—friends and experiences and a language. She wished she could understand what they talked about, could hear her mother in her chosen tongue. How different their relationship would be if they could communicate. Perhaps she could confide in her mother about school and acting, if only she could find the right words in the right language to express how important it was.

As Nhi and Trieu left the adults in the kitchen to speak in their unintelligible tongue, Nhi inwardly reprimanded herself for thinking of them as "adults," and of herself as "child." She was nineteen, she lived on her own and worked on her own, and she made her own decisions. She needed to begin considering herself an adult, or her father never would. They'd left the kitchen, in fact, because the "adults" had begun talking about them as if they weren't sitting at the table.

"Trieu always has her head in the clouds," Nhi thought her mother said.

"Well, Nhi has no discipline," Nhi thought her father said.

It was difficult to be sure. Nhi translated her parents in a vague way, her brain detecting the general meaning, but passively and without conscious effort. She never knew the exact sentiment, something always lost in the conversion. It was like she could see a few cogs grinding away, but could not see the whole machine, did not know what the cogs were powering.

She did not have an understanding of this discrepancy until she began taking French classes in high school. The literal translation, word by word on the page, was a much different, more laborious, more deliberate act of understanding. She had to work for it. But she thought she could understand the intentions of the words, more clearly define the boundaries of meaning. She heard Vietnamese from behind a veil, the words suggesting a feeling, a gist, an imprecise emotion, but never full clarity.

The two sisters explored the house together. It was a large home for only three people. Aunt Lan and Dr. Danh were rich, something their mother complained about ever since they'd gotten married two years ago.

"It very tacky," Xuan said. "Bác Sĩ Danh a very tacky man. He use to be poor, that why he always buy very ugly thing. He marry very young woman before because he have no class or respect. He very lucky to have Dì Lan now, she help him."

But walking through the house, Nhi could see that Aunt Lan perhaps had had little effect on Dr. Danh's taste. She noticed when they first met Dr. Danh that he was wearing a diamond-encrusted Rolex. Her mother's stare had lingered on the watch, lips pursed, holding a distasteful word on her tongue. The house had other such things as a large jade statue of Dr. Danh himself, a Jacuzzi bath with jets in each of the bathrooms, and matte gold curtains in the master bedroom and in Phuoc's room, whose floor was littered with broken toys and empty gadget boxes.

"Get out!" Phuoc said when they stopped by. There was a hoarseness on the edges of his voice, a bite that was unexpected.

"We didn't mean to bother you," Nhi said.

"Get out! Get out! Get out!" he said. He began slamming with each hand a plastic fire truck and a magic eight ball lying nearby on the rug. "Get out! Get out! Get out!" The rattling of the toys against the tile floor and Phuoc's screaming made it difficult to think. Nhi felt a dry hand on her bare shoulder.

"Phuoc, be nice to our guests," said Dr. Danh. Phuoc stared at his fire truck. It was a foot long and had a to-scale, fully rotating and extendable ladder attached. The truck had many of the details in miniature of the real thing, although some of the paint was cracked, some of the more delicate parts had broken off. Dr. Danh rubbed Nhi's shoulder. "I'm very sorry about my son. He is still learning manners. You two make yourself at home."

Nhi hadn't looked at Dr. Danh up close before. His face had deep lines, heavy crow's-feet and laugh creases. His eyes were small and black, hooded by drooping lids and framed by triangular, sparse eyebrows. He looked much older than Aunt Lan, who was in her late fifties, although she'd gotten a lot of cosmetic work done, so perhaps she wasn't a reliable measurement of age. He smiled at them both, a closed-mouth smirk that was more leering than friendly.

Trieu grabbed Nhi's hand. "Thank you, Bác Sĩ Danh. We will be sure to tell our parents about this. About how hospitable you are." She smiled back at Dr. Danh, full teeth. There was fear lurking under her confidence, but only Nhi could detect this. She knew her younger sister well.

"Phuoc, don't make me come back here to remind you." Dr. Danh's smile flickered. He gave Phuoc one last admonishing stare before going to the kitchen, where the voices of their parents and Aunt Lan were echoing against the rug-less tile.

"You're ugly cunts," Phuoc said.

"You little piece of shit," Trieu said. She advanced into his room, but Nhi, still holding her hand, pulled her back.

"I hope you die in the hurricane," he said. "Get out of my house."

"Make us," said Trieu, whose voice had taken on a childish tone of its own.

"Calm down. He's ten years old," Nhi said, embarrassed. Here they were, sparring with a child surrounded by broken toys. But Trieu's comment had rendered him silent. He could not make anyone do anything, the burden of his youth more apparent to himself than ever.

They left him and sat together in the guest room with the door closed. They cranked the wind-up radio and listened to coverage of the city evacuation efforts, even though the electricity was still on and they could technically use the electric radio. They kept winding and winding, the zipping noise as the plastic arm rotated a kind of soothing, a kind of calm.

When the storm passed over and the electricity finally did go out, they wound the radio up together in the kitchen until their father told them to stop.

"There are reports that water is rising in parts of the city, already at ten feet in the lower Ninth Ward and still climbing. Footage of residents left behind show their desperation and hunger…" The voice of the radio host crackled into the still, dimly lit kitchen. Xuan's cork sandals smacked against the floor as she paced the adjacent room, slurping on a cup of hot tea made on the portable gas stove on the back porch.

"Thank god, thank god," she muttered, "I bless the house before we left. I hope God protect us."

"Ten feet?" said Nhi. "Doom and gloom. They're exaggerating." She didn't even know what ten feet looked like. What was the height of a house, or a tree? How did the water compare? In her mind, she recalled the flooded streets when it rained too much, ankle-deep water that surged into the sewer in front of their house. She was incapable of imagining water any higher than that.

"I don't think they're exaggerating," said Trieu. "How could they be? It's the news."

"They always exaggerate. Think about the numbers, it's just crazy."

Trieu did not respond. The walls held in the hot moisture from outside, the air stagnant. The stale smell of old water enveloped the house, although Nhi had become nose-blind to it. The adults were on the back porch, their father smoking a cigarette while their mother heated the kettle for another cup of tea. Aunt Lan sat on the patio furniture, painting her nails a shade of Sally Hansen magenta. Only Dr. Danh was inside, cloistered away in his office where his Bowflex machine was. They could hear his muffled grunts from behind the closed door.

Trieu stood up, shared a conspiratorial look with Nhi and glanced around the room before cracking open the refrigerator and peering in. The temperature of the fridge had already begun to intensify the odor of pickled cabbage and wilting vegetables. She opened it wider and grabbed the box of pinot grigio on the top shelf before making a slow jog toward the guest bathroom. Nhi took the wind-up radio with her, cranking the arm on her way to the bathroom.

Inside, Nhi turned the cold bath tap all the way as Trieu rummaged in the cabinet under the sink. She held up a pink bottle of Mr. Bubbles. The radio sat on the bathroom counter, still delivering news of the storm.

"Looks like that little brat still takes bubble baths," Trieu said, before unscrewing the top and pouring a liberal amount of the syrupy liquid into the stream of water rushing from the tap. Nhi pressed the spout on their stolen boxed wine and filled their cups up to the rim. They both stripped off their clothes and stepped into the cold bath, wine and cups in hand.

Nhi felt no self-consciousness about her body, none of the way she felt in audition waiting rooms while fully clothed, sitting next to women who were taller and thinner and bustier and whiter. In Trieu, Nhi saw her own body—a boyish frame covered in the softness of feminine skin. They both had the Trung belly, a thin layer of fat on their abdomens, the first place they would gain weight when they were older. They were incredibly thin but had no muscle mass. Trieu and Nhi both had bad acne after puberty as well, an affliction that Trac had never struggled with. They were envious of her pearly smooth cheeks, which she'd inherited from their mother. They had gotten their father's skin, porous and oily, bumpy and easily tanned. When they were little, Trieu and Nhi took many baths together, and when Trieu's body began to change, Nhi showed her how to shave her legs and underarms, showed her how to pluck the coarse black hairs from her bikini line, instructed her as she used her first tampon, brought her to the mall and bought her a proper bra with her own money, showed her how to press her fingers against the red bumps on her face, drain them and hide them with skin-colored liquids and powders. She showed her all the things their mother never showed them because their mother did not have their coarse hair or their bad skin, did not use tampons and did not think children needed new or expensive bras.

Sitting in the bath together seemed to calm Nhi down, reminding her that there was a stable feeling in the world. Trieu grimaced as she sipped the warm white wine. The water was refreshing and cool to their hot skin at first, but became tepid within a few minutes. The bubbles made a sizzling sound as they popped, and they sat in the water without speaking, tart white wine against their lips.

"Images taken of families on their rooftops have emerged, many people forced to axe their way through attics as water rises steadily in their homes…"

It was still gray outside. The flat light of the sky gave the bathroom a strange glow. The bath tap dripped water. Nhi wondered if the jets worked, if that would drown out the sound of the dripping.

"…reports of rescues being made by residents with canoes or kayaks. There is some criticism of state and federal response to the storm, as water continues to surge into the city…"

Nhi looked up to the door, and through the crack she saw a crinkled crow's-foot pointing to a beady black eye. Trieu hadn't seen him yet. She stared into her cup of warm wine, unaware of the dripping and the overcast light and the eyes. Their parents were right about Trieu, even if she wouldn't admit it and got upset to hear them say the things they said—she had her head in the clouds. She was always lost in extravagant and unrealistic ideas, overconfident in her ability to achieve. Nhi had always considered Trieu the most ambitious of the three of them, but the least equipped for success. Ambitious in her lofty goals, ambitious in her standards for herself and the world, but those ambitions were never in reach. And part of the reason they were never in reach was because Trieu had no sense of the world around her. Dr. Danh's eyes stared at them through the crack in the door, and Trieu remained entrapped in her own mind.

"New Orleans police are asking that anyone with access to a boat please consider joining the rescue effort. An I-10 ramp is now being used as a boat ramp. In many cases, people who need to be saved have had to resubmerge themselves in floodwaters to access rescue boats…"

He moved the door ajar just a bit more. He looked at Nhi, their eyes meeting, but this did not seem to scare him away or make him ashamed. It was as if he were watching a television program, and the subjects of the show had become aware of their onlooker, unable to break free from the scene into which they'd been placed. Nhi pushed her foot against Trieu's, who followed her sister's gaze to the man in the doorway. Neither of them made a sound. Nhi thought about this moment through-out her life and replayed it over the years, trying to puzzle out why they didn't scream or rush to cover up. Why they remained submerged in bathwater, why they stared at him in defiance and total silence. The older she got, the more she forgot the reasons of her youth.

But in the moment, it was a battle of wills. Screaming and shouting seemed a concession, an admission of fear. Covering up, an admission of shame. Leaving the bath, a rejection of the water to which they would be unable to return, and Nhi loved the water too much for that. And buried underneath the de-fiance was unease, not of Dr. Danh, but of her parents, of the trouble and embarrassment it would cause for them.

"You see these people walking through the water, and they look shell-shocked." The radio spoke to them from what felt like a thousand miles away. The hum of static underlying the reporter's voice.

The door clicked when it shut. Nhi and Trieu breathed.

"They look like refugees. They *are* refugees."

7

TRAC

Trac was in Belinda's living room eating bad Chinese food straight from the to-go containers as she complained about Francis. The television glowed, a news segment about the hurricane on low volume. A pixelated, multicolored mass swirled toward shore in the meteorologist's predictive computer image. The screen flickered throughout their viewing, full of static, each time Belinda cursing the cable company, or hurricane winds, or the electricity, and each time, Trac would see the form of a woman on the screen, gone so fast Trac sincerely wondered if she was going crazy.

It was as easy as a tilt of the head, as quick as two seconds and a blink for Belinda to press her lips, greased with lo mein oil, against Trac's.

Trac didn't feel anything at first, only a numb, struggling comprehension. But when Belinda pulled away, her own heart was beating so fast that her chest hurt, the spaces behind her eyes were tight, and her hands were clenched, fingernail marks on her palms. It was only later Trac realized these reactions as symptoms of thrill. She was hot and cold at the same time, sick and excited.

Belinda was beautiful, the kind of woman who might not appeal to everyone, but who possessed a magnetic personality, large blue eyes and perfectly symmetrical lips. Her features were so exaggerated, she sometimes looked alien, a simultaneously austere and kind face. She had a dainty, pointed chin, a charming widow's peak, and cheeks always flushed pink.

In the office, Belinda wore conservative cardigans and buttoned-up blouses. She was always dressed in slacks. When they went for lunch the first time, Belinda confessed she used to wear pencil skirts, that when she first got the job, she was so excited to buy business clothing, couldn't wait to wear preppy skirt-and-blazer sets. She'd gone to J.Crew and bought three full-priced suits in black, navy, and khaki. But one of the older lawyers, one of the partners, always made comments about her legs.

"Not anything too off-color," she said. "Just stuff like, 'Look at those legs!' and 'Legs for miles!' and there was just something about even *knowing* he looked at my legs that made me feel kind of dirty."

Trac had never experienced this in the office, but she didn't find it difficult to believe. She'd seen the secretary and the legal interns and the paralegals navigate similar, deceptively innocuous office interactions. But Trac herself had never had to put up with Barry sitting on the edge of her desk, or Stephen touching the small of her back as he passed her on the way to the office kitchenette.

In fact, Trac had a theory she had developed about this as an undergraduate when she was in a sorority. She realized she existed in a state of in-between. Her friends often forgot she was not-white, but, if this were possible, at the same time always remembered she was not-white. Because she wasn't Black, they did not feel the need to remember, had not been taught in school, by parents, from society, to be defensive around her, uncomfortable about the histories that loomed above her. The South was a strange and complex place, something Trac only realized once she'd left for Columbia Law School. In a place like New York, people were racist without realizing it, and in fact, thought it was impossible that they ever could be. But in the South, people acted out of resentment and self-righteousness. They'd been told all their lives that they were racist, reminded of their past sins, accused by the rest of the country of being backward, last in every list. The result was a more self-aware and insistent stubbornness. You think we're racist down here? Well, we don't trust Black people for a reason—poor, and criminal, and uneducated by no fault of ours. You think we're stupid? Well, you don't understand our way of life.

But by this logic, Trac was not a part of "we" but was also not fully a part of "them." She saw this in her forced inclusion at parties and events with her sorority, and how the men at these parties and events never approached her, both uninterested and slightly discomfited by the reminder that they were, indeed, white, simply by her existence in the room.

When Trac went to the beach on spring break, she wore a full-length cover-up to prevent from getting too tan. Her mother's voice whispered, *too dark*. But her friends did not see *too dark*. They did not see *too brown*. They saw tan, as if Trac had the same skin as them, and if they sat out in the sun for long enough, they, too, would be as tan as Trac. But sometimes, Trac could not help hearing the word *tan* as a code word for *not like us*. It never went away, that voice. And during Rush when Trac was a sophomore, the first-ever Black girl went through and the chapter deliberated on her admission to the next round of parties. Hunter Duchene said, "We can't be known as the Black sorority," and Trac said, "Do you think we're known as the Asian sorority?" and Hunter said, "Trac, you know what I mean. You don't count," and Trac joined the polite chorus of laughter, and she raised her hand to contribute to a unanimous vote to cut Sidney Freemon.

She didn't count, even though, as they got ready together for winter formal, Missy Bossier told her she was "so pretty for an Asian." She didn't count, even though she certainly felt as though she counted when the first and only boy she'd had a one-night stand with asked where she was from, said he liked how submissive Asian girls were, and the excitement she'd felt at being desired by a man had disappeared as suddenly as it had appeared, the realization that the same thing about her that made every other white man uncomfortable was the sole thing, and nothing else, that made this particular white man want her. She could not escape it. She would always be defined by it or against it, but never without it.

And so, in the law firm, the men never touched her, did not make any comments about her as a woman, as if she might not be a woman at all. They asked her questions about things she didn't know, about lawsuits that involved complex numbers, about travel tips to places she'd never been and wasn't from. They always assumed her competence, she could sense that, and she was thankful for this, but could not shake the insecurity that this, too, stemmed from her appearance.

Belinda had so many anecdotes about being treated like an idiot: the time Francis sent her from the room to retrieve coffee for the other lawyers, the time Stephen explained to her how to read a document that she herself had drafted, the time Barry asked a male clerk to proofread her work, apropos of nothing. Belinda had gotten her law education from Georgetown, and still, Archie seemed to address only the men sitting next to her, even when she was the one giving a presentation.

"He'd speak to the air next to my head before he'd ever speak to me, it seems," Belinda said.

But Belinda and Trac had developed a system in group meetings to make sure they were heard. Whenever one of the male lawyers interrupted them, Belinda or Trac would interject and acknowledge what the other had said, as naturally as if Archie or Stephen or Barry had said it. The system had started without premeditation. It was a spur-of-the-moment decision. Trac had been interrupted, Stephen talking about her idea as if he had had it, and Belinda took the chance between his breaths to say, "I think what Trac suggested is a good idea, and we should implement that."

After that, Trac began doing this for Belinda as well, and soon enough, they were getting lunch and after-work drinks almost daily. They rarely collaborated on the same cases because Belinda worked under Barry and Trac worked under Francis. But they sought each other out, a feminine reprieve from the blustering of men all around them.

Trac had only started in the summer—the hottest month, August—right out of law school, and when Belinda took her to lunch as a welcoming gesture on the first day, they walked along the hot, bright sidewalk to the brasserie down the street. She could smell Belinda's perfume mingled with sweat. Top notes of bergamot fading down into orange blossom and grapefruit and salty skin. The sun pulsed off the skyscrapers that walled them in, heat throbbing from black tar freshly laid on Poydras Street. Dirty blond baby hairs stuck to Belinda's forehead and at the base of her neck, beads of sweat gathering at her hairline. Trac refused then to acknowledge these observations for what they actually were: the beginnings of desire.

But there in the living room, Belinda's hands meandered her body in the way a man's never had. Careful, full of tenderness.

Belinda's place was the kind of apartment Trac had always dreamed of having. It was one half of a historic double gallery shotgun in the heart of Uptown, a block away from the river. The house was a lovely shade of seafoam green, the shutters a bright purple, the door left its natural wood tone. Original floors and windows, high ceilings, and a tasteful blend of midcentury and traditional Southern interior. Everything appeared both impeccably in place and lived-in, comfortable but designed. Belinda, it was clear, was a woman who cared about looks.

They sat on her couch in their underwear. Belinda's body reminded her of a ripe peach, supple and easily bruised, the texture of washed velvet. She tried not to look, embarrassed and unsure of what it was she should want to look at, afraid of what it might mean about herself. She had had flings with other women that disappeared, but Belinda was someone she worked with. The stakes were never this high, as in the past Trac always created situations where she could exit.

"Katrina reached a Category 5 storm earlier today, which means the storm sustained winds higher than 157 miles per hour, but still may weaken. Mayor Ray Nagin has opened the Superdome to residents who were unable to evacuate," the meteorologist said, pointing to the path the storm could take on the screen behind her. She wore a pink blouse that clashed with her red hair.

"How much you wanna bet Francis will still call at four in the morning during this storm to tell me I have to come into work?"

"No bet," said Belinda.

"The mayor has put out a mandatory evacuation order," the redheaded meteorologist said, "and has asked residents who are not leaving to stay indoors with water, food, and other hurricane emergency essentials."

"Are you evacuating?" said Trac.

Belinda rolled her eyes. "I grew up here and have lived almost my whole life here, and I've never once evacuated."

"We never have, either," said Trac. "My father used to say it was like monsoon season in Vietnam. *Why leave?* he used to say. *Why leave when you know it will happen?* I never understood that logic. You wouldn't leave, either, if you *didn't* know it would happen."

"My parents used to throw hurricane parties. They were ragers, too. My dad was an alcoholic, though no one except me would ever admit that now. He would make this rum punch and wear his Hawaiian shirt. He'd say it was like we were in the Caribbean with all the heat and the rain."

Belinda's hands were clasped in her lap. It was an odd place for them and looked uncomfortable as she leaned back against the short arm of the couch. Trac knew Belinda had shared something private, however small and seemingly casual. "What were the parties like?" she asked.

"I was pretty young when my dad died, twelve years old, actually. But the thing I remember most about the parties is how excited everyone was, like the adults were getting away with something. He required everyone wear beach clothes and all the neighbors would show up. They came with beers and chips and dips. Our housekeeper, Regina, was Filipina and she'd bring over homemade cassava cake, and I'd eat so much of it while my parents danced. I always had a sugar headache by the end of the night."

"Were there other kids, or just you and the adults?"

"I invited my best friend over. She lived down the street. But we mostly just sat in the breakfast nook and watched all the adults get trashed on punch and sangria wearing Hawaiian shirts and straw hats. I didn't realize it then, but I think the thing I was so fascinated with was how carefree they appeared, like the hurricane had given them permission to discard their obligations."

"This is the exact opposite of how I remember my family's reaction to hurricane season," said Trac. "My mother's fear permeated the entire house."

"That's the thing, though! My mom is so uptight, normally. She's a part of New Orleans high society. She still gets invited to the Spring Azalea Ball every year. *So* boring," (here, Belinda rolled her eyes again, as if to show Trac she didn't have any part in this), "and I think she took her role a little too seriously. But during those hurricane parties, it was like some water spirit possessed her and made her a different person. I think I probably loved her best during a hurricane. She would dance and drink and kiss my father like she was a teenager."

Trac thought of her own mother, what she might be doing to prepare for Hurricane Katrina. She could hear the maddening ding of her jade bangles as they clanked against one another. She believed they warded off evil and harm, and so, she wore multiples to increase her protection. Her heavy sandals clacked against tile. She'd slam cabinets shut after rifling through, choosing which items to wrap up in newspaper and secure in boxes. The television would be on its highest volume, newscasters yelling facts in the living room about wind speeds and projected paths. Feeling a loss of control as she watched the television with rising panic, Xuan would take out her ruler and draw charts on bits of old paper, scribbling cardinal directions and prayers, lucky colors and possible dangers. She'd make them all look at her drawings, unexplained, as if they could read her secret language. Trac had always thought it interesting her mother wrote everything down in pen, her fears, materializing on paper, never open to change or movement. She felt bad for Trieu and Nhi, who were home right now while their mother no doubt paced the kitchen and then the garden, looking into the sky as if it held the forecast for their future.

No, Trac definitely did not love her mother best during a hurricane. The nostalgic affection on Belinda's face was so far away, in a place that Trac could not access, had no idea about, and she felt an inexplicable annoyance. It appeared sneakily, a quiet itching. Trac did not at first notice it was there or where it came from, its presence so natural to her childhood: it was a feeling she had often around her mother, an irrational rage she was forced to smother and contain for fear of transgressing her place as the child. It showed itself when her mother did something beyond reason, when she forced Trac to do the thing beyond reason, too. Small things: wearing a winter hat when it was seventy degrees outside, insisting Trac buy a toaster oven, scolding her for wasting money on full-size trash bags instead of reusing plastic grocery bags, drinking distilled water even when Trac explained it was devoid of nutrients. Her mother's worst inclinations seemed to be all mixed together and made extreme during a hurricane.

Yet, the thought of this alone was not what irritated Trac. It was the fact that Belinda would never understand. She knew plenty of people like her, after all. They thought they had it bad, their New Orleans Junior League moms who made them go to etiquette classes when they wanted to smoke pot and do whatever else it was that white people were allowed to experience. Belinda's mother in a bohemian dress as she danced, for once, to Jimmy Buffett while wind and rain whistled outside, this image of a woman whom Trac's own mother could never become, even if she tried or wanted to—and Trac thought with a sad jolt that her mother probably *had* tried and had wanted to, but simply couldn't. Couldn't stop herself from buying life jackets, couldn't stop herself from storing gallons and gallons of water in the garage, couldn't bring herself to walk around the neighborhood without their father by her side and carrying a gun, couldn't help seeing the danger in her children going to a sleepover, couldn't see the sense in going to a therapist, couldn't trust the contractor in the house because he would steal or rape or murder, couldn't throw out any of the rotting food in her fridge, couldn't stop buying more, couldn't stop worrying, couldn't, couldn't, couldn't ever dance during a hurricane.

How could she tell this to Belinda? She couldn't, not without sounding petty. She'd tried before with other friends, but how did you tell someone the sound of your mother's bracelets made you angry? That somehow, a lifetime of little things your mother did amounted to a flash of rage over jangling jade bangles? Even then, people responded bracingly with an anecdote they deemed to be equal. "My mother has done something like that," they might say, embarking on a story of their moms worrying about their sleep habits or their too-frequent brunch spending. It was never the same, though, and the only ones who had ever understood that were her sisters. Nhi scoffed at their mother's superstition, and Trieu begrudgingly measured herself against it like a yardstick with all the ways she fell short. But Trac viewed their mother's horoscopes as a challenge—Xuan made thoughtless, niggling comments about the Goat's people-pleasing tendencies, its smallness, not in so many words, but in suggestive implication that someone else might brush off or forget. Trac did not forget, and in fact, her whole life had tried to transcend it, to prove her sign wrong.

Trac suddenly wanted to rid the moment of her mother. Already, she could feel the memory of their bodies together tarnishing. Belinda stretched on the couch, her feet on Trac's lap, unaware of what was happening. This unawareness made Trac more annoyed. Everything was tinted with a haze of resentment. Outside, the hurricane had not arrived yet, but a wind rustled the crepe myrtle tree outside the window so that its branches clicked against the side of the house. She couldn't let the feeling sit.

"Let's go," said Trac.

"Where are we going?"

"I just want to go outside, feel the breeze," Trac said.

Belinda pulled on duck boots over her pajama pants. She wore a pink tank top with no bra. Her hair was in a messy bun, stray wisps along her neck and forehead. Trac rarely saw her this disheveled and couldn't help but feel herself warm to Belinda, her irritation disintegrating at its edges. They walked in a zigzag through the neighborhood, up Freret onto Cherokee, down Maple to South Carrollton, where they crossed the short distance to the Mississippi River, traversing Leake Avenue to stroll along the river trail right next to that hulking snake of steady, drifting water. Trac took Belinda's hand and twirled her. They held each other and swayed as a light mist of rain coated their hair and clothes.

The Mississippi sloshed forward, lapping sound of water against water. It was muddy and opaque and wide. Trac had never realized just how wide it was until she'd seen other rivers, discovered what could be considered a river in the first place. She'd taken the Mississippi for granted, having lived right on it all her life, and had always thought it an ugly thing. Brown, the most boring color in the world. Brown like dirt and cardboard boxes, brown like wood waiting to be painted, brown like the towels her mother had bought at Wal-Mart, brown like her skin after weeks at summer camp, brown like her eyes, the most boring, ordinary color. What could be worse than brown?

Belinda walked so that her shoulder, sticky with humidity, brushed against hers. The wind whisked the mist of wet from their skin. It was late, probably past midnight by now. It was hot, too, but there was something strange in the air. The summer heat's usual weight was absent, replaced by a lightness that felt pleasant, crackling with energy, full of sighs and song. Normally, a walk in New Orleans even past midnight was an oppressive affair, requiring the willful push of your body through dense, smoldering air. But Belinda and Trac strolled, shoulder to shoulder, bodies floating. They walked past and behind the zoo, onto the grassy banks of the Fly, where locals had picnics during the day. They sat down under an oak tree and looked out across the river. It was uncanny and beautiful. Trac looked down into the brown water, and its opaque surface shimmered under the outdoor lamps, a glittering that both drew her eye in while obscuring what lay beneath.

Her mother was waiting farther down the riverbank. Trac stood up and walked to the edge of the grassy area, squinting to look at her. Her mother would never leave the house at this hour, let alone before a storm. But there she was, long, elegant neck and high-bridged nose.

"What's wrong?" said Belinda, but Trac squinted to see more clearly. Her mother had a framed portrait of herself when she was young, a black-and-white photograph that had been colorized, like a drawing. Xuan was young, her hair long. Trac had never seen her mother with long hair. But the face in the photo was unmistakably her mother's, the familiarity of her jaw or cheeks or eyes unaltered by age, as it was for many others. This woman standing a few strides away along the river was young, too, much younger than her mother. Her hair was in a braid, and she wore a military-green jacket. Her body had the posture of someone prepared to fight, straight backed, unafraid to occupy space. She stood akimbo. This couldn't be her mother, and yet Trac could not help but think they must know each other.

"What are you looking for?" said Belinda. She must have stood there in silence for several minutes. Why couldn't she speak? She wanted to point to the figure standing near the water but was paralyzed, arms like sandbags. Wind whistled through the oaks and the woman moved like the breeze as she fell toward the river.

The waves swallowed her up, closing over her head. It rushed on, indifferent, brown, and glittering. The sound of wind and water, shaking leaves and the breath of Belinda behind her. Trac searched for her mother at the edge of the river but couldn't find her.

8

XUAN

Xuan had dutifully purchased the new issue of *Best Lunar*'s annual horoscope book every year since Trac was born twenty-two years ago. The tome was thousands of Bible-thin pages and included a chapter for each lunar zodiac sign. She first bought it because Trac was an accidental pregnancy, destined to be born under the Year of the Goat in the element of Earth. Had Xuan had the choice, she certainly would not have picked the Goat, of all signs, for her first child to be, especially not an Earth Goat. It wasn't that it was a bad sign—it was that it was a forgettable one. No one talked about Goat years because Goats were not known as movers or shakers, for beauty or dominance. They were no Dragons or Tigers, or even Snakes or Monkeys. Goats were people pleasers and worked hard, but they were never dazzling or revered or charismatic.

When Xuan discovered she was pregnant, the first thing she did was drive to the bookstore and ask if *Best Lunar* had already published its annual issue for the coming Goat Year. She pored over the pages, learning that Goats are very private and have few intimate friends. Auspicious colors are brown, red, and purple. Their lucky direction is north. So, Xuan wore brown and red as much as she could while pregnant, and every morning woke up and walked north. When Trac was born, she always remembered that Goats were secretive, and as Trac got older, Xuan never shook the suspicion that she did not really know her daughter.

And she did that every year after, reading each page of the book like a very important yearly report. Twice, she abstained from wearing white for the entire year because it was unlucky for her sign. And recently, she had been sleeping in the guest room, on the futon in the office and on the living room couch, because the bed was in a room facing an unfavorable direction for Metal Tigers.

She told each of her children exactly what they should do for their signs as well. They often didn't listen, fully inculcated by American society as they all were. She supposed she couldn't be too mad at them. She prayed for this and had been successful.

Best Lunar for 2001, however, was difficult to read. Xuan spent so much time obsessing over *Best Lunar*'s star charts and horoscope calculations. While they helped Xuan to plan her upcoming year, to predict to the best of her ability the dangers in store for her and her family, the book was still purposefully abstruse and broad in its proclamations. Now it was September, and she continued to look at *Best Lunar* every day, trying to decipher its star charts. The year before, she'd done the same, expecting some catastrophe. The year 2000 was a portentous number. She had expected something, anything—and then, as if to confirm her fears, they began to talk about it on the news. But, they treated it like some technical issue, that computers would be unable to handle the date change. Xuan did not trust the news coverage. She felt the beginnings of danger in her bones. She bought life jackets and hundreds of cans of Spam and green beans. The coat closet was packed with woven bags of jasmine rice. She stocked a foil emergency blanket, two flashlights, and a wind-up radio for every room in the house.

Her children said she was overreacting, but Xuan knew what they could never know: danger never left or disappeared. It merely hid in wait. New Year's Eve leading into the year 2000 came and went, as uneventful as any other night, but Xuan still felt a disaster was impending, lurking in the shadows to strike when it was most opportune. Danger was all around them, happening all the time, and the inescapability of this fate only made Xuan search for ways to control it more. If she prayed every day, if she scattered holy water around the house, if she offered food on the altar, if she wore protective oil—would these things change the inevitable?

In Vietnam, her mother and grandmother always prattled on about reading their horoscopes to predict outcomes. Sometimes Xuan closed her eyes and imagined herself in her home again, in Saigon, warm air and the scent of burning herbs, the bustle and clatter of the city outdoors. Even in her anxiety to protect her children from the catastrophe sure to arrive, she mourned that they would never know the things she'd given up, the life she had lived, however scarred and dangerous it had been. It was like an entire history had disappeared into thin air. She was the only person, now, to carry the memory of it, and once she was gone, that memory, too, would be gone with her.

Before the girls went to school one morning, she flipped through *Best Lunar* and burned the bagels. She always overtoasted, never able to get a handle on the sensitive toaster they'd had for close to ten years now. Xuan was not about to wait at the toaster's side, peer into its glowing orange slots and monitor the bagel's brownness. She resented having to make breakfast for her children at all. It didn't help that American breakfast was unnecessarily labor-intensive, its ingredients and appropriate meals limited to a narrow set of eggs, bread, and bacon or sausage. When she was in Vietnam, the maid had made her breakfasts. It consisted of heated leftovers from the night before, or a bowl of rice with fried eggs and bone broth. Her mother was an entrepreneur, busy with her money lending and her businesses. Xuan was very fond of Yen, the maid (perhaps *maid* was the wrong word). She made breakfast every morning, and when Xuan was lonely or bored, Yen would sit with her on the family home's back veranda and tell her tales from her old village, Panhou. She had a horrible northern accent, slightly squashed by a developing Saigon lilt. When Xuan was older, she and Yen would walk together in the mornings to have a bowl of pho at her favorite restaurant. She wondered often, usually these days when the bagels burned, what happened to Yen in the chaos of Saigon's fall. There were people she could ask, who she could send letters to or call, but Xuan never did. She didn't really want to know.

"Thanks, Mom," Nhi said, as Xuan handed her the bagel in a napkin. Her daughter grimaced as she took it. The bagel, to Nhi's credit, had been inconsistently scraped with a butter knife, so that patches here and there were blackened.

"I do not put cheese on it because I know you like to do it. You want cheese?" Xuan said. She rushed to the refrigerator and pulled out half a block of cream cheese, its silver foil packaging crumpled and covered in stray crumbs from bagels past.

"I'm late for school, Mom. I'll just eat it like this. Trieu! Hurry up, we're late," Nhi shouted to the ceiling from the kitchen. Trieu stomped down the stairs and accepted her burnt bagel.

"You want cheese, my love?" Xuan asked her youngest daughter.

"We don't have time for cheese, Mom," said Nhi. "We're going to be late for the bus."

"I want cream cheese, though," said Trieu.

"I do it for you, quick." She smeared cold, unmalleable cream cheese on the bagel. "Here, for you, my baby," said Xuan. Trieu took a bite of it.

Nhi grabbed Trieu's hand and led her forcibly away. "We will miss the bus," she said. Xuan did not follow them as they quarreled on the way to the door. They did not say goodbye to Xuan, who was left in the kitchen still holding the butter knife. When she heard the groan of the front door against its jamb, Xuan walked to the foyer and watched her children through the window. Nhi opened the lid of the trash can waiting at the end of the driveway for garbage collection and tossed her napkin-wrapped bagel into it. She held the lid aloft for Trieu, who did the same, and then they walked briskly down the street toward their bus stop.

Xuan ripped the toaster's plug from the wall and marched outside to the street. She, too, lifted the lid of the garbage can, and stuffed the toaster into it. Despite how hard she was on Trac, an Earth Goat, she knew her oldest daughter would've never thrown the bagel away. Trac was a considerate child, always thinking about how her actions affected others. While Xuan thought there were other career paths that were a better fit, she had to admit, Trac was at least well suited to a career in law in this one way, to analyze consequences and solutions, never impetuous.

Even though Trac was in law school as they wished, had been a compliant child, had never caused any problems, Xuan felt a detachment from her. Trac bore on her shoulders a responsibility that Nhi and Trieu did not. She felt guilty for admitting it, but that was just the way things were. Nhi, a Fire Tiger, only thought of herself. She had been a quick and rushed labor, but a difficult baby, and Xuan knew it was the Fire in her. She could never settle, and now, in the throes of teen selfishness, Nhi did and said things small and hurtful, like dozens of paper cuts that stung over and over, just hurtful enough that Xuan held and collected them in her closed, tight fists, carrying them with her but never saying anything. But Xuan was a Tiger, too, and perhaps that was why Nhi could get away with saying and doing the things she did, which Trac was not permitted.

And Trieu was her baby, a captivating Dragon tempered by her Earth element. Trieu was already thirteen, and she struggled against her mother's love and expectation, which Xuan suspected was smothering. But she could not seem to stop herself from hovering above Trieu, poking and prodding, pushing and prying, her last chance.

Nhi's Fire enriched and renewed Trieu's Earth, and the two sisters huddled together like thieves—trading secret notes with drawings on them they thought their mother didn't see later, sharing candies, holing up in their rooms to conduct private fashion shows—excluding their mother, who was too oppressive, too bumbling, too overbearing. Xuan did not know what it took to be a mother and she did not know what it meant to be herself. How had she failed so spectacularly at toasting a bagel? Xuan turned the television on as she left the room to retrieve the toaster she'd thrown in the trash. She watched the garbage truck as it made its way from the end of the street toward her home, two men in gray jumpsuits walking alongside it as they tossed trash into the back. Her hand was on the doorknob, dead bolt unlocked. But she was frozen to the welcome mat, hand welded to the knob as she watched the truck move, house by house, toward her own. The green garbage truck idled for a moment in front of it as the men upturned her trash can into its compacter, the slightly yellowing toaster tumbling out first, then quickly obscured by the bags of trash beneath it.

She went back into the living room, where, on the television, smoke plumed from the Twin Towers in New York. Xuan stared at the news coverage, the looping images accompanied by news anchors' voices. The smoke and crumbling building, muted footage of people hurtling earthward. Xuan could hear the destruction clearly over the anchor's voice, like bombs that drowned out all other sound. She imagined the people in New York. People who saw the disaster from both close and afar, watched in awe and fear, and then, eventually, continued on with their lives. She knew this disposition like a learned prayer. That familiar, low buzz of panic fluttered inside. It never really left the hollow of her chest, there since she first heard the blasts of actual bombs, lying awake in bed with her sister.

Xuan picked up the phone and dialed Trac's phone number. The line rang, and her answering machine picked up. "This is Trac. I'm probably studying. Leave a message!"

"Hi, my baby, how you? Call me. It your mom," she said. She dialed again, and let it ring. She left another message. "It your mom," she said. "I see if you okay. Call me." She punched the rubber numbers again on the cordless phone and let it ring. "It your mom. I call to see if you okay. Please call," she said. Again, and again, and again. The sound of the ring was empty, like an echo, and every time she dialed Trac's number, its ascending melody matched the pounding of her heart.

9

TRIEU

Trieu's mother hated going to parent events for school. If at all possible, Xuan avoided attending PTA meetings or parent conferences. Cuong also abhorred going to these required meetings on the progress of their children. They already knew how their children were doing in school because there was only ever one option.

However, Trieu's math grades started suffering last year in pre-algebra. She got her first C on a unit test. When Ms. Fredricks laid the page of radicals and exponents on her desk with a large, red "78" scrawled at the top, Trieu began to cry right there. She had to excuse herself and go to the bathroom without asking permission, any fear of being reprimanded by the teacher outweighed by the embarrassment of being seen crying over a C-plus. In the bathroom mirror, she stared at her blotchy, snotty face and wiped all the salty fluids off her nose and eyes with the school's horrible, earth-friendly paper towels. She felt ill thinking about what would happen if her parents found out. To Trieu's surprise, when she returned to the classroom, the teacher did not comment nor admonish her. Instead, Ms. Fredricks called Trieu to her after the bell rang.

"Trieu, I noticed you were upset after receiving your test today. There's been a steady drop in your homework grades this quarter, too. Are you struggling with the material? It's getting harder so that you can be prepared to take Algebra I next school year," said Ms. Fredricks, not unkindly. After Trieu did not respond, she added, "There's nothing to be ashamed of if you need to ask for help."

"No, I'm okay," said Trieu. "I just didn't study hard enough."

There was a long pause as she waited for Trieu to tell the truth, trying to determine if she should push a little harder. "I want your parents to sign the test even though it's only a C-plus. We need to make sure we address this before the end of the year." She took a stamp and pressed it down on the test, which she took from Trieu's clutches. It left a signature box in purple ink.

Trieu was mortified. She rarely ever spoke to teachers, managing to make the grades on her own, even if the class or textbook or teacher were horrible. She never asked her parents for homework help, as it almost always ended poorly. The last time she asked her father a math question was in the fourth grade, and he didn't understand the specific, state-mandated curriculum for decimals and fractions. When Trieu tried to explain this requirement, he threw her workbook on the ground and told her if she knew how to do it, she might as well not ask. She cried and cried, and he told her she looked ugly when she cried. Trieu had since developed an intense fear of speaking to authority figures. She overheard her mother complain to a friend once on the phone in Vietnamese, "She's a Dragon, she's supposed to be more outgoing. I don't know why she's so timid. Maybe it's the Earth in her. I know a Metal Dragon would never, ever be so shy."

Trieu felt a very particular kind of shame from this comment that she could not exactly explain or pinpoint. It felt ridiculous to confide this in even her best friend, Rebecca, who lived down the street and who was very white and who would not understand the kind of deep embarrassment Trieu felt. She let her mother down in a way she couldn't help, her supposedly innate gifts conspicuous by their absence. Her mother had born a Dragon child expecting her to be much greater than she was, and she instead had received a normal, perhaps less than mediocre daughter. The truth was that Trieu was good at many things. She had a natural gift with visual art, and consistently received praise from her art teachers. But she was painfully shy, and she was scared of disappointing her parents. She carried this simultaneous confidence and insecurity all her life, beginning projects with self-assurance and eventually abandoning them in order to avoid the all-encompassing possibility of failure, a pattern that became inexplicable to even herself.

So, Trieu did not give her C-plus test to her parents. Instead, she forged her mother's curly script signature and handed it back to Ms. Fredricks the next day, who suspected nothing thanks to Trieu's good penmanship, particular talents in art, and general air of trustworthiness. Her parents would never know because they rarely went to the parent-teacher meetings. Trieu would just have to work harder to bring her final grade up.

Despite this wishful thinking, there wasn't time before the end of term for Trieu to hoist her grade up from a B to an A. And when her report card arrived, the B printed next to Pre-Algebra looked like an infection upon the skin of the cheap transcript paper. This, she could not conceal.

When her father saw the report card, he sat for a moment at the dinner table, gripping the piece of perforated paper with both hands. Nhi and their mother both sat as still as wax figures, staring fixedly at spots away from him. Trieu wished they would look at her. He stood up and picked up her table setting, piece by piece. He slammed her bowl full of rice and broth into the kitchen sink, the sound of china shattering, and when he came back to the table, the transcript had been crumpled into a ball, which he stuffed into her full glass of water.

"Your grade is unacceptable," he said. "You live in my house, you pay your debt to me. Work harder or you cannot stay in this house and eat my food."

After this incident, she cried in the privacy of her sister's room, who was nice enough to let Trieu use the set of colored pencils she bought from the art store. Nhi went into her closet and used her stepladder to reach the top shelf, which was shoved full of old totes and stuffed animals. She pulled out a red plaid tin, something once given to them by a neighbor with home-made Christmas cookies. The cookies were long gone, given to the Vietnamese Sunday school class. "Cookies will make you fat," said their mother, who always said she never baked for this very reason.

Nhi opened the tin to reveal that it was full of old Hallow-een candy, a packaged Nutter Butter bar, and a treasure trove of various, forbidden sweets.

"Voila! Dinner is served," said Nhi.

Trieu ate fun-size Milky Ways and KitKats until she felt sick.

The school uniform, which was newly implemented at Shirley Verret Middle School, was a good idea in theory. Many of the school's low-income students were able to afford the piqué polo and Dickies khakis, and adolescence could be that much easier without the stress of buying the latest styles. Administrators also thought it would be easier to police the students' dress, which they felt was the gateway to gang initiation. If students were not allowed to wear ratty white T-shirts and do-rags or low-hanging pants, then students couldn't possibly join gangs. At least, this is what the vice principal said in her long-winded speech at parent orientation the June before the school year started.

Trieu was not supposed to attend, but Xuan didn't trust her to be home alone even though she was thirteen. She sat next to her mother in a metal fold-up chair, wishing she could turn the same dull tan color as the seat. In reality, none of the other adults paid her any mind. They didn't even look at her. She was as invisible as she hoped. But Trieu knew that what the vice-principal was saying was not meant for her ears, and this made her acutely aware of her body in this forbidden space.

Since school was let out for summer break, Trieu practiced problems in her pre-algebra workbook every day. She did this now, while her mother sat straight backed and attentive to the meeting's agenda. Trieu redid each question she'd gotten wrong in Ms. Fredrick's class over and over again, until she memorized the answers. With each declining grade she had received last semester, her father had become more and more angry. Her mother did not scold her, but instead, took out her horoscope book and pointed to incomprehensible symbols.

"This year you have struggle and conflict. If now you know, you can prepare better," her mother said. Trieu decided she would be ready for algebra when school started in a month.

Vice Principal Bucher moved out from behind the podium and motioned for someone to walk onto the stage. The school secretary wheeled a clothing rack into view, the squeaking of the rolling metal rack and the clacking of her kitten heels echoing in the auditorium. Wire hangers swayed on the near-empty rack, a sample of each uniform piece hanging from the bar: a pair of khaki pants, a pleated khaki skirt, and piqué polo. The secretary held each piece of the uniform up for the audience to see under bright auditorium spotlighting. The polo was a deep shade of orange, and on the left breast, an embroidered tiger head above the words Shirley Verret Middle School. The tiger was clawing through the shirt, its mouth thrown open in a vicious snarl. It was an odd placement: on the girls, it looked as if the tiger were ripping a giant hole over the boob.

"Students will have the option of wearing either khaki pants or pleated skirt, and they will all wear this polo shirt, allowing them to show school spirit every day," said Vice Principal Bucher. Trieu thought the shirt was hideous, so bright it appeared fluorescent in the light. "We will require that students wear a black or brown belt and black or brown, closed-toed dress shoes. This will be in addition to our dress code rules already instated that regulate hair style, body art, piercings, and nail art."

Trieu felt an odd sense of relief as the vice principal droned on about skirt lengths and acrylic nail bans. Since Trieu had started middle school, she'd had a shocking set of realizations about herself. The first was that she was, in fact, Vietnamese. The second was that, contrary to what one might assume, the other Vietnamese kids did not like her. And the third was not only that she was not cool, but that such a concern existed at all and, even more surprisingly, mattered to her very much. These epiphanies had been triggered by Trieu's transfer from the elementary school down the street to Shirley Verret, which was the closest middle school to their home. Xuan and Cuong would never pay for private school when their tax dollars ("Our stolen money," Cuong called it) paid for one right in their neighborhood.

But Algiers Elementary School for the Arts and Sciences and Shirley Verret Middle were very different. Algiers Elementary was a public school for gifted children who had to test in with an IQ exam and a critical thinking skills assessment designed by child education specialists, all in an effort to make college prep school "accessible" to children of all economic backgrounds—although they were currently embroiled in a lawsuit about racial bias in their testing procedures, but the Trungs knew nothing about that.

Shirley Verret Middle, on the other hand, was just your run-of-the-mill New Orleans public school, which is to say, it had no money and no IQ exam and fewer resources and too many students. At Algiers Elementary, most of Trieu's classmates were white, although there were a few Black students and one Hispanic student. She was the only Vietnamese American child enrolled, but this was never a problem for her. Rebecca and all her other friends were white; her teachers were white. It had never occurred to her that she was not-white. She knew she was Asian in that way one knows she must wear a child-sized áo dài on culture day or must hide the odor of her paper bag lunch of shredded pork skin, rice, and fish sauce. But it was one thing to know you were different, and another thing to be *not* something, not-white.

Shirley Verret was school to predominantly Black students, with the next-largest demographic being first-generation Vietnamese American kids. They all lived in Woodmere with the exception of Trieu. The Black kids left Trieu alone for the most part, sometimes heckling her from the bleachers in gym class, or laughing at her awkward jog during kickball. But, she was ignored or forgotten more than bullied.

What Trieu had been wholly unprepared for was what she now knew to be her test of entry with the Vietnamese kids, which she had failed, and had failed abysmally. In the locker room in second period PE on Trieu's first day, a girl named Tina applied a slick of bubblegum-pink gloss to her lips. She wore lavender eye shadow, which matched her lavender headband. She spoke in rapid Vietnamese to her friend Mai, who wore the same headband, perhaps in an attempt to look like Tina, but of course could not pull it off quite as well. Tina had the air of a popular kid, the self-confidence of a girl who knew her own effect on people. Every action had its reaction, and Tina was fully versed in the physics of her choices.

"Hey," Tina said. "You're Trieu, right?" She jerked her chin up. Trieu thought she would never look as cool doing that with her chin.

"Hi," said Trieu. She jerked her own chin up, too, and already knew it had been a failed attempt. "Yeah, that's my name."

Tina turned to Mai, speaking in Vietnamese. They smiled and looked expectantly at Trieu, who could only stare. A familiar dreadful feeling gripped her, her stomach on a never-ending roller-coaster drop. Her ears and neck were hot. She only ever felt this way around her family. In school, she was used to being in control, understood.

"You don't speak Vietnamese?" said Tina.

Trieu stuttered through her response, a mix of English with the few Vietnamese words she knew. "I know a little," she said, finally, in English.

Tina said something to Mai, and they laughed.

"You a Twinkie, huh?" said Mai.

"What's a Twinkie?" said Trieu.

"Yellow on the outside, white on the inside. *Americanized*," said Mai. She elongated the end of the word, pronouncing *ized* like *iced*.

"A bitch who think she too good for us," said Tina.

"I don't think I'm too good for anyone," said Trieu, but they had already gotten up and were gathering their things. As they walked through the locker room, they chatted again in that opaque language Trieu did not know, their words echoing, tinny and clamorous against the concrete of the locker room.

From that point on, the Vietnamese kids did not speak to her, only conversing in Vietnamese when in her earshot. Trieu got snatches of words, sometimes the word *Americanized* hidden in the garble of language, sometimes *my trắng* bubbling up above the unknown phrases. She knew they were making fun of her, but about what, exactly, she was unsure. She got the feeling it was about the way she dressed. She didn't have any evidence to support this, but when they were around, staring at her, she felt naked, like they were looking at each piece of her and deciding to discard it, deciding the pieces were not up to scratch until she stood before them entirely bare.

This was an inevitable daily anxiety of Trieu's around the Woodmere crew (which she had privately dubbed them), as she would start each morning already unhappy with her clothing.

She was never unhappy about her clothes before, but her outfits had also never been as obviously different. Most of her closet was already comprised of dresses or skirts before the uniform. She wore penny loafers to school, and all of her socks were accidentally dyed pink by her mother in the wash.

"Aw, you put your socks in the wash with something red, huh?" said her Louisiana history teacher one day in front of the entire class. It was the first time Trieu ever regretted sitting in the front row. It was also the same day Mr. Beckett had started their unit on the Civil War.

"The Civil War was about states' rights—*not* about slavery," he'd said. "Confederate soldiers were fighting to protect their land, and today, they are considered American veterans and patriots. This will be on the test, so I don't know why no one is taking notes."

After the lesson, Tanisha stormed out of the room and rumors swirled all day that she'd been suspended for "disrespect" and skipping class. Trieu wrote the notes down and held this fact with her all the way to college, not once thinking to relinquish it until a professor her sophomore year would teach an entire lecture on the Lost Cause myth.

But it was while Trieu wrote these notes down that Mr. Beckett scolded the class. "See Trieu? She's taking notes. Everyone should ask Trieu for tips on note-taking. Clearly, she's the only one who knows how," he said. It was then that he noticed Trieu's socks. Trieu would reflect on this moment for many years to come, and later realize it was wildly inappropriate for Mr. Beckett to make such a comment. She would never know, however, that Mr. Beckett had started the Civil War unit with apprehension, that he was fully aware his proclamation about states' rights would be cause for a tense lesson, having been a Louisiana history teacher for going on thirteen years. Most of his students were Black. But he couldn't stand to perpetuate the misconception that the Civil War had anything to do with slavery. His great-great-grandfather was a Confederate veteran, and it pained him to think that many of his own students, whom he cared for deeply, believed his own ancestors were racist. Trieu's socks, it turned out, were his lifeline.

After the door slammed behind Tanisha's disappearing back, Mr. Beckett could barely tolerate the claustrophobia of the room. Thirty-two pairs of eyes on him, pens frozen with the exception of Trieu's. And there her pink socks were, Adidas crew socks wedged into the shiny leather of a penny loafer. It was both pitiful and silly.

The whole class broke out into giggles, some craned to see her socks. Mr. Beckett secretly breathed a sigh of relief and went on to talk about the War of Northern Aggression.

So, when Trieu sat in that auditorium with her mother during parent orientation, the vice-principal displaying each piece of the uniform onstage, she felt a weight lift, a relief that she no longer had to notice the low-rise jeans she did not own, the tight, bejeweled Bebe T-shirts her mother would never buy for her. Even her socks might be less noticeable simply because clothes, in general, would be less noticeable. They went together to the uniform outfitters and bought two of the highlighter-orange piqué polos and two of the pleated skirts. Her mother did not buy the Dickies khaki pants for her.

"It for boys," her mother said. "I wear school uniform in Saigon. I know what is right for uniform."

And Xuan was right—girls in Saigon were not allowed to wear pants. Pants were for boys, and skirts were for girls.

But in America, it became clear to Trieu, almost everyone wore pants.

She didn't notice on the first day of school, or the second or third. After the first week, it wasn't even about the pants. It was that no one was following the dress code rule about shoes. Spongy, white leather Nikes were everywhere, despite the requirement for black or brown colors. Trieu had thought, finally, her penny loafers would not be out of place. Especially with a pleated skirt, her loafers only looked a little bit strange with the bright orange polo. But no one followed the dress code on the matter of shoes, and no one seemed to be enforcing it.

The Nike sneakers everyone wore were seventy dollars. Trieu went to the mall with Rebecca that weekend to examine them. Rebecca did not care about the shoes, which annoyed Trieu. Rebecca could afford to be blasé about the matter because her mother bought her anything she wanted if she did all her weekly chores, a fact about which Trieu could not help but be jealous. Who had ever heard of someone being rewarded simply for doing what they were supposed to do? Trieu inwardly laughed at the thought of her father giving her money for taking out the trash or doing the dishes. The idea was preposterous.

After the mall, Trieu went to her mother, the one more likely to buy her something she deemed unnecessary. Trieu had to convince her that the shoes *were* necessary. She needed them, Trieu had discovered at the mall, needed them if it meant she wouldn't have to endure another school day of hostile, linguistically obscure remarks, another day of suspected malignment. The worst part was not knowing what they were saying, her imagination inviting her to invent and build up, taking a tone or a look and creating a whole encyclopedia of what might be wrong with her existence in their spaces.

"Mẹ," Trieu said, "I have to buy new shoes for school."

"What shoe? You already have shoe," said Xuan.

"I need new ones for gym class."

"Why you need?"

"The gym teacher said I need better shoes."

"Your teacher said?"

"I might not do well in class if I don't have these shoes," said Trieu. Her mother looked skeptical, still, but Trieu could see the gleam of doubt washed across her mother's original assuredness.

"You make bad grade, why?"

"Because if I don't have the right shoes, it's hard for me to participate in the activities," Trieu said. The lie poured silkily out of her, like it had been waiting there all along. Truthfully, the last activity they did in PE was square dancing, and before that, badminton. Her hand-me-down Skechers were fine, even for the kickball she played last year. But utility was not the need, however much Trieu might present it that way.

"Okay," Xuan said. "You take me to the store, I buy the shoe." Trieu was sure her mother did not believe her, but she also was sure her mother wouldn't take a chance on Trieu's grades. Trieu was right, but wrong about her mother's motives. Xuan wanted her daughters to make As, yes. And, Xuan felt that during the Year of the Snake, all of her children would be more concerned about their appearances, because the Snake could be a vain sign that cared about luxury and looks. But mostly, she wanted her daughters to survive her husband's rage. She wanted to preserve how good they were. It was too late for Trac, who at twenty-two was as hard-hearted as her husband, and already she could see bitterness begin to spoil Nhi's heart, like a spreading bruise. But Trieu was still young. Xuan wanted to see into Trieu's future, find the places where she might become damaged, and she wanted to stem the rotten infection, eradicate it if she could. The hardest part of being a mother, Xuan decided, was watching her children be disappointed by the world the way she surely had, the churn of history making its way around and around, and she, a helpless witness to the inevitable turning.

The car did not cool down in the time it took for them to drive to the mall. It was still August, after all. It seemed the school year began earlier and earlier in the month. Trieu heard on the nightly news (which her mother had on at high volume while she cooked dinner every evening) that they did this in anticipation of hurricane days the school district projected they would need.

At Teakwood Mall, heat shimmered over the black tar parking lot, its surface as still and smooth as dark water, white and yellow paint lines bright and stark. The blast of air-conditioning inside made Trieu's eyes water, and as they walked through the food court and among shops on the east side of the mall, they got drier in the cold, recycled air. They passed a candy cart and a Great American Cookie stand, and Trieu looked longingly at all the junk food she knew her mother would never let her have. It would all be worth it, Trieu thought, if she left today with a new pair of shoes.

At the store, Trieu led her mother to the wall where the sneakers sat on a plastic floating ledge among dozens of other display shoes. Xuan picked up the white Nike, her dusty-rose–painted nails grazing spongy-soft leather, baby blue metal swoosh, unblemished white laces. She placed it back on its ledge and began to peruse the others.

"What about this one?" Xuan said. She picked up a shell-toe Adidas. "Or this one?" In her other hand, a sportier, more practical, and cheaper Nike.

"No, it has to be the one I showed you," said Trieu.

"It overprice. Why so expensive?" *Esspensive.*

"I don't know. I have to have it for school." The lie tasted a little more acrid in her mouth each time she told it.

"It look cheap, but it so expensive," said Xuan. "Look at this other shoe, made of nice material." She handed Trieu a suede Skecher. The sneaker was black, a blocky leather *S* that, for some reason, infuriated her. She hated the Skecher. But it wasn't just that. It was shoe after shoe her mother picked up, cheaper or different or just not exactly what Trieu had asked for. A blistering rage overtook her. It was her mother's grating accent, the missing verbs and wrong tenses, the fragments and the sloppy pronunciation. She had told her what she wanted, handed her the exact thing. Trieu shoved the Skecher into her mother's arms and rushed out of the shoe store. She ran through the mall, back to the food court, and sat at one of the metal tables in front of the Popeye's. She stared at the people waiting for their orders, the salt and deep fryer air wafting her way. Another reminder of something she wouldn't get even if she asked for it.

Her mother walked up to the table and handed her a plastic bag. In it, an orange Nike shoebox peered up between the handles. Trieu could hardly believe it. She didn't open the box at that food court table, and her mother briskly walked toward the exit after handing her the bag. Trieu did not want to open the box in the presence of Xuan, thinking it might somehow flaunt her mother's moment of weakness. Or else, it could jinx it, shattering the illusion that it might after all be the shoes she wanted. What could be worse than thinking she'd finally gotten the desired object, only to open the box and realize she'd been foolishly disappointed?

She rushed up the stairs on her tiptoes, careful not to jostle or crinkle the plastic bag. She did not want her father to hear, although he had shut the door to his office and would not have heard anyway, being deep in the world of his newspaper. Trieu took the box out of the bag, holding it by the tips of her fingers, gingerly like she was handling a small and scared animal. When she opened the box, those white shoes glowed under the ceiling light, fresh with the smell of new leather.

She tried on the shoes with her pleated khaki skirt and orange polo, her dyed-pink crew socks, and felt both proud and embarrassed. She finally had the shoes she wanted, and yet, something about the bright white leather, the newness of it, shouted for attention, especially with her uniform, which was already different from what everyone else wore. What Trieu wanted was not attention, but to be the same, to the point where no one could notice her.

She stared in the full-length mirror, looking squatter than she actually was because the mirror was warped in the middle. The problem had been her penny loafers and her socks, yes, but Trieu could see the problem went beyond that as she studied her reflection. Her skirt needed to be pants, and her pants needed to mask her socks. It was an entire system that could not be fixed simply by taking out one component, by swapping loafers for Nike sneakers.

She went into her mother's closet, which was stuffed full. The walk-in had a rod on each side, and every wire hanger, an assortment Xuan collected from dry cleaners and thrift stores, had something hanging from it. The shelves near the ceiling were packed with half- and once-folded shirts and cardigans, shorts and pants. One could see that Xuan had begun piling clothes on the carpeted ground with her purses and hats, neatly stacked in some organization unknown to anyone but her. Trieu plunged into the closet, climbing the step stool and reaching up to rifle through the pants folded on the top shelves. They tumbled down around her in mounds as she rushed through the stacks.

From the depths of the closet, Trieu pulled out a pair of beige, wide-leg pants. They were high waisted and pleated, and also the closest to Shirley Verret's Dickies khakis. The color was so light, it looked almost yellow, but Trieu could not find anything better. She brought the pants to her room and took out a sewing kit she'd gotten one birthday from her mother but had never had any interest in. She used it once to hand sew a pillow, but the pillow turned out lopsided, the stitches visible and uneven because Trieu had hurried with the measuring.

They did not have fabric scissors, so Trieu would have to be more patient as she began to cut her mother's wide-leg pants along their seam on the inside of the leg. She felt a burst of energy, a feeling of control. Her mother always said Dragons were creatives, and finally, she felt the power of this. In her mind's eye, the figure of her sign loomed large, and she imagined her own body wore the skin of this Dragon like a coat. It was slow work, as expected, but Trieu sawed the scissors carefully toward the pants' crotch. They left a jagged and stringy path behind, but she wasn't worried about that. The uneven cut would be disguised once sewed again.

She put the pants on inside out, and sitting down, Trieu used a pencil to mark a line on the fabric where she wanted to sew, fantasizing about the straight-leg fit of her classmates' Dickies. She would not be wearing a skirt tomorrow with her brand-new shoes, that much she had determined.

The needle in the kit was large and dull, its gaping eye the size of a grain of rice. It was meant for beginners, and the white thread loped easily through it. Trieu began to sew along the crooked pencil marks she'd made, holding the fabric up close to her eyes, so that each stitch had her undivided attention. The trail of white thread moved slowly up to the crotch, where she tied it off in a double, triple, quadruple knot. When she straightened up the pants, she saw a stitch here and there suddenly diverging off and then back on, a path of indecision and inexperience. Trieu did not fret over this. When she turned the pants right-side out again, the stitch marks would be invisible. She moved onto the other pant leg, marking out another stitched path.

The pants precariously slid over her legs. The seam stretched against her skin, straining along the path where the stitches were large or uneven. But Trieu looked at herself in the mirror and beamed. They were too tight, but they were better than her skirt. Little strings and bits of thread flitted from the edges of raw fabric here and there where she'd run out midleg and had to tie off early, starting afresh with a new length from the spool. From far away, without close inspection, who could notice that her pants were sewed by her large needle and too-close eye and clumsy hands?

She wrestled her orange polo over her head and tucked it in, slow and careful, afraid any movement too aggressive might make the whole thing fall apart. She pulled her pink socks on all the way up and patted the hem of her pants over them. Only a sliver of pink showed at the bottom. She put on her new shoes, drawing the laces tight section by section, making sure they lay flat and untwisted, the bow even and double-knotted. Trieu felt an excitement and happiness and fear all at once. She would never go back to wearing a skirt.

The next day at school, when her pants split apart in algebra class, it was during a pop quiz. Trieu had not read the assigned unit, "Introduction to Functions," in their textbook. As she stared at the questions, the numbers and letters began to swirl and blur. All she could see was the jumble of equations she'd memorized that summer from her pre-algebra workbook. The directions at the top of the quiz came to her in fragments, a hot panic spreading in her chest. She crossed her legs and felt the seam of her pants slide apart against her inner thigh (not fast, not dramatic—but slow and silent and unstoppable), the cold air a shock to her bare skin.

Provide a definition for the following terms: function, domain, range, relation. Function, domain, range, relation, function, domain, range, relation. She chanted the words over and over in her mind, as if thinking them again and again would make them mean something. Then the seam on her right leg opened up like a zipper down her leg. Trieu, powerful and creative, draped in the clothes of a Dragon, capable of anything, crumbled.

Trieu ran to the girls' restroom and sat in the stall on the toilet. The stalls were painted peach, but they were covered in names and phrases. She was amazed at how many people carried permanent marker with them. *Tina sucks dick*, written in purple marker and curly cursive. An arrow pointed at the remark, beneath written in bubbly print, *Bitch can't read this cuz it in Engrish.* Another addition, in red, cramped writing, *Ching chong ching! Bing bong bing! Ding dong ding!* and next to *dong* in more cursive, *Her favorite snack.*

Trieu stared at the comments written above the toilet paper dispenser, and found herself feeling jealous, jealous that anyone found the time or energy to write about Tina in a bathroom stall, that anyone thought about Tina enough they would externalize it somewhere, even anonymously. It was Trieu's own jealousy that allowed her to recognize these mean little notes were written out of another form of jealousy, too, that other people felt the same way Trieu did, and as she stared around at the stall walls, covered in handwritten graffiti, she did not see a single thing about herself. No one felt jealous of her, no one cared to write a mean little untrue thing about Trieu because no one knew who she was.

She stared down at her legs and waited for the bell for next period to ring, and then another ten minutes to ensure no one would be in the halls. On the way to the school's front office, she walked with her hand on the thread to keep the pant legs from falling open. Trieu called her mother, who brought a new pair of bottoms, and the vice principal gave her an infraction slip for wearing nonissue uniform pants.

10

NHI

The encyclopedia set was from 1986, the year she was born.
She hauled out the black-and-brown leather-bound volumes
she needed from her father's office and skimmed the small portions of text dedicated to Vietnam, Vietnam War, and Southeast Asia. It didn't occur to her to research Indochina, because
she was thirteen and had heard nothing of such a place. And she
didn't do any reading on French colonialism or the relationship
between China and Vietnam, because what she *had* read in the
encyclopedia was self-contained, had not pointed in any other
direction outside of itself. The pages dedicated to the topic to-
taled four. It was finite and confident of its own truthfulness,
saying to Nhi, *You are done. This is all you need to know.*

She asked Trac, who was twenty and in college, for help, but
she told her little that she didn't already know.

"Grandma Tien told me a story, once," Trac said, "about a
Vietnamese woman who fought pirates on a boat like a warrior.
But I think it was just a story. She never told me much about
Vietnam, and anyway, I was really young when she died. I don't

remember her very well. You should just look up the information in some history books."

It did not occur to Nhi to ask her parents for help. They did not talk about the war. In fact, they did not talk to their children at all, really, about anything, not in the way Nhi had seen her friends speak to their parents, with warmth and informality, about colored hair extensions, sock hops, and school crushes. Nhi could not imagine a universe in which she even uttered the words *colored hair extensions* within earshot of her mother or father. Their relationship was one of obligation, one in which Nhi had been gifted with life and was obligated to spend the rest of it paying back the debt.

Her mother watched from Nhi's bedroom door as she pasted color images printed at the school computer lab onto a trifold presentation board, but Xuan did not offer any help or commentary. Her father, of course, did not even know the project was an Social Studies class requirement. Each fold of the board was titled "History," "Culture," and "Government," the encyclopedia itself having used those section headers, as if history and government and culture did not intersect or overlap, but remained firmly in their own divisions of the trifold presentation board.

At Shirley Verret Middle School the next day, Nhi stood at the front of the classroom with her board propped behind her. She gave a brief overview of the Vietnam War—none of the details concerning the deeply entangled international and cultural conflicts that undergirded it, but instead, the dry, flat facts, the dates and names of battles, the climate of American politics.

She said, "'Rice is a dietary staple of the Vietnamese people,'" a sentence word-for-word extracted from the encyclopedia. It wasn't until she had to stand at the front of the classroom, said so obviously that "rice is a dietary staple of the Vietnamese people," that she acquired the acute feeling of self-awareness, the gaze of her many other Vietnamese classmates burning the hairs on her arms from their intensity. In planning the presentation, she had only considered her teacher, Mrs. Gillman, as an audience, had completely forgotten who would actually comprise the mass of people before her.

"Many Vietnamese farm rice," she said. "But they are also known for a distinct cuisine. They are known for dishes such as pho, a rice noodle and beef broth soup."

Eric Nguyen raised his hand. "Why you keep saying *they*, like you ain't Viet?"

"Eric, please be respectful," said Mrs. Gillman. Nhi teetered back and forth on the balls of her feet. She wrung her hands together, and found she could not bring herself to look at her audience. Instead, she turned toward her presentation board and pointed to a map, which she had printed out in black-and-white and colored in with crayons.

"Vietnam is a coastal country, and most of its industries involve the water," she said. She had printed out all of the images from Microsoft Encarta, an online encyclopedia. Where else could she have looked? When Nhi got older and went to college, before she dropped out, she would take an introductory Vietnam history class. She would learn from the professor that there were dozens of specialized books, written by people who'd done hundreds of hours of research on just the things she hadn't known about. She would read some of those books for her class and feel deeply foolish, inadequate even, for not knowing.

But even now, not yet knowing what she didn't know, and standing in front of her classroom with what seemed a wholly insufficient presentation poster, she felt foolish and inadequate anyway. It was a foolishness and inadequacy that was always near and would never leave, would trail her into that Vietnam history classroom and through adulthood, its presence so customary, she'd go through the world without ever realizing it needn't be there. She sought out the spotlight, yearning to correct this moment, and even when she arrived there, she would still question herself, always the feeling of an imposter.

"Fishing is a major source of revenue for Vietnam, and they—we—they," Nhi stuttered, "largely export shrimp, catfish, and tuna."

"Ngu như chó," Eric said. There was a murmur of laughter. Mrs. Gillman looked uncomfortable, unsure of what do. Would it be racist for her to discipline Eric? She opted to pretend she had not heard.

"Thằng chó!" Kieu said. She blew and popped her bubble-gum. Her classmates laughed louder this time, some of them waving to Nhi as they repeated Kieu's words.

"Okay now, let's not be disruptive," said Mrs. Gillman.

"We just trying to help our classmate, Mrs. G—offer her some moral support in her native language," said Eric.

Mrs. Gillman hovered between annoyance and indecision. "Go on, Nhi."

Nhi wished she could understand what they were saying. "*Chó,*" they kept shouting, *dog*.

"Vietnam in recent years has increased its tourism. It is a single-party socialist republic," she said. She had copied that directly from the section entitled "Government," which did not offer any backstory or explanation beyond that Vietnam simply *was* a single-party socialist republic, and Nhi had not had the time or the desire to do more research on what exactly that entailed. On her presentation board, Nhi pointed to the Vietnam flag, and a photo of the country's party leader.

"Chó chết," said Andy Nguyen.

"Chó đẻ," said Lucy Tran.

"Đụ mẹ mày," said Vu Ngo.

The insults had a sting to them, spit and poison.

"English in this classroom, only," Mrs. Gillman decided. "This is an American public school, and you will speak English."

As the bell for the end of period rang, Eric shoved Nhi's board to the ground on his way out, and the stream of her classmates shoved her, too, with their shoulders as they passed. Mrs. Gillman sat at her desk, determinedly staring at the stack of papers before her, and Nhi gathered up her things as fast as she could to avoid being alone with her. The poster was awkward to carry. She dragged it down the hallway, its outer flaps banging open and hitting her knee with every step.

At lunch, Nhi sat outside at the metal picnic tables near the gymnasium with her friends. Most people ate in the cafeteria, but Nhi and Haley and Emily liked to sit outside for its privacy. The tabletop, coated in purple thermoplastic, crisscrossed in a diamond pattern, its holes through which Nhi's sandwich crumbs tumbled onto the patchy grass below. The trifold poster board leaned against the table, as obtrusive at their lunch spot as it was in Nhi's mind.

"Don't worry about them. Fuck them," Emily said. The word *fuck* was louder than the others. It propelled from her mouth, full of trepidation and defiance, though she was clearly unaccustomed to saying it. Nhi appreciated the support. Emily's mother was Vietnamese and her father white, and sometimes they shared in the misery of being bullied. But Nhi thought sometimes, and guiltily, that she bore the largest burden for a failure to culture. Of course, Emily encountered her classmates' attitudes her whole life and felt even more an outsider, someone who belonged nowhere. What was funny was that they both belonged nowhere, and perhaps that was why they were friends. Emily, who was neither wholly white, nor wholly Vietnamese, and Nhi, who was Vietnamese in name and looks, but not, apparently, in culture. Nhi would never voice it, but always secretly wished that she had even a drop of white in her blood. Wouldn't it make her life easier, better, to be less than what she currently was, to cut her blood with whiteness?

Haley was white, one of two white students in their grade. The other was Jacob Ketterling. He didn't count, according to the kids at school: he had always lived in the same neighborhood and been friends with all the Black kids at school. Jacob's skin glowed whiter than Haley's in the sun, but he wore a do-rag and regularly got sent to the disciplinarian's office for breaking dress code, his socked feet clinging to their Adidas slides as they slapped against the pavement. Sometimes they called him Eminem, although Nhi was unable to tell if this was ridicule or friendly teasing. Haley, however, was, in Jacob Ketterling's words, "Cracker-ass white as fuck."

The three of them sat every day in their self-imposed quarantine after discovering the tables during first period PE one day. Nhi had been struck in the head while playing volleyball. Students waiting their turn in the bleachers laughed, and she ran out the back, discovering the hidden nook behind the gymnasium dumpsters populated by four boys sharing a cigarette. Emily had followed her out, and the boys gazed at them, unconcerned.

Nhi and Emily took Haley to the alcove, where the table sat empty at lunchtime, remnants of cigarette ash beneath it. At first, people poked their heads around the cinder-block wall but quickly withdrew seeing the three of them eating their lunches. Now, people barely ever showed up. The hidden table had been claimed by the three of them, the social order reflected in the geography of the school in the rigid ways it was during adolescence.

"The worst part was," Nhi told her friends, "I didn't know what they were saying."

"I hate when they talk about us in Vietnamese," said Emily.

"Well, I knew a little bit. Words here and there," said Nhi. She felt embarrassed by the fact that she wasn't fluent, and wanted Emily and Haley to know that she knew the words, even if she didn't know how they strung together.

"Ya lyin'," said Eric. He walked around the cinder-block wall that partially obscured their table. Andy was right behind him.

"You're a communist," said Andy.

"What are you talking about?" said Nhi.

Eric pointed to her presentation board. "Why you come in

here with that communist-lovin' shit?" The early-afternoon sun was still high in the sky. It cast the boys' shadows onto their table. Nhi had always felt their lunchtime niche to be a school day relief, an escape. But now, Eric and Andy blocking them in, their growing teen bodies looming over theirs, it felt for the first time like a trap.

"Go away," said Haley. "Please leave us alone."

"Why are you calling her a communist?" said Emily.

"Why are you friends with a communist?" said Andy.

"We're not communists," Emily said.

"I know *you're* not, white girl," said Andy. "But your friend is."

"I'm half-Viet," Emily said.

Andy laughed. "Well you look all-white."

Eric kicked the presentation board to the ground and stepped on it. He bent over and peeled off the printed, encyclopedia image of the red flag with its yellow star, ripping it to pieces. "Don't bring that communist shit to school ever again."

"What kind of Vietnamese girl don't rep her own flag?" said Andy.

Nhi stared at the fragments of ripped paper on the ground, her face as red as the flag. Of course she didn't belong with them, with people like Andy and Eric. Of course she hadn't known the particular pain that would be caused if she put the official but incorrect symbol beneath "Get to Know Vietnam," which she had painstakingly cut out and pasted letter by letter at the top center of the poster board. Eric spit on the dirtied project, and when they left, Nhi did not try to save it.

That night, Nhi and Trieu slumped together on the couch. *Entertainment Tonight*, which their mother had been watching, was over. Nhi snatched the remote up before her younger sister could and began flipping through the channels. They didn't have very many, as their father found it necessary to purchase only the local news, boxing, and the game show network.

Nhi's mouth had the filthy feeling it always did after eating a dinner with fish sauce, the sugary, vinegary aftertaste coating her mouth. They had fried fish and tofu, rice and nước chấm, thawed frozen spinach sautéed with garlic. They ate a variation of this, sometimes with broth, every night. Nhi ran her tongue over her teeth as the television flashed before her.

"Have you voted yet for which Big Fat Loser you think will win the challenge tonight?" said the television host. "It's not too late to call 1-800-BIG-PHAT and tell us who your favorite is!" The host was standing on a beach with a microphone. There was a live audience before him that applauded, and behind him, in the ocean, the contestants swam toward a platform in the distance. Some of them had to stop midlap and tread water to rest. Lifeguards on Jet Skis loitered on the edges of the swim area, ready to rescue. One by one, the contestants heaved themselves up onto the platform, where a Last Supper–style table was set with plates of heaping food. A tiger paced the long stage, but it disappeared before Nhi could point it out. She blinked, searching for where the tiger might have gone.

"What's going on?" said Trieu.

"It's a fitness show," said Nhi. "They compete to get skinnier."

"Why?" said Trieu.

Nhi had to think about this. The most obvious answer would be that they were trying to lose weight. But as she watched the spectacle before her, the camera absurdly close to the contestants in their stretched uniforms, emblazoned with the words BIG FAT LOSER, she knew that this was the wrong answer to Trieu's question.

"It's about being on television," she said. That was closer to the truth. What Nhi meant, but didn't know how to articulate was, *It's about being seen.*

Their mother walked over to the living room and stood

watching. "Chời ời là chời," she said. Her curved, pink nail pointed at the screen. "Look at the Vietnamese boy!"

He dragged himself across the platform, his uniform sopping wet. He dripped and slipped, stumbling as he clutched his side before finding his seat in front of a plate piled high with bánh mì. He began eating the sandwiches so fast, she wasn't sure how he could be chewing. The sheen of sweat and water on his face, the flecks of sandwiches flying as he bit into them was grotesque, but Nhi could not look away.

Her mother clicked her tongue. "He so fat. Very American. His parents must be very embarrass. I don't understand why he do this."

A fitness trainer wearing a metallic purple unitard stood near the man's ear, shouting at him. "This is why you're fat," she screamed. "A big, fat loser!" He was crying into the sandwiches even as he continued to shove bread and slippery meat into his mouth. Below this image, a ribbon with his name and occupation: Minh, IT Specialist. The television flickered, the antenna needing to be adjusted, and Nhi thought she saw the image of a woman, wearing fluttering, yellow silk, before it blinked back to *Big Fat Loser*.

Nhi understood perfectly why he would do this. She gripped the remote, her palm sweaty, afraid someone might try to change the channel. She felt to her core that she understood this man, this *very American* man. She was American, too.

"Vietnamese don't do this," her mother said.

But, for once, Nhi did not feel ashamed upon hearing these words. She was right—Vietnamese didn't do this. Yet everyone in the room, even disapproving Xuan, stared transfixed at the television. Even the camera could not pan away from this man that looked like them, but who, according to her mother, was not like them, didn't act like them, didn't *do* like them. Perhaps if she had the same steel of this man, she could face the ugly thing itself, stare it in the eyes rather than shrink away when her poster board got thrown to the ground, when other people told her she was not welcome, when she accidentally did not do like Vietnamese—even if it meant crying, or failing, or being humiliated. She wanted to be like this very American man.

At school the next day, while standing at her locker, Andy and Kieu banged their fists on the lockers next to her. The hollow sound of fists against metal clanged near her head.

"What the hell you staring at, banana?" Andy said.

"You," she said. She wouldn't turn from his gaze.

Kieu slammed her locker door shut and they walked away.

She didn't feel afraid at all. The ghost of someone stood at her back. *Big fat loser*, she said to herself. That was what she was. Big, fat, American loser, and she didn't care one bit.

11

TRIEU

In a strip mall painted a shade of golden sand, Red Dragon Restaurant almost disappeared between a jeweler and a Vietnamese video store, both facades adorned in multiple flashing neon signs. The humble but popular lunch spot was run by a couple who specialized in hand-cut egg noodles. It was Trieu's favorite restaurant, but she hated going there with her family because she couldn't correctly pronounce the food she wanted to order. The word for egg noodles, mì, dipped much deeper in its pronunciation than Trieu could ever properly manage. When the adults around her corrected or resaid what she had tried to say, it was always with an air of ghastly disbelief, as if saying *mì* half an octave higher than she should've was a sin. She was turning seven this year, but already, her lips could not hold the sounds right, and they never came out the way she thought they would. She mixed up inflections and words and ideas. What she learned in school and what she heard in every other space melted together. When she said *mì*, the word floated from her mouth warped and deformed. The older she got, the more she overthought it, the worse it all sounded.

During Lunar New Year, Red Dragon had the best múa lân dance. People from all over town came to see it, and the restaurant put out a wonderful spread to welcome prosperity and good fortune. They were saying goodbye to Year of the Dog and ushering in Year of the Pig. Trieu and Nhi were dressed in matching clothes: pleated linen dresses with a square lace neckline and puffy sleeves. Their collars were adorned with handmade rosettes. Nhi's dress was yellow, and Trieu's was red, lucky colors for Tết. Trac, who was fifteen, wore thrift store jeans and a holey Better Than Ezra T-shirt. The pink-and-blue tie-dyed laces on her suede Skechers were dulled from dirt. In fact, they were late to the Tết celebration because Trac and their mother had gotten into an argument about what she was wearing.

"Why don't you wear the new dress I got you?" their mother said.

"I don't want to," Trac said. "Please, Mom."

"You want to wear old pants, old shirt. It has holes in it. And tennis shoes. Why don't you wear the new shoes I bought you!"

"I like my shoes. They look cool." Trac looked reluctant to continue arguing.

"You don't care about your family," said Xuan in a swirl of panic. "Bring bad luck on us by fighting with me about your clothes."

"I'm not fighting with you," she said, but still, did not explicitly agree to change her clothes.

You weren't supposed to fight or disagree during the New Year. Trac did not budge, and so, Xuan let it go. What was worse—her daughter looking like trash at one New Year's festival, or casting the whole Year of the Pig in the dark shadow of their argument? She could not control Trac's shoes, but she could stop them from arguing. Xuan wore a new red áo dài and hoped that it would help make up for this lapse in good nature.

Trieu hid under her mother's bed and listened to this entire fight. Her new dress, which she had worn without protest, was now covered in dust.

Upon entry at Red Dragon, the children were given a gift bag full of toys and red-and-gold foil envelopes full of money from the Vietnamese Community Association. Even Trac, a teenager, got a goody bag full of plastic trinkets and money. These kinds of celebrations had a tendency to self-segregate. Trieu and Nhi exchanged some of their toys with the other kids, cousins and the children of their parents' friends. They ran around Red Dragon and got on the empty stage to dance. There was a reckless freedom in the restaurant, as parents mingled and drank, and their children took advantage of the rare lack of supervision.

Trac sat with the small gang of teenagers, who all pretended to sulk, but would be loath to admit they found it all exciting. Trac and a girl named Linda amused themselves with a cartoonish plastic boy that peed when you filled him with water and pulled his plastic shorts down. They filled him bit by bit by suctioning tea or water from their cups with straws and releasing it into the toy's cavity. When they pulled down his pants, water squirted from the hole in the smooth plastic expanse of his pelvis, and Trac and Linda laughed, flicking water onto each other. Neither Nhi nor Trieu had received one of these toys in their bags.

"Go ask Trac if we can play with hers," said Nhi.

"What if she says no?" said Trieu.

"Tell her both she and Linda already have one, and they can share."

"You tell her," said Trieu.

"If you ask her, then I'll give you any of the toys from my bag that you want."

Trieu went over to the teenagers' table and tapped Trac on the shoulder.

"What do you want?" she said.

When Trieu asked her for the toy, Trac looked at Linda, expectantly, who responded before Trac could make a decision, "Yeah, go ahead. I'm bored with these toys now anyway. I'm gonna go find my little brother, I'll see you outside for the dance!" As she walked away, her long, black hair swung back and forth with her hips.

"What the hell, you little shit," said Trac.

"What did I do?" said Trieu.

"I was in the middle of something and you interrupted. And now, Linda left and is *bored*," said Trac. She took the peeing toy and shoved it violently into her paper bag. "You can't have it."

"But you have to share with us," said Trieu.

"I don't have to do anything," she said, her chair screeching as she pushed away from the table in search of Linda.

Trieu couldn't believe this. What was wrong with Trac, anyways? She had been moodier as of late, but she rarely lost her temper or spoke to her younger siblings like this. And, she always shared her things, even through complaints, sighs, or eye rolls. Trieu decided that she would tell her mother, who would straighten Trac's attitude right out. She stalked over to where Xuan stood with another adult. All of their parents loved to stand back and talk about their children, saying terrible things about them in underhanded bragging.

"Van has no friends," said Mei to Xuan. "I'm worried about him. He spends all his time doing schoolwork. He's number one in his class. I said, Van, you need to spend time with friends! Don't have to be the best at everything all the time."

"That's so nice Van can be top of his class when he's only seven years old. I tell my daughter Trac she needs to spend less time with her friends, too, because high school is much harder. She has so many. But I guess, if she still has all As, it's okay to have friends," Xuan said. Trieu watched this conversation unfold while waiting patiently for her mother to notice her.

"What is it?" Xuan asked her.

"Is this your youngest?" Mei asked. She had a frozen smile on her face. "She's so cute! Child, how old are you?" The words her mother and this woman were saying were rapid fire, although Trieu understood them perfectly well. It was hard to explain, like watching subtitles superimposed over the sounds coming from their mouths.

"Say hello, be polite," Xuan said.

"How old are you?" Mei asked again, pinching Trieu's cheeks.

"I'm six and a half," she said, in English.

"She doesn't speak Vietnamese?" Mei said, eyes wide. "Oh my goodness, you didn't teach her?"

"I did," said Xuan. Pink tinged her cheekbones. "She knows how to speak Vietnamese. Answer her properly, Trieu."

Somehow, Trieu knew what they were saying, their Vietnamese morphing in her brain into understanding. But, when she tried to think of the specific phrase herself, the words for *I am six*, she could not accomplish this simplest act of translation.

"All my children know Vietnamese. I always make them speak it at home," Mei said, with a condescending laugh.

Xuan was the one, now, with a frozen smile. She turned her back on her daughter to continue conversing with the woman, and Trieu recognized this as a dismissal.

They gathered in the parking lot, firecrackers popping and hissing against cracked pavement. Trieu stuffed her fingers in her ears because the sound of it made her body want to curl up somewhere, hidden and safe. From inside the restaurant, the undulating bodies of two dragons snaked their way among the crowd. A man put his whole body into the beating of a large drum. The dragons, with their flapping mouths, fluttering feathers, their bulbous eyes, got closer to the audience. They jerked back and forth, threatening to knock kids and elderly over but staying just far enough away. A man in a moon-shaped, smiling mask hopped between the dragons. A ripple of laughter through the crowd as the man, with his papier-mâché mask, pretended to stumble, tumble, and mime laughter by patting his large belly.

The clownish man was terrifying. He approached each child, getting suddenly near their faces in what Trieu took as an act of intimidation. Every child found him to be delightful, engaging in his dance, laughing and running after him like an endearing uncle.

Trieu knew she was next. He walked toward her in a zigzag, labored and drunkenly, but toward her all the same. The drums beat louder. A new set of firecrackers exploded and popped and sizzled against the ground. She looked at Nhi, who stood next to her with an anticipatory grin on her face, hands balled up into fists. She had always loved attention, and this cartoonish little man guaranteed all eyes would be on them. How did Trieu escape? She saw her parents standing together with some other adults, laughing and clapping like nothing was amiss.

Ông Địa stood right in front of her now. His mask was painted an unsettling shade of orange. It glistened in the afternoon sun. He stooped down to eye level with her, dragons dancing on either side of him, looming above and casting a wavering shadow over her. Their cartoonish faces—bulging eyes and grotesquely flapping mouths—were monstrous and menacing. She did not feel a sliver of good fortune from these beasts, despite everyone's insistence that they were the bringers of luck.

Ông Địa jumped back and forth in a deep squat like a monkey in front of Trieu and Nhi, the crowd cheering. Trieu took both of her palms and laid them flush against his shoulders, a surge of strength pulsing to the tips of her fingers as she pushed him backward onto the rocky asphalt. An intake of breath could be heard, even over the loud pop of firecrackers and the stutter of the drum. Trieu ran inside the restaurant as fast as she could.

★ ★ ★

The restaurant was empty. Everyone was outside. She wondered if the dragon dance had gone on, her indiscretion forgotten. Trieu knew better, though. While the ritual continued, she would pay for her actions later, at home, when her parents were able to discipline her without embarrassment. She sat at one of the restaurant's large, round tables. It could seat eight to ten people, easily, and had a lazy Susan laden with half-drunk beer bottles and glasses of iced tea or soda. There were some unclaimed goody bags for kids, their contents spilling out on the table. The doors were propped open, the drums and firecrackers reverberating within the still quiet of the restaurant.

Trieu went to Trac's paper bag of goodies and took the little peeing man. She pulled his blue shorts down, and old iced tea trickled out. It cheered her, for some reason. She tested each of the straws in the various cups left on the table, but they were all empty.

The bathroom, where she would fill him up in the sink, was at the end of a long, dark hallway. It was always dirty, and you could hear everyone in the kitchen working, usually, because it was right next door. But right now, there was no one bustling around, and she tried to be brave in the dark, windowless hallway. The swinging bathroom door was propped open with an old brick.

Trieu stood at the bathroom's threshold, gripping the peeing man. The fluorescent light flickered, although it wasn't needed. The small rectangular window above the sink and near the ceiling had sunlight streaming through it. The solitary mauve bathroom stall was occupied. The sound of quick and harried inhale, exhale, the sighs of desire. In the gap under the stall door, two sets of feet faced each other, one, a pair of ballet flats, and the other, suede Skechers with dirty tie-dyed laces.

"Trac?" Trieu said.

There was a long stretch of silence. Trieu's own patent leather Mary Janes snapped against the tile. She dragged the child's stool to the sink so that she could reach the faucet to fill the peeing man with water.

12

TRAC

On Valentine's Day, the kids at Trac's elementary school brought
little paper valentines, which they had bought in neat boxes full
of sheets of perforated cardstock. Her classmates shared Sesame
Street and Muppets valentines. Some of them brought Popples,
Rainbow Bright, and Care Bears cards. Others handed out generic cartoon animals hugging hearts scrawled with messages:
Be Mine, Happy Valentine's Day, Be My Valentine.

Valentine's Day was right after the Lunar New Year, when the
busy hustle of cooking and praying, the loud popping of firecrackers, the crowded Tết fairs were finally over. In her mind,
the holiday was organized, bookended by the nostalgic retelling
of the zodiac myth her mother did every year, and the quiet of
making valentines at home, Trac on the floor of the living room
with Xuan every February 13. Xuan neatly cut out symmetrical hearts with a pair of her daughter's safety scissors, and Trac
colored them in with pink and purple crayon. She lay the paper
hearts over a scrap of lace before coloring, the texture translat-
ing into crayon not quite as well as she envisioned. Xuan would

pencil those words, *Happy Valentine's Day* in her tidy script, and Trac would trace over them with black marker.

As her classmates passed around their store-bought cards, Trac would pull the flimsy paper hearts from her brown paper sack with shame, hoping that each one would be buried beneath the piles of other cards on her peers' desks. At home, she laid all of the valentines she'd received before her in rows and picked each one up, staring closely at the Care Bear surfing a cloud, Big Bird hugging Elmo, Rainbow Brite skating on a rainbow, generic cartoon caterpillar inching toward *Happy Valentine's Day*, generic cartoon kitten cuddling *Be My Valentine*. She saved her favorites in an old cookie tin.

Last year, Trac made the paper valentines on her own. She cut them into hearts in the waiting room of the hospital where her mother gave birth to her younger sister, Nhi. She wrote *Happy Valentine's Day*, in uneven, childish script, letter by letter, checking against the valentines saved in her cookie tin to ensure everything was spelled right. This year, after having made them alone the previous Valentine's Day, Trac realized she had looked forward to making them with her mother. Before, she had always been jealous of her classmates' store-bought valentines and embarrassed about the homemade quality of her own. But, when her mother gave birth to Nhi, and she'd had to sit and make them by herself, she felt, for the first time, the sensation of loneliness. Even after her mother came home, even after she delivered Nhi, small and bundled in her arms, into the cradle of their family (or, perhaps, because of this), Trac continued to feel alone. It was this feeling that made Trac yearn for that ritual of making valentines with her mother, to recall how things used to be.

At lunch a few days before Valentine's Day, Tommy Hebert, who sat across from Trac at the lunch table in the cafeteria, waved his hand in front of his nose.

"What's that smell?" he said. "It's Trac! Trac smells like *fish*."

The other kids laughed, embarrassed by her. "Ew," said Clara Thomas. "Is that really you?" She unrolled the Fruit Roll-Up from her insulated Barbie lunch box.

Trac shut the tin lid of her own lunch box. Her mother had packed a Tupperware of rice and fish sauce, shredded pork and pork skin. Oily green onions and pickled-carrot garnishes were smashed beneath the plastic cover. The pungent odor of room-temperature pork and fish sauce had drifted from her lunch box and sat in the air.

"Smells like garlic fish farts," said Tommy.

A woman stood behind Tommy. She had her hands on each of Tommy's shoulders, the threat looming over his diminutive body, and yet, he did not acknowledge her, didn't seem to know she was behind him. "Don't let him speak to you like that," she said to Trac.

"Or like my dad's BO," Tommy continued.

"Don't speak to me like that," Trac said. "What's BO?"

His mouth was full of strawberry yogurt. "You smell bad," he said.

"Tell him what you think," said the woman. She was wearing a rice paddy hat and a gun slung across her chest.

"I'm going to tell you what I think," said Trac.

Tommy laughed. Little bits of yogurt peppered the table.

"Tell him the truth," said the woman.

"You're ugly," said Trac. "My mom says you're white trash." His eyebrows and mouth tautened, pulled downward by some invisible string. His cheeks reddened. Trac felt a surge of satisfaction.

"You stink like rotten shrimp," said Tommy.

"Always tell the truth," said the woman.

"I don't stink like rotten shrimp," said Trac, although she didn't know if that was the truth.

"Are you Chinese?" Tommy said.

"Show him you are Vietnamese," said the woman.

"No," said Trac. "I am not Chinese."

Tommy pulled up at the corners of his eyes, and then down. "Are you Chinese, Japanese," he said, "or dirty knees?" He slapped his knees under the table.

"You will not disappear," the woman said.

"Chinese, Japanese, dirty knees," he sang.

"Stop it," said Trac.

The woman began to sing, too. She had a high, beautiful voice, a nasal pitch full of longing. "*Que sera, sera…*"

"Chinese, Japanese, dirty knees."

"Whatever will be, will be." Her mother sometimes sang this song while cooking or preparing for bed.

Trac stood up.

"Chinese, Japanese, dirty knees." He slapped his knees every time he said the last phrase, the sting of it snapping in the air.

"'The future's not ours to see…'"

"Stop it!" Trac said. The woman's singing and Tommy's rhyme filled up her ears with unbearable noise.

"Chinese, Japanese, dirty knees!" he said, louder, over her protests.

"You will not disappear," the woman said.

Trac leaned across the brown laminate cafeteria table and pushed Tommy off the attached teal seat. The yogurt he was holding splattered on the floor beside him, where he was sprawled with an expression of bewilderment.

In the principal's office, Trac did not cry. She almost never cried. Mrs. Fremont gave her a demerit slip, which had to be signed by her parents. She was being sent home early, Mrs. Fremont said. Tommy's parents had been called, and he was also being taken home. Trac would have to apologize formally tomorrow, Mrs. Fremont said. She looked at Trac's file and picked up the phone, glancing back at it periodically as she dialed the home number. The telephone rang and rang. Trac was sent to sit outside the office on the bench near the door as Mrs. Fremont pressed the telephone hook and dialed the number again.

Trac watched through the propped administrative building's door as Tommy Hebert's mother escorted him away while ruffling the hair on his head.

"Can we get ice cream?" he asked his mother.

"Maybe," she said, although Trac felt sure that meant yes. Mrs. Fremont poked her head out of her office.

"Do you know where your parents are during the day?" she said.

"My mom is at home and my dad is at work."

She receded back into her office. Trac waited on the bench. She hoped her mother would still make paper hearts with her that night for Valentine's Day tomorrow.

"Do you want to go home?" The woman from the cafeteria was back. She wore a fluttering, red silk áo dài, the gun slung across her back. The closer Trac looked at her face, the clearer and more blurry she was, like someone she'd met before but could not place, like everyone and no one at the same time.

"Yes, I want to go home," Trac said.

"If you want something, you have to take it," the woman said. "A Goat is strong, with horns that push all obstacles aside."

Trac took her hand, which felt firm and supple and cold, just like her mother's. The woman led Trac out the front entryway. They walked on the cracked and uneven sidewalk, underneath the shade of the neighborhood oak trees. It was easy leaving, and home wasn't far away.

They crossed the street to walk the rest of the two blocks to Trac's home. It was warm outside, and there was a wetness in the air that would cool once the sun set. February was a strange month for weather. It was the descending nighttime chill that made Xuan force her daughter into too-heavy coats. But it was still sunny outside at this early-afternoon hour, and Trac began to sweat in the pink down-filled puffer coat. She unsnapped the buttons and unzipped the zipper, shedding and draping the jacket over her right shoulder. It was heavy for her skinny, young arms. Trac thought about asking the woman to hold the jacket for her, but something about her did not invite it. It was the same something that would not allow her to ask her own parents to do anything of the sort. Tommy Hebert could freely ask his mother to go for ice cream. Even if she said no, he could still ask. Trac would never pose the question in the first place, the inquiry itself a liberty taken without permission.

Along their short, sun-streaked walk, a carport filled with junk sat in the shade of a looming oak tree. Trac paused. She didn't want to carry the coat. In fact, she hated coats, which she was forced to wear regardless of the weather. She took the coat, which Xuan had bought new with tags from the Goodwill, and placed it on top of the yellowing chest freezer.

When Trac and the woman arrived home, the door was, of course, locked. Her mother was usually there at this time of day. She only worked part-time as a secretary. Trac sat on the doorstep with her back against the door, backpack leaning gently against her leg. Though she was shaded by the front porch awning, the afternoon sun still scorched. Her companion paced the yard, not anxiously, but firmly, like a sentinel doing her job. The sun moved slowly across the sky as hours passed, and Trac thought of all the things she wanted to do. Make Valentines, drink Coke, go swimming across the street at Mrs. Matthews's house (which she'd never actually done—she could see the glimmering cerulean water through the cracks in her wooden fence), push Tommy Hebert to the ground.

No one at school noticed she had gone without permission. Mrs. Fremont assumed her parents had picked her up without saying hello in the office. She'd spoken to the Trungs before and could never quite understand them. Xuan and Cuong had only been in the US for twelve years, after all, and their English was still garbled around the ends, still blurred in the middles of words, just enough for someone like Mrs. Fremont to opt out of listening at all, even to the parts that were clear and crisp and practiced. *They wouldn't want to speak to me,* Mrs. Fremont thought, *because it must be too difficult for them. They took their daughter and left—that's what I would've done.*

Except that Mrs. Fremont never got in contact with them on the phone, so it wouldn't make any sense for Cuong or Xuan to know their daughter was being sent home early. She dialed and dialed the number, but then her secretary cracked the door and said the HVAC repairmen had arrived, and Mrs. Fremont went to speak with them about the HVAC trouble, the shoddy job they'd done last time, the estimated time of repair, and she went with them to the east wing and never went back to her office to contact Trac's parents.

After taking Nhi to a doctor's appointment and then buying groceries, Xuan had gone to school at pickup time to find her daughter missing. Mrs. Fremont kept saying, over and over, "You got her earlier, remember?" as if Xuan were stupid and couldn't remember she'd picked up her own daughter.

She drove all over town in a panic, Nhi screaming in her baby seat. The car was full to the brim with different kinds of fear. Xuan's fear about Trac's disappearance. Nhi's instinctual fear, the kind that only very small children have. And Xuan was afraid to tell Cuong. She feared his response, and she feared being exposed as the careless and inept mother that she was. So she didn't tell him. She hoped she would find Trac before he got home. And, that hope was funny because it never occurred to her to check *home* in the first place. Maybe it did not occur to her because Trac did not treat home like somewhere she would want to go. Xuan took the car to the park and ran through its large baseball field, yelling out her name. She drove all through the neighborhood, imagining Trac hoisted in trees. She drove to her friends' houses, knocked on their doors and asked in garbled, frantic English if they had seen her. And, at 5:00 p.m., Cuong pulled into the driveway and saw the figure of his daughter as he walked up the path. From the street, she was obscured by a large potted plant at the edge of the front porch. She slumped against the door frame, peacefully sleeping, and sat with her right hand lying palm up. Her companion had held it until Trac fell asleep, then disappeared as dusk fell.

That night, Xuan and Cuong argued, both of them feeling foolish and scared, though neither would admit that to the other. Trac did not get to make valentines with her mother. She came to school empty-handed the next day, and delivered her formal apology to Tommy Hebert. He did not accept her apology, at least verbally, and instead, without looking her in the eye, handed her a Care Bears valentine with a lollipop taped to it. Clara Thomas and Abby Benson were nearby and giggled. They started singing, "Trac and Tommy, sitting in a tree. K-I-S-S-I-N-G." Trac stared at Good Luck Bear and the four-leaf clover on his belly to avoid looking at Clara and Abby. She felt inexplicably ashamed. She turned her valentine over and, on the back, in shaky handwriting, it said, *From Tommy,* and next to *To:* was a simple drawing of a fish.

13

XUAN

When their mother died, Xuan and Lan didn't know what to do. If they'd been in Vietnam, there were many things they would've done out of sheer practicality, a natural progression led by common sense: clean the body, prepare the grass mat upon which to lay her, set up the altar for prayer, open their home for visitation, guard the body in the night from spirits, and cook food during the time unoccupied with the previous duties. There would've been an abundance of voices in the room: neighborhood women to offer advice, plenty of immediate and distant family to boss them around, elders to reminisce about their traditions and rituals, the exact matters of death and how to conduct them.

But, in America, they weren't allowed to keep the body in their home. And while they were surrounded by people, no one knew exactly what to do next in these new circumstances.

The first time their mother fainted, the ER doctor told them it was because she had diabetes and needed to regulate her blood sugar. He asked them if their family had a history of diabetes. They said they didn't know. He went through the medical forms they were supposed to fill out and verbally asked them the questions they couldn't read. They said, yes, no, I don't know, but really, the answer for all of them was just, I don't know. He gave them a prescription for insulin and a referral for another doctor.

At the primary care doctor, they learned their mother's American diet was to blame. She loved sweets, and at the gas station near their house, she would walk and buy a candy bar at least three times a week. She was homesick, and so, she cooked dishes from home that made her feel less lonely, as if the food would fill the spaces between her bones, that hollow feeling, wherever it might be located. She made fish stewed in caramel, eggs and pork in sugary coconut broth, added a little extra sugar to her fish sauce, formed homemade sweet rice into blocks wrapped in banana leaves.

"You can't have refined sugar, Tien," the doctor said. "And when you do, you have to measure it." They all nodded their heads yes. After demonstrating how to use it, the doctor proffered a small box containing the device to measure her glucose levels. They took it without question or complaint.

But they did not measure her glucose because they didn't know how to read the instructions, couldn't remember what the doctor had done. They never filled the insulin prescription because it had to be injected with a needle. Xuan, who was supposed to be Tien's caretaker, was not permitted to mother her own mother. Tien lived with Xuan and her family but refused to relinquish control, insisting on cooking her own meals, doing her own shopping, deciding upon her doctor's appointments, whether or not she would take medicine.

For dinner one night, Tien made sweet and sour soup, canh chua, with catfish and pineapple, stewed tomatoes and bean sprouts, oysters and shrimp, an extra rock of sugar. She made chè chuối with purple yams, the bananas slimy and ripe. The dessert was cloying and coated their mouths in a candied slick. She told Trac to turn the television off so she could play the piano in peace. Before bed, Tien ate a Hershey's chocolate bar, letting each piece melt in her mouth, savoring and consuming the sweetness.

The next morning, she wouldn't wake. The body didn't feel cold, exactly, but like it was quickly losing heat that could not be regained. Her feet and hands were swollen, the jade bracelet she always wore imprinting itself against her skin.

They called the paramedics, who arrived and pronounced her death at 9:12 a.m. The time of death was important, the Buddhist monks told her later, but Xuan didn't know what it truly was. Tien had been still and fading in warmth when they found her. How long did it take for a body to get cold? Did it happen right away, quickly, no heart to pump, no blood to warm?

Lan had let out a terrible and prolonged choked sound, but Xuan just stood there and stared, unsure of what to do. That was the predominant feeling she had then, staring at the newly dead body of her mother, and throughout, in conversations with the funeral home director, the Buddhist monks, the Catholic priest, the florist. Everyone only ever seemed to reveal step by step what it was she was supposed to do, the end objective or bigger plan shrouded. Was she supposed to bury her? Cremate her? Were they supposed to host a wake, a memorial? It was like these people had a bird's-eye view of her mother's death, could map out its progression and its end, while Xuan was two inches away from the body, right up against it, unable to see anything else. Xuan's family was Catholic, but her family had also done many of the Buddhist traditions and rituals of prayer. They'd gone to church, but they also had an ancestral altar in their homes for as long as Xuan could remember, to which her mother and grandmother had prayed, offered food, and burned incense. She didn't know what she was supposed to do, so she called both the Vietnamese Catholic Church *and* the Buddhist temple, which happened to be only two blocks from the church.

At the funeral, Xuan, Lan, Cuong, Trac, and Lan's husband, Hieu, tied bands of white linen across their foreheads. An altar with a framed photo of Tien was next to another altar with a small Buddha statue. They held sticks of incense and knelt on the ground, bowing when the monks told them to in between their long, clamorous chants. Women in purple robes stood on the periphery of the ceremony, hitting bowls and chimes. Xuan had no idea how long the ritual was, no idea what she was supposed to do and when she was supposed to do it. When they bowed too slowly, or misread the signals and acted at the wrong time, the monks gave them dirty looks.

People who knew Tien in Vietnam, and throughout the small Vietnamese community in New Orleans, other elderly women who tended to the community garden with her, came to the funeral to pay their respects. People walked around them as they bowed, moving back and forth between the two altars, and finally, when the ceremony was over, the priest stood to give a sermon at the podium near the open casket.

"They put too much makeup on her," said Lan.

"And they did her hair wrong," said Xuan.

The body in the casket did not resemble their mother at all, so much so that Xuan wondered if it was even the right one. This suspicion was made worse by the fact that the funeral home had misspelled their mother's name on the placard outside of the funeral parlor. Perhaps this was the body of some woman name Ten Tung, after all, and all of this was a joke, the real Tien Trung crouched behind the casket and ready to spring up in surprise. She imagined this lifeless, stiff body had been stuffed with cotton, face painted on like a doll. The longer she stared at it, the less she could conjure up the face of her mother, its detail and movement: the way the lips crinkled at the corners, the way her brows almost met over her nose when she frowned, the fluttering of loose gray hairs fallen from her bun when she laughed, how all of her features had crumpled when she realized they would have to leave Vietnam.

Instead, this body floated to the surface of her mind and took up all its space, and when she tried to push it away, in its stead, a blank face. It was this, more than anything, that Xuan thought about that night in bed.

They left the body at the funeral parlor overnight. The monks told them they should pray through the night and be ready to complete their prayer ritual in the morning before bringing the casket to the crematorium. The Catholic priest told them to let him know when they got the ashes, so they could be put in the cemetery crypt. The Buddhist monks reminded them the temple needed a small photo so they could continue to pray for her for forty-nine days while her soul roamed the earth before rest.

"Are they being competitive?" Cuong said as they walked to the car.

"Of course not," Xuan said, although she wasn't sure why she said this, since it was clear the priest and monks had been jockeying for power all day. Perhaps to reassure herself they'd made the right decision in choosing both religious ceremonies rather than one.

She had never asked her mother what it was she wanted when she died, which was the cause of all this. At first, Xuan thought they should do a purely Catholic funeral. But then, Lan said, what if she wanted an altar? What if they messed up so badly, their mother's soul drifted through the earth and spirit world without purpose, upset that her daughters never did the proper rites? This indecision was exactly the thing Tien would have criticized her daughters for.

As the first light of day filtered through their plastic blinds, Xuan closed her eyes and let the brightness of morning cast an orange pall on everything. She listened for a moment to Cuong's loud and steady breaths, then got up to pray, she guessed, both to Buddha and to God.

Xuan experienced the last part of the funeral as if in fast-forward on a videotape. She went through the motions, but at some points she came back into her body and was surprised to find herself there at all. The monks chanted and sang, voices ringing out at a pitch that twisted her insides. The Catholic priest, who became agitated with the length of the Buddhist ceremony, loudly began his own prayer for Tien over the monks' song. Everything was rising and falling, the noise, the room itself, the people in it. Xuan rubbed her eyes. She was so tired. Her mother sat up in her coffin, except that she didn't look like the corpse that Xuan had last seen. Tien looked like she did when she first woke up in the mornings, eyelids fighting the weight of sleep. She turned to look at her daughter, the small, closed-mouth curve of a smile and the feeling of love persisting.

After they carried the coffin to the hearse, followed in a procession to the cemetery across town, walked through the rows of looming marble tombs, pushed the coffin into the incinerator, stood outside in the warm air—Trac held her mother's hand and Cuong smoked a cigarette behind the Herbert family crypt—they drove home, Lan with them, and walked around the house, each of them, with a kind of purposelessness. What did you do after a funeral? It seemed jarringly wrong to continue on with mundane life as if nothing was amiss, and yet, what else was left?

There were so many things lost, and now, another thing. Xuan wanted to go home, the place where her mother was, her face unlined and bright, the opposite of that wooden, dead face in the coffin. The more she thought about her old life, the less she remembered. There were no physical things to tether her to its existence, all of them absorbed into the anonymity of war. She knew her house, full of people and sound, felt like the sun on her skin, that sitting on its roof and eating corn stolen from the kitchen felt like wind on wet. But those things didn't make sense when she tried to say it out loud, and she couldn't put anything concrete to impressions—not the color of the walls, nor the shape of her mother's hands. She wanted to gather up all the things she lost and surround herself with them. All her custom dresses, probably being worn by the wives of communist leaders. Her jewels, probably divided up and sold on the black market. All of the herbs in jars at their family apothecary, the furs imported from Paris, all the books from their library burning, the trees in neat rows on their rubber plantation, her beauty pageant trophy.

Of all the things she couldn't bring, the trophy was the one she dwelled on the most. On the night they left, Xuan had filled her pockets with food and money. She wore as much jewelry as she could, arms and neck weighted like a shackle. She stared at the trophy, trying to figure out a way. Perhaps she could hold it under the flap of her jacket. Or, she'd convince her mother it could be used as a weapon, because certainly it could be. It was a solid silver cup. But she knew that it was too heavy, too cumbersome even to lift, let alone carry for sustained amounts of time. No bag would hold it comfortably. There was not a way to hide it, and it would slow them down.

She stood and stared at that trophy one last time before leaving their house. It was the last thing she looked at, the light from the moon outside gleaming on the round surface of the silver cup. The trophy had caused such suffering. Yet Xuan found she could never turn from it, the memory of what she'd done to bring it home. It reminded her of her friend Bambi, with whom she'd entered the beauty pageant in the first place.

She wondered where Bambi was now, if she was still in Vietnam, if she was dead or on the streets. Xuan didn't even know who to call or where to write if she wanted to find her. A lot of people had become homeless after the war. But, she liked to think Bambi was too resourceful. A hustler, someone who, against all odds, survived. It was the very thing her own mother had disliked about Bambi. She was scrappy and shrewd out of necessity, because she came from nothing. She used her body to get the things she needed. Trashy, her mother called her. Well, her mother was just as dead as Bambi surely was, so what did trashy matter in the end.

Xuan barely had a memory of the drive. She'd taken the keys without explanation and drove alone to the trophy store. It was a small, cinder-block building off the West Bank Expressway. It shared a gravel parking lot with another cinder-block building, which was recently painted tan and served as a new apartment complex. Finding a parking spot was difficult because the lot was crowded with tenants' cars. Xuan parked poorly and had to squeeze her body through the tiny gap between her door and the adjacent car.

The store was crowded with shelves and plastic trophies, but otherwise empty, a bright fluorescent light casting everything in a sheen that hurt the eyes. The store filled her ears with an imperceptible buzzing. There were some very expensive- and heavy-looking trophies behind the glass case, but mostly there was a variety of plastic awards in a rainbow of colors. Little lamps, music notes, miniature karate figures, and tiny graduation caps perched atop pillars. There were some trophies that simply had giant numbers at the top, descending to as far as thirteen. Xuan wondered who would order something to commemorate thirteenth place.

"Do you need help?" A man walked in from the stockroom. He had a loose cigarette hanging, unlit, from his lip. An LSU baseball cap pushed his hair down over his forehead.

"No, I okay, thank you, sir," said Xuan.

"Well, what are you looking for?"

"Nothing," she said. "Thank you."

The shopkeeper chuckled. "Most people know what kind of trophy they need when they come into a trophy store."

She was looking for a feeling, and how did she describe that to him?

"Beauty," she said. "I won a contest for beauty."

"And you need a trophy for it?" he said.

"Yes," Xuan said. "I need a trophy for it."

"They didn't give you a trophy when you won?"

"I loss it," she said. "I loss in the war."

He walked down the second aisle, beckoning her to follow. He crouched and pulled trophy after trophy from the shelf, lifting it up for her to see.

"No," she'd say, "not right," and he'd place it back on the shelf, lifting up the next, to which she'd say, "No, not right," again, and he would continue showing her more.

"What is that?" she said, pointing to a display of trophies beneath a taxidermy deer mounted on the wall. "What kind of trophy over there?"

"Those are hunting awards," he said. No one ever bought them—who bought a hunting award? The trophy was the dead animal. If you needed something with longevity, then you stuffed its head and mounted it on a wall.

She went over to the display and held a small trophy, about the length of her forearm, with a big cat figurine on top. The single pillar was blue with two vertical holographic stripes, and on the white base, a blank metal plaque.

"You sure?" he said, although it was clear he didn't care what she bought. "Want something engraved on the plaque?"

"Yes, I want 'Miss Saigon' engrave on the bottom." And she went to the counter, taking a pen and scrap paper from her purse to write it out so he didn't misspell anything. But even so, when she got home later and looked at the plaque, Saigon was written incorrectly: *Sagon*.

She spread newspaper out in the backyard. She taped over the engraved plaque to keep it clean and covered it in a fine mist of metallic silver spray paint. *"Are you having a breakdown?"* Cuong had asked, but she honestly didn't know. Ripping off the tape, she wrote *Miss Saigon 1973* in thick permanent marker over the barely visible engraving.

Inside, she moved the trophy from place to place. The dinner table, the mantel, next to the television, near her bedside. Each time, standing back to look, to remember, silver paint and beauty.

14

XUAN

At the American grocery store, Xuan learned exactly what she needed. She never lingered or browsed the aisles, she never double-checked. She knew. She knew what she needed, and she knew what they would have to offer her. They had lettuce and carrots and cucumbers, vinegar and eggs and garlic. There were even items Xuan had discovered and now added to her list: Braunschweiger liver sausage, which was almost exactly like pâté, bagels from the bakery, two liters of Coca-Cola. Sometimes they had gingerroot, but most of the time they didn't. They had white rice, but it was never jasmine. They had fish in the meat department, but never whole. Instead, clean, portioned flesh shimmered, wet and bright in the case. No head, no bones, no tail.

In New Orleans, there was no Vietnamese grocery. Only a small Chinese store that offered some of the things Xuan might need. Soy sauce, rice vinegar, jarred chilies in oil. She could not find fish sauce, and nothing had the salty pungency to replace it. She heard a rumor from her cousin that there was a man in town who possessed it. He had family in Thailand.

"He has a whole pantry full of Thai fish sauce," cousin Khanh said. "That's what Diep told me. He went to Thailand and filled his suitcase with dozens of bottles in case he never had another chance."

Xuan rubbed her belly absentmindedly. Her daughter pushed against the walls of her body, restless. She would be Year of the Goat, not a year she would've picked on purpose. She wondered if her daughter would ever taste fish sauce. Thinking of this made Xuan miss home so intensely that the corners of her eyes got hot. "I wonder if we can buy a bottle off of him," she said. "Who is this guy?"

"I don't know. It's just a rumor. I heard another rumor that this guy is actually a communist."

"Everyone here thinks everyone is a communist," said Xuan. It seemed at every party, someone would gossip about someone else, a person invariably missing from the party and unable to defend themselves, saying that they were a secret communist.

"Think about it, though—how else would he get the fish sauce? It's a great idea, actually," said Khanh.

"Why would it be a great idea for a communist to come all the way to America to hoard fish sauce?"

"Because there's obviously nothing being exported from Vietnam right now. This guy has the monopoly on fish sauce in America! He could charge whatever he wanted and send the money back to the regime. He's asking fifty bucks a bottle— *fifty bucks*! That's more than my utilities every month. I might still pay it, though. *Fifty dollars*," she said.

The story seemed both far-fetched and totally logical. "Who did you hear this from?"

"I already said, Diep told me."

Diep was a gossip. Her lips were thin, but her mouth stretched large and wide. She had small and unkind eyes. She was polite enough on the surface, but there was something in her face that was untrustworthy and a little bit mean. Despite this, or perhaps because of it, Diep was popular. Xuan found this baffling. She did not understand how a woman so openly disliked by most people was also always surrounded by company.

"I told Khanh that story about the fish sauce because I wanted to test her. I knew she would tell someone," said Diep.

"So, there's no fish sauce?"

"Oh, there's fish sauce."

Diep led her through the kitchen, which was poorly lit and mostly orange laminate, and through the back. The metal security door banged against the house's brick when Diep accidentally pushed too forcefully. Xuan's ankles prickled, insects darting around her as she waded through the uncut grass. Diep opened the combination lock on a small beige toolshed.

Inside, there were crates stacked to the sloped ceiling. Nearer the door, Xuan peered into an open crate. Rows of bottles filled with brown liquid. There were a few empty spaces where Diep must've taken some to sell or use.

"You want one?" said Diep. "You can have one, only twenty dollars."

"Twenty dollars for one bottle?" said Xuan. "Are you talking about American dollars?" Twenty was high, but she already felt she was getting a better deal than Khanh. Should she buy them now before the price went back up? She wondered if this was Diep's selling strategy—spread the rumor to get customers, create the demand, and then make them feel like they're getting a steal even when they aren't. It was funny to think Diep had concocted a tall tale about communists selling fish sauce when she was running the most capitalist hustle Xuan could imagine.

"Yeah, you know how hard it is to get this here?"

Just yesterday, Cuong had come from the grocery with the items Xuan had requested. She sent him back to return the eggs because he had spent ninety-nine cents, about ten cents more than the usual cost. He'd gone to the wrong store, the more expensive store, because it was closer to their home. She certainly could not rationalize a twenty-dollar purchase for a single bottle of fish sauce.

"It's good quality," said Diep. "You wanna taste it?" She took a bottle out of the crate and popped open the plastic white cap. Xuan cupped her hands as if receiving communion, and Diep squirted some of the sauce into them. She lifted her hands to her face and inhaled the odor of rotten ocean. She dabbed her tongue against her palms. It was so salty it stung. The baby inside her kicked and tumbled.

The fish sauce, Xuan could tell, was not good. It should taste like fish, not fishy. The liquid should be amber, the shade so deep it might be opaque if you didn't look closely enough. Xuan lifted the bottle to the light to peer through it. Mud-colored water sloshed around as she swirled it like wine. But still, Xuan admitted, it was fish sauce.

"How do you get this?"

"Why do you want to know?"

"I want to buy them bulk and sell them in a grocery store."

"Who's gonna buy *my* supply if you're selling them for cheaper in a grocery store?"

"No, you misunderstand. I want to buy my supply from you, and sell them in a grocery store. New Orleans's first-ever Vietnamese grocery."

Diep told Xuan that she and her brother had gotten separated during the chaos of April 30, 1975. She'd waited for Duc as long as she could, and then left with her children on the boat she'd arranged for the family. Duc was trapped on a crowded city street, and random violence began to break out in the way random violence breaks out when people begin to panic. Duc was knocked down, and he woke up next to a shop door, shoved against a wall. When he finally got back to his house, everyone had gone.

Duc did not wait. He knew they were gone. The house had a different feeling, a house mourning the loss of its charges. None of the furniture had been moved, very few things taken, and yet, the space felt vacant, as if it had been unoccupied for years rather than hours.

"He went to Thailand. The way he tells it in letters, it sounds like he was the last man in Vietnam to leave." Xuan had heard that so many times. Every man had been the last man to leave Vietnam—God forbid a man just admit he had been one of many to leave, driven out like common cattle.

"How did he get to Thailand?"

"I don't know, really. He changes what he says, and he's vague. Sometimes he says he took a boat to the Philippines first. That makes the most sense, doesn't it? But sometimes he implies he walked the whole way, straight through Cambodia to get to the Thai border. I don't believe he could've done that without being captured and killed, though," she said. "But other times, it sounds like he was trapped in Vietnam for a long time before he could leave. He won't say in his letters outright, and I can't afford to call him. Even if I did, I don't know where to call. I really don't know what's true anymore."

Duc had a friend in Thailand, a friend who let him sleep at his house for months. This friend knew a guy. That guy worked in a factory packing Thai fish sauce. He let Duc take whatever amount he needed for a price.

"Listen," said Diep. "I pay two dollars per bottle, and a lot more on shipping. That's why I charge twenty dollars. But if we go into business together, I'll only charge you six dollars a bottle to stock in your store if you open one. You have to buy a whole crate at a time, though."

Six dollars for a bottle of fish sauce wasn't twenty or fifty, but it was still a lot. That made each crate seventy-two dollars.

How much could Xuan charge before people weren't willing to pay? Seven dollars a bottle? Eight? Ten? People could barely afford to buy rice. But, she had a feeling the fish sauce would sell no matter what.

When Xuan proposed the idea to Cuong, he was watching television. The screen was the size of Xuan's small handbag. Their sponsors, Bob and Diane, had gotten the TV as a refugee donation from St. Mary's Catholic Church. "God is good," Diane had said, as her husband handed them the small black-and-white television. Xuan wasn't so sure about God being good, or if he was there at all. She went to confession at the urging of their sponsors, and she never heard back from him. If losing her house, her homeland, her family was the work of God, then he must be cruel. She imagined him watching them from above, manipulating them in absurd situations like contestants on an American game show.

Cuong loved game shows. "I'm learning," he would say as participants picked letters on *Wheel of Fortune*. He sat on the mustard yellow couch, also given to them by St. Mary's, with his elbows propped on his knees, muttering guessed letters and phrases under his breath.

That night, when Xuan came home from Diep's house, Cuong had already eaten dinner. The remnants of toast with butter lay on a plate in the glow of *Wheel of Fortune*. Xuan sat next to him and he absentmindedly placed his hand on the globe of her stomach. *Wheel of Fortune* ended and a new program glowed on the screen.

"Anh, I met with Diep, today," she began. Cuong was unwrapping a strawberry candy he got for free from the church's entryway candy bowl. The crinkle was loud and distracting. Xuan told him about Khanh's gossiping the week before, her conversation with Diep, the brother in Thailand, the crates and crates of fish sauce hidden in the shed.

On the television, the title for the next game show vibrated on-screen. *"$2.00 Beaauuttttty Queeeenn!"* a man shouted into a microphone. Dick Martin wore a plaid suit and stood in front of a stage. Goldie Hawn stood next to him in a sequined gown.

"Welcome to *$2.00 Beauty Queen*, America's favorite traveling beauty pageant," he said into his microphone, "where women of all walks of life have a chance to wear a crown. Different shapes and sizes here, if you know what I mean." The sound of the crowd laughing. "We're in Dallas this week, finding the country's most beautiful."

"You have the chance to win *big money*," said Goldie Hawn. Again, the crowd laughed. Xuan didn't know why this was, but she had long accepted this as an American habit. Laugh and laugh and laugh, even when something wasn't funny, even when something was uncomfortable or sad. Americans laughed at everything.

A string of women strolled onto the stage behind the hosts, which was lit with giant bulbs and the flashing neon letters of *$2.00 Beauty Queen*. All of them were wearing bikinis and pumps, a white sash across their chests. Xuan could barely see what the sashes said from the tiny screen of their television, but she felt a sudden, deep sense of longing for one of her own. Goldie and Dick walked up to the women and interviewed them one by one.

Some of the women weren't very attractive, Xuan thought. This was another thing Xuan had learned about Americans. Their taste in women was repulsive. She and Cuong watched the show with rapt attention as contestants raced and strutted and talked. The women performed their talents, which in some cases were utterly ridiculous. An accordion player, a jump roper, an Irish step dancer, none of whom were very good.

At the end of the show, a curvaceous redhead stood alone onstage as Goldie Hawn crowned her. She had a big mole on her lip, and her rippling breasts were in danger of spilling out of a too-small dress. Her talent was spinning plates on poles, but several of her plates had crashed and shattered on the floor. If this was the winner of the beauty pageant, surely Xuan had a chance at winning? The contestant in last place stood next to the redhead. Goldie put a dunce cap on her flowing blond hair. The loser was much more beautiful than the winner, in Xuan's opinion. Everything was backward in America.

As Goldie handed a giant check to the winner, the crowd laughed, but Xuan barely noticed.

"Do you think they win a lot of money?" said Xuan.

"Probably. It's an American game show," Cuong said.

"If we won, we could buy fish sauce and lots of other things. We could rent a space and open our own grocery store. I think we would make a lot of money. It could be our big break."

"We could sell all the produce from the gardens the other refugees started. Bean sprouts, Thai basil, bitter melons," Cuong said. She knew she had him now. The seed of an idea had sprouted in his mind, and his voice took on the edge of determination when he decided something.

As if on cue, the credits finished scrolling and Dick Martin's voice-over brought Xuan's attention back to the television. "If you're in these cities," his voice said as a list of places appeared on the screen, "then come see us! Audition to be on the best game show in the biz. Nontraditional applicants encouraged!"

Xuan scanned the list before it could disappear, recognizing a few of the cities right away. New York, Los Angeles, San Francisco, of course. But, a jolt of excitement as she saw how long the list was, what other places it contained. Washington D.C., Chicago, Philly, and other major cities. Nashville, Seattle—New Orleans. Xuan scribbled down the 1-800 phone number and turned to Cuong, beaming so much her cheeks hurt.

At the audition, Xuan had a moment of panic. Her child kicked against her stomach and her feet ached, swollen in the low heels she wore. She was pregnant and huge, and at an audition for a beauty pageant game show. What was she thinking? The women on the show had been American and mediocre. Xuan knew she was more beautiful, and when she wasn't pregnant, at least five waist sizes smaller. But Xuan *was* pregnant—eight months, in fact—and it had been a moment of pure delusion to believe she could be picked for a televised beauty competition.

But Xuan didn't leave the waiting room of the brick warehouse building, and when a plain-looking woman called her name ("Ex-Ooh-Ann? Sue-Awn? Swan?"), Xuan pushed herself out of the chair with difficulty and followed her into the interview space. A woman near the door measured her. Three men sat at a table, and when Xuan entered the room, they looked at each other with curious expressions of excitement. Where are you from? *Vietnam.* How old are you? *Twenty-nine.* Do you speak good English? *I speak pretty good.* What's your talent? *I can sing, maybe.* They looked at each other again. They didn't want her to sing. *I can do whatever you need.* They told her to come downtown next Wednesday; they were filming an episode that day and one of the girls dropped out. Wear a dress, they said, and tennis shoes. Make sure you talk like that on the show. *Like what?* Thanks for coming in, they said.

When she showed up at the downtown game show location wearing a lucky red dress, her pregnancy bump voluminous beneath draping fabric, she felt stupid in her tennis shoes. They were comfortable, but she hoped the showrunners would provide other clothing. She arrived empty-handed, no gowns and no other shoes.

The warehouse was full of lights and people. Assistants were filing audience members in, cameramen dressed in black T-shirts and jeans ate their breakfast sandwiches, and the other contestants stood in a cluster. Xuan joined them, her sneakers squeaking on the concrete floor.

"Ah, you must be—" the producer scanned her list "—how do you say this? Is it *Swan*?"

"That fine," said Xuan. The producer's eyes gave Xuan the once-over, lingering on her enormous baby bump. She waited for her to say *sorry* and send her home. She waited for her to check her list again and ask if she was sure this was the correct show. She waited for her to laugh at the sight of her, like all Americans did. The producer didn't do any of those things, though.

"Okay, wait here with the other contestants, and we will direct you where to go," she said, slowly and looking Xuan directly in the eyes, as if that might help the language barrier.

The other contestants were also wearing tennis shoes and dresses. There were women in formal evening gowns, others in short, sequined party dresses, and some in too-casual sundresses. Heels hung from hands here and there. Xuan could see that she was not the only contestant who was told little about what she might need to wear or bring.

"Line up, line up, line up!" Assistants, more assistants than Xuan could've known were there, swarmed the crowd of women and began shuffling them into a single-file line. They swayed and bobbed into place, submissive in their confusion. Xuan was near the front of the line. She, and many of the other women, still clutched their personal belongings, their purses. One woman, who wore a full face of makeup and electric-blue eye shadow, still held a half-eaten granola bar, her pink lipstick dotted with crumbs.

"Go, go, go!" they were told, and each of them stumbled out onto the brightly lit and hot stage, facing a faceless audience. Xuan held tightly to her shoulder bag, resting her other hand absentmindedly on her pregnancy bump. As they stared into the blinding lights, the audience let out a low rumble of laughter.

Dick Martin strode along the stage as he spoke into a microphone, staring into Camera A. "Welcome to *$2.00 Beauty Queen*, where dreams come true for every woman! Here we have twenty beautiful specimens of *all* shapes, sizes, colors, and creeds." He paused in front of Camera B and winked. His tartan suit looked too hot for the weather. Goldie Hawn stood at the other end of the stage in a floor-length dress that looked like molten gold.

"Hi, Dick!" she said. "How are you enjoying the Big Easy?"

"Heya, Goldie!" he responded. "*Laissez les bon temps rouler,* am I right? Can you give our viewers the lowdown?"

"Sure, Dick! Today our beautiful contestants will compete to win the two-dollar crown by participating in three competition categories: evening gown, bikini, and talent show! It's the beauty pageant you're all familiar with, but with a twist." A tittering of laughter and a healthy round of applause.

"And what's the twist, Goldie?"

"The loser in last place gets dunce status!" The crowd *Aw-ww*ed.

"Well, there you have it," said Dick Martin. At the break, Dick Martin's white smile cracked, and his face melted into its natural state of boredom. "Get my water," he snapped at an assistant.

The contestants were shuffled off the stage. "What the hell is happening?" the woman next to Xuan said. She talked out of the corner of her mouth. She had a smoker's rasp and the kind of Southern Louisiana accent that Xuan found difficult to follow.

"I don't know," said Xuan. "I don't remember this on the show when I watch with my husband."

"They always do this at the very beginning, so maybe you missed it. I thought they prepped all the contestants on what the plan was ahead of time, so they were in on the joke, but they've just been ordering us around two seconds before we need to do something." The woman gave Xuan an exasperated look, as if they were old coworkers commiserating about an incompetent boss. "Where you from? You don't sound like you're from around here. What's your name?" *In on the joke.* How could you be *in* something that wasn't a place?

"My name Xuan and I from Vietnam. Where you come from and what is your name?"

The woman slapped her palm into Xuan's and shook hands while patting her back with the other. "Nice to meet ya, Xuan. I'm Darlene. Drove in from Prairieville for this. My boyfriend's favorite show, he really gets a hoot out of it."

Xuan didn't yet know what a hoot was, what it meant to be *in* on a joke. Fatigue had squashed out any hunger she had had for knowledge. In school, English was her favorite class. She loved learning languages. French was beautiful and sophisticated, a language her father had taught her, but English was bold and crass and, in some instances, completely illogical. She had once loved it for that. But now, she hated it. All the expressions she didn't know only served to make her feel even more moronic than she already did. Her coping method was to simply disregard all the things she didn't know, learning only exactly what she needed to survive.

A man dragging a cart piled high with dresses walked down the line of women and handed them each an evening gown. Xuan lifted hers up by its thread-thin straps, and saw that they had haphazardly hemmed it to suit her measurements. It was baglike, Xuan assumed, to accommodate her pregnant body. The other women began stripping their clothes off on the spot, leaving little mounds of crumpled dresses, slacks, and blouses around them. Xuan did the same, the studio air-conditioning blasting her exposed stomach and causing a spine tingle. Her baby pulsed inside her, as taut with energy as its mother was. She wondered if this child would be beautiful, possess the kind of beauty fit for a pageant. Goats were timid and compliant, but some people said they were also physically appealing because of their inherent agreeability. But that didn't necessarily mean a Goat *would* be beautiful, only that someone might perceive them that way because they were kind, which was just another way of saying, in Xuan's opinion, that someone wasn't actually beautiful. Goats weren't like Snakes or Cats, who were usually described as pleasant to look at without all the hemming and hawing. But, you never knew, really. Maybe a Goat could be beautiful, too.

Xuan pulled the shapeless fabric over her head, and when she looked around, saw that the room was full of the same hideous chartreuse-and-bubble-gum-pink fabric of her own dress. The psychedelic floral print made her eyes swim, the people moving beneath them strangely rippling through the air.

Darlene's dress, which had long sleeves and a train, was so lengthy that Xuan was afraid Darlene might trip. "They really know how to keep the show interestin', huh?" she said.

The assistants pushed them out onto the stage again. They were to walk down to the other end, do a twirl, and walk back to line up. Xuan's tennis shoes were still visible; her evening gown stopped above the ankles.

At the edge of the curtain, an assistant watched Darlene walk out and waited for her to reach the end of the stage before nudging Xuan into the light. She shuffled out, the rubber soles of her shoes catching on the shiny stage floor. The farther she walked, the longer she was on the stage, the more self-possessed she began to feel. The noise of the studio was muted and far away. Her legs felt stronger, the lights felt familiar. She straightened her back and raised her chin. Suddenly, Xuan's body wasn't bloated, a vessel for the human inside her. Suddenly, she was thin and floating, the kind of confidence born of comfort. She felt the affirming weight of a crown resting on her sleek, black hair. At the end of the stage, she turned and paused to smile, a subtle, closed-mouth curve and the barely noticeable twitch of her shoulder that men had always found so alluring. As she walked back to stand next to Darlene, where the rest of the contestants stood in a line, the next person was sent back out.

That contestant was so tall and sturdy, Xuan wondered if she was a man. What was this person doing here, at this pageant?

As each new contestant walked past her to the end of the stage, Xuan began to realize: they weren't beauty queens at all. A short woman with leathery skin and bleached hair, an older lady with a hunchback who struggled to walk, a girl with an unfortunate unibrow. The last woman to stroll across the stage was the only one Xuan would consider fit for a beauty pageant—tall, waifish, and all-American, she could've been a stunt double for Goldie Hawn herself.

During the bikini competition, Xuan's breasts, heavy and tender, were barely contained by two cloth triangles. The string of her bikini top rested on the ledge of her stomach. She couldn't see her bikini bottoms or the nude heels on her feet when she looked down. The heels, which would normally still be a size too big, felt snug against the bulging flesh of her feet. As she walked across the stage a second time, air-conditioned gusts rushing against her exposed body, she felt for a moment as if she were outside of herself. Before, she had floated across the stage, buoyed by the fleeting familiarity. Now, she floated like a ghost, witnessing her human form stumble clumsily toward Goldie Hawn and Dick Martin, themselves bathed in the protective glow of beauty. The room was full of other ghosts like her, women wearing sashes, armor, rags, and gowns. They trembled in the cold warehouse, as if the space were hostile to them. They fluttered on the edges of the audience, squatted in the rafters, flickered in and out of existence along the margins of the stage.

"Xuan is from Vietnam!" said Dick Martin, as she took her place next to them for her brief interview. "Xuan, say a few words about yourself."

"Hello," she said. "I would be honor to win the money so I can make my life in America."

"That's a bona fide all-American narrative if I ever heard one," he said.

"So, tell us," Goldie Hawn said. "What brings you to *$2.00 Beauty Queen*?"

"I use to be in beauty pageant in my home country. I win a few year ago, and have a big trophy for it. I hope win today, too." Above the undulating roar of laughter of the audience, she could hear a man in the crowd coughing, a woman's high-pitched cackle.

"Well, we hope you win," said Dick. She was sent to stand with the other women. Her baby kicked against her, reminding her again that this body didn't belong to her. Every limb was bloated, so that when she looked down at her feet beneath, or glimpsed her hand outstretched, she wondered who they belonged to. The knowledge that they were hers made Xuan feel disoriented, this daily confirmation that reality did not align with her experience.

Backstage, an assistant handed her an index card. On it, the words *Talent: Singing* and *Song: Vietnamese national anthem*.

"Any questions?" the assistant said. "You said your talent was singing, right? We want you to sing this song. We think it will be a hit with the crowd. Can you play up your accent more? The level you had it at was great, but we want to keep crowd response high."

Xuan did not answer as the assistant stood there.

"Hello? Do you understand me?" She huffed. "Whatever," she said, moving onto the next person, her stack of index cards in hand.

The Vietnamese national anthem? Xuan stared at the neatly printed text. What anthem? Which one? What nation? Her vision blurred. When she looked up, some workers were preparing a prop table for the final portion. They set down the winner's cardboard prize check, which was laughably oversized. Wasn't it worth it to stay if it meant she might win? The competition was so slim. She was pregnant and yellow skinned, but still, she had been chosen for the show. She walked over to the check to stare. It was blue and looked exactly like a check would. On the amount line, fake cursive text had been used to write, "Two dollars and 00/100."

There was more money; this, she felt, had to be true. But, if anyone had asked her, she could not say exactly how or why she thought that. Facing this giant check, everything she thought to be real was suddenly tainted with a healthy portion of doubt. She felt this contamination in her confidence daily—at the grocery, wondering if she'd said *oil* correctly based on the puzzled expression of the worker from whom she'd asked about aisles; on the bus, as she was exiting and, for a moment, couldn't recognize where she was despite all her assuredness when she had pulled the bell cord; at McDonald's, when she received her order and it was not what she thought she'd so clearly said to the cashier.

She tried to remember watching the show with Cuong. Why hadn't any of its truth been apparent to her? In her memory, the competition had been cultured and rigidly structured, beholden to tradition, full of women who belonged in a beauty pageant. Now, onstage, she saw Hang and Bian and TuVy and Phuong in their silk áo dàis, floating, and Dick Martin and Goldie Hawn in full color, sparkling in the Saigon sun onstage. But that couldn't be right. Hang and Bian and TuVy were probably dead, and Phuong was still in Saigon, waiting for the return of her husband from reeducation.

Xuan had watched the show on a tiny, black-and-white television. The sound didn't work well, so they watched the women stroll and strut without music or commentary. At times, Xuan had barely watched, and so, she had missed the chaos, the stunts, the hilarity. She had not been *in* on the joke. She had barely talked to the other women there, and as she looked around, she realized that, perhaps, everyone else had known. The girl with the unibrow, the hunchback—was that a real unibrow, a real hunchback?

Pulling her lucky red dress on over the bikini, she clutched the rest of her loose belongings to her chest. When she reached the exit, she turned around to stare one more time. Maybe if she looked long enough, she could see what she had missed. But the lights were bright and the skin of the figures milling far away glistened, and when she blinked, she thought she saw them again. Her friends in their áo dàis, floating gracefully to and fro, beautiful and terrible to behold.

15

XUAN

The party was in the apartment above the garage. The house in front was a ranch-style brick home in Metairie, and at the end of the cracked, shifting driveway on the right, there was the garage where the Fosters stored their tools, extra furniture, and car parts. The car itself was parked on the street because it was too low to the ground to go up the driveway without bottoming out.

Xuan and Lan had carpooled with Linh, who was able to buy a used car last month. The three of them stood at the end of the drive, staring at the illuminated windows of the garage apartment. White, peeling paint flaked from the exterior, and the side stairwell, the metal kind that looked like a fire escape, was dubiously attached to the building. Vague, dark shapes moved behind translucent curtains. Music was audible but incoherent, as if someone had shoved cotton in their ears.

Xuan almost didn't come, and now, she deeply regretted her decision. The party wasn't even in a house. They were relegated to a space above where unwanted things were stored out of sight and mind. It was insulting, really. The memory of clean, cavernous ballrooms, black-and-white marble floors, low burning chandeliers—they seemed so close in her mind. It was what made it all the more difficult to face this new reality, the peeling, sinking pile of wood where they were supposed to socialize.

"It's not so bad," said Linh. "Don't be dramatic."

"I didn't say anything," said Xuan.

"I can see it in your face. You always judge things too early."

"It's just embarrassing," said Xuan.

"Everyone in there is like us," said Lan. "There's nothing to be embarrassed about. Weren't you saying you missed doing stuff like this?"

"I meant a real party, one where I didn't feel wildly overdressed." Xuan adjusted the strap of her green dress. She'd spent so much time on her hair and makeup. She and Lan pooled their extra money together and had bought a blush-and-powder compact, kohl eyeliner, mascara, and a tube of mauve lipstick and shared it all. They didn't have enough extra cash yet to buy a brush or sponges, so Xuan applied the blush with the cheap, wiry miniature brush that had come with the compact. She tapped her ring finger onto the pressed rouge and rubbed the pigment onto her eyelids, too. She had smudged dark brown kohl liner around her lash line. She and Lan both wore the same face, and each, her best dress. Xuan's attire felt disproportionate to the structure they now stood before.

"Just go in," said Linh. "You can see some of my friends from work. We'll just meet the others." *Others*, Xuan thought. Linh did not like to say out loud the word *refugees*. There was something shameful about it. "We have to meet them all eventually, right?"

There was a notable number of displaced Vietnamese in New Orleans, and the issue of meeting them had been frequently discussed. They all lived in different places across town, some of them in garage apartments they could afford on the outside of the city, others in the spare rooms of their sponsor's home until they could afford their own place. Most of them did not have cars in this country only navigable by car. Lan and Xuan lived in a cramped, one-bedroom apartment with their mother. Tien slept in the bedroom while Lan and Xuan shared a mattress in the living room.

Xuan took a deep breath. She was lonely, after all.

The stairs creaked and groaned. The door at the top was ajar. Light spilled out into the darkness. A Chinese elm grew against and around the stairwell, its trunk pressed against the metal spindles like flesh bound by rope. Xuan ran her hand against the flaky lace bark. The apartment felt like an oven, and the door was open to help circulate air from bodies and their mingling heat. There weren't many people, maybe twenty, but right then it felt like a hundred crammed into that one-room apartment.

"Have I died and God is rewarding me for my brave, virtuous life?" A man in a white shirt and loose khakis pushed through the crowd to sling his arm around Linh. He clutched at his heart, as if mortally wounded by their beauty. His shirt was speckled with oil and what appeared to be tomato juice.

"Shut up," she said, but she looked pleased. Xuan could not believe this flirtatious expression would ever grace Linh's face in the presence of this dirty, forward man. "Oh, Hung, this is Xuan and Lan. We went to school together in Saigon."

"Rich girls!" he said.

"Hung and I work together at the restaurant," Linh said, and Hung's stained shirt made sense. Linh worked at a diner, but she was only allowed to bus tables because she didn't speak English very well. Xuan guessed this man was probably a dish boy. His hands looked dry, likely from soap and hot water, with dirt under his fingernails. He had the posture of someone with a few drinks in him.

In the back corner of the apartment, people crowded around a table where men played cards. Loose bills and coins sat piled in the middle, and smoke from their cigarettes hung in the air above them. They hooted and shouted, thumping the table, people egging them on or rooting for particular players. Others milled around, men with Heinekens in hand or women with clear plastic cups full of ice cubes floating in cheap wine. Xuan had never been to a party like this before. Bambi sometimes sneaked her into the bar when she worked, but otherwise, this was far from what Xuan knew to be a party.

Hung disappeared and reappeared clutching green longneck bottles against his body. He handed them each a beer, a gesture so generous, Xuan felt her distaste ebb away.

"What's going on back there?" said Lan.

"They're gambling. You should go put some money in the pot," said Hung.

"But I don't know how to play the game."

"You don't need to know how to play the game," he said. So she began making her way to the table, the neck of the sweaty beer clutched in her hand. Xuan wanted Lan to stay next to her. She felt empty and lost without Lan there, open to attack.

"Is this your beer?" Xuan said. They all struggled so much to make ends meet, she felt guilty taking the free drink.

"No, that guy over there bought all the drinks for this party," he said. He pointed to a man standing over the gambling table, yelling at one of the players to put more money in the pot. Lan was over there holding a five-dollar bill, unsure of what to do with it. Xuan wished she wouldn't spend it. "He won really big the other night playing blackjack and wanted to spread the joy. I'm not complaining." Hung put his lips to the opening of his beer and took a long drag, smacking his lips after. Her benevolence toward him vanished. Hung was handing out beers with the generosity of a man who had paid for nothing. Linh took small sips of her beer, grimacing.

"This tastes terrible," she said.

"You only say that because you're a woman," he said.

"What does that mean?" said Xuan.

"Women don't have the stomach for alcohol."

"Or, women know when something is cheap." Xuan took a long draw from her beer while staring at Hung, and willed herself to remain stoic.

"Cuong," Hung yelled across the room. The man making the ruckus at the gambling table looked up. "Cuong, this girl over here says the beer you bought is cheap."

"I didn't say it was cheap. I said I could tell if *something* was cheap."

Cuong weaved through the crowd, now, making his way toward them.

"You, yourself, don't seem like a cheap date," Hung said. "Must be hard to get guys to go out with you, you're so uptight." He grinned, some menace there. Her attitude was being interpreted as an invitation, a challenging pursuit, rather than a deterrent. How quickly he had abandoned Linh. He'd even withdrawn his arm from her shoulders, his body leaning toward Xuan in an unconscious display of desire.

"Linh, do you want to go to the bathroom with me?" Xuan asked. She wanted to get away.

Linh shook her head—she wanted to stay here with Hung. She didn't notice his change in interest. She'd always been bad at reading social situations. At the Cercle Sportif Ball a few years ago, Linh had accidentally cut the chairman's wife off midsentence to announce the pâté was delightful. She failed to notice the wife's coldness towards her and didn't know why she wasn't invited to the chairman's garden party later that month. When Xuan told her, she had no memory of tense relations during the Cercle Sportif Ball. "But the pâté *was* delightful," Linh said.

"Hello, ladies, do you need me to take care of this guy for you?" Cuong swiped the beer from Hung's hand. "You shouldn't drink any more, man. You turn into a real creep."

"Come on now, we're fast friends, aren't we?" Hung wedged

himself between Xuan and Linh, putting an arm around each of them.

"I'm Linh. Hung and I work together."

"You probably work. Hung just shows up," Cuong said. A sighing laugh slipped from Xuan.

Hung turned his head toward her, nose almost touching her hair. "You think that's funny, Xuan?"

Cuong picked up Hung's arm like a dead animal, and placed it gently against his side, patting his hand. "Excuse me," he said, "I gotta show Xuan something more interesting than you. Enjoy my beer." Although she hadn't introduced herself, her name sat easily on his lips. Without explanation, he steered Xuan by the shoulders away from them, into the crowd, beading sweat on skin brushing against them both as they passed through a sea of bodies.

"Eat shit, Cuong," Hung yelled from behind.

"Where are we going?" Xuan said.

"Away from him," said Cuong.

"Well, we're away, now. What's next?"

"You're going to put twenty dollars in the pot," said Cuong.

"Where are you going to get twenty dollars?"

"Come on. Trust me. I have a feeling, you're going to win big."

Xuan did not have twenty dollars to give him, but she didn't want to say this. She had never not had enough money, and now she was lucky if she had a few extra dollars for makeup or food or a beer after work. "I'm not giving you twenty dollars."

Cuong turned to the man standing next to him. "Hey, Duy, lend me five dollars." Duy took a five-dollar bill from his pocket and handed it to Cuong, who immediately handed it to Xuan. "Okay, put five dollars in the pot. Everyone," he said, raising his voice, "Xuan, here, is adding five dollars to the round."

"Yeah, and you're announcing it because? Record your bet like everyone else." A man sitting at the table, holding his card close to his chest, was pointing his free hand at Cuong. "Stop delaying the game." A flash of gold from his mouth.

"No time to add our bet to the list, that's why I'm announcing it. Lots of witnesses, see?"

Someone handed Cuong a pair of dice. "Blow on these for me." He held his open palm up to her mouth, and she blew on them. The dice knocked loudly as they rolled across the wooden table, and Xuan didn't even get to see what he landed on before the entire table erupted into groans and cheers, people standing, both to collect winnings or to sulk away from the table. Cuong took ten dollars from the pot, handing her five, and giving the other five to Duy.

"You must be lucky," he said.

"Tigers aren't known for luck," she said. "So, it must be you."

"I'm a Dragon," he said, knowing well that the Dragon was regarded as the luckiest sign in the zodiac. His mischievous grin made him even more handsome. "So, I guess you owe me a favor for lending you some of my luck and winning you money."

Cuong drove a brand-new red Mustang. It was bright and noisy, just like Cuong, all his charm and magnetism palpable the second he entered a space. There was something dangerous about him, too, the way people spoke to him—Hung had told him to eat shit, but with the tone of someone who would retract it in a second if Cuong chose to turn around. Perhaps that said more about Hung than Cuong, but Xuan could not explain the thrill, the breathlessness she could not control all night, wondering what he might do. Even though he had not done anything to suggest a unique inclination for insanity. Maybe it was the sheer confidence—removing Hung's arm from her, lifting his hand to her mouth to blow on the dice, his announcement to the room that people actually stopped to hear—that both drew her in and made her nervous. That much confidence could be dangerous.

"I'm taking you to dinner," he said.

"Now? But it's almost nine."

"I know a place," he said. And she accepted his vagaries without question, although she could hear her mother's voice in her ear. *You barely know this man, there's no one there to chaperone you, do you want to date a man that gambles, how can he afford this car?* Xuan would learn later that Cuong had leased the car and irresponsibly spent all of his paycheck to afford it, and this was an accurate reflection of his attitude toward everything. He expected more from everyone but himself. He was reckless and did what he wanted. His own recklessness was often the source of his troubles, and, she would later see, anger. People were charmed by and also scared of him. But, in this moment, Xuan could not disentangle her reason from desire. He drove fast and looked over at her with a smile that made her feel seen.

The restaurant sign glowed against the dark sky. It was a Chinese restaurant attached to a gas station. Xuan had not had Asian food in a restaurant since a rainy day in April last year, in Saigon. She'd gone to a cafe near the house for noodles.

"It's good," he said. "I've been here a few times now. A couple of other Chinese places I've been to are weird. It's usually just American food with soy sauce. But this place tastes just like a restaurant I used to go to in my neighborhood. It's not Vietnamese food, but there aren't any restaurants yet. I guess we're supposed to open one of those ourselves if we want to eat in a Vietnamese restaurant." He laughed, seeming more nervous than he had all night. "Did you want to try?"

"Yes," she said. "Yes, I want to try."

And so, he rushed out of the driver's seat and around to the passenger's side to open her door, extending a hand to help her out of his car. She walked with him into the brightly lit, dingy restaurant with her arm linked through his. He ordered egg noodle stir fry and dumplings, green beans in garlic, crispy fried shrimp. A steaming pot of jasmine tea, loose leaves floating in their small, cylindrical cups, sat on the table among their plates, given without request. She stared at him through the steam floating above their food. She felt an overwhelming flood of homesickness, and was sure it was because Cuong reminded her of home.

PART II:
1975—

16

TIÊN

Tiên wore every piece of jewelry she had. Gold necklaces adorned her neck, pendants cold against her skin. Jade bangles and diamond-encrusted bracelets clinked against each other on her delicate wrists. She sewed loose jewels inside her jacket. And, in an unassuming cotton bag slung across her chest, forty thousand in soon-to-be-irrelevant currency. Along the hem of her shirt, she had sewed six ingots of gold. And tucked in her waistband, a small silver knife she used to cut up herbs and medicines. Her mother gave it to her.

It was difficult to appear unencumbered. She felt heavy for more than one reason. Outside, the scurry of panicked fleeing and mass chaos intruded upon the usual peace of their home. Their neighbor had woken them up in the night to tell them the North Vietnamese were only a few days from taking the city. This came as no surprise. The NVA had been advancing for weeks, each city falling with little resistance and no leadership. This whole civil war, Sài Gòn had remained relatively unharmed. There had been an attack on the US embassy during the

North's Tết Offensive, but other than that, encroachment upon the city could have been much worse. The hissing of bombs falling earthbound, then their thunderclap as they crashed, a never-ending feeling of terror—Tiên had lived in fear every day, yes, but their beautiful house had remained unharmed up to now, and they, themselves, had remained unharmed, too. What did harm really look like, anyway? Tiên thought that perhaps they lived in a constant state of harm so they could no longer tell.

When Nguyễn Văn Thiệu fled Sài Gòn six days ago, though, it was like a giant sign billowing above them with the words *We're In Trouble*. Big Minh had taken over the presidency, but what was he if not completely useless? Having a president was ceremonial, at this point, something they did just because they couldn't imagine not having someone at all. It was alarming that this symbolic gesture was, and perhaps had been, the only thing holding their tenuous state together. Big Minh only cared about tennis and going to the country club. If Big Minh was their last hope, then it was clear they were fucked. Whispers about fleeing, finding a way to France or the US increased in intensity and urgency. People wanted to bring their whole families, but such a feat seemed impossible. Her neighbor, for instance, had twelve children, and they, in turn, had children themselves. How could she possibly hope to escape with them all?

Tiên had only her daughters, Xuân and Lan. They were both unmarried, all the marriageable men dead or gone or already married, or all three. And she, herself, had not heard from her husband in five years. She assumed he was dead or as good as, although the military would not confirm it. Even if he was alive somewhere, she wouldn't wait for him. The city was packed with bodies. Refugees from the Highlands, Quảng Trị, from Tam Kỳ and Huế, Chu Lai and Đà Nẵng. They crowded themselves into Sài Gòn, their fear permeating every inch of space.

Tiên knew she had to get out. The city had erupted into chaos. With the loss of hope, people began to loot and riot, get drunk or violent. Emotions were strung tight and people were behaving as if they might not see tomorrow, mostly because they probably wouldn't. But, she had a lot of connections. She had money. People came to her for loans, which she lent them under the assurance they would pay them back with interest. She accepted their jewelry and valuables as collateral in case they were hesitant to clear their debts. Although, this was rarely a problem, as she sent her collector, Huy, to every house to make good on their loans. He was a convincing man. She was helping people, people who were poor and wouldn't be able to afford food or shelter or necessary things otherwise, and, sometimes those people needed a little extra encouragement to pay her back. Poor and pitiful they might be, but Tiên had to pay her own bills, too.

But now, bills had no meaning. What if she didn't pay the fish market vendor or the laborers at the rubber plantation? What if the man who owned the meatball stand never paid her back after gambling all his profits in one last game? What if she never restored the fortune-teller her jewelry? None of it mattered. The fish market vendor had been beaten and looted. Their rubber plantation laborers had all abandoned their jobs, disappearing. The meatball stand man had gambled everything away because he knew this was the end. Might as well enjoy it.

The fortune-teller was probably gone or hiding. Tiên sometimes accepted fortunes in exchange for herbs. The woman had last predicted that there was water in her past and her future, that it moved around her, and she, with it.

"Follow the water and find the source of trouble. Find the source of trouble and destroy it," she had said. Tiên gave her dried jasmine with reluctance, secretly thinking the fortune was nonsense. Now, she waited for her boat to be built, about to venture into the water, and felt foolish for her arrogance. Yet as the self-satisfied expression of the mystic who owed her money floated to the surface of her mind, she did not feel even a shred of guilt as she pushed her bony hand through the fortune-teller's jade bracelet.

"How much does he want?" Tiên asked. She and Huy sat across from each other with a steaming tea set between them in her apothecary, where she conducted all business matters. She'd sent him to speak to a man who could build them a small boat. Huy said the man wanted to remain anonymous, but that he knew him well and could be a liaison.

This had been almost a year and a half ago, after the Americans had withdrawn all their troops, after they'd signed the Paris Peace Accords. Tiên read her horoscope, suspicious of their proclamations of tranquility. She had done all the math for her sign and its planets. She even had her predictions double-checked by an astrologer. All signs pointed to disaster, and all hope of refuge was directed to the element of Water. It seemed obvious to Tiên that, should trouble arise, they would need to go to the sea.

So, Tiên had asked Huy to facilitate the transaction with the anonymous man and his boats.

She had tasked him with this months ago. Come January, when North Vietnam broke their promises of peace and began coordinated attacks with a clear final destination of Sài Gòn, Tiên asked Huy about the progress on their boat. Was it done?

"He says it's almost complete, but he won't finish it unless you pay him more," Huy said now. Tiên carefully measured dried ginseng on a scale. The neighbor had inflammation problems and his wife had asked for some herbs.

"More money? We already agreed on a price. His last payment is next month, contingent upon the completion of the boat," said Tiên.

"He said that was then, this is now. Demand has gone up and he wants what the boat is worth."

Tiên slammed her balled-up fist on the table, the copper scale rattling. "He's hustling us. We agreed on the price, why do you think I asked for this job so long ago? What am I supposed to tell the families we're splitting the cost with?"

"It doesn't matter," said Huy. "Look, you're lucky, Co Tiên. He might be jacking up the price, but at least he's willing to part with the boat in the first place, to even finish building it for you. There are a lot of people who have no way out because they didn't think to prepare as much in advance. They're trying to buy entry onto freighters or other boats, on helicopters or airplanes for three times the amount you have."

Regardless of right or wrong, Tiên had no choice. If she wanted the boat, she had to pay this man whatever he wanted. She visited each of the two other families who had helped pay and told them of the increase. They pooled their money together and, with it collected in a cloth bag, Tiên handed over the small fortune to Huy. She had not heard word from the boat builder until the day Big Minh took office.

Huy came to her home with a message. "The boatbuilder says you must board the boat at night, and tell no one you are leaving. The NVA has the entire city surrounded. It will be a matter of days if not hours before they penetrate and the city falls."

Tiên sent word to the other families. She gave them a day to get their affairs in order, to gather the few things they would take. The boat was small and wouldn't hold that much. Xuân and Lan each packed a small suitcase with clothes, valuables, and photos. They each lit a stick of incense and prayed at the altar to their ancestors, putting some fruit and tea there as a last offering. Tiên wished her mother were alive, could be there with them. Perhaps this was the best scenario they could hope for, the three of them still young enough to plunge into the unknown, and the spirit of her mother whispering guidance into Tiên's ear, pushing her to make decisions for the rest of them.

★ ★ ★

At midnight, the outside shuffle of noise and war and people did not cease. However, a strange gloom of secrecy fell over them all with the darkening of the sky. Tiên wore her hidden wealth and carried only a bag full of cash and fruit. Her daughters wore valuables, too, and carried their small bags of clothes and photos. Lan and Xuân had wrapped rice balls in paper and stashed them in their pockets. The other families were cloaked and quiet when they met in the alleyway near the dock Huy had instructed them to come to that night.

Huy led them to the site of the boat, looking into the streets and around corners before signaling them to move forward. The city was full of movement and panic. Tiên doubted whether anyone would stop them any more than they might stop someone else.

The gathered at the end of a dock where a small boat was tied. It was guarded by three men holding guns. "If you want to board the boat, you have to pay us more."

Us, Huy said, who was also pointing his gun at them. Tiên knew she was foolish to not see it before now. She had never met with or spoken to the boatbuilder herself. All of her information, all of the demands had been delivered by and from Huy, who now had no more reason to preserve their relationship.

One of the men waved his gun in Tiên's face. "Drop your bags, drop them now!"

The clunking of objects as the bags hit the deck. The men rifled through them, taking out the cash or loose valuables and leaving their other belongings in disarray. They didn't touch the fruit. She held her sleeves against her palm, hoping they didn't pat them all down for jewelry, but she was lucky—they seemed to be in just as much of a hurry as the rest of them.

The boat was small, with just enough space for fifteen people to sit cross-legged on the floor. It was a sailboat with one large mainsail and a jib. Mr. Bui was a fisherman who'd learn to sail from his father, also a fisherman. He sat at the stern, hand on the tiller so he could steer. Hot air and ocean salt. The boat was buffeted by a strong wind, cutting across waves in the South China Sea. It was strange for a boat to move with confidence when they had nowhere to go, no destination in mind. The water was black and choppy, and Tiên felt vulnerable in what amounted to a small pile of wood on this vast, endless sea. She thought about their house, rooted to its one spot. Full of their things, things accumulated over lifetimes. And now none of it was theirs. The communists could easily set the house on fire, erase them from memory, and who would know or remember, who would be there to refute?

Tiên and her daughters could die, in fact, were likely to die out in this deep and infinite water, and no one would ever mourn the loss of their bodies.

They sailed for hours until they couldn't see land in any direction.

Where did they go now? At first, it felt like this might be temporary. A trip to the beach gone wrong. Being physically removed from Sài Gòn helped with this thinking, since they had no idea what was happening there now. They sailed southeast, then west, then east again, then more south, each time sailing until nightfall, sleeping, waking up and sailing again in a different direction. They each ate their food small bite by small bite, savoring their morsels of life. The bites became smaller and smaller, and soon, there were no more things to eat. They ran out of water after a week. Lan and Xuân could barely chew or swallow their rice cakes, no matter how little of them they ate. Tiên found a solution to this, offering up her fruit to them. They ate one small bite of lychee with one small bite of rice, the lychee's sweet juice making their mouths slick enough to swallow. Others on the boat followed suit, eating slowly, carefully. They were cramped and close together. The boat was full of bodies and their waste. At first, this was a source of embarrassment and indignity, but the longer they were on the boat, the less they cared about such things. Tiên tried to clean the floor, using her empty canvas tote to toss waste into the water, soaking the tote in seawater, wringing it out, and scrubbing the boat as clean as she could. The boat become more and more soiled the weaker Tiên and the rest of them became. Once they were out of food, they all lay there, bodies piled upon bodies, barely alive. They had a boat, they had escaped Vietnam, but what good was that when they belonged nowhere else? Tiên did not know who she was outside of that place she could no longer call home.

On the tenth day at sea, Mr. Bui pointed to a figure in the near distance. As it approached, they could see it was a wooden boat, not unlike their own. Some of them cried tears of joy. Maybe whoever was on that boat had water and food for them. Maybe they would let them join their crew, take them to a welcoming port. The boat got very close, beside them, almost. Men on board were singing. It was a rowdy song, and some of them raised their beers in the air. It must mean they were close to some shore, some place where people lived and sang and bought beer.

Two of the men jumped onto their boat, rocking dangerously on the water. They dragged the prone bodies up by their collars and shook them. They were not Vietnamese because Tiên could not understand the words they were saying, but she could see tattoos along their forearms in Thai. Pirates. How naive of them to hope for this.

The pirates began to jump onto their already cramped boat. It was reckless and unwise for them to do this, but they were drunk and felt powerful. Mr. Bui had pushed one of the pirates into the sea. The others did not notice that their friend struggled against the current in his inebriation. It was clear the pirates had no plan other than to follow their own impulses. Tiên's head whipped back and forth as chaos ensued around her, each man pursuing what he wanted: gripping necklaces around a woman's neck, hauling children up by the armpits and tossing them overboard to make more room, pawing at a girl's legs as she shut them tight, the girl's father stabbed as he looked on, back pressed against the bow. Tiên closed her eyes tight, gripping each of her girls on either side. They huddled up against the side of the boat hoping to disappear.

Under the weight of a shadow, Tiên opened her eyes. One of the pirates was leering at her. He grabbed her wrists, pulling her up to her feet, and pushed back the sleeve. He tried to pull the jade bangles past her wrist, but they butted up against her bones. Drunk and rushed, he shouted unintelligibly, pointing at her jewelry. He wanted all of the valuable things on her body. Perhaps once he had stripped of her everything, he would use the body itself, too. He pointed at Lan and Xuân, screaming. Tiên did not need to know what he was saying to understand what a man like this demanded. She had seen this all her life, this expectation coupled with violence.

They would take their things, violate them all, and leave them here to die, to disappear in the water. Tiên felt a rush of anger expel from her mouth. Was she shouting, too? There was a loud ringing in her ears. Her hands seemed to move independently, as if strung up like a puppet. She felt the pressure of a body behind her pushing and pulling her own, even though she was pressed against the side of the boat. *You will not disappear,* a voice said. Maybe it was her own voice. The boat seemed to be full of girls and women, though she could barely see through the fog of her own rage. Tiên looked down to find her hand gripping the hilt of the dagger she used to cut herbs, the one her mother had given her. It sat soundly above the pirate's heart. His eyes bulged and his mouth formed a little *Oh*, as if he didn't quite know what was happening. Tiên put her hand to her mouth and was surprised to find her jaw was pried open. She was emitting a long howl, and she could not stop. It shook in her chest before ricocheting from her gaping maw. She watched herself, as if watching a television program, wrench the hilt of the dagger from his chest, stagger over bodies and sink the dagger again and again into pirate after pirate. None of them expected her, engrossed in their own violations, and when she had determined the outcome of their lives, they lay on the floor of the boat, on top of other bodies, with an expression of utter bewilderment.

When Tiên woke up, everyone on the boat was still. Perhaps everyone was dead. The shadow of a ship cast upon them had woken her. They lowered a rope ladder and Tiên crawled among the bodies, looking for her daughters.

"Lan," she screamed. "Xuân, wake up. Wake up. Wake up. Wake up, please, please, please."

The pile of bodies began to stir, and she saw her children move among the mass of flesh on this little boat meant to save them.

17

XUÂN

Her mother, Tiên, thought beauty pageants were a waste of time. Xuân would never live up to her expectations, her mother who owned local shops and businesses and helped the needy and cooked and did everything. Xuân couldn't be expected to do any of that, especially when she had no skills to do so. She wouldn't even know where to start. When was she supposed to learn to cook when all of her meals were cooked for her? Clean, when the house was tidied by the maid? How could she help the needy or start a business when she didn't have any money of her own, and wouldn't know the first thing about making any?

It was after the bike factory burned down that Xuân signed up for the beauty pageant. Her mother had been in a manic rage about the fire, understandably, and she'd taken it out on her children.

"You are good for nothing," she'd said. "Our livelihood is in ruins and my children can't support their mother in any way. What will you do when I die?"

"But, don't we still have the apothecary and the jewelry store and the rubber plantation?" asked Lan.

"That's not the point," their mother said. "The point is that we had a bike factory last week, and now, we have nothing where it used to be."

"We have plenty of money," said Xuân, who knew immediately that her comment was not befitting an obedient daughter.

"Where do you think we would be if I didn't know how to do things? Do you think I would have survived? You are ruined by comfort and luxury. One day you will need to survive and you will not know how." She slammed the door behind her, leaving the dinner preparations to Yen, their maid.

The next day, Xuân told her friend, whose name was Thắm but who was nicknamed Bambi after the American cartoon, that she wanted to join the pageant. Xuân was sure this was not what her mother had had in mind, but there was something about the pageant that lured her in. Perhaps it was the idea of glory or recognition that was within her reach, some feasible success. Xuân would never be able to start her own business. But a pageant?

If she were entirely honest, her mother's tantrum had also nurtured in Xuân an unshakeable resentment, a youthful desire for rebellion. But, of course, Xuân was not entirely honest. She piled onto this resentment persuasive lies to herself about the impressiveness of the pageant, the seductive fantasy of winning it, so that the resentment was obscured.

Many of her friends had already agreed weeks ago to walk in the pageant. Hang, Bian, TuVy, and Phuong, with whom Xuân had gone to private school, had all heard about the pageant, in fact, through Xuân. Bambi had enlisted her for help getting local elites to join, to give the pageant a sense of exclusivity and, ironically, create more public interest in it. Bambi had been trying to convince her for weeks to sign up, and now, Xuân could tell her she'd changed her mind.

Bambi's American boyfriend was, for some reason, there with the US military but didn't seem to be involved with anything remotely related to the war. Xuân was unsure of what exactly it was he did, and Bambi didn't seem to know either. But he was the founder and organizer of Sài Gòn's first beauty pageant, and there were cash prizes and sponsors. It was going to be televised for the American GIs, apparently.

Lenny's eyes sometimes lingered uncomfortably long, but he was charming and personable, and he was surprisingly proficient in Vietnamese. He had sun-bleached hair and skin consistently scorched pink by the sun. While Xuân knew nothing substantial about Lenny, somehow it made perfect sense that he would be the force behind such an event. What was more Western than a beauty pageant? Of course, the only white man Xuân had ever spoken to would be behind it.

At a sidewalk café, Bambi led Xuân to an empty wicker table for four. "We saw this table first," she snapped at another girl approaching the empty chairs in the otherwise crowded outdoor dining area.

Bambi wore a miniskirt that hiked up her thighs. She was not afraid of yelling at strangers, and she was not afraid of miniskirts. Xuân wasn't allowed to bring Bambi to the house because her mother thought she was trashy. Bambi wasn't trashy, Xuân had argued at the time, but she had secretly admitted to herself that her friend lacked a certain amount of modesty. And, it made sense her mother didn't approve—Bambi wasn't a friend met in private school or from political functions. She would be immediately ostracized in either of those spaces. Bambi was a bartender that Xuân had only met last year, when she'd skipped school with her sister. They'd gone into the bar, having heard it was a regular hangout for American soldiers, and because the novelty of skipping school required they do things like this to make the day worth it. What they found in the bar was no one, because it was 10:00 a.m., and Bambi, who was sweeping the floor in a go-go dancer's dress.

"Lenny, baby, Xuân wants to join the pageant," said Bambi. Lenny had just arrived at the table wearing aviators and smoking a hand-rolled cigarette.

"Xuân! You beauty, you gorgeous woman. Come here, let me get a good look at you," he said. Lenny was wearing a Vietnamese tunic that she was sure he'd bought at one of the market stalls for too much money. He placed his hands on Xuân's shoulders and stared into her face. His cigarette hung limply between his lips. He twirled his finger in the air. "Turn!" he said.

"There's a cash prize, right?" said Xuân.

"Of course. One thousand dong, sponsored by an American metals company out of North Carolina called Smith and Yancy."

"North Carolina," she tested with her tongue. *"Smith and Yancy."*

"How'd you get them to sponsor it?" said Bambi.

"One of the owners' sons is stationed here. He said what he misses most is beautiful women. And I thought, how can he miss beautiful women when he's here in Vietnam? He must not know what his options are."

"What do I need to do? What are the rules?" said Xuân.

"Just be beautiful," said Lenny. He laughed and swiped his tongue over his lips while ashing his cigarette onto the pavement. This was certainly true, Xuân learned, but it was not the only requirement. While there was no entry fee for the pageant (a fact Lenny had been sure to brag about), there were still costs incurred. Xuân needed a new áo dài. She also needed an evening gown and a swimsuit. She needed high heels. The pageant required all participants be under the age of twenty-five, unmarried, and childless.

Xuân used her mother's money to buy a new áo dài. The seamstress measured her to make a custom one out of green silk.

Xuân asked if she could make her an evening gown, too, the kind that American starlets wore. She gave her a page she ripped out from *LIFE Magazine* of Audrey Hepburn at an awards show.

"I can make anything for a price," the seamstress said. And Xuân used her mother's money to buy a new evening gown, too. She already had a swimsuit, which, incidentally, her mother's money had also bought, but she resolved to erase all her debts with the prize money. She needed her mother's support now for the cost of a few items of clothing, but not when she won the competition. Her mother would no longer get to say her children were good for nothing. She might not be happy about the idea of a beauty pageant, but could she be upset if Xuân won? The glow of potentially taking first place would surely dim the hot burn of her mother's judgment afterward.

When the evening gown was done, she tried it on for Bambi and Lenny at the apartment Lenny rented above Phở Huong. The dress was pale yellow satin and glistened in the low light filtering through the plastic window blinds. It was too tight around her rib cage, but her décolletage looked quite lovely with the off-the-shoulder neckline. She had a small waist and small breasts. Xuân often envied Bambi's figure, which would be considered fat by any Vietnamese standard, but which was obviously coveted by Lenny, who found a way to touch her in any situation—the graze along her lower back, the rub of her arm, the light squeeze of her waist, the casual grasp of her wrist.

Men never touched Xuân like that. She didn't know then that it wasn't for her own lack of touchable body, but for lack of opportunity. Her mother made sure to shelter her daughters, had thought it was possible to shield them with money and position. In fact, Tiên was obsessive about this. Xuân was only ever in spaces with men who wanted to marry her, and even there, she was rarely allowed to linger for long. If Tiên knew anything for sure, it was that a woman's worth depended entirely on her innocence, or at least the perception of it.

As Lenny's eyes roved her body, Xuân realized this was the longest a man had looked at her. She couldn't decide if she liked the attention or not—what was it she was feeling? It was an alien emotion, one that did not fall into *like* or *dislike*, but perhaps something entirely its own. Discomfort and power simultaneously. A large silver cup gleamed behind Lenny's head on top of his dresser.

"Is that the trophy?" said Xuân. It was huge, big enough to hold a watermelon.

"First place, sweetheart. Solid silver," he said. "Bambi, baby, go to the café and save us a seat. I have a craving for iced coffee."

Bambi looked between them. "How long will you be?"

"I don't know. I want to give Xuân some advice about her dress for the pageant and then we'll meet you."

"I'm not sitting at the café alone for twenty minutes. You send me off like some assistant to save your tables and leave me waiting."

"Just go and find a table. We won't be long."

"Then it shouldn't be a problem if I wait here until all of us are ready to go together."

Lenny huffed and ran his hands through his hair. He took a bag of tobacco out and began rolling a cigarette on his dresser. They all stood there without speaking until Bambi finally said, "Are you going to change, Xuân, or are we waiting here all day?"

Xuan rushed to change. "Let's order cake at Café Paris," said Bambi. She smiled and ran her hand along Lenny's face. "I heard they have flan today." Lenny shrugged but grinned as he rolled his smoking paper. For the first time, Xuân recognized that Bambi was an excellent actress.

The pageant was held in Paris Square, near the flower garden of the Notre-Dame Cathedral. Xuân thought it was embarrassing, all these memorials to a culture that was not theirs. Paris

Square, Notre-Dame—couldn't they think of anything more original? The Virgin Mary statue stared across the road at them as they ridiculously paraded around in their dresses. An audience area had been set up for the American soldiers, who all stood in the hot sun in full uniform.

Xuân's face hurt from smiling, and she couldn't remember what it was exactly she'd been doing for the past two hours. All the walking, the waving, smiling, it had been performed by some other body, some programmed machine walking, waving, and smiling without thought. A contestant being asked a question by Lenny, the host, shrieked, and then laughed. It brought Xuân back to earth. The girl (because she was a girl, a girl who couldn't have been over the age of sixteen) was being patted on the shoulder by Lenny. It had come to this, in the end: Xuân, Bambi, and the Girl, standing onstage in their evening gowns. The others, Hang, Bian, TuVy, Phuong, and a dozen others, all stood behind them in a straight line, onlookers.

Suddenly, Xuân was next to Lenny. When she had walked toward him, when the Girl had finished answering, she didn't know. But here she was, standing next to Lenny, so close she could see the sheen of sweat and spit on his microphone.

"Xuân, what do you think is the solution to the conflict between North and South Vietnam?" he said. His teeth were yellow and gray. He had asked the Girl something much easier, something about Sài Gòn beautification, or what she thought about helping the homeless. The answer would obviously be yes to both. Xuân didn't know how to talk about North and South Vietnam. It was complicated. It required centuries of context. What was the solution to the conflict? She wondered if she could answer with more questions, an endless ream of inquiries. That, at least, would be true to the situation.

She looked out at the crowd, bathed in hot sunlight. "The solution to North and South?" she said, in English. "The solution is America!" She put the flat disc of her hand to her forehead, pulling it down in a salute, her other hand on a cocked hip. The men cheered and whooped. Some whistled. As she walked back to her spot at the end of the stage, Bambi winked at her.

The women were corralled into the church, where they sat in the pews or milled about in the nave, speaking to each other in excited and low murmurs or staring up at the stained glass. The three judges, a first lieutenant, a second lieutenant, and a captain, were deliberating outside with Lenny.

He strolled in with a few of the soldiers. "Ladies," he said, "meet and greet some of the men while the judges talk."

The men scattered into the crowd, making beelines for women they'd had their eyes on during the pageant. Their voices echoed into the arched ceilings of the cathedral, creating a cacophonous din. A heavenly illumination, multicolored shapes cast onto the stone pillars, the wall, the ground, as light streamed through stained glass made the room feel otherworldly. Xuân watched as Lenny guided the Girl by the small of her back through a door near the altar.

"Chao, Em," a man said to Xuân. An awkward pause. "Do you like American music?" He was a soldier, blue eyes and brown hair. He'd taken off his camouflage hat and held it against his stomach.

"The Beatles," said Xuân. "I like Beatles."

"Which songs?"

"All songs," she said. Her mouth felt full of cotton. She had lots of favorite Beatles songs, and some she didn't like. John Lennon when they'd just become famous was the most handsome Beatle, "Hey Jude" was her favorite track, and "Help!" her least. This soldier looked a bit like Lennon through the jaw and chin. But she couldn't seem to think of the words in English, and this boy (man? He looked quite youthful), didn't know any Vietnamese. She could tell from the flat, dead tone of his greeting.

"I don't like the Beatles, really. A little too much for boy-crazed girls in the beginning, and now they're just weird," he said. His smile was nice. They stood there without speaking for what felt like too long before Xuân left him, weaving between the other girls standing in the aisle.

"Toilet," she said to the boy before walking briskly off. "I have to go to toilet."

Her shoes shuffled against the floor as she walked toward the altar, which seemed to loom above. The door to the sacristy looked like the dark wood paneling of the church walls. It was a windowless room, and as her eyes adjusted to the darkness, she pushed down a feeling of dread. Lenny's back faced the doorway, the Girl propped up on her arms on top of the vestments' cabinet, her legs pried apart as Lenny thrust into her, handles of the top drawer rattling against his pelvis. Lenny didn't turn around, didn't notice the door had opened. Xuân and the Girl stared at each other until Lenny thrust one more time and leaned his forehead against her chest. Xuân left before he could turn around, leaving the door ajar.

When the Girl was crowned Miss Sài Gòn, Xuân was not surprised. But witnessing Lenny writhe against her in the sacristy, and then watching him grin as he placed a sparkling tiara on her head, had given her what felt like a constant state of heartburn. Xuân had received first runner-up, and Bambi second.

When Xuân came home that evening, her mother was in the garden waiting for her. Tiên sat on a bench and watered her apricot blossoms. Xuân knew the ruse was up. She hadn't told her mother about the pageant, but by now, news must've traveled to her, one of the most well-connected and social women in the city. Xuân did not bother to lie.

"Mama, I only entered the pageant because I thought I could win."

"And did you win?"

"I know the man who organized it and he said I had a good chance."

"That means you didn't win."

"No, but I was second place."

"So, you whored yourself out to this man for second place. A nice compromise for everyone."

"Second place is good. There were twenty other women and none of them got second place."

"You don't strive for anything, it seems." She snatched Xuân's bag from her hands and upended it, her pageant clothes, delicate and beautiful, floating to the ground. "You have always been selfish, and you never think things through. A horrible combination, Metal and Tiger."

"You never even acknowledge me," said Xuân. "It's as though I must jump around to catch your attention, performing like a circus animal."

"What could I acknowledge you for? If you ever have a child who is only as interested in themselves as you are, I will know God has taught you a lesson."

The idea of the pageant suddenly seemed so foolish, and Xuân knelt to the ground to pick up her clothes. The image of the Girl, the pants of her áo dài tossed carelessly on the ground in the sacristy, flashed in her mind. Her mother was, of course, correct. She didn't know what luck kept her from having the fate of the Girl, naive as Xuân was, so willing to believe in her own exception.

"Doesn't it bother you that you didn't win?" Xuân asked Bambi. They sat in the empty bar where Bambi worked. It was early morning, just past dawn. Xuân couldn't sleep and she knew Bambi often slept in the bar's back room on the cot when she wasn't at Lenny's. Her family lived in a two-room apartment, and all seven of her siblings slept on the floor of one room. It was common for families to do that. When Bambi slept at

Lenny's, it was the first time she'd ever stayed someplace where she could stretch her arms out and touch empty air. Lenny had bought the cot for the bar's back room and helped her set it up. "In case you work late," he said to her, and she often did. It was just another reason Bambi forgave Lenny for his flaws; despite everything, despite his wandering gaze and bouts of impetuousness, he did things for Bambi that helped her survive. No one had cared about her survival before. Xuân had never brought Bambi to her home because her mother would never allow it, but she also breathed a sigh of relief that she would never have to. There was something shameful in their wealth, a shame that could not be so easily ignored if Bambi saw with her own eyes the excess, the grandeur.

"I don't know if I care about the pageant. That girl could've deserved to win," said Bambi.

"But you're his girlfriend," said Xuân. "Surely, you care."

"It's not like he was a judge. He was just the host. He just organized it." Xuân let out a derisive snort. "What? You don't think so?"

"I think Lenny had a lot more influence than that."

"I think I would know if he did. Lenny is my boyfriend."

"*Sure,*" Xuân said.

"How can you come in here before the sun rises, wake me up, and tell me my boyfriend is a liar? How disrespectful."

"I'm not trying to be disrespectful. But why are you sleeping here, at the bar? You didn't work last night. Yesterday was the pageant. Why aren't you at Lenny's?"

Bambi couldn't admit that Lenny had asked her not to come. That he often told her not to come. That he also often told her when to come. Bambi would never admit it to Xuân, but she came and went at Lenny's request like a prostitute.

When she asked Lenny why, yesterday after the pageant, he said he didn't owe her any answers. "I bought all the clothes on your body, all the beautiful dresses you wore today," he said. "I pay for your life."

"What's that got to do with why I can't come over?" she said, and he stormed away back toward the church, where many of the women and soldiers still lingered to socialize. Bambi didn't come over last night, or any of the other nights, even though she knew she could show up at any time and find out what it was he was hiding. Lenny was right, after all. Everything on her body, everything in her life, was purchased by Lenny. He owned everything she had and owed her nothing.

"We should go to that girl's house and steal the trophy," said Xuân. "It's not right that she won."

"It's not her fault. You should stop blaming her. Besides, the trophy isn't at her house."

"Well, then, where is it?"

"Lenny said it's solid silver. They were never going to give the trophy away. It was for the pictures," said Bambi. "The plan is to use it year after year for every pageant."

"Even better. We know where Lenny lives. Let's take the trophy from him." All Xuân could hear was her mother's voice. *You don't strive for anything, it seems.*

"How are we going to do that? He's not just going to hand it over nicely. Besides, what does it matter? The trophy is just a symbol. Neither of us won, whether we have the trophy or not."

"That girl won because Lenny said so, not because she was better than us. She doesn't have the trophy. So, who won the pageant, then? Who's the winner? It can be us if we take it for ourselves."

"She gets money and a trip somewhere nice. She gets photos in the paper. She won."

"She didn't *win*. Lenny gave it to her."

"There were judges," said Bambi. "What's your obsession with Lenny? That's my man you keep shitting on."

"Lenny *is* shit, and I saw the moment he handpicked his winner in the church after I walked in on him and that poor girl."

Bambi did not look surprised, and Xuân did not expect her to. But, she was unprepared for her face crumpling, the cracking open of Bambi's mask. Her cheeks sagged, lips apart and somehow slack, as if even the muscles in her face, which were tense and at attention all day, had given up. They stood there as Xuân allowed her space and silence to feel ashamed, and then, she grasped Bambi's hand and led her outside.

When they arrived at Lenny's apartment, they stood in the dark, wet hallway outside his door. The building's walls were thin, and they could hear the echoing thud of heavy footfalls and the low murmur of the television and, below them, the bustle of the morning phở crowd in the restaurant on the first floor, which seemed to swell in volume as time wore on. By then, it was midmorning, and warm tendrils of sunlight were finally falling through the window at the end of the hallway.

Xuân had a nervous energy; the sensation of heartburn had not ceased since she'd left the sacristy. In fact, it had intensified, creating a discomfort, an inability to sit still, a dissatisfaction. Now that they were here at Lenny's, her heart strained even more against her chest—in anticipation of what? She felt at an utter loss since the pageant about what she could do. She didn't even know to what end she was doing, but *do*, she had to *do* something.

You don't strive for anything, it seems.

She looked at Bambi to see her body shrinking from the door. She hunched her shoulders, folded her arms, as if to make herself disappear. Xuân herself stood up straighter to compensate, to help hold Bambi up with her own presence. She'd never seen her act so meek. It inflamed her.

"I want you to open the door," said Xuân, "and I'll run in and grab the trophy."

Bambi nodded, and despite her timidity, Xuân was impressed to see her move confidently toward the door and grip the knob with resolve.

She opened the door easily (Lenny never locked it when he was inside), but instead of rushing in, as Xuân had imagined, they both stood frozen.

The Girl held a small, sleeping baby, as Richard Nixon gave a speech on the television. Lenny sat on the end of his bed peeling banana leaf away from sticky rice. It was a domestic scene, one of such familiarity for the inhabitants. It was like looking at a moment immortalized in a documentary photograph about families. Lenny and the Girl looked up at them, expressions of people who'd been caught doing something harmless, like children who'd stolen candies.

It was this offense, more than anything else, that caused Bambi to scream, a high-pitched, raw scream that woke the baby, and which prompted it to let out a similar scream, an uncontrollable, animal cry of fear, anger, panic. Their expressions of mild surprise were a breach, the final breach upon Bambi's dignity. Lenny showed no alarm at their arrival, no indication that the scene before them was a transgression, hidden deliberately and perpetually from her.

"Get out!" she screeched, pointing her finger at the Girl and her child. "Get out, now! Get out," she continued to scream, "Get out get out get out." The Girl ran, clutching her child and tripping on its dragging swaddle cloth. She looked so young, even younger, if it were possible, when holding the infant. As if, by holding the baby, Xuân could see more clearly how close in age they were. She felt sorry for them. Lenny would leave eventually, and those children, the girl and her daughter, would be forgotten. The noise from the phở bistro below had picked up, the outside street sounds buzzing in their ears.

"Calm down," he said. "Stop screaming!"

Lenny was on his feet, approaching Bambi. Xuân ran to the

dresser and dragged the trophy down with both arms. It was heavy and difficult to remove from its height. She moved it, trembling, to the floor, then wrapped both arms around the base. The Miss Saigon 1973 engraving pressed into her arm. Bambi continued to scream. Lenny slapped and pushed her to the ground.

"Stop it!" he said, his voice hard. He kicked her. She continued to scream. He kicked her. "Shut up," he said, "shut up!"

Xuân lifted her arms and braced her body, muscles tense and shaking. Then, a steadiness, as if her arms were being held up for her, and a release, as she smashed the trophy against Lenny's head. He fell to the floor clutching his skull. Xuân stood above him and dropped the trophy on him. She picked it up and dropped it on him once more. She picked it up and dropped it. Again, and again, and again, and again.

18

TIÊN

She helped her aunts wash her mother's corpse, wiping papery skin with wet cloths. Tiên knew she should be sad. She *was* sad. But Tiên did not associate anything about her mother with this cold, stiff body. It was like dabbing down a terrifying and life-size doll. Perhaps she was in shock.

Or perhaps she had been preparing for this event for the last year, her mother having left them ages ago, her personality drastically different from the woman she had known. The house reeked of incense and rotten flesh already. They dressed her in funeral clothes. They wrapped her stinking corpse in white cloth and laid her on a grass mat made of tea leaves. In her mouth, coins. Between her teeth, chopsticks. They stooped over her, their prayers a hum in the air mingling with smoke and fumes.

She was nestled into the plain wooden coffin, the grass mat hugging her, enveloping her like she'd been there for years. Under her coffin, a lamp kept her spirit warm. It was important to put her in the main room of the house, which, in their case, also served as the storefront for their herbal medicine shop. They had pushed all the shelves—old glass bottles clinking against each other, housing dried plants or ground seeds or oil mixtures—against the wall and placed her in the center. Her feet faced the door; Tiên hoped her mother was ready to leave home for the afterlife. Where was it that she would go? She couldn't imagine leaving home, leaving Sài Gòn, leaving Vietnam. It seemed the same as leaving the world. Tiên's entire life only knew home as a place at war: war with the French, war with the Japanese, war with themselves—but still, she could never think about being anywhere else. She supposed that was why they'd been fighting for so long. No one wanted to leave, and new people kept arriving.

Where was her mother now? she wondered. It seemed likely that she, too, would never leave Vietnam, that she would wander its bustling streets and market stalls for eternity, float among the neatly planted rows of rubber trees on her plantation.

The street up to their home was lined with white flags, and visitors began to appear at their door bearing white flowers and money. The altar was grand, full of oranges and lilies. A photograph of her mother standing among those rubber trees in her favorite áo dài stood in the center of the altar. Neighbors and friends approached, billowing incense between their palms as they bowed to her photo.

Quỳnh's body remained in the house for five days. Each day, people came to say their last respects. It was hot, the middle of July. Burning incense, heat, and the decaying corpse of her mother made their home a difficult place to be. She found the week hard to recall, the atmosphere of the house itself creating a strange distortion to her memory.

In fact, she was having a hard time remembering the face and person of her mother. Every time she tried, she could only see the wooden and lifeless corpse that had been displayed in the main room of their home for the past week. Even in the photo on the altar, her face looked blurry, like the camera was shaking. Had it always been like that? Or, now that her mother had died, evidence of her life was slowly being erased as time went on? Every day of the wake, she stood at the open coffin and stared down at her mother's body. It looked like a stranger.

Tiên rummaged through boxes that stored dozens of family photographs. Some of the photos were very old—special portraits of elders, most of them already deceased, and probably the only photos ever taken of them. Even if their rubber plantation burned to the ground, their grand home bombed to rubble, her mother had always said these boxes of photos were proof of their wealth. Not many could afford photographs now, and especially not then. Poor people disappeared once they died, their bodies the only thing that had tethered them to living memory. But the Trung women had a record of their existence, proof that they had lived on this earth. And, in their obsession with record keeping, they had passed their names to their daughters, would continue to do so, insisting they preserve the matrilineal line. Women kept their names even when they married, and fathers rarely cared about their daughters as long as their sons could carry on the male line. Whatever else they may have sacrificed in marriage—dignity, autonomy, freedom—they insisted upon preserving their name.

Tiên shuffled the photos one after the other, scanning each one for her mother's face, but she saw again and again a blurred blotch where she should've been. Other photographs, in which she had been sure her mother was present, bore no trace of her. She went through the boxes, searching the stacks of photos once, twice, three times, each time more frantic than the last, before dropping the photos unarranged in their boxes and shoving them away, frustrated.

Quỳnh was the kind of mother who was generous, the kind of mother who did not expect a return for her generosity. But she was also stubborn and emotional, a bad combination, especially when mixed with Tiên's own inflexibility, her impatience with the feelings of others. In a lot of ways, they were the exact same person: popular, honest, compassionate. People who loved plans and tidy spaces and who hated compromising on their ideas. Her mother endearingly called her *dê con*, kid, like a baby goat, because she, herself was also a Goat. Quỳnh never said it, but Tiên knew she was her favorite simply for this fact.

But those things that made them the same were also the things that caused strife in their relationship. Quỳnh said it was because she was born in the element of Fire, and Tiên in Metal.

"Fire heats up Metal and makes it angry," she had said. This certainly felt true at times. Her mother's melodrama agitated her, a reaction not well suited for a daughter toward her mother. Quỳnh was particularly hard on the help, assuming the worst of them: always suspects for theft and never competent enough for even the simplest tasks. Tiên found her rigid expectations embarrassing. Even when her behavior was warranted—when the maid *had* stolen cash from the wooden box inlaid with mother-of-pearl, when the gardener *had* lied about his horticultural credentials and ended up killing all their lilies—Tiên still never gave her mother room to be right, and Quỳnh was loath to ever admit being wrong.

"You are moody, my little Goat," said her mother, often, which only served to make matters worse. Now that she was dead, Tiên begrudgingly admitted: it was the fact that they were so alike that they had ever fought, Metal or Fire irrelevant.

After her illness, the most intense parts of Quỳnh's personality seemed to swallow her whole, grow and pulse, a disease itself. For weeks, she heaved her rice porridge into her lap, the vomit swirling orange. Her skin looked permanently stained, too, although they couldn't tell if they'd convinced themselves of that because they knew it was in her body. She threw fits, screaming and lashing out in anger when things were not the way she wanted them. She clung to ideas against any logical dismantling. She was convinced someone was lurking in the dark and stealing a single diamond each night from her favorite necklace, despite her family's reassurances that she was quite alone, despite showing her the necklace each day, intact. She sometimes woke up thinking they were at the rubber plantation, and that all their trees were stripped bare, even though she hadn't been well enough to visit there for months. *Bones,* she kept saying, *bones in the earth,* but her family could not make sense of that, either. The more contradictory evidence she was presented with, the more Quỳnh doubled down in the illogic of her own reality.

Her head hurt so much, she lay for hours, days, clutching it. Her honesty was laced, now, with meanness.

"We are the unluckiest sign in the zodiac," she said.

"We can change our destiny," Tiên said, trying to cheer up her mother.

"I was unlucky enough to have an ugly daughter," she said. "And I'm unlucky enough to die here with her at my side."

"That sounds lucky to me," Tiên said. "To have a loved one by your side."

"I'm sorry," Quỳnh said. "I'm sorry." She had come to her senses, apologizing again and again. "I don't know who said that. I don't know who I am," she'd say, looking afraid.

Often, she would speak for extended periods about the fire. "Do you feel it?" she might say, or other times, she chose to scream, her body convulsing in some unseen burst of flames. "The fire! The fire!"

Tiên would take her mother's hand and drape it over her shoulder, helping her walk. Maids had drawn a bath for her, just warm enough to comfort her inactive body. Her hands and feet were always cold, even though it was the hottest part of the year.

"A bath, Mama," Tiên said. "Water puts out fires."

Tiên helped the Fire Goat step into the bath, a ritual she always complied with. The mention of water always seemed to calm her, remind her there was balance.

"Did you feel the fire?" her mother asked, soaking in the bath one last time.

"I felt it. It was burning hot." She wasn't lying, technically—summer in Vietnam felt like they were all burning alive.

"Leave me," she told the room, and they all left her.

The water in the bath swirled around her as she slid her arms across its surface. She stared down into the water as it unfurled between her fingers. Before her illness, she used to take long walks. She loved strolling by the river. It was comforting to know water had come from somewhere and was going elsewhere, that it had done so for thousands of years, that it had carved a path through earth and rock and grime, persisting forward. The sound of it rushed into her ears as she thought of walking along the riverbank with her children, each of them eating a mango she'd bought them at the market. Eyes shut and ears full, dreaming of rivers, she didn't notice as the bath swallowed her whole.

Tiên's brother, Phúc, had to sit by the coffin for the past four days. He was the eldest child. He did the same when their father died three decades ago, except then, Phúc had only been eleven years old. Tiên was two years younger than him, only nine at the time, but she had the stark memory of small and silent Phúc sitting next to their father's coffin, room hazy with smoke.

Now, Phúc was forty-one, stocky and strong. He hung out with Americans a lot at the US embassy. They nicknamed him Mr. Fuck because they couldn't pronounce *Phúc* properly, and thought it was hilarious.

Phúc had been sleeping on a cot near the coffin all week, guarding the body. It was the last day of the wake. Tomorrow, they would start the procession to the burial site. He looked disheveled and unrested. He called Tiên into the room and pulled her into the corner near a bookshelf, whispering, as if their mother might hear him.

"Tiên, I think mẹ is alive," he said.

"Why do you say that? It's been a week and she hasn't woken up," she said. It was part of the reason the wakes were so long. Stories of men and women waking up in pitch darkness, the coffin already buried, were not just folktales.

"I heard her move in the coffin last night. I didn't sleep well because I kept hearing noises. When I brought the light over to see, I didn't recognize her. It looks like a different person in there. I'm scared tonight there will be more noises. What if she's trying to get out? Or what if she was stolen, and now she's trying to get back in?"

"It's her. She just looks different because she's dead."

"There's something wrong. Today, cousin Cới yelled at me. We forgot to put the banana on her belly. How could we forget? I feel like we didn't know what we were doing. Mẹ was the one who planned everything. And now she's gone, and we don't know anything."

"I don't think it matters, Phúc," she said. It surprised her that now, suddenly, he'd chosen to believe in old wives' tales.

"Her spirit could've escaped last night. Maybe that's what I heard?"

"Did you see a half cat half snake demon jump over her coffin, too?"

"Don't mock me," he said. "I don't know what I saw. Maybe I did see that."

Tiên didn't tell him about the blurry faces, the photographs. They were both being tricked by grief and despair.

That night, Tiên slept in the room with Phúc and her mother's body. She lay on a mat on the ground, back to the coffin, and stared at the spines of horoscope books and farmers' almanacs. She drifted in and out of sleep, the line between dream and reality as hazy as her mother's face in her memory. Tiên rolled onto her other side to look at the coffin, which seemed to glow in the flickering lamplight. Her brother's snores were wet.

In the corner, she saw the creature slink along the wall, its bright green eyes shrewd and reproachful. The angular, feline face of a cat, its two front paws padding quietly on the stone floor, and the body of a dangerous-looking snake, its tail dragging and undulating behind it. The figure of her mother walked after it, but then, the flash and flicker of her body as she dived into the ground, swimming through it. Her face bobbing above the surface, young and clear and bright. Was it a demon that had led her out, as they were always told would happen if you didn't guard your loved one's body well enough? Or had her mother been released by some spirit they never understood properly, limited and earthly as they were?

When Tiên woke up, the sun streamed in through the front windows. Phúc had opened the coffin lid and stared down. She stood next to him and saw their mother, gray and papery, perhaps a different body altogether. It was the day of the burial.

"I hate to bury her," said Phúc. "She would detest being trapped to the earth, covered in dirt, even if it's just her body."

"I think she might be swimming," said Tiên. "Flowing with water, free somewhere."

19

QUỲNH

The rubber plantation was three hours by car northwest of Sài Gòn. Quỳnh made a point to visit at least twice a month, usually leaving on Sundays after church. She bought a new car every few years because she could, and she didn't see why not. Many people thought it extravagant, but she didn't care. She was in her sixties now and had worked all this time. She enjoyed being ogled at in her shiny new vehicles. Besides, she drove them to and from the plantation in Bình Long Province at least twenty-five times a year on poor roads bordering the wild. She hated to admit it, but her anxiety was based in the fear that her small body would fail her in the face of violence, even though she frequently denied to men that this obstructed her ability to wield authority. They already didn't think she could manage the brutality involved in the plantation; she was a weak-stomached woman, they thought. She could never admit that being a woman made her afraid of all the things they said she should be afraid of: men, her body, other women.

She brought a male house servant with her on these drives,

just to deter possible guerrilla soldiers lurking in the dense jungle that surrounded the route. She sometimes suspected her house servants sympathized with, were perhaps even members of those hated Việt Cộng. She was always suspicious. It seemed impossible that anyone who wasn't rich wouldn't hate her family for it. She had started driving a Simca Aronde because it was both a popular car and inconspicuous, inconspicuous enough that communists had started using them, it was rumored, to transport their own illicit supplies. Her brand-new car was a lovely shade of green because she believed the color would be lucky for matters of money. Luck was something she could use, unlucky Goat that she was. The unluckiest sign in the lunar calendar.

Though the war in recent years seemed bleak for the South, Quỳnh was always searching for moments of fortune. Despite having a generally inauspicious zodiac chart, Quỳnh was optimistic. She was a Goat, after all. Vietnam could use more Goat-like dispositions, in her opinion.

The US's Agent Orange campaign had helped to clear portions of her path to Sông Plantation. She drove past the destruction regularly on her way to Bình Long, sometimes sick or dead bodies piled along the road, her line of sight to orange-powder-draped villages free from the thick tangle of green that had been there previously. While the ruin was devastating for many, Quỳnh couldn't help but think the Agent Orange was a blessing. She didn't have to jump at every movement on the road now. She could see straight ahead and on either side of her car, at least for much of the beginning of her drive. It wasn't until she approached the plantation that the brush began to thicken again, and, while this may have been false security, she felt safer the closer she got to her property, to its ordered design and meticulous upkeep. Few things lasted, but as her mother, Thảo, said, the land was always there. It accumulated memory, stood as a physical testament to their existence. It would remember, even after their whole family had gone. Legacy, Quỳnh knew, was more important than anything.

Sông Plantation was a smaller parcel of land than some of the others. Her mother had bought the property from a French colonial bureaucrat, Monsieur Rodier. A bachelor and a generally odious man, François Rodier had been quite reluctant to sell his land to their family. He wanted to sell it to another colonial, to keep it in white hands, although it wouldn't have mattered much if he had anyway, as they were pushed out by the Japanese and then Hồ Chí Minh's cronies not long after he had relented to sell to Thảo.

"He thinks we're uncivilized," explained Quỳnh's father. He, too, was a colonial bureaucrat, and regularly had to deal with Rodier. Theirs was one of the few Vietnamese families that could float among those pasty-white Cochinchina partisans. They worked at a deficit constantly, maneuvering within the narrow perceptions the French had of them. Elite, Quỳnh's family might consider themselves, but she knew they were just as uncivilized, dirty, and dumb as their Vietnamese countrymen who lived in the streets, who toiled on the plantation.

It didn't matter how much wealth they had, and it didn't matter that they came from a long line of scholars before the French arrived. In fact, this very circumstance might have worked against them, as the French were looking to create their own elite subordinates and strip the preexisting elites of power, choosing their own sycophants, and educating them with approved French curriculum. Quỳnh's own family would have been ousted from political positions if her father hadn't joined a program to attend university in Paris, a kind of French colonial pipeline to bureaucratic success for the Vietnamese. "The French way is better," they said, and that was why all the old Vietnamese scholarship had to be expunged from public memory. All of the scholars knew this was just a less violent, more polite way of colonizing, although there was plenty of actual colonial violence to last a lifetime outside of the academy.

It was laughable that the French considered them of subpar intelligence, when in reality, Quỳnh knew those weak-minded Westerners would balk at the multilevel, decades-long process to study for and pass the Confucian civil service exams in order to be a true scholar. Perhaps that was why the French had permanently suspended the exams more than fifty years ago.

Quỳnh's great-grandfather and great-great-grandfather had achieved trạng nguyên, and her own father regularly told them stories of ancestors who had achieved bảng nhãn or thám hoa. It was an achievement to merely sit for the exams, let alone be the best at them. But the people had already forgotten about them; the exams were exclusive and reserved for those with the time and privilege to spend many years immersed in study. People like Quỳnh's forefathers viewed themselves as the guardians of Vietnam's cultural history, the only ones who remembered languages and rituals despite all the Chinese, and then the Japanese and French, who tried to squash it out of them, who tried to say *You are just an extension of China, Japan, France.*

And yet, a mere fifty years out from the disintegration of centuries' worth of scholarly tradition, the Vietnamese people barely had a passing memory of its existence. Did their history exist without those who kept the records?

It all made sense to Quỳnh, though. She had thought about this often in her silent drives to and from Bình Long Province. Commoners hated the exams because they weren't included in them—why would they decry their dissolution? They didn't understand the loss. And the French? Of course, they would want to be rid of this guardianship of Vietnamese culture. How could they civilize the Vietnamese if they allowed them to harbor their Vietnamese ways? It hadn't gone well, this civilizing of theirs.

Even so, Quỳnh suspected this was why she obsessed so much

about the family plantation. Her mother had instilled that in her, even though they knew their labor left the trunks open for disease. Those lines of rubber trees arranged in a neat, unnatural grid. It took so much effort to clear the brush that grew on the ground, brush that would actually offer protection for the trees to grow. The French had been obsessed with the aesthetics of their plantations, and Quỳnh, and her mother before her, grew obsessed, too. They knew better, and yet, they still followed suit, afraid to be labeled uncivilized, just as Rodier had accused them.

Deep down, Quỳnh loved the beauty of it. If she could be responsible for the beautiful symmetry, order, and control of her own land, then perhaps that meant she, too, could be beautiful.

"There's always the feeling of being a younger sibling," her mother had said about the colonials one night while preparing to attend a Christmas party a number of years ago, when the plantations had been more plentiful in number and before the French had fled. She had been invited to a fete at another plantation. As elites, they were considered the least savage of the natives. Of course, none of the colonials said this to them, and Quỳnh doubted whether or not the colonials themselves were even aware they thought this of her family and her people. Quỳnh hadn't understood then what her mother had meant about being a younger sibling.

"No matter how much you try to catch up, they always view you as something to teach, to be coddled or disciplined into something more attractive," she said. "Don't fall into that trap, my love. Know yourself well enough that you never try to achieve the thing they envision for you."

Quỳnh thought her mother was the most beautiful woman in the world that night. She wore an emerald green cocktail dress from France, her hair in an elegant chignon. She fastened pearl earrings to her lobes and rubbed her lips together to smear the pale pink lipstick she'd applied.

"And most importantly of all, my little Goat," she said in the foyer, "remember life is just one big performance. Learn to act well enough that everyone thinks you're what they wanted all along." She tucked her lips underneath her teeth and gave her a lipless kiss on the cheek before leaving to get in the back seat of their Peugot humming idly on the bricked circle driveway.

The trees had been stripped down and stood naked and erect in rows, like some obscene and immovable display of nude soldiers commanded to remain at attention. Quỳnh tripped over her own feet exiting the car, leaving the door ajar as she gaped at her rubber trees. The bark had been skinned right off, down to the pale, delicate flesh beneath. The trees were ruined, and the sap could not be collected. Normally, a spiral was carved in the bark, guiding the sap into a tin basin. Now, there was no bark. Quỳnh was lightheaded and propped the palm of her hand against a tree. It was sticky and viscous.

Her workers had abandoned the site. Where was the plantation hand in charge of keeping them all at their tasks? She got back in her car and drove down the long path, past the rows of trees. They flashed like blinding rays of sun in her periphery. She ran up to the house, which was on the highest ground on the property. It sat on a small hill, where she could look down at her life's work. The neatly arranged trees were mesmerizing if you stared at them too long. They sometimes looked as if they were moving, shifting back and forth. She'd close her eyes and they'd be still again, but not for long if she didn't look away.

The house looked untouched, even though the door had been left open. She suspected they'd done it on purpose, her workers. Let her know they were there, had been inside, were always on the land she only sometimes set foot on. But they hadn't taken anything from the house. Instead, they had destroyed her plantation. It looked like the trees were leaking tears of sap. She was crying, too. Her cheeks felt hot, angry, her stomach swirling.

"What's wrong, Madam Quỳnh?" asked her house servant, Cam.

Quỳnh jumped at the intrusion. She hadn't expected anyone to be in the house after such a crime had been committed. "What are you doing here?"

"Madam Quỳnh, I am always here. I clean the house daily in the morning. I have also been preparing dinner because of your arrival today."

"I know *why* you're hired," snapped Quỳnh. "I mean, what's happened?" She could feel flecks of her own spit on her hands as she waved them wildly.

Cam stared at her. She appeared unsure of what to say, apparently unaware of the situation outside, but also afraid to offer the mistress of the plantation her silence, or, even worse, the wrong answer.

"I don't know what you mean," Cam said.

"The trees! Our trees!" said Quỳnh.

Cam's eyes widened, her utter bewilderment plain. She looked like she might cry. She was perpetually afraid of losing her job.

"Oh, get yourself together," Quỳnh said. "The trees, what happened to the trees, stupid girl? Did you see anyone out there last night?"

When Cam failed to answer again, Quỳnh snatched her hand and led her outside. They hurried down the porch stairs, running as fast as Quỳnh's low heels would allow toward the eerie uniformity of the rubber trees. A strange fog hovered above the ground as dusk approached. Quỳnh placed her hand on the trunk of a tree. Its bark was completely intact.

"I don't understand," she said. She continued to walk down the row of trees, placing her hand on each one the farther into her artificial forest she went. All of them were unharmed.

"Madam Quỳnh, are you all right?" Cam's voice sounded tinny from the distance between them.

"The trees, they were stripped and destroyed."

"The plantation overseer gave me a report of the property this morning," said Cam. "Nothing seemed amiss."

"They were completely destroyed," she said, again. Cam did not respond. She waited for her mistress to say more, but there was only silence from Quỳnh, who was both relieved and terrified. "Go back to the house and finish preparing dinner. I'll be back in a moment."

When Cam left, Quỳnh walked briskly back to the Simca, and drove the way she came, back to the edge of the plantation. The trees had been stripped, she was sure of it. Perhaps they had only managed to reach the trees farther away from the house, the ones near the end of the long driveway? That would ensure Cam wouldn't have seen them in the night. It was strange, though, that any of her workers would do this. She treated them well enough, and this was a tactic normally exercised against the French during the war, already more than a decade ago. She was rich, but still, she wasn't French. She gave them a living wage and shelter and medicine. She knew their children and their wives. Quỳnh could never shake the feeling, though, of deeply rooted resentment.

She stopped her car in the middle of the road and got out to greet the trees. They were all in good health. Her hand pressed against the bark, as if pushing harder might reveal it to be an illusion, might make it disintegrate. Her palm was clean when she examined it. Quỳnh looked into the dark, infinite tunnels of trees before her. Dusk was falling rapidly, and the lines of plants created the effect of endlessness, like an optical illusion. She'd driven a friend up before to spend the weekend, and she had remarked on how odd it was to exit the exuberance of the jungle and enter this vast, orderly, and geometric space.

"It doesn't feel quite natural," she'd said.

"Well," Quỳnh responded, "that's because it's not."

How odd, Quỳnh reflected now, to think that they had managed to make something as natural as the tree feel wholly artificial, perhaps even clinical.

A woman with dirt-caked skin revealed herself from behind a rubber tree farther away.

"Hello?" said Quỳnh. "Who are you?" She had a sudden, soaring feeling of vindication. Strange things *were* happening. She wasn't crazy. The woman did not respond.

"This is my land. You can't be here," Quỳnh said. Behind the woman, more people stepped out, tree trunk by tree trunk. They wore rags and were filthy. Some of them had horrible gashes and wounds on their heads and limbs. Some of them wore no shirts at all, revealing awful lash marks. Others, still, were morbidly thin and sickly looking, malarial if Quỳnh could say so.

"If you don't leave, I'll call the authorities," she said. She was afraid of them, afraid of the evidence of their suffering, and afraid of their numbers. The sound of moaning and crying, of many people crying, echoed in the air, and yet, none of her visitors had moved or opened their mouths. And when she closed her eyes to pray, and opened them again, they were gone.

Sitting on the front porch furniture as she drank her coffee, the sound of aircraft whining in the distance, Quỳnh watched the sun rise. The glowing orange orb and flat periwinkle sky failed to soothe the feelings of unease she had had all night. She barely slept, imagining the men and women walking past her broad bedroom windows, or in the hallway of her home. They were never there when she looked up, peering through the panes of glass or past the threshold of her door. She wondered what they were all doing here on her plantation, why they were haunting her.

It was because of the orange rising sun, the mellow golden glow that it cast as it moved slowly upward, that Quỳnh could not at first distinguish between the sky and the bright orange dust dropped from the planes that had appeared. The orange powder sat in the air as it plumed and fell in cascades on the landscape below. A cool morning breeze swept it along in waves like the ocean, covering everything in sight.

20

XUÂN

Her mother clasped Xuân's hand as she walked ahead, dragging her like a towboat. She wove through the bodies crowding the sidewalk near the Presidential Palace, its front gardens green and verdant in the June heat. They were going in the wrong direction. Her mother paused, people rushing around them, and made a sharp about-face in the direction they had come.

Tiên wore a white tennis dress, her ponytail still styled despite the fact that she'd played vigorously. Normally, Tiên would never leave Cercle Sportif in her exercise clothing, racket in its bag slung over her shoulder. Xuân was in trouble, of course. She was quarrelsome and prone to bouts of sulking when told to do something she didn't want to do, especially now that she was thirteen. In this case, she'd been left to play with the presidential adviser's son at the pool. Tiên had met him to play doubles tennis with two French women, Barnabé and Martine, the children of landowners who never left after the French did. Minh and Tiên against Barnabé and Martine—Vietnamese against French.

The trouble was, Minh was extremely good at tennis and extremely competitive. Tiên was neither. But they had had a long conversation at the Cercle Sportif annual ball one year about tennis, and Tiên had pretended to play more frequently than she really did. She went to extraordinary lengths to keep up the charade by meeting him for matches, and Xuân took advantage of this. She loved going to Cercle Sportif, which always seemed to feel freer than taking walks in the city, which were always chaperoned, and definitely freer than their home, even though they lived in quite a large house.

While her mother played match after match with the presidential adviser, she swam alone in the teeming pool, its blue surface sparkling in the open air. She held her nose and dunked her head underwater, pretending to be a mermaid. Sometimes she'd kick her feet against the tiled wall, propelling herself forward like a bullet, and pretend she was a shooting star. Adults ignored her and she stayed out of their way. American politicians and diplomats, elite French expats, and wealthy Sài Gòn families whirled around her like she didn't exist. She found this a relief, and, in the water, she felt a calm she never felt otherwise.

Xuân had always been stubborn for a daughter, but her adolescence had made matters worse.

"Metal and Metal," Xuân had heard her grandmother say more than once before. "They clash."

Xuân didn't know much about the lunar zodiac yet, but what her grandmother said seemed true enough. It felt like her mother was constantly trying to mold her, bend her into the shape she wanted, like a sculptor. And Xuân tried her best to adhere to the expectations of a good Vietnamese daughter. Obedient, submissive, and most importantly of all, silent. But how could she take her mother's advice when the woman herself showed none of those qualities she yearned for in Xuân?

"You have to be silent sometimes," she said. "You have to know when to not speak. That will be your greatest weapon. A woman who is silent is dangerous."

"You're never silent. You always say what you think."

"That's not true. You only think that because I speak to you so much."

"I've seen you say things to important men. You've insulted politicians to their faces before."

"And I had control. If you heard everything I thought in my head, you'd know how much I really do remain silent. Never lose control," she said.

Xuân remembered this advice when, upon arriving in the art deco lobby at Cercle Sportif, the presidential adviser presented his son, who looked to be a few years younger than her, and already wearing his swim trunks. The presidential adviser smiled, his mouth gummy. Many of his teeth had been pulled, the rumor was, when he was a prisoner of the Việt Cộng.

They were left in the lobby together when the adults left for the tennis courts. Xuân was displeased she would not get her pool time ritual, and she could already tell the boy would be unpleasant. He had the air of many of the boys she was forced to socialize with, that familiar look of someone well cared for and given too much attention: the plump cheeks of a well-fed child, carefully combed hair, and arrogance in every gesture. Everyone wanted a boy, and if you got one, he was treated like a show animal. Preened and fattened and given every advantage, but also, ultimately, expected to perform in top form. But boys got away with much more. They weren't taught to be silent, and if they messed up, it was easily excused as boyish nature.

"Don't bother me," Xuân said. She walked to the pool without waiting for or inviting him, but he followed after her anyway.

"You can't talk to me like that," he said. Even his voice confirmed to Xuân that he was exactly as she thought. Entitled and overconfident.

The sight of the pool gave Xuân a thrill. Droplets glittered and twinkled in the air as water splashed. She and the boy dodged waiters carrying trays of cocktails. Instead of using the ladder, she sat herself on the edge of the pool and lowered her body into the water against the wall. It was still cool, despite the crowds of bodies and the hot sun.

The boy jumped in feetfirst, splattering water in her eyes. When he came up, his black hair flowed in a sheet over his eyes, and water rushed down the crevices of his face.

She sputtered and wiped her eyes. He jumped up, placing his hands on her shoulders and dunking her down below, putting all his weight into keeping her under. She thrashed, her mouth stupidly inhaling and filling with water. Under the surface, she could see the legs of the other pool patrons milling around, and an animal, a kitten suspended and swaying limply near the bottom before she was able to come up, gulping mouthfuls of air. He jumped up and did it again, before she had time to gather her senses. She opened her mouth involuntarily, liquid in her throat. Underwater, the pool appeared empty. Where had all the bodies gone? She shut her eyes tight. He let her come up, and she could hear him laughing as she coughed, gripping the side of the pool. She couldn't see, hair in her face and water blurring everything.

"What is wrong with you?" She was sputtering, had been coughing up water. Her throat was raw and her mouth tasted salty.

"You told me not to bother you," he said. "And that was rude."

"Get away from me."

"I'm sorry, I thought it would be funny. I didn't mean to hurt you." The change in his tone was abrupt. Xuân did not expect it. He sounded contrite and genuinely concerned for her. She pushed her hair away from her face.

"It's fine," she said.

"Can I give you a hug to show my remorse?" he said.

"I guess." She wondered if this was how he was forgiven at home. Though not much younger, he was still a child, after all, couldn't be older than eleven. He came close to her but did not extend his arms to hug her.

"Will you hug me instead?" he said. She wanted this to be over, this uncomfortable moment. Why had she said it was fine? She didn't feel fine. She didn't know how to act. She wrapped her arms around him, child hugging child. Against her leg, she felt his hands fidget against their crowded bodies, as he pulled his trunks down and pressed his penis against her crotch, rubbing its flaccid tip up and down. She pushed him away.

He was laughing. She didn't remember doing it, but her palm stung badly from its contact with the boy's right cheek. He wasn't laughing anymore as he held his pink face, eyes watery.

The boy left a trail of dribbling water all through the lobby and onto the tennis courts, where he told his father what had happened. Tiên stormed out of Cercle Sportif, Xuân's offending hand in a tight grip, all the while berating her in a low tone so that passersby might not hear. She was so mad that they had walked in the wrong direction and had to turn around to come back the way they came. They walked southwest again, a few blocks to the extra apartment they had in that area of town. It was a small condo they sometimes used when they went to social events, which frequently happened near the Presidential Palace. Xuân's skin was already hot from all the walking. She missed the pool and wished she'd had a longer time there.

In the apartment, Tiên threw her things down. "I told you to be in control," she said. "Why did you slap that boy? He's the oldest son of a very important man."

"He wouldn't leave me alone," she said.

"I told you to entertain him."

"He tried to drown me."

"You're bigger and older than him," said Tiên.

Xuân didn't know why she couldn't tell her mother about the hug. There was something shameful about it. She *was* older and bigger than him. She still didn't have any control, and that was embarrassing. Even so, the truth lingered on the tip of tongue, pushing against the inside of her lips. She wanted to tell her, but how could she? She was mortified of the word *penis*. Wasn't silence easier than saying it?

Her mother did not give her the chance. With an impatient huff, she walked to the balcony and stared down onto the street below. She left the French doors to the balcony ajar, and Xuân could hear the sounds of the city outside. It was both louder and quieter than normal—louder in the sounds of people, like there were more crowds filling a small space, and quieter in the lack of cars, curiously absent in honking and rubber against concrete.

Xuân walked to the French doors and looked through the paned glass but did not join her mother outside. She could see the crowd gathered just outside their condo in a ring of spectators. The innermost barrier of people were Buddhist monks, bald and wrapped in saffron-orange robes. One monk sat lotus style in the center of the circle and handled a necklace of wooden beads in his hands. The sweet odor of gasoline wafted to their balcony on the wings of a hot summer breeze coming east from the river. Another monk had upended a five-gallon container over the head of his fellow as a prayer was said. The liquid crawled around the sitting monk. The fluid motion of a striking match, ablaze as the fire grew, engulfing robes, man, body, flickering on the surface of the road like a tar swimming pool set alight, the monk sitting on water like a god. He remained seated, his skin and body withering and blackening. He was silent, completely silent. Xuân marveled at his expression, his grimace, which looked as if he was undergoing some mild pain or nuisance, but which did not betray any urge or remote desire to save himself. Dark smoke billowed and flames licked the air. She would never forget the odor of burning flesh.

As his body burned, his composure slowly came undone. His body fell over on its back, heart toward the sky, the sound of it masked by wailing onlookers. He was surely dead now, Xuân realized, and it was as if the sound had turned back on. People were crying and praying. A monk said again and again into a microphone, "A Buddhist priest burns himself to death. A Buddhist priest becomes a martyr. A Buddhist priest burns himself to death. A Buddhist priest becomes a martyr." As the fire subsided, the monks covered the smoking corpse with robes. They attempted to pick him up and put him in a coffin, but his limbs were immovable, baked into place. One tried with futility to shove his bent leg into the narrow box, like packing an overfull suitcase. His arm protruded still from the top of the coffin, but they gave up, carrying the wooden box away from the scene.

He burned himself to death, he became a martyr. Her mother turned away from the railing and went into the kitchen to prepare something to eat. She didn't speak, her face as opaque as the burning monk's. Xuân suddenly wished she could be in the pool, alone. It was hot here, in this room. She wanted to wash away the smell and the memory of the burning man, of the fire, of the silence, but she knew she would never be allowed back at Cercle Sportif with her mother until she apologized to the boy. And she would never, she decided, do that.

21

THẢO

Quỳnh had her father's eyes, his forehead, his nose. His fair skin.
But she had her mother Thảo's jaw, her hair, her gentle and diminutive hands. Thảo reminded herself of this when she looked
at her own daughter and thought, for a flash, she saw Rodier's
expression hover like a mask over Quỳnh's face. It seemed to
be happening with frightening regularity, especially now that
Quỳnh was an adult. The older she got, the more like Rodier
her features seemed to age. Perhaps Thảo was finally paying
the price of having kept this secret for more than twenty-eight
years. She had hoped that by never speaking it into existence,
the secret might be erased, its memory disappearing into the
anonymity of time.

She hadn't seen Rodier in a long time. He was an old man,
now. When it became clear that Thảo was pregnant out of wed-
lock, her belly growing ever larger even as she wrapped it tight
with a linen cloth to try and flatten it, her father locked her
for two days in the ramshackle building where their laundress
cleaned the clothes to punish her.

The first night, her mother sneaked outside with food for Thảo. She cupped her daughter's face with cold hands.

"It is the greatest shame possible to your family to have a child out of marriage," her mother said.

"I'm sorry," Thảo said. She supposed this was what she should say.

"Who is it?"

"If I tell you, it will be an even greater shame than if you didn't know," Thảo said. Mixed children were ostracized, ridiculed, abandoned. Thảo wondered if they would even be able to tell that her child was half-white if she didn't divulge it. She was right. When Quỳnh was born, no one could know unless they were looking for the signs, the traces of Rodier there in the space between her eyes, there in the curve of her brow. For a moment, as she stared at the bowl of cold rice her mother had brought her, she had been seized by the desire to drink the now-tepid lye water that sat in the laundry basin behind her. A memory from her childhood stopped her, of their laundress coughing into her shoulder, leaving a spray of blood behind, smiling her gummy smile.

"Did you hear that Francois Rodier is selling his plantation?" Han said. They were walking home from the market. Thảo had a bag of shrimp and her sister carried bundles of herbs. Quỳnh held her daughter's hand and, in the other, a sack of some baguettes.

Han's face shone in the morning sun. She had smothered herself in old oil left from cooking fish. The night before, she'd mashed bananas and aloe vera and applied the homemade cream to her skin. The night before that, she'd made a turmeric paste and patted it onto her nose, her forehead, her cheeks. The old women next door had shared all their remedies for wrinkles. They told her Pigs were prone to blemishes, too, because they indulged too much, and Han bought everything they had to sell. She smelled terrible. Thảo had given her sister remedies for all these things, remedies she'd made Quỳnh use when she was younger for her adolescent skin issues, but Han insisted they hadn't worked for her.

"Who is Francois Rodier?" Quỳnh said.

"He's no one," said Thảo.

"He's an old Frenchman who used to throw the most elaborate parties," said Han. "He lives in a beautiful house on his plantation, but poor man doesn't know a thing about trees."

"But he owns a rubber plantation?" said Quỳnh. Tiên stumbled on the sidewalk, but Quỳnh continued to drag her down the street by the hand. She was only four years old, but Thảo could see the slope of Rodier's nose in her grandchild even though Quỳnh had married a Vietnamese man with a wide, flat nose. She wanted to flush Rodier out of their blood, to erase him.

"Yes, he owns it," said Han. "But he didn't ever seem to know what he was doing. I always wondered if his workers were purposefully leading him astray, since he treated them terribly and expected them to keep everything alive."

"Is that why he's selling?" asked Thảo. "Because everything's dead?"

She remembered how sad the plantation always looked whenever they attended his parties. She would stay outside on the porch, or wander the grounds to avoid being alone with him. The trees never seemed to grow as much as they were supposed to, and the land was bare. Was it some blight, or just Rodier's incompetence? She would sit among the sad trees, staring at the glowing house full of light and people. It was a relief that he never searched her out, but it was also an insult—she was a speck in the grander journey of his life. Why would he think to search for her? He barely remembered her, she was sure, his expression devoid of recognition every time he glanced her over. He was always drunk, after all. And, the older she became, the less interest he showed.

"I don't know why he's selling," said Han. "I think the trees are fine. He's probably hemorrhaging money. He has a terrible gambling problem, I've heard. Anyway, he's having a party."

"But, why? He hasn't had one for years," said Thảo.

"I think he means to use the party as a selling tactic. You know, spruce up the old mansion and make the grounds look as appealing as he can. Try to get his friends to buy because he'll probably get a better payoff. It's easier to ask for more when it's a friend. But I don't think he can ask for much."

"Why not?" asked Quỳnh. Thảo could see the childlike curiosity in Quỳnh's face in times such as this, and it reminded her of what innocence her daughter still possessed. Quỳnh was a Goat, gentle at her core. She might be stubborn, occasionally argumentative, quick to temper because of her Fire element. She certainly could stand up for herself. But, Thảo wondered if that had more to do with her environment, a trait Quỳnh had developed in order to adapt, perhaps to the meanness that sometimes spilled from Thảo, uncontrollable. At her daughter's basest level, she was kind. And Thảo didn't like that, because she worried that kindness would bring heartache to her doorstep.

"Why not? People think it's haunted. Bad luck. Nothing grows there! And rumors of ghosts, mean spirits," said Han.

"When's the party? Oh, Auntie, do you think we'll be invited?" said Quỳnh.

"Invited?" said Han. "Of course we're invited. Why do you think I'm even mentioning it?"

Tiên tripped on the uneven road, again. She fell on her knees, her wailing loud enough to send the birds in a nearby tree flapping into the sky. Tiên sat down, rubbing dirty hands against streaming eyes. Her knees were scratched and covered in dirt, the gleam of wet and pink where skin had been ripped away.

"I wonder what I'll wear," said Quỳnh, as she knelt down to help her daughter.

"You'll look beautiful no matter what you wear," said Thảo, and what she wanted to say—*Don't go to the party*—died in her throat.

There was little Rodier could fix to make the plantation look any better than it was. The house was magnificent simply because it was a mansion. But the land had never looked worse. What could he do? It's not as if trees grew overnight. Wilderness creeped onto the property, unkempt and unmanageable.

"Where are your workers? Do they come with the plantation, or will you take them with you to other projects you have planned?" a pasty-faced man asked with interest.

"Many of them have died. You know, they don't have the same fortitude as us French," said Rodier. Thảo stood on the edge of this gathering, eavesdropping at the party. Rodier was circulating, trying to sell the property to all his friends in attendance.

"Ah, yes," the man said. "And are they responsible for how pitiful your trees appear?"

"I don't know if *pitiful* is the right word. But I think yes. The incompetence of the Vietnamese workers, at least my own, has been a burden. But I assure you, the land itself is full of potential."

"And how much does potential cost?" asked Thảo. The men turned in surprise.

Rodier looked flabbergasted for a moment, and then burst into laughter. "Potential is priceless, my dear."

He turned his back to her and asked the men he had been speaking to if they'd like another drink. He left the group, weaving among the packs of people. Thảo followed him from a short distance. She could see his head easily above the others. He was still a tall, imposing man in his seventies. He looked the same, with grayer hair and more laugh lines, a small belly and slightly sagging neck. It seemed unfair he would still have that quality of carelessness even as he stooped with old age, while she felt the burden of worry and fear creep into the dark circles under her eyes, in the bow of her back. Rodier stopped to speak to a servant, and as he finished giving his request, Rodier grabbed the arm of her daughter, Quỳnh, as she walked past.

From where she stood, Thảo could not hear them over the string quartet and the buzz of conversation. Their mouths moved soundlessly. Quỳnh's lips parted in a polite but charming laugh. Thảo recognized in Rodier's expression, this old man, his desire.

By the time Thảo and Rodier had their meeting, he had already been coughing blood into his linen handkerchiefs for a few weeks. His servants had sent word to her about it. He came to Thảo in Sài Gòn, to the home she had grown up in and was now hers. Her parents and brother were dead. Han lived with her husband and in-laws. Her father must have died unwillingly, knowing this would be the outcome. Even after he collapsed, couldn't move any of the right side of his body, his speech slurred and garbled out the left side of his mouth, he still managed to tell her to leave his bedside each time she came to sit near him as his life ebbed away. His estate going to the daughter he loved the least, the one who disappointed him the most.

Rodier did not take his shoes off. She led him to the formal sitting room, which had rigid wooden seating. The elaborately carved chairs and table were inlaid with mother-of-pearl.

"Do you have gin?" he asked. "It's supposed to help with my health. I've been feeling unwell."

"I'm sorry to hear that. We don't have any gin," she said. Then, to the maid, she directed, "Get our guest some rice liquor. With some lime to make it taste better."

"Nothing to worry about. I'm sturdy as an ox."

"The rice liquor has a strong flavor. We bought it from a

woman nearby whose mother distills it in a village on the out-skirts of Sài Gòn."

They sat uncomfortably across from one another while wait-ing for the maid to return with his drink. Thảo took a sip of her hot tea, cradling the egg-shaped teacup in her palms. "I'd like to buy your plantation," she said.

He laughed, accepting the crystal glass from the maid. "I wouldn't sell it to you," he said. He drank from the glass dain-tily, pinkie finger out, and scrunched his nose in distaste. How-ever, he continued to take a long sip. "Everything has tasted bitter lately. I'm eager to get this sickness over with. Makes ev-erything tastes bitter. Even my sweetest whiskey has this taste."

"Why won't you sell the property to me?"

"I think we both know you're not fit to have it for more than one reason."

There was a beat of silence. "Who will buy it?"

"Well, there are a few interested parties—"

"There aren't any," she said.

"Excuse me?" Rodier stood up. "Your father and I were long acquaintances. To think his daughter would speak to me like this."

"I know there aren't any offers."

"How would you know?" He seemed to realize he sounded petulant. "I've spoken to several other French colonials who want to add to their land holdings."

"That was weeks ago. I know because I've told them the land is barren. And, because I've paid them not to put an offer in. It wasn't difficult since they didn't really want to buy it in the first place."

"This is insanity," he said. Droplets of condensation flickered into the air as he slammed his empty crystal cup onto the table. "I'll simply correct them of your lies."

"Or, you could just sell the land to me." Rodier was caught

between his pride and practicality. He didn't want to sell to Thảo because she was Vietnamese and a woman. But he wanted to get the land off his hands as quickly as possible. He whipped out the linen handkerchief in his pocket and coughed into it. There was a spray of blood spreading when he lowered it.

"I'll buy it right now. We can draw up an agreement, and I'll pay the amount you offered to others," she said. She could see the weakness in Rodier's face. He coughed again into handkerchief. "Would you like a second drink? You can stay for another and we can discuss the details." They sat together, the clink of Thảo's porcelain teacup being set on the low table between them. She could hear the rustle of clothing, and felt behind her the light brush of someone walking by, but when she turned to look, the air was still and empty. Rodier had made the same motion, looking behind himself, but there was no one. He picked up his empty glass in a nervous gesture and rubbed its moisture on his pant leg.

"Yes, I think I'll have another drink," he said.

Thảo bought new dresses for Quỳnh and Tiên. They each smoothed the creases from their skirts after traveling to the plantation. Thảo's short heels crunched on the branches strewn across the walk up to the plantation house. Quỳnh held Tiên's hand again, dragging her along.

The house still had much of its furniture, as Rodier had had nowhere to take it, and now he was dead.

A hot breeze whistled through the trees and rustled the debris Rodier hadn't bothered to clear. In the afternoon blaze of sun, Thảo thought she saw dozens of eyes stare out at them through the large front windows. She blinked, and there was only the elegant drape of green velvet hangings.

"This is ours, now," said Thảo. She looked back at her daughter and granddaughter. For once, their round, glowing faces did

not remind her of Rodier. She was reminded, instead, of fra-
grant lilies, of coconut desserts, a cool breeze from the Eastern
sea, the soft caress of a child's skin, a feeling of joy.

22

QUỲNH

Quỳnh was born in the element of Fire. Her mother said this was why she had a big temper despite being a Goat, and also why she didn't like baths, the former of which was drawn out whenever she was forced to do the latter. Quỳnh liked to help tend to the garden, watering and pruning and picking the medicinal herbs that Thảo grew for their shop. There were large rows of aloe plants, which Thảo liked to cut, soak in salt, and mash into a paste for burns, wounds, and acne. Sometimes she would force Quỳnh to drink a mixture of muddled aloe, lime juice, and salt for her acne. It was disgusting, but Quỳnh learned to gulp it down before her tongue had a chance to taste it. Her skin was fair but prone to redness and oil, blemishes and uneven tone. None of the other women in their family had these skin problems, nor her fair tone, and Thảo often blamed her daughter for the painful bumps that marred her face, as if Quỳnh could control them. They began appearing in the last year, right after Quỳnh turned twelve years old. Of course, Thảo also attributed their appearance to her Fire element. "Hot-blooded," she said.

"It makes your skin red and angry." But Quỳnh didn't feel hot-blooded or angry. She only felt ugly.

Quỳnh's mother didn't want her to work in the garden any longer. While the sun turned Thảo's skin a golden tan, which she also tried to prevent by wearing long sleeves and a large hat, Quỳnh's skin merely turned pink, peeling and flaky. Yet Quỳnh enjoyed working her hands in the dirt. She would leave the garden covered in grime and mud and loose foliage, her nose red from sun exposure and hat nowhere in sight. Sometimes she would loosen the dirt just so she could plunge both of her arms up to her elbows, and lay her face against the warm earth. She imagined burrowing deeper and deeper, until the ground ate her up, and underneath she would savor the cool, dark peacefulness of being alone, away from the judgment of her mother's sharp eyes.

But she could never really wish for that, because she loved working in their shop too much. People in the neighborhood came by every day for medicine, advice, and treatments. They came to borrow books, which had, in the past, primarily been about ancient health remedies, but soon came to encompass books of all subjects. Many of them were in French—Jules Verne, Guy de Maupassant, Emile Zola, Voltaire—and Quỳnh would spend hours sitting at the table reading, waiting for people to ask after her mother for advice concerning their illnesses and Gió Độc, the toxic winds that entered their bodies and were the source of all their ailments. One woman came in weekly because she could not figure out how to make herself an inhospitable environment for the Trúng Gió that was causing fainting spells. Other women came for treatments like Giác Hơi or Cạo Gió, even though most people had their family members do this. Thảo was known throughout Sài Gòn for her ability to siphon away sickness, create tinctures that healed, make the body release what it needed to let go. She specialized in fertility and menopause, helping many to survive the bodily pain of being a woman.

From her garden, she harvested many herbs. Dried them, boiled them, crushed them. There were many ways to prepare and store the herbs for use. Ginseng, wolfberry, cinnamon twigs and cinnamon bark, ginger, licorice, peony, rhubarb, salvia. Herbs to treat the lung, the spleen, the heart, the kidney. Help for the stomach, liver, bladder, and intestines. All matter of medicines for joints, for hearing and sight. And even things one might not need: bountiful hair, bright eyes, strong teeth. Herbs for every taste. Pungent, sweet, hot, bitter, acrid. Their medicine pantry was packed with colorful jars full of oils and powders, whole leaves and chopped roots. There were so many sicknesses that needed healing, each body a unique ecosystem that had to be evaluated and diagnosed.

Her mother did this healing through herbal medicine and physical touch. Quỳnh saw her mother touch a lot of people, hands strong and sure. In doing Dật Gió, for example, her sturdy fingers snatched at the skin, pinching it away and letting it spring back, over and over in the problem areas. She pressed her palm against the abdomen, against the back, the neck, pressure points on the face. And yet, Quỳnh could not help but notice, her mother did not like to touch her.

It was difficult to ignore this fact when she watched her mother touch, without hesitation, different people every day. And, even though Thảo had herself read the same French books that Quỳnh now read (they had arrived in the house's library because of her, after all), when she saw her daughter's nose buried in those books, she usually said something mean. "Why don't you do something useful instead of reading these silly French books?" she sometimes said, or "You'll leave an oil mark on the page, your nose is so close." Her eyes would linger on Quỳnh's blemished cheeks and jaw, her red, slick skin, a constant cause for concern. Because Quỳnh was a child, she did not know she herself was not the source of her mother's repulsion.

To avoid being swallowed up by her own self-hatred, Quỳnh blamed her skin problems on Gió Độc. It was not, she insisted, something from inside that caused these welts. The ugliness did not come from within, but rather, something from the outside, some wind that blew and blustered into her, created these pustules and rashes on her cheeks. Certainly, it was some toxin, invisible like atoms in the air, sticking to her skin and leaking through her orifices, snaking into her organs. It didn't help that Quỳnh hated taking baths. This was exacerbated in the last year, in part, due to her mother's tendency to scrub her raw, thinking if she scrubbed more or harder, that her daughter's blemishes might slough off, melt into the hot water. Herbs would wilt and bloat in the near-boiling bath, Thảo hoping they might make her daughter look like her, or at least like someone else other than the person she was.

In the heat of midfall, Quỳnh dug her hands into the earth to wrestle the roots of a lemongrass plant into the open air. As damp dirt crumbled through her fingers, she uncovered bits of bone, hard like slivers of steel. She panned the dirt to find more, pulling shards of what used to be. She gathered them into a small pile, holding the hem of her skirt as a basket. Brushing off the fine coat of soil, she displayed them like figurines on a shelf alongside herbs for menstrual cramps.

That night, she slept fitfully. The room was full of women and their murmuring voices, overlapping whispers that rose and fell with the rise and fall of her chest. They sat on the edge of her bed and felt her hot, bumpy skin with the back of their hands, gently moved stray hair against her forehead. They paced around, opened the window and let in the breeze. The room flooded with hot water, steam rising and beading up along the wall and furniture, and when Quỳnh woke up, her sweat had drenched the linens, hair wet against her scalp.

She discovered the sticky residue of blood between her legs, and beneath her, the glowing, angry wound of red on her night-dress and bedsheet. She gathered up the sheets and crumpled her nightdress and underwear with them, sneaking into the garden in the night to bury the evidence. She used her hands to scoop and pull away dirt to make a hole, balling up the linens as tightly as possible to place in her hiding spot. The patter of her hands piling dirt as they buried her secret was a comfort.

But, Quỳnh's handiwork was clumsy in the darkness. Upon discovering the sheets were gone and finding the shadow of a bruise on the bare feather mattress, their maid informed Thảo that her daughter had had her first blood. They heated up buckets of water on the fire until it was bubbling, carrying it to the tub and filling bucket by bucket until it was brimming with boiled well water. Sprigs of lavender had the air smelling of calm and possibility. Quỳnh stepped into the bath, an almost unbearable temperature. The dried blood between her legs bloomed.

Thảo soaked a washcloth in the perfumed bathwater and gently ran it across Quỳnh's skin. Her daughter was a woman now, she supposed, and she mourned the person she could no longer be, her body propelling impossibly toward a life of dis-appointment, at the whims of fickle and mediocre men. She would grow old and suffer, forgetting how youth yearned, de-sired, and believed. They all forgot, eventually, history burying itself under more and new grief, so that all they could do was survive their present. Who would remember for them, what it felt like to be young?

Quỳnh held her breath and submerged her head underwater, praying that when she resurfaced, her skin would be smooth like a pearl so that her mother might look and love. But Quỳnh knew it was fruitless, lips pressed resolutely shut, toxic wind trapped inside, rattling her to the bone.

23

THẢO

Francois Rodier had rushed the land clearing and the building of structures so that he could at least start planting trees on some of the sprawling property he'd bought in Bình Long Province. It made sense, Thảo's father had mused. It took at least seven years for the trees to be ready for tapping. The profits from a rubber plantation could only come once the sap was flowing, and the initial expense was large, even with colonial government assistance. The tradeoff was, of course, the well-being of his workers, who suffered from overcrowded living quarters, difficult work without proper tools, little gruel to eat. Rodier had hired a hulking man to intimidate the laborers, Theo Boucher, who had also been in charge of finding people to work the plantation. He'd gone north to the Tonkin bearing promises of a dependable wage each week. He arranged boats to take them south to Bình Long Province, where they were far from their families. They received meager payment, which was frequently withheld if the workers didn't behave the way Boucher wanted. Where would they go if they escaped? The plantation had been made into their entire world.

But, Rodier didn't concern himself with that. He was a numbers man, and he obsessed over his numbers daily, the growing debt he had accrued trying to take part in the rubber craze so many of his friends had benefitted from. He was embarrassed to tell his friends, all of whom had fully fledged operations, who were cutting down more trees, clearing more land, to expand.

The main house, at least, was done. And a grand house it was. The rooms were large so that the air would rise, and the windows were floor to ceiling. Rodier threw the shutters open and rarely closed them, letting in a breeze. The light as it bloomed on the maple-brown floors was something Thảo would always remember.

The first year Rodier had a Christmas party at Sông Plantation, Thảo was sixteen. Her father sat her and her siblings down before the party, looking stern.

"Don't embarrass me or your mother at Monsieur Rodier's party," he said. "I am permitting you to come because you're old enough, and it's time for you to ingratiate yourself to our friends. Dũng, you should socialize with the men who can help you in your career. It's time to stop playing around." He waved his crooked finger at their brother, who stared at the ground.

"Yes, Father," he said.

"Thảo and Hân," their father said, "you're young women. Soon, you will have to marry. There will be some Vietnamese families with their sons. Don't humor the advances of the white colonials, but don't shame me. I still have to work with them."

With that, he left the room to prepare for the party. Thảo, who was younger than Hân, was scared. "I feel like I'll do something wrong," she said.

"You probably will," said Hân.

★ ★ ★

In the back house where the laundry was soaked in a giant basin of hot water, the distinct odor of ammonia and floral burned her nostrils. Their laundrywoman, Hương, stood on a stool as she stirred the basin with a wooden paddle. She was soaking their clothing in lye and lavender. Thảo's mother bought imported French lavender because she'd heard colonial wives scented their laundry with the plant.

"Hương, where is my favorite white dress?"

"I'm washing it now, my dear," she said. Hương coughed into her shoulder because her hands were wet. On her sleeve she left specks of crimson.

"You've been coughing blood," Thảo said. She pointed to red dotted on her yellowing shirt.

"It's all the work I do," she said. When she smiled, there were dark holes where her teeth were supposed to be. "Not to worry, child. A little blood doesn't hurt."

"But, are you sick?"

"It's the lye," she said. She picked up a tin can and shook it. She winked at Thảo and smiled her toothless smile. "It's dangerous being a laundrywoman." She laughed and laughed at her own joke as Thảo took the can from her, prying it open to find white powder inside.

"It gets in my throat because of the steam," Hương continued. "I do a lot of laundry." She shrugged.

Thảo decided to wear a different dress in yellow. They'd had dresses made in the Parisian style. Long and frilly, and too hot for the weather. A low neckline that revealed a lovely collarbone. It was the most of her neck and chest she was ever allowed to reveal.

The house glowed in the settling dusk as they walked up from the road. It was white, but looked like mostly windows, framed by natural wood shutters. The terra-cotta roof tiles cast beautiful shadows, and the steps leading up to the grand entrance of Rodier's home were tiled in a colorful, intricate design. Everything about the house contrasted strangely with the plantation land itself, which was either covered in the wild green of uncut jungle, or haphazardly cleared and lined with rows of hevea tree saplings. A few other buildings stood in the distance. Thảo could tell they were shacks meant for the workers.

Some of those plantation workers now wore servers' clothes and had their hair combed. They walked about the party holding trays of jeweled-colored bites, looking like they belonged just enough so that they were invisible, until Thảo spotted barely healed gashes or heard them whisper to each other in rural dialects. Hân had abandoned her at the beginning of their arrival. She stood near some other girls she knew, and they chatted with the men there. When they were young, Hân and Thảo used to do everything together, perhaps more because they were close in age and were often paired up because of it. But Hân outgrew her sister, who always got in trouble for saying the wrong thing or losing her temper or acting out in a way unbecoming of a Vietnamese daughter. Hân wanted all the things Thảo didn't, and Thảo judged her for it, she had to admit. It was unfair. The gap between them had widened incrementally, day by day, so that, when she finally realized, it could no longer be bridged.

Thảo explored the house on her own to avoid speaking to men. She was a Metal Tiger, independent, and rebelled against the decisions forced upon her. She enjoyed the freedom of exploration, often going to new places with her family and losing them upon arrival. Tonight was no different, as she wandered from room to room, moving quickly enough so that no one could stop to engage her.

The main spaces were full of people, and they were getting louder the more they drank. It was a curious mix of languages that buzzed around her in a cacophony of sound. People spilled out onto the front porch, everyone in their best clothes; dozens of black three-piece suits and a rainbow of full-length dresses milled about in the elegant home. It was hot for such clothing, even in December. Shadows from the dangling chandeliers in every room made patterns on the hardwood floors.

On the stairs, Thảo didn't check to make sure she was seen. She knew it was rude to go upstairs, where the private quarters were. But she'd learned from her father that, even if you didn't know what you were doing, or if you knew what you were doing was wrong, you should pretend otherwise. Nothing alerts people to your actions so much as self-doubt.

The upstairs was dark and quiet. Thảo could hear the murmur of voices beneath her. On the landing, there was a sitting area and library. Shelves full of books and furniture upholstered in emerald green velvet. She wondered how much it all cost for a single man to live in a house like this.

Rodier's footsteps were loud. He gripped the banister for guidance, and when he reached the landing, Thảo could see he'd sweated through his white shirt. His hair fell ungracefully into his eyes.

"What are you doing up here?" His Vietnamese was terrible. "What's your name, girl?"

"I needed some peace," she responded in clunky French. "My name is Thảo. We've met before. You work with my father."

"Ah, your French is very good," he said. He approached her, and she could see he had an empty glass in his hand. He set it down on the bar behind her and uncorked his decanter to pour himself another. "Would you like one?"

"Yes," she said. He was very close and smelled like old tobacco and salt, and slightly sour. She could see the pits and mounds on his face. He was tall. His hand was clammy on the back of her neck as he pulled her toward his lips, which he licked before smashing them against hers. She parted her mouth and felt his tongue thrust inside. He tasted the same as he smelled. She'd never been kissed before, but usually imagined it with other girls. Her popular classmate, Mai, to whom she never spoke, or the young woman who sold her fruit every afternoon on her way home from school.

His other hand began to palm at her dress to lift it up, but it was too long and heavy. She pulled herself away and smoothed her skirt down.

"Monsieur Rodier," she said, "I don't think I should."

He grabbed her by the waist and breathed against her cheek. "Why shouldn't I," he said. He didn't seem to be inside himself, his voice speaking from a harried, dreamlike state. Thảo pressed her palms against his wet shirt, trapped between his body and the ledge of the bar that cut into her back.

Staring at her feet as they pattered one in front of the other, she didn't glance back at him, afraid he would be there, closer than she knew. Mouth against her neck. She wondered what lye and lavender could do for her dress, if it would be enough to erase the way it felt against her body now.

The party came into view as she descended the grand staircase. Bodies moved, swaying hypnotically against the chandelier's shadows and the flicker of firelight. She was a ghost looking down upon the festive cheer. The collective sound of voices and laughter had brought a feeling of excitement, an opening up into possibility. But now, what did she feel?

She wove her way among the bodies, out onto the front porch and down onto the barren plantation land. A long, bright rectangle of light stretched out through the open front door when she turned around to look. Thảo wanted to be away from the house, away from the sour smell of Rodier. Would the lye and lavender scrub that from her nostrils, too? Perhaps she was imagining it. Why couldn't she be like Hân? Her sister could surely push moments like this outside of herself, like tucking items neatly into a box and closing it shut.

Thảo took her shoes off and walked barefoot on the earth

toward the shacks. They were far from the main house, and felt farther in the dark. She almost missed the little saplings planted in rows, which already looked withered. She wondered if Rodier knew anything at all about rubber trees, if he knew anything about plants, about nurturing living things to grow.

Her eyes had adjusted to the darkness, the faraway silhouette of uncut forest becoming clear to her in its details: the curve of banana leaf, the crooked arm of a tree, the scuttle of creatures around the trunks of dense wilderness. As she approached the buildings, she could hear the stricken moan of someone unseen to her. The unmistakable sound of slapping skin stung the air.

"Quiet," said Boucher. "Be quiet."

They were behind the shacks, obscured by the building. Thảo stopped, leaning against the trunk of a tree. She didn't know if she could go any closer, but she couldn't turn away. She waited in the darkness until there was silence, and when the overseer walked away from the building, he didn't notice her eyes following him. When his body disappeared with distance, she turned to stare at the shack, which she knew must be full of dozens of workers. It was still and quiet, and yet, Thao had a strange humming in her head that she knew could not be real. She was dizzy and full of that sensation, that leaden sensation, which she now knew to be dread.

24

LADY TRIỆU

It wasn't my sister-in-law's cruel words, or even the sting of the lashes on my back that made me crack, made me give in to that feeling of rage (although surely those things had contributed, built up over time).

My brother had left me here with her while he camped in the mountains, gathering men for a fight against the Chinese. I stayed at home and fed the pigs, washed our clothes, bathed his wife. I did my chores every day, rising in the darkness before first sun, and ending with the cooking of the last meal. Perhaps I would have continued doing so if she hadn't tested the limits of her own cruelty. Or, perhaps I would've been engulfed by my rage no matter what.

For dinner that week, my sister-in-law wanted pork.

"Slaughter the pig," she said to me, even though the pig was meant for my brother's return during New Year.

"I don't know how to slaughter the pig," I said.

"You've seen your brother do it."

I went out to see the pig. He was still small, and I felt even worse about my task. We sat together and mourned its life. I looked at the pig and told him he would die soon. He did not respond, but when I laid him down and slit his neck, as he bled and bled and bled, his little eye stared at me in reproach. I held his body with my hands and his blood poured out of his neck and pooled underneath and around him. It stained the hem of my shirt. It was red, so red. How could a lucky color make me feel so horrible?

I took the knife, covered in my victim's blood, and went inside. I wiped my hands on my shirt, leaving more red marks. It would be terrible to do the wash later, to have to confront my deed again as I wrung it from the fabric. The thought of the chore was almost unbearable.

"Did you slaughter the pig?" she asked.

I plunged the knife into her heart. She died with a look of surprise on her face. I let her blood pour out onto the floor and had a moment of regret. At the creek behind our home, I filled a bucket with water and wet a rag. I wiped my sister's body clean. She was difficult to carry, but I was able to lay her on a bed of dried grass where the pig used to sleep. She looked angry even in death. My apology and prayer did nothing to change her, and I left her there, knowing I would never call that place home again.

The creek washed the dried blood from my hands. I stripped off my soiled clothes and let them be carried by the current, away from me. I stepped into the water and let it stream around me. It felt good to be free, even if the cost was death.

I needed to find my brother in the mountains, so I followed the creek. I took the knife with me for protection. Near our house, the creek was shallow and the current was gentle. The farther into the mountains I traveled, the deeper and wider it became, growing into a river that cut through dirt and rock. The sound of it lulled me to sleep at night and woke me with the sunrise.

Every day, when the sun was setting and I no longer wanted to walk, I jumped far below into the rushing river water, washing the dust and dirt from my body. It was hot all day, and the sun made me heavy. But when I splashed the water on my skin in the receding daylight, it refreshed and cooled me. It made me feel so different from what I felt before, and in that, it reminded me of who I was. It reminded me that there were places I could go and people I could be who were so far outside the bounds of my imagination that I could never imagine them until I arrived, until I became.

Even my home, my sister-in-law, I couldn't remember them only a week after we'd last met. They had a blurry quality in my memory, and this new life—the wilderness around me, the chill of river water, my freedom—overtook me. If you had asked me last week, last month, last year, if I could imagine this place or myself as I was now, I would describe a much different circumstance. It made me wonder what other futures I could not imagine for myself. If the future, too, would remember me, once I was in the past.

I walked farther and farther into the mountains, eating wild berries and herbs along the way. I cupped my hands and drank river water from them. Sometimes I vomited into the river, and it was swept away downstream. It was the reaction I had when I thought about all the blood of the dead pig.

There was no sign of any men until the seventh day of walking, when I arrived at the edge of the earth. The path had come to an end on a small cliff overhang, and I was elevated over the land below. I saw in the distance those specks of men and their camp. I made my way to them, going back down the small hill to take another path.

The woods were thick, but it was easy to find them because they'd trampled the way before me. I sneaked up as close as I could to their camp and hid behind the brush. They seemed relaxed, like they had been there a while. They looked like boys playing together. Some of them were boys. I searched for my brother but did not see him.

When I revealed myself, I knew immediately I had made a mistake. The danger was palpable. These men would not spare me regardless of who my kin might be. In my ragged clothes, dirty face and hair, I am sure I did not look like the kind of woman they fantasized about at night. Of course, this is a naive misconception held by a woman who didn't know enough. Any man will treat your body like a pig's after he is done with it. You can dress it up in silk and jewels, but the outcome is the same.

They descended on me quickly, pulling me into the center of their gathering. They pawed at me, hungry for touch. I wondered how long they had been here, alone with each other. Why weren't they fighting, as we all thought they had been? Tales in the village of male honor, bravery, and sacrifice. It seemed they had been in this outpost without moving, settled, ready to stay until they died of hunger or natural causes.

One of the more brazen ones held me against his chest and smiled at his friends.

"I go first," he said. The men cheered. He turned me around to face him. I caressed his chest and his shoulders relaxed. He wouldn't have to restrain me, he thought. I grabbed the short knife hanging from a crude rope belt on his waist and stabbed him in the neck. He screamed and stumbled back, ripping the knife from his neck as blood spilled out. The men did not help him. They stared on in shock.

He was on the ground now, clutching the wound. The sound of his crying sat uncomfortably in the air. I kicked him so he lay flat on the ground, staring up at me. I put my foot on his chest. I wanted him to look at me as he died.

25

THE TRƯNG SISTERS

My sister and I met another girl here, at the edge of the sea. Sometimes we walk through the rivers, all of them. We follow the rivers to the end of the earth, where water meets water, and we wash away all the things we feel burning in us. There is always something burning, trapped by the armor we refuse to take off.

Each of us is always fighting a war. Me and my sister are fighting our war, and the girl is fighting hers. Maybe it's silly to differentiate between us—maybe we're all sisters. There are more of us. Women and girls in the clothes of warriors and in rags, in silk dresses and in nothing at all. They are walking in mighty rivers, looking for the sea. It feels like a race, even though we have all the time in the world. We stand on Heaven's shore and stare out into infinity. I can hear the fighting and then, sometimes, I am *in* the fighting. It never ends, but I suspect perhaps these wars are over. I suspect we must be dead. I suspect we must be ghosts. Do you ever suspect yourself to be dead? I must certainly be, however alive I may feel, however many times I may say, *See me.*

I can see the present and the past. I see the buildings taller than the trees, and I see the burning buildings of old villages long gone. I see metal and wheels and dark smoke, and I see my sisters riding alongside me on elephants, tails swaying to and fro. I see the ghost of my sister straddling a man, plunging a spear into his heart again and again. I see myself doing this. I see the river that we throw ourselves into while holding each other.

Each memory is a room that I can visit. Each memory happens at the same time. Who says time must move forward? I am always riding the elephant into a horde of men, I am always holding my sister's hand, I am always crossing the river, I am always burning. I am, always.

★ ★ ★ ★ ★

AUTHOR'S NOTE

My mother's pageant trophy always sat on top of our piano. Trying to memorize the sweep of my fingers without looking down at the keys, I would fix my gaze on the imposing silver cup. In the way we always know trophies commemorate exception, I knew the trophy was exceptional. But it had been a permanent object in my childhood periphery and had therefore taken on the misleading sheen of the ordinary. While my mother had often mentioned the pageant she was in, I never asked more. Adolescent self-absorption, along with a restrained parental relationship that did not invite confidences, has been the source of many silences in our family.

It was not until I tried to write about this trophy in 2016 for a graduate creative nonfiction workshop I was enrolled in, that I realized how little I could definitively say was true. All I knew was that the trophy existed, and that its existence was proof a beauty pageant had happened. When I tried to research the pageant, I was directed to sources I did not want. When I tried, for the first time, to ask my mother specific questions about her experience, she gave me vague, circuitous answers. I wondered about the history of this object, the practical questions of its survival across an ocean to the top of the piano in our sitting room in New Orleans. How did it get here, through the chaos and danger of Saigon's collapse? Did my mother drag it, out of all the precious items she could bring, onto the escape boat where she and other passengers were stranded for weeks, almost dying of thirst? What was the pageant like, and how could something as frivolous as a pageant even happen during a civil war? Each answer I invented seemed simultaneously possible and unlikely. In this exercise, I realized that I had similarly filled in other gaps in our family history with some convenient and innocuous lie, rendering questions I should've asked unnecessary. I was ashamed. I was guilty of participating in the erasure of my own family.

That shame was at the center of my writing *Daughters of the New Year*. My mother and father didn't volunteer much about their lives in Vietnam while my siblings and I were growing up. I was an adult when I confronted the fact that their memories were too painful, that the silences in our family were a method of survival. What they told me was often a version of the truth, the happy or exciting moments of their former lives; in sharing only these parts, they reshaped this truth, almost creating an entirely different one. I imagined a family just like ours (and indeed, many Vietnamese immigrant families *are* just like ours), children purposefully and maddeningly separated from a cultural history too difficult to recall. What was interesting to me was not necessarily the damage wrought in the present, but rather a subversion, an unraveling of the past. What happens when we have the ability to go back, uncover a truth that is, in reality, forever obscured? What would we discover? How often does history repeat itself without our knowing, the same pain and joy experienced again and again? The irony is that in writing this book, I am still, even now, inventing a truth, filling in the gaps.

My father passed away in January 2021. He was born in 1940 and had come of age in a Vietnam that no longer exists. I was acutely aware of the loss. The loss of a father, yes, but also the loss of a memory. Even though I asked, I will never know what happened or what it was like for him, a South Vietnamese soldier who lost a country. Even though she is still alive, and I can still ask, I will never really know what it was like for my mother, an affluent beauty queen from Saigon who lost everything: a home, a language, a life. If I was guilty of erasure, though, I hope this book is a penance. That trophy, after all, did what it was supposed to do. I didn't know the particulars of its story, its origin, its history, and yet, the fact of its plain existence would not allow me to ignore, would not allow me to forget.

ACKNOWLEDGMENTS

This book is indebted to the work and unwavering belief of many people. I am so grateful to Eloy Bleifuss for taking a chance on me—our chats are a balm during a long and opaque process. Thank you to Grace Towery for seeing the potential in my book, editing it with kindness, patience, and extraordinary compassion. Thank you to the entire team at Hanover Square Press and HarperCollins for the often-unseen labor that goes into creating and promoting this beautiful literary object. Thank you to Gigi Lau and Ness Lee. And I am thankful to Logan Harper, for believing in me first.

Thanks to the programs and institutions that contributed time and space in this novel's conception: the Sewanee Writers' Conference, and the Ohio University and University of Mississippi Creative Writing programs.

An endless well of appreciation for Eric LeMay, who encouraged me to write about Miss Saigon, and to Patrick O'Keeffe, for always telling me to "keep going." Thank you Dr. Amritjit Singh, Dinty W. Moore, and Dr. Alec Holcombe. This book would not have been possible without Christine Adams, Susanna Hempstead, Greg Tolliver, Angie Mazakis, Sarah Minor, Madeline ffitch, and Burnside Soleil, all of whom read my work, supported my voice, and created a community where my writing could thrive.

Tommy Franklin's LEGO gift many years ago (which still sits on my desk where I work) reminds me I am a superhero when writing. Megan Abbott encouraged me to embrace difficult narratives about girls and women. Beth Ann Fennelly asked me to pay closer attention to the line. Jack Pendarvis, Jimmy Cajoleas, McKay McFadden, and Liam Baranauskas, original purveyors of good ideas, are always in my head, squashing self-doubt.

Gratitude and love to Lesley Ferguson. Thank you, Melissa Tran and Diana Cope. Roger and Handsome Luke made the hard writing days bearable. Thanks to Rosie, Cathy, and Quan, my older siblings, who always protected me and gave me an example of how life could be lived on your own terms, so much of which was poured into this novel. The list of people who created a literary support system are innumerable, and I am so thankful for them.

I will never be able to thank Josh-Wade Ferguson enough, for his endless support, unconditional love, and an almost delusional belief in my abilities. Thank you for cheering me on and guiding me through grief.

This book would not exist without Miss Saigon: my mother, a survivor. And for my father: cảm ơn, ba, for giving me everything I ever needed, language and all.